Men Times Three

Also by Bonnie Edwards

BREATHLESS

THIGH HIGH

MIDNIGHT CONFESSIONS

MIDNIGHT CONFESSIONS II

BUILT
(with Amie Stuart and Jami Alden)

THE HARD STUFF
(with Sunny and Karin Tabke)

PURE SEX
(with Lucinda Betts and Sasha White)

Published by Kensington Publishing Corp.

Men Times Three

Bonnie Edwards

APHRODISIA

KENSINGTON BOOKS

http://www.kensingtonbooks.com

APHRODISIA BOOKS are published by

Kensington Publishing Corp.
119 West 40th Street
New York, NY 10018

ISBN-13: 978-0-7582-3827-6
ISBN-10: 0-7582-3827-4

First Kensington Trade Paperback Printing: October 2010

10 9 8 7 6 5 4 3 2 1

For Alexis Morgan
My friend Pat
And Ted, Always

Men Times
Three

TJ O'Banion

1

"You're a good brother, TJ, you know that?" His middle brother Deke, slid to the ground beside TJ's open passenger door. He slumped left when right would've been better. TJ held him up by pinning his shoulders.

"Yeah, yeah, I know. And you're pissed drunk again." How the hell had it come to this? His family was a mess, his business in the crapper. Why? Because his family was a mess! "Can you stand?"

Deke shook his head. "Can't drive, either."

"No shit." TJ got hold of him under the armpits and heaved. Deke rose about six inches then got a foot under himself and helped. TJ wrestled his ass into the passenger seat. "Pick your feet up. That's right, now swing them inside." He bit off a comment about how disappointed their old man would be. Deke had suffered enough.

And going through old shit wasn't going to make anything better.

Once Deke got his feet inside, TJ buckled him in and ran to the driver's side.

"You okay to drive?" Deke's head swayed with each word while TJ climbed in and started his pickup.

"I'm not the family drunk," he grumbled, but he doubted Deke could even process the comment. His brother hummed under his breath. The neon from the bar's sign put a green glow on his face. Or maybe he was green around the gills. "Don't puke; I just got the truck detailed."

"S'okay. Did I tell you you're a good brother, TJ?"

"Tell Eli; he's the one who won't come home." And TJ needed him here. He had a busy summer ahead and Eli was the best electrician on the Olympic Peninsula. When he was home.

"Eli's in—no, wait a minute, that was last month. I know!" Deke tried to snap his fingers, but they wouldn't work for him. TJ sighed and waited until Deke gave up. After a moment the light of remembrance lit his face. "Eli's in Malaysia or Morocco or someplace with an *m* in it." The announcement was made with drunken pride.

"Yeah," TJ confirmed, "that'd be the place. Always looking for the next thrill, that's our baby brother." TJ didn't bother to track him anymore. Eli would come home when he was ready, and not a day before, no matter that his refusal grated on every one of TJ's nerves. Eli was the most stubborn O'Banion and would eat glass before he'd admit he was better off at home.

Rumor was that Eli was like their uncle. Wanderlust had killed him in the form of a rhino in a bad mood in Africa. Eli knew the story as well as any of them, yet he shrugged it off.

Deke put his head back on the headrest. He stared at the ceiling, blinked a couple times. "Why'd she do it, TJ? Why'd she take him that way?"

TJ sagged at the pain in his brother's voice. "I dunno Deke. Women do what they do." He pulled out of the parking lot and headed home. "There's no figuring them out. Best to let it go."

The clouds had moved off, leaving the sky black as ink and alive with stars. He liked driving in the quiet of night. He heard a sharp intake of breath but he didn't look over. Deke's pain was private and the beer had eased his tight control. "You know, Deke, it's time to quit drinking." He looked straight ahead. Deke wouldn't want him to see the sheen in his eyes.

"Soon as it stops hurtin', I'll quit drinkin'."

"Know what'll help?" TJ glanced over.

Deke stared at him, bleary eyes gleaming from the dashboard lights. "Yeah, I do. I'm gonna get laid."

"I was talking about work, but getting laid always sounds good." He chuckled, glad that Deke had at least thought of a way out of his morass of pain and loss.

Deke nodded as if he'd found the answer to life's biggest question.

"I'm gonna fuck every woman I can find. Fuck 'em all."

"That'll take you all of two days." Local women were few and far between and the O'Banions had burned a lot of bridges among the female population. Tourist season—and the fresh crop of women that came with it—was still weeks away.

These days, TJ didn't see much point in messing with tourists. He'd spent years in the passing pursuit of pussy, but now he wanted a woman who'd stick around. He slammed down on those thoughts; they never led anywhere but to a cold shower.

"I heard Maribeth Anderson's available," he suggested. "You went to high school together, right?" She'd never interested TJ. No flare. All his appreciation went to women with flare.

Lots of flare.

Flare and the Olympic Peninsula didn't go together.

"Maribeth's divorced," Deke grumbled. "I don't do divorced women. Not anymore. Not ever again."

"They're not all like Misty."

Deke snorted. "We're out of beer. Stop at the store."

"No. We start clearing the land tomorrow at Jon Dawson's place. We're up bright and early."

"What'll we do if the heirs don't want the cabins built?"

"My agreement was with Jon." Besides, Jon had taken care of that problem before he died.

Deke nodded and subsided into his seat. Drunken reflection oozed out his pores, but the silence lasted for the rest of the trip home. TJ pulled into his sprawling parking area and shut off the ignition before his brother spoke again. "You're a good brother, TJ. Have I told you that?"

He chuckled. "You need to quit drinking so I can get some work out of you in the morning." He slapped his brother's knee to startle him toward sober.

"Fuck 'em all. That's what I'm gonna do." Deke's head lolled back on the headrest and TJ decided to leave him there. He took off his jacket and covered his brother with it. A snuffle told him Deke would be out for the night.

He walked into his house, wondering what time it was in somewhere with an *m* in it. Not that he cared.

All he wanted was the youngest O'Banion brother home and at work again. He needed Eli to work on those cabins at the Friendly Inn. He needed Eli to come home so they could be a family again and build the business together the way they'd always planned.

As he shut his front door, he studied the slumped figure in his pickup. Deke needed Eli, too. His brother's pain was hard to see and, being the youngest, Eli had always been able to make them all laugh.

TJ wasn't sure why his youngest brother had taken to wandering so far. Maybe knowing he had such deep roots here had let him stretch his wings.

Whatever it was, it was time for Eli to settle down. Here, where he was needed.

Marnie Dawson nodded to her bartenders as she crossed the dance floor of her club, BackLit. She only managed a nod because if she walked over and chatted she might lose her composure. BackLit was her dream and, with the rotten news she'd just received, she didn't want to cry in front of the staff.

Wailing about the economic downturn and stingy-ass bankers was bad form for a business owner. Especially one known for her cool head.

So the nod of greeting would have to do. The club was an hour from opening and the bartender they'd just hired had to be brought up to speed. What the hell, she threw her a wave and pulled out her cell phone. The woman waved back and grinned with a thumbs up.

Seemed happy enough. At least something was working out today. Now, if she could just get Holly to agree to sell their joint inheritance, she could buy out her partner, save her club and life could be normal. Maybe not normal as in nine to five, but at least she'd be in charge without a pain-in-the-ass partner.

"Holly, you never pick up anymore. Call me," she said into her phone. It was almost as if her cousin had gone into hiding. Probably hiding from Jack. He was a possessive jerk and couldn't accept the divorce, no matter what Holly said. She still didn't get that Jack was a little off center, but the divorce had brought a ripple of relief to the entire Dawson family. "I'm heading to the Peninsula in a couple hours. Let me know when you'll be there, and I'll have your room ready."

She pushed through the door to the back stairs then began the climb to the second-floor office she shared with her partner, Dennis. Her voice went low because this was family business, not club business. It certainly wasn't Dennis's business.

"We'll spend a couple days at the not-so-Friendly Inn and decide how much to ask for it. I need to be in and out, so our newfound cousin had better not throw us any curve balls." If Kylie Keegan did try to hold things up, Marnie would call the lawyer she'd contacted ahead of time. She disconnected and turned her mind to clearing her desk so she could leave.

There were paychecks to sign and the new bartender's paperwork to be done. This trip to the Peninsula had come at a bad time, but if she wanted to save her club, she had to go.

Besides, lately there hadn't been a convenient time for anything. Her grandfather's funeral had come hard on the heels of another family tragedy. Her Aunt Trudy had died in a car crash before a major rift between Grandad and Trudy could be mended.

Distracted by the family sadness, she opened the office door and walked into a scene from a porn flick. She halted half a step into the room. "Whoa," she muttered and backed up.

But her desk was littered with paperwork and damn it, she had to get out of Seattle. If she left, there was no telling how long Dennis would indulge, and she didn't have time to wait.

Three intertwined bodies writhed on the floor in the dusk of the unlit office. The square of light that splashed the trio didn't make any one of them raise so much as an eyebrow. They were all too involved, too close to coming, to care that she'd walked in. She should have clued into the action when she saw the closed door, but she'd been preoccupied.

Dennis usually waited until after closing before he indulged his penchant for group sex. She didn't recognize the women, but she rarely did. Not only did Dennis like groups, he liked variety.

"Excuse me, all, but I have work to do," she said, to no avail. They either didn't hear her or didn't mind an audience.

Dennis sprawled on the floor, naked. She knew it was him because of his crooked baby toe. It hooked up over the one next to it. She couldn't see his nod of welcome because his face was bracketed by the strong thighs of a brunette. His muffled voice came to her in a breathy groan. "Marnie, come join us. The girls will like you."

The brunette looked at her with heavy-lidded eyes, her

makeup smeared from the sheen of perspiration that covered her face. They'd been here a while. The woman dropped her pussy lower and Dennis's voice muffled out as she covered his face with a sigh of satisfaction.

She clasped her breasts and squeezed her nipples while she rocked over his mouth. Her moans grew in intensity and Marnie held her breath in a purely physiological reaction to the unfolding scene. She ignored the moistening in her panties and put on an air of nonchalance.

Dennis knew how to work a woman, or so she'd been told. She had no interest in finding out for herself.

A blonde faced the brunette and rode Dennis's cock. She rolled over him, her head thrown back while she bounced so hard her ass jiggled. The brunette released her nipples to slide her hand to the other woman's clit. The blonde squealed at the touch. "Oh, yeah, yeah."

Deep powerful groans reverberated through the room. Dennis, she assumed. The musk of sex permeated the air. Envy warmed Marnie's low belly while her nipples peaked hard. She hadn't been laid in, what? Three months? Didn't seem fair. Dennis was as discriminating as a sailor on shore leave. No, she didn't envy the way he behaved, the easy sex, the nonchalant attitude.

It was sharing the physical release she missed. She was so tired of coming alone. "I've got a lot of work to do in next to no time. You going to be long?" She directed the question to the gyrating women.

They laughed and kissed each other. The blonde wiggled her fingers at Marnie in a gesture meant to coax her closer.

Marnie shook her head. She never shared her men. But it was impossible to look away. Besides, she had every right to expect to work at her own desk in the middle of the afternoon.

Normally, she would back out of the office if she stumbled

into this, but with no time to waste, she closed the door to wait it out. If she left, they might go for another round and she'd suffer rush hour traffic all the way to the Peninsula.

She leaned her butt against the desk to wait. The only lighting came from the three security monitors on the wall next to the door. One screen showed the club's entrance, another the delivery door in the back and the last showed the bar itself and the cash register. She watched the bar for an idle moment while she flexed the muscles at the top of her thighs. She found no relief from her frisson of need. She shifted, flexed harder then distracted herself by watching the monitors more closely.

Everything looked routine. Tuesday meant a slower crowd so it was a good night to train new crew.

The moaning from the trio got louder. The scent of sex grew stronger. She crossed her legs at her ankles, admired her new boots and pondered whether she should strip and join the fun. Just once. Now *that* would blow Dennis's mind.

On the other hand, if she fucked Dennis once, he'd never stop trying to catch her with her defenses down again.

Loneliness was no reason for unsatisfying sex. Next time she got laid, she'd hold out for something great. No ho-hum sex for this girl. Not anymore. She wanted to be so overwhelmed by lust that she had no choice but to fuck the guy. She wanted hard, fast, bucking sex that made her heart stop and her lungs explode.

She wouldn't get intense from an anonymous quickie.

The rare times she had indulged in casual encounters had been major disappointments. Sex fueled by alcohol and loneliness was the worst, and that's all she'd found in too long.

She wanted seduction. On her part, and on his. She wanted to be wooed into bed, wanted in a way that drove all thought out of her mind, took her to a new place of mindlessness. She wanted Zen sex.

Unfortunately, in the club scene *long and slow* meant fifteen minutes of eye contact and a sloppy conversation that usually centered on such meaningful shit as what kind of car the guy drove and how nice her tits looked in that top.

A sigh rose from the pile of naked limbs and rolling hips as Marnie pondered the idea of finding a real relationship in her unreal world. Just as soon as she returned from the Peninsula, she'd find someone she could have a conversation with. A man who made her crazy with lust. A man.

Not a man-child. And not a hound dog. An honest-to-God grown-up male who wanted her in his life.

In the meantime, this was some hot action. But cold and mechanical at the same time. A loud moan signaled the end for one of the women. The blonde's body shook as she rocked her clit over her friend's hand. Her ass shimmied and guttural groans from the brunette spurred her on.

"Yeah," the brunette crooned. "Fuck him. Rock that cock."

She soon joined the other woman in ecstatic moans as the brunette stiffened over Dennis's face. "Unh. So good." She cried out as the blonde pinched her distended nipples while she came.

Two down one to go.

Marnie took her seat behind her desk and reminded herself to pick up batteries on the way to the Friendly Inn. Long and slow with BOB would have to be enough until the right man caught her eye.

Once the inn was sold, she wouldn't have to put up with Dennis and his women again.

She had to hand it to him though; he tried to make his women feel good about their efforts, so he always yelled when he came. He figured they appreciated it. Dennis shouted his release a moment later and the pungent odor of sex and musk bloomed.

From what she'd seen, the blonde and brunette were more into each other than into Dennis. They kissed and petted as he relaxed, until a light tap on the brunette's haunches signaled the end. After a moment the three partners rolled off and away from each other. The women stood, looking mussed and sated.

They intertwined their fingers and kissed each other deeply.

Marnie pointed at the piles of feminine clothing. "You can dress in the hall," she said in dismissal. "Turn on the lights on your way out," she said in a tight voice.

The women each kissed Dennis with fervor, giving his cock and balls one more long stroke each before they gathered their clothes and pranced out holding hands.

Dennis stood, stretched and scratched his flaccid cock. "Sticky," he said with a grin.

Marnie shook her head. "We didn't get the loan."

"You love to ruin the glow." A filled condom dangled as he scratched his balls absently. He headed into the office washroom. Water ran into the sink, the toilet flushed and out he came again, grinning like a fool. "It's okay, I've got a plan." He bent to pick up his clothing and began to dress.

Not nearly fast enough, she thought. "Why am I not surprised you have a plan. You always *have a plan.*"

He grinned and zipped his slacks. "It's a great plan."

"Unless it involves a winning lottery ticket, I doubt it'll help."

He bent over and picked up his shirt. While he pulled it on, he grinned wider. "The club needs a new direction."

"You're crazy. We're about to take off."

"You've said that for months, but apparently. . . ." He waggled his brows. The man was bright enough on his good days. But lately, she'd seen fewer and fewer good days. ". . . Apparently all the banks in the state disagree with you."

"It's the economy, the mortgage crunches, not the club. And do not even think about going anywhere else for a loan." Dennis liked to think he was connected. "I won't have any silent partners. Not the kind that you'd bring in." Of course they'd been approached with ways to make extra cash, but Marnie refused to play and had made it known police personnel were always welcome in BackLit. She'd quietly put the word out to thwart any of Dennis's wilder, illegal schemes.

"We still need to change things. The thrust, as it were." He stepped in front of her chair, slipped his hands to her shoulders and squeezed lightly. The faint scent of pussy wafted by.

She pulled away. "You're a pig. You didn't even wash your face."

"I like the smell of women."

"You're getting more strange all the time." He'd never been fastidious but this was gross.

He laughed and took his seat behind his desk across the room. Maybe it was stress. They were in a crunch. The economy had gone flat and put pressure on them to keep their prices lower while increasing staff. Expenses had climbed and their DJ had threatened to jump ship and go to the competition. He had a following and brought in a lot of regulars. "What's the word from Mike?"

"He wants at least ten percent more."

"Damn. We can't go that high and he knows it." Not with a new bartender they absolutely needed. Pressure built behind her eyes. She downed a painkiller from the bottle she kept on her desk. She no longer needed water to wash them down. What did that say about her lifestyle? She sighed and refocused on Dennis.

"That's why we need a new direction," he said. "I'm tired of being held hostage by that guy. If we change things up, he can go and we'll never need another DJ."

Whatever he had in mind wouldn't matter if they sold the inn. He'd sell his half of the club to her and disappear from her life. "We don't need a new direction; we need patience." She pulled out the company checkbook and started signing paychecks. She'd like to do direct deposit, but the waitstaff turnover was too rapid. She could never keep on top of the changes. "We'll talk about everything when I get back. In the meantime, keep Mike happy and tell him we'll discuss his salary at month's end."

"Right, yeah, sure." But his eyes were focused inwardly as his mind whirled.

Damn, he wasn't going to let this rest, but she knew when to leave things alone. Dennis could be unpredictable and she didn't have time for an argument.

She tapped her pen on the checkbook and waited for him to remember she was leaving him on his own for a few days. This was a first and she fought down the bitter fear of Dennis in charge.

His eyes dropped to the floor under her desk. "That's the reason for the ugly boots. You're heading to the Olympic Peninsula, where they've got that tree museum, right?" Dennis hated the outdoors and everything to do with it.

"If you mean the Olympic National Park, then yes, that's where I'm going." Close enough. The Friendly Inn sat on several acres of second-growth timber on Seduction Cove. "And my boots aren't ugly. They're practical. Stilettos won't work up there."

"When will you be back?" The gleam in his eye made her want to cancel.

Shit.

"As soon as I can." If all went well, she'd be free of Dennis and his unpredictability. "Promise me you won't make any changes while I'm gone. We *will* have a discussion when I get back," she promised.

He shrugged. "Sure, I want to work out some details anyway." He snapped his fingers and pointed at her. "I'll make a business plan and give you a professional presentation. You'll like it."

His strength. That was what had convinced her to take him

on as a partner in the first place. He had a head for marketing and sounded like a shark when he was on a roll. But the man had no follow-through.

With a partner like Dennis, the other half would always have the lion's share of the work. Applying himself to a presentation would occupy him while she was gone. Satisfied, and aware of the clock ticking toward rush hour, she signed the last check and began stuffing envelopes.

"Fine, you get your ducks in a row, and when I get back, we'll have a serious discussion. Now, all I want to do is hit the road. The sooner I leave, the sooner I get back." She passed her hand over the frown lines etched into her forehead. Maybe the inn's peaceful surroundings would help her find her equilibrium again.

"In the meantime, I'll take care of everything," Dennis said with a grin that made her belly clench. Selling the inn quickly was her best option for getting Dennis out of her life and Back-Lit to springboard onto Seattle's must-go list.

2

A car barely bigger than a toy bumped across the grass-covered parking lot in front of the misnamed Friendly Inn. TJ and Deke watched the vehicle from the deep shadows of the front porch. "What the hell is that thing?" Deke asked.

"One of those European cars that get a million miles to the gallon." TJ didn't care; it was the driver he was interested in. Must be one of the heirs. One of Jon Dawson's granddaughters.

Deke snorted. "It's two seats with a roof. Golf carts are bigger."

The car stopped and the driver's door opened. A sensible boot, small enough to be a woman's, landed on the grass, quickly followed by a shapely leg in blue jeans. A woman emerged from the car wearing a gold-colored blouse and green fleece vest. Nice.

Even better was the mane of red hair that topped her off.

TJ loved redheads. Always had. This one had flare and cranked his temperature just by breathing.

Her jeans rode low on her hips and her tucked-in blouse

emphasized her curvy waist. A redhead with curves and lustrous long hair that hung loose and free.

He swiped the cobwebs and bits of debris from his hair, shirt and jeans.

She swept a handful of hair out of her way while she reached inside the car for something.

He took a long deep breath and sucked in the beauty of the day made better by the arrival of this gorgeous woman. She leaned back into the car to grab something off the passenger seat. His heart kicked into high gear at the sight of her shapelier-than-average butt and Deke's suggestion of getting laid moved into the realm of TJ's personal goals.

Deke's low whistle set TJ's teeth on edge. He'd forgotten Deke was getting the same view he was.

He cast his brother a sidelong glance. He'd slapped at the dirt that clung to his clothes, too. He smoothed his hair as TJ watched. "Not a chance, little brother. She's mine."

Deke shot him a challenging look. "You always want the redheads."

The redhead in question straightened to her full height, with a canvas knapsack in her hand. Her mouth moved in an animated conversation, but snatches of the conversation drifted away on the wind.

"She must have a hands-free phone stuck in her ear," he said. "Either that or she's talking to herself."

Deke snorted. "You like the wacky ones, too."

"Once, I picked a wacko once, Deke. Everyone's entitled to one mistake."

The redhead laughed, touched her ear to hang up then gave the car door a hip shot to close it. Her breasts jiggled on impact. He sucked in another breath and the effect of her whole package charmed him: shapely curves, hair, expressive face and smiling mouth.

And flare. Lots of *flare*. He'd be damned if he knew what it was, but she had it.

"That a car?" Deke called. "Or a scooter with a roof?"

She looked startled by Deke's voice and stopped in her tracks. She took a wary step backward while squinting into the shadows on the porch.

They each took one step into the sun, so she could see how harmless they were.

Like hell he was harmless. He wanted to stalk and chase, pull her down and cover her head to toe. Naked.

He grabbed Deke's forearm, looked him in the eye. "You're going to walk away, Deke. Now. Seriously. Walk away."

But Deke always was a butthead. He shook off TJ's hand and went straight toward her.

"Takin' your life in your hands, Bro." TJ threw his voice low so only Deke could hear as his brother moved toward the redhead. TJ kept the threat softly spoken but clear.

Deke surprisingly veered left and headed for her tiny car instead. "Mind if I take a look at her?" he said, bright as a yokel.

"Help yourself. The door's unlocked." The beauty sized up his brother with one flick of her eyes then trained her gaze on TJ.

His heart stuttered and his cock stirred to life. It wasn't her eyes or her figure that had him by the 'nads; it was her mouth. A man tended to remember his first kiss, and his had landed square on that incredible mouth.

If he thought hard, he could probably still conjure the taste of her lips.

Strawberry lip gloss. Yeah, that was it. Sticky, and sweet as sin. But under that, where the female taste really lived, was the sweetest flavor known to man: invitation.

He hoped the invitation still stood, because now that she was full-grown, he could take her up on it.

He flat-out wanted to take her, nearly as much as he wanted to take care of business here at the Friendly Inn.

A pair of Paul Bunyans stepped out of the shadows on Grandad's veranda and took three long strides toward her. Plaid shirts, blue jeans and tan work boots convinced Marnie she'd stepped back in time. Who dressed like this today?

Still, two huge men coming at her with interest plastered across their faces took her back a step. She put her hand on her car door handle although they could probably run faster than she could accelerate.

"It's a Smart car," she responded to the familiar question with the same calm tone she used with drunks at the club. Friendly but firm. "A two seater from Europe."

The bigger, broader, black-haired one gave the younger, shorter one a quiet instruction meant for his ears only. Whatever was said made Bunyan the Younger change course and head for the car rather than for her.

As he drew near, she realized "shorter" was relative. He was a mere half inch under the six three of the older one. He was brawny and had his plaid flannel sleeves rolled halfway up his forearms. Clearly they were brothers. They sported the same square jaw and dark hair, although the younger had brown hair. He stared with curiosity at her car. "Don't pick it up and carry it off, okay? It's my only transportation."

She glanced back at the older one and got caught in the force of his primal, watchful gaze. Hot as sin. The question, "Who are you?" fell out of her mouth before she could stop it.

The attention in his gaze heated to smoldering. An expression she'd seen before . . . somewhere, a long, long time ago. His mouth lifted in a grin that looked halfway familiar.

Warmth oozed around her chest.

She knew that mouth. Firm lips, agile tongue and a ready

smile. She recalled the feel of him with delicious clarity. A woman tended to remember her first kiss and especially her first taste of desire.

For one crazy moment she wanted to go back to that awkward summer, that tender first kiss. She smiled wider, in recognition and welcome.

"Marnie Dawson," he said, his eyes glowing warmth. "You've grown some." His gaze flicked down her body, heating her to sun-warmed chocolate.

She put her hands on her hips and cocked her head to the side. "Thomas John O'Banion. You've filled out some."

His grin went wider and stole her breath. "You spent the summer here with your grandfather when you were thirteen."

She walked three steps closer. His outdoorsy scent was fresh and tangy. The breadth of his shoulders could block the sun, and even better, her peripheral vision caught a glimpse of his naked left ring finger at his side. Lifting her face to his, she smiled and put every bit of allure she had into the look they shared with equal intensity. Threads of memory tightened between them as she recalled long warm days spent in his company.

He'd been a couple years older and bored that summer. Grandad had him doing chores most days, but after dinner, he spent his time with her. The night before she left for home he finally let his lips skim hers. Once, twice, then full on until he pulled back. "Best summer of my life," she whispered.

He chuckled. "I've had a weak spot for redheads ever since."

"Thank God for that." Marnie laughed with TJ, easing back from the sparks that could catch fire if she wasn't careful. She felt absurdly pleased to see him. The sharp tang of desire reverberated through her memory.

First crush, first love, first kiss. Whatever they shared, it felt good to see him. "You still live here? I'm surprised."

"The Peninsula's home," he said simply. "I'm a building contractor now."

"For a moment there, I thought you'd grown into Paul Bunyan." He certainly smelled like a woodsman. "Those chips look suspiciously like cedar." She tilted her head toward a sprinkling of bright yellow shavings on his boots and ankles that he'd missed when he'd slapped at his clothes.

He laughed a deep, booming laugh that he hadn't had at fifteen. The sound warmed her with its honesty and made her think Bunyan thoughts again. She wanted to look for an ox and an axe. "I build log cabins, so you're not far off."

All those rough hewn logs. The scent of wood. The strength it would take. Oh, mama. A man who built solidly snug log cabins by the strength of his own hands. "Seriously sexy, TJ."

"Thanks. I think." He scrubbed his large hand over his thick hair and went an interesting shade of red under the stubble on his jaw. "Never had the job described that way before, but I'll take it."

She wasn't talking about the job, but he knew that. "So, life's good?" she asked.

"Now that Deke's back, yes, life's good. I've been after him to come home for a couple of years and last month, he showed up just in time."

She glanced over her shoulder at the younger Bunyan, er, O'Banion and grinned as he tested the weight of the car by lifting the rear. "Hey, put that down. Very funny." She rolled her eyes at TJ. "I don't remember a brother."

TJ snorted at his antics. "There was a time he wasn't as smart as he is now."

"That, I can believe."

"For a few years in our teens the three of us couldn't stand being in the same room, never mind the same family." He chuckled. "If I could get Eli, my youngest brother, to come home, the business would be set. Eli's our electrician when he's not globe-trotting."

"A triple shot of O'Banions?" Three log-cabin-building brothers, built like mountains. "Whew, you boys must be hell on the women around here." A moment of mutual admiration stretched until TJ's eyes darkened.

"Not lately," he assured her.

"I'd say that's a shame but I wouldn't mean it."

His brows dropped to a frown as he studied her. "Sorry about your Grandad, Marnie. Jon Dawson was a character."

"That's a nice way to put it."

He gave the rambling building behind him a cursory nod. "Don't know why he pretended this was still an inn. He didn't mix much with strangers."

"He didn't mix much with family, either. Not for years. The only reason I got to stay with him that summer was because my parents parked me here. I never knew whether I was welcome or not."

TJ nodded. "Sounds like Jon. He was crusty, but for what it's worth, he missed you after you left."

"He wasn't just crusty. He was crotchety, difficult and rude. None of the family had seen him for years." She had her regrets about that, but she'd only done as he'd asked and stayed away. "Still, he left me this place." She glanced at the weather-beaten inn. It would have been quaint in its day. But the land was valuable.

"You and a cousin, right?"

"Mine and Holly's. Actually just his female grandchildren. A quirk of his?" she asked. If TJ was a friend of Grandad's maybe he knew more about the strange details of Jon's will than the family.

TJ shrugged. "Maybe he figured his grandsons were better equipped to support themselves. Jon had some old-fashioned ideas about men and women and their roles."

"And their abilities," she said. The old man had always favored his male descendants, at least until it came time to read his will. Holly and Marnie had brothers, but they'd been left stock certificates and bonds. No real estate. Holly and Marnie's parents had been left incidental items with more sentimental than monetary value. "Have you met my cousin, Holly Dawson?"

"Can't say that I have."

"How about a Kylie Keegan?"

His lips firmed. "Oh. Kylie. She a cousin, too?"

At his regretful tone, her bullshit meter buzzed like a saw. "Yeah, Kylie. Has she already been here?" She and Holly hadn't even met her yet.

"Not since before Jon died. After she drove off in a huff, he pulled out a bottle of fine scotch, blew the dust off and talked about regrets all night."

"Specific regrets?"

"Nothing in particular." A flicker deep in his gaze said he knew more than he was saying. Loyalty to his friend. She understood.

Interesting. Poor Aunt Trudy died before knowing her father might have had regrets about kicking her out on her ass without a dime. All because of one baby born out of wedlock. This Kylie Keegan. Trudy had been so angry with her father, she'd changed their surnames from Dawson to Keegan when Kylie was born. No one knew where she got that name or if it had any connection to Kylie's father.

"That explains some things we've all wondered about," she said vaguely. But not everything. Bitterness raised a flag, but she fought it. Still, sharing a major inheritance with a stranger was a big problem. If she were Kylie, she'd keep a low profile. If Kylie wanted nothing to do with her mother's family, everything could be handled through lawyers and she would never have to meet her cousins.

Except for that damn codicil.

All Marnie wanted was to sell the place and get back to work. Any reasonable person would want the same. She just hoped Kylie Keegan was reasonable.

One-third of this place would set Marnie up perfectly. She couldn't begin to guess what Dennis had in mind for his new direction for BackLit, but if things panned out here, she'd never have to know. She'd be able to buy him out of the club.

Deke's voice drifted across to them. He was still gawking at the car. "This thing looks like it's cut in half. Where's the rest?"

"Very funny." But she answered a couple of his questions by rote while she felt the all-over study from TJ. After she tossed Deke the keys for a test drive, she turned back to the O'Banion who interested her most. "Like what you see?"

"You had me fooled when you stepped out of the car. I saw jeans and boots and figured you fit in here. But I was wrong. You're city. Completely city."

"That's a bad thing, I take it. What gave me away?"

"Manicured hands, designer labels and your face hasn't been turned up to the sun in too long."

"I'm pasty-faced?" She pretended to be insulted, which brought an answering chuckle.

"Let's just say, your skin looks too soft to be outdoors much."

"That's better." He was quick. And funny.

"Seattle isn't all that far, but it's a world away. We have lots of fresh air and a slower pace."

Which all sounded great. Maybe she'd stick around a while and soak up some R and R. "I bet you're just the man to encourage me to relax and enjoy everything the Peninsula has to offer."

"Could be." He turned and wedged his full-sized hands into his jeans pockets as he looked up at the inn. "What are your plans for the place?"

"I want to sell as fast as possible," she said. She looked at the second story and sighed. "But it's in sorry shape." She hoped the interior was in better condition. "Holly's got a knack for making things look good." She frowned and checked her watch. "She's supposed to be here soon. Let's hope she can work some magic on short notice."

"Walk with me, Marnie. There's something out back you need to see." She set her knapsack on the top step of the porch and let him lead her around the two-story inn. Up close, the wood looked weathered and beaten by years of neglect. It could need more than fresh decorating to bring it up to saleable condition. Her hopes faded with every step. "You'll want to check this out before you make any plans," he said on a grave note.

"You're giving me the willies, TJ. How bad can it be?"

They rounded the corner of the building and she gasped at the horror before her. "No way. What's going on?"

He had the grace to look apologetic. "We'll be finished before the summer's over."

Marnie stared at devastation on par with a nuclear blast. Heavy equipment littered an area she remembered as a stand of tall cedar. Very tall cedar. Beautiful serene tall cedar. Not old growth, but mature and lovely. So dark the green looked black at the first sign of cloud cover. It was gone, all of it. She blinked at a sudden wetness at her eyes. She dashed at her cheeks. "It used to be so lovely." She took a couple of steps, mouth gaping at the loss. "You've got to be kidding me."

The equipment looked like giant versions of little boys' toy trucks and backhoes, except for the life-sized destruction. She felt sick. Wronged in some way. "What do you mean, you'll be finished? With what?" There were still acres of forest behind the clearing, but she'd be damned if he tore out one more tree. "You're not logging the whole acreage, are you?" What she saw made no sense. He was supposed to be a builder not a destroyer.

"This will all look better by tomorrow," he promised, indicating the big yellow machines. "We'll clear the stumps. Bring in a grader, then we put in the footings, pour the foundations and—"

She raised her hand and cut him off. "Stop right there. This property is going to be sold. Listed for sale tomorrow. Just as soon as Holly gets here and—" She quit. She'd forgotten Kylie, the unknown cousin. "Never mind. This!" She raised her hands in horror. "This makes me sick. We can't sell with this ugly mess right behind the building." Not without a drastic cut to the asking price, and in this market, the cut would be too deep. She needed every dime.

The fresh scent of cedar assailed her. Clean and lovely, the cedar blended with the earthy smell of torn up roots. "We thought Holly would spruce up the interior of the inn, maybe get a painting crew in. We expected cosmetic work. Decluttering and staging."

"Dee what?"

"Tidying up the inn. Making it fresh."

He snorted. "You haven't been inside. Believe me, there's almost as much work in there as here."

Her stomach knotted with worry. "This is a desecration." Her memories of Grandad's land were nothing like this. Holly would be sick when she saw it.

She turned, slowly, trying to get a grasp of the nearly total destruction of at least an acre. Roots sat torn from the earth, soil still clinging to the stumps: roots that were larger in circumference than she was tall.

"This is the ugliest time. It'll look a lot better soon, I promise." She heard his speech but the words made no real impression.

In her state of shock, she'd forgotten TJ was with her.

"You." She glared at him. "You did this. Without permission? Why?" The timber of course. The trees were worth a fortune. "Grandad would never have agreed to logging his land."

He had the grace to duck his head. "Not logging. Developing. Jon wanted me to build three cabins back here. He paid me up-front for them. They're going in."

"They are not. You stop right now." She tried to superimpose her memories over the devastation, but she couldn't. The torn earth was too ugly, the roots of the trees too naked to be glossed over.

"I gave my word to a dying man." His tone was clipped, definite. "The work continues."

She sagged because he was right. The work had to continue.

Grandad had added a codicil to his will that any improvements being made to the inn or grounds had to be completed before the property was sold. Not that this looked like an improvement, but the work had begun and had to be finished.

TJ's attitude made her think he knew about the codicil. So much for her plans to sell fast and get Dennis out of her club.

TJ dropped his hand to Marnie's shoulder. The gesture felt familiar and comfortable. That summer they'd shared had been filled with easy touches and friendly gestures. He'd taught her to fish, held her hand while they'd been hiking and she needed help to get up, down or over rocks and trees. Not much more than children, the touching had been free and easy.

On her last night, while they were swimming, she'd gotten warm all over, let him kiss her and childhood slipped away.

The hand on her shoulder was meant to comfort her but she shrugged him off. "We can't sell the place like this." She tested to see if he'd mention the codicil.

"Sorry I jumped the gun on the work, but when I give my word, it stands. When his daughter was killed in that accident, Jon called me. He was heartbroken, so I promised him I'd build these cabins and that's what I'll do."

She blinked the wet out of her eyes. To drive a daughter away, only to have her killed with no chance of reconciliation. Even Jon Dawson would feel a hit like that. "Did he look sick? Complain of feeling ill?"

"Like I said, he was broken. I'd never seen him that wrecked before. He may have had some remorse, but he was still a stubborn bull-headed old man. Knowing Jon, he probably expected your aunt to call and make the first move."

At Trudy's death, he was broken. She squeezed her eyes shut. Such a waste!

But mourning two people too stubborn to reconnect was not going to get this property fixed up and sold. That was up to her and her cousins. Holly would be okay with the idea, but Kylie felt like an open noose around her neck. At any moment the noose would tighten and her future could blank out.

"I'm going in to see what needs to be done with the interior." She strode around to the front of the inn. "I can only imagine how bad things are on the inside."

He caught up to her as she turned the corner. Deke pulled in to park and honked the horn. He unfolded himself from the front seat and put on a show of stretching out the kinks. She flipped him the bird.

TJ spoke in her ear. "Jon didn't have a housekeeper. He lived on the main floor, mostly in the kitchen. Most nights he sacked out in his lounger in front of the television."

"I'll deal with you later," she said, her voice icy. "Don't think I don't know that you jumped the gun, as you so aptly put it, just so I couldn't stop you."

"Smart, too. I like that."

She swung on him. "Don't think I'm going to sleep with you, either."

He took a step back, put up his hands in mock surrender. "Not this minute. I'm not that kind of man." He kept his expression serious.

"Oh. Go to hell." She stepped onto the veranda and headed for the front door, bracing herself for what she'd see when she opened the door.

"You tell me to go to hell and flip off my little brother. I'm starting to think you don't like us. Or maybe it's just me."

She ignored him and pulled out the key the lawyer had given her.

"If you'd like to see the pond again, I can take you. Remember the pond?" His voice was a low sexy rumble that steamed down her spine and sent shivers along her nerve endings.

Incorrigible. But fun.

Inside the inn's foyer, Marnie suppressed a grin. "The pond," she muttered as she turned the lock to keep the O'Banions outside where they belonged. "I can't believe he remembers."

Heavy draperies shut out the light in the expansive living area so she flipped on the light switch by the door.

At first sight she wanted to shut the lights off again. Instead, she took two steps in and stared at the living area to her right. The fireplace. The furniture. It was all here as she remembered, but—"Oh. My. God."

3

With a fumbling turn, Marnie opened the door at her back. Both brothers stood outside the inn. "You didn't tell me it was this bad," she said. She opened the door wide and waved them in.

The two huge men crowded her, but she was not moving farther into the room without backup. She might step on something scurrying across the floor. She shivered.

"It wasn't this bad last time I was inside," TJ said, shock mounting as he looked around. "Must have been kids."

Litter was strewn across the floor. Wine bottles, cigarette butts, beer bottles and—"Is that a condom?" she blurted.

Deke nodded, eyes round. "Safety first, I guess." He pointed to another one in a corner.

A wide set of stairs rose on her left and the lobby counter sat in a corner nook by the staircase. A pair of ancient sofas faced each other in front of the stone fireplace. "At least they didn't spray paint the stone," she said.

TJ snorted. "They've done everything but."

A round coffee table sat between the sofas. The table had

been beautiful once, but now it was an ashtray, with butts and burns scoring the fine wood. "Grandad made that table. I remember him putting the finish on it." She felt ill at the sight. Her stomach clenched as she remembered his hands rubbing, rubbing, rubbing polish into the wood.

TJ nodded. "He made a lot of the furniture. He was a craftsman."

"How did they get in?" she wondered. "That door hasn't been used in a while; I had to shove to open it."

"Deke, check the cellar door. I'd have noticed if they'd broken in through the back door in the kitchen." He went to the windows and tugged at the heavy draperies. The rings screeched across the rod. "Been a while since these were opened." Dust billowed around him. He coughed and waved the dust away. "Jon lived in his own area beside the kitchen. It doesn't look like he ever came out here."

"How sad. All of this is just so sad." No matter that he'd been a crusty old geezer, no one should spend their last days alone in the dark, away from friends and family. *Knowing that his estranged daughter had died before they could mend their fences.*

"Jon grew more reclusive every year. For what it's worth, he lived with a lot of regret."

"Thanks, I'm getting a pretty good idea. Beginning with the time he kicked his only daughter to the curb."

"That would do it." No surprise in his tone told her he already knew about the estrangement.

"Our dads tried to keep in touch, but Aunt Trudy had her pride and refused to have anything to do with her family. When she died in that car accident, it was the first time I ever saw my father cry."

She shook her head at all the foolish loss and vowed again to never lose touch with her brother.

At the dust-laden registration desk she found an old-fashioned rack of square cubbies with ten keys hanging on hooks. Even if the inn was fully functional, she didn't see how ten rooms would provide enough cash flow to keep the doors open. She did some rapid calculations.

"Do you remember Grandad operating this place? Ever?" He'd been closed for renovations the summer she'd been here. She remembered watching him planing wood and turning out spindles in his shop out back.

"He preferred woodworking. This coffee table would kill him if he saw the burns. Bastards."

"I remember his woodworking shop. Is it still there?"

"Yes. Still functional. In fact, it's all just as he left it, unless the kids broke in there, too."

"I hope not." This was bad enough, but to vandalize his tools and equipment would be sacrilege.

Deke returned from the basement. "They got in through the cellar door. There's an overgrown lilac bush out there. That's why we didn't notice they'd ripped out the boards we nailed into place when he died."

TJ nodded. "His workshop's fine then. We'd have noticed if the padlock had been broken off or the windows busted."

She gave him a grateful nod. "Thanks for seeing to the locks and things." It was a shame about the interior and ironic that the O'Banions had torn out every living green thing out back except that lilac bush.

Deke agreed with the assessment of the workshop but went off to check anyway while TJ picked up her bag. "You can't stay here tonight. There's no telling how many people know it's being used as party central, or how dangerous it can get here. Come home with me." He grinned a wicked smile that offered its own invitation. "I've got a guest room with a full-size bed. Clean sheets, too."

"Be still my heart." She fluttered a hand over her heart. "You really know how to seduce a girl."

A whole night within reach of TJ O'Banion. She glanced at Deke, who walked in, then did an immediate about-face and left again.

No way. She couldn't handle a night in the same house as TJ. She'd said she wouldn't sleep with him and she meant it. He'd deliberately sabotaged her hope of selling the place by tearing up that acre out back and she held on to that reminder like a life ring. "There's got to be a hotel room around."

"Probably, but I live closer than all the hotels. Plus, Deke and I will be around if you need any help with humping."

"Excuse me?"

"Furniture. Moving furniture." His look was all innocence, as he continued, "You don't want to sleep on a filthy bed in this place. God only knows what's gone on upstairs."

Bad, oh no, it could be bad. She felt color drain from her face as she dashed up the stairs to see for herself. The rooms ran along an open hall that overlooked the main floor. Trashed, all of them. And all the furniture had been stolen.

She stepped back to look over the railing at the brothers. "No beds. They've been stolen, I guess." Back when she'd visited, Grandad had told her he was making headboards and footboards. He must have gotten some furniture installed.

TJ frowned. "The inn never actually took in any guests. It's possible there was never furniture up there."

"Never?"

Deke shook his head to confirm. "I saw a lot of stuff stacked in the cellar. Could be Jon stored it down there rather than asking for help to get it upstairs."

"An old man who refused to ask for help. Sounds like Grandad."

"Where did you sleep when you were here?" TJ asked.

"In a tiny guestroom in his suite behind the dining room and kitchen." The room hadn't been much bigger than the single bed and small dresser Grandad had crammed in. She shuddered to think of the condition of that single bed all these years later.

"Ready to reconsider my invitation?" TJ smiled up at her, innocence and sex appeal personified. Damn him.

She warmed all over and need lit a match in her sex. He flashed her a smile that melted her panties and teased her with promise.

Tease. The idea held a certain allure. It could be a lot of fun to tease him for a few days. Payback for ripping the shit out of the land out back.

He may win the war, but she'd give him a hell of a run before she surrendered. Oh yes, she'd hang him by his blue balls until he begged for it.

She smiled back at him and put enough heat in her expression to sizzle steak. "I'll take you up on that offer, TJ, seeing as you were such a good sport to offer me a guest room. To myself."

"Guess I'll move out to my camper then." Deke muttered beside TJ.

TJ slapped his palm on Deke's shoulder to hold his brother still. He stared up at Marnie. "That's great, Marnie. Jon would be pleased to know you've accepted my hospitality."

She walked down the stairs much more slowly than she'd run up, her expression serene and sultry. The sway in her hips promised him a good old-fashioned chase.

A chase he was definitely up for. *Up* being the operative word. His cock had been on alert since he'd first set eyes on her.

"Deke, get your shit out of the spare room and move your camper to Lyle's place. I have a guest that smells a lot better than you."

He'd won this round, with the help of the kids that had ruined the inn. As sad as it was to see the condition of the place, he rejoiced at his good luck.

Marnie had accepted the cabins and the interior of the inn was guaranteed to keep her out of his hair through most of the project.

Best of all, he'd have a whole summer of contact. She wasn't the kind of woman to leave work to others and she'd be on site more often than not.

He had a handle on the woman she'd become: sexy, bright, driven. He wanted to know if there was anything left of the girl she'd been, the funny, smart kid who'd laughed with him and caught his heart in the first blush of attraction.

He had a whole summer to learn about Marnie Dawson. A whole summer to seduce her, starting now.

Holly Dawson glanced at her call display. Marnie. Guilt made her answer. "Finally," Marnie said by way of greeting, "you picked up."

"Only because you made me feel guilty about not answering. I've been busy. New place, new job, yada yada." Avoiding her ex-husband had been high on her list, too. She juggled her phone, her purse, her keys, while listening to a wild rant from her favorite cousin.

She opened her apartment door and left her key to dangle in the lock as she listened. "You won't believe the devastation. All those beautiful trees gone. Uprooted as if they never existed," Marnie wailed.

Holly didn't get a word in while Marnie blasted through some more complaints about a guy named Paul Bunyan who was immovable as a mountain. She got hopelessly lost in the details, none of which made sense.

The best thing to do when Marnie got on a rant was to let her wind down. She set her purse on the shelf in the hall closet, while Marnie complained in her ear about stubborn mountain men in plaid shirts.

"Paul who?" She leaned on the wall, prepared to listen for as long as it took. Marnie in a panic didn't happen often, so it must mean serious trouble at the inn.

"He tore up an acre of trees to build log cabins."

"Paul Bunyan?" Marnie was frazzled if she was imagining fictional folk heroes. "Have you seen his ox?"

"Yes, no, don't be a pain and *listen*." Marnie's exasperated voice rang through the phone. "His name is really TJ O'Banion, but he reminds me of Paul Bunyan. He's big and brawny and builds log cabins."

"And he's cleared the back acres? All of them?"

"One. But you'll recall the codicil Grandad added to his will? We thought it was odd, but now it makes sense. He paid the O'Banions to clear the land and build log cabins behind the inn."

"What was he thinking?"

"After Aunt Trudy died, he added the codicil and paid TJ in advance. The work has to be finished before we can sell." Marnie stalled out.

"If the cabins increase the value, then I'm fine with the whole idea." She looked forward to spending a couple of weeks away from Seattle and the chance to spruce up the Friendly Inn couldn't have come at a better time.

For lots of reasons, getting gone worked for Holly, but Marnie wanted in and out and a sold sign on the lawn. This time on the Peninsula was time Marnie couldn't afford.

Holly understood, but at the same time, she wanted the peace and quiet. She needed to sort out her life and a couple weeks away fit the bill. Marnie still ranted, but one detail came clear.

Grandad had always been an out-of-the-box thinker, a man who forged ahead with ideas without a thought for anyone else.

She couldn't decide if that made him strong and decisive or just plain selfish.

He would never have consulted with his children about such a move, even though the land and the business would one day be theirs.

But he'd fooled everyone by skipping a generation in his will. He'd passed all his land down to his granddaughters with the stipulation that no male descendants could visit the inn until one year after his death.

"I wish our fathers could go up there and see what's going on. I have to wonder what else the old man had up his sleeve."

"Doesn't bear thinking about. But in a way, I'm glad we only have each other and Kylie to deal with when it comes to decisions about the inn. Surely three people can find common ground sooner than an entire family of stubborn Dawsons." A hint of humor laced through Marnie's words.

"We'll manage, but—" A pair of strong arms caught Holly around the waist, cutting off her words. She yelped in shock but recognized the scent of the man who held her.

"Holly? Are you okay, what's going on?"

"I have to go, Marnie." Jack nuzzled her neck. "I have unexpected company." Her ex nipped at her ear, while he dangled her keys over the hall table. She heard him kick the door shut as she disconnected.

Damn, she should have seen him lurking outside the building.

She flipped her phone off and turned into Jack's arms, thinking fast. He snugged her hips tight to his.

His cock rose, ready and hard between them. Holly let him kiss her while she tried to think of a reason to get him out of here before the inevitable happened.

Too late.

His hand slid up her skirt to her pussy with expert knowledge and pressed against her in a rocking motion. He knew she'd be wet for him in seconds. Sex had almost always been good with Jack.

It was everything else that was wrong.

Moisture built while he sighed into her mouth. "See, babe? It's so right for us." He tore her panty hose open then hooked a finger around the crotch of her panties and pulled them down so he could open her and plunge into her moistening channel.

Damn, this was good. She tried not to like it, but her knees went weak as she opened into a bloom. She hadn't seen him in two weeks and she'd hoped he'd take the hint and let these booty calls come to an end. But Jack had never let anything go easily.

"Jack, we need to talk." He rubbed his thumb over her clit. "Really." But, oh, it felt good. So good. She let her head roll as he rubbed at her. They'd talk later, after he'd woven his magic. She was such a sucker for this. Did it make her weak to want sex this much? Her clit plumped as he rolled it under his thumb.

She shifted to give him more room while he tore at her hose again. If she was lucky, he'd drop to his knees and eat her raw. But she refused to ask. He'd like hearing it too much.

"Done enough talking, Holly," he said into her ear. His chin rasped the delicate skin of her neck. "Right now I want you and you want this. You're so hot, so needy every time. I'll never get enough of you." He kissed her again, hard, testing, tempting. "There'll never be another you."

He was right about her need for sex. She was easily aroused and he'd taken advantage all through their marriage. Knowing he was doing it again didn't stop the sensations, though. She was a sucker and let him play her like one.

But one more time couldn't hurt. She moaned as he bared her breasts and suckled each one. Tension rose and orgasm beckoned.

She bit back the next moan as desire heated deep in her belly.

A flare of anger burned along the passion as he kissed her neck with a stream of nips and nibbles that drove her toward release. Her hips pumped in response to the steady plunge of his fingers. "Jack." He made her so wet.

"Hear that, baby?" He moved his finger faster, sliding into her slickness. "You're wet for me. Just for me. Tell me, Holly, tell me."

"Just for you, Jack," she lied and panted for breath, and heard the wet slide as he worked her toward a fast first come. Her plumped clit distended toward his thumb and he laughed in his throat when she rolled her hips for more. He burrowed his thumb and rubbed harder. She groaned and opened wider, giving him the invitation he craved.

She rolled her head again and touched the frame of her hall mirror, but Jack didn't stop. He knew all her signs and kept up a steady assault on her senses.

"Unh," she groaned the way he liked and stopped pretending she could put the brakes on this with him. He took her over the edge into weak release.

"That's it, baby," he crooned as her pulsing orgasm faded. It had been a couple of years since she'd had a really great orgasm, but Jack never bothered to notice.

There was a lot he didn't want to see, and Holly had unconsciously entered into a conspiracy of silence with Jack. Their marriage had slipped away while neither of them noticed. Conversation had deteriorated, shared time had disappeared. The only thing they still had was *this*.

Three months after the divorce even the sex had faded to a shadow of what it had been.

Yes, a conspiracy of silence cocooned them.

A silence that had to be broken.

Later.

Right now, she didn't have the heart to throw salt into his

wounds, so she took him into her bedroom and into her body, one last time.

She tugged off her shredded panty hose and panties and settled back on the bed while Jack shucked out of his jeans. She passed him a condom and smiled when he whined about it. She cocked an eyebrow. "We're not together, Jack. I don't know where you've been."

He used it, but he was pissed off enough to drag her by the ankles to the foot of the bed. Then he bent her knees to her chest, opened her legs wide and rammed into her. He grunted with the force of his powerful thrust while Holly clutched the bedspread and counted plunges.

Should take four, but, hey, Jack was in fine form today with six. He spurted into her and rode out his orgasm in a burst of enthusiasm she didn't feel. Two weeks ago she'd at least managed to feign interest.

Booty calls with her ex. How pathetic. But this was the first time he'd come to this new apartment. Other times she'd gone to him and it shamed her that she had. But sex with strangers wasn't a sure thing and Jack came with a guarantee. Marnie often said a vibrator did, too.

Jack tried to shift to his usual side of the bed but she scooted over and moved into place to block him. "You, ah, have to go now, Jack. I'm busy tonight." She held her breath while he took in the comment.

He frowned. He liked everything in its place and she was on the wrong side of the bed. Her bed. Her new bed, that up until now, had had no trace of Jack in it.

"I want to have dinner, watch a movie," he said. "Do what we always do."

"Which is the problem, isn't it?" She should have been more careful with her keys. She set her forearm across her forehead and stared at the ceiling. Plastic stars and moons glowed at her from the ceiling.

He saw them, too. She knew because he made a clicking sound with his tongue. He disapproved of whimsy, and the glow-in-the-dark celestial bodies smacked of lightheartedness.

Thing was, she loved feeling light and happy and it was time she said so. "I like my stars," she said. "They're mine and I like them."

He smoothed his cock and left sticky tracks on her brand-new sheets. He'd always been lazy post coitus. He wouldn't leave unless she pushed harder.

"What are you busy with?"

"Packing. I'm going to the Peninsula to meet up with Marnie."

"Why? You never go there."

"Family meeting. Everyone's going." The lie came more easily than she expected, but she'd say anything to ease this moment. She didn't want to end things with the bald truth. She didn't have any feelings for Jack anymore: not love, not anger, not even dislike or disappointment. There was just a big void where her feelings for him used to live. And sorry, sad sex couldn't fill that void any longer.

"Your Grandad sick? He's got that inn, right?" Jack always liked the idea of her coming into her share some day. It was a mistake to mention the Peninsula. He could be dogged when he got wind of something.

"No, he's not sick." A technicality because Jon Dawson had died months ago, in the early days of their separation. "But we thought it was a good time to get together." She scrambled to think of a reason that would work to put him off the scent. "It seems we have a cousin we've never met. My Aunt Trudy's daughter. No one's met her."

He snorted and rolled to sit up. His back showed his recent weight gain. Love handles bulged at his waist. Not that she cared, but it proved he was still stressed over their divorce. He liked to blame her for his fast-food diet, but when they were together he'd done a lot of the cooking. According to Jack, her skills were never quite up to snuff in the kitchen.

"You need to move on, Jack. This has to be the last time we're together."

His back stiffened. "Why? We're talking now. Isn't that what you want? To communicate?"

"Fucking when the mood strikes isn't communication. It's been months since the divorce. I've got a new place I like. A job I enjoy," she lied again. "You need to find the same kind of positive things." She wanted to pat him on the back, but he'd see it as an invitation for more sex. "Take this time while I'm away to focus on what you want out of life. You may find someone you connect with."

He turned to face her. "When are you coming back?" His voice was quiet, soft. His eyes shimmered in the twilight that filled the room.

She hesitated, because she wasn't sure how much time he might need. She shrugged. "I took a couple of vacation weeks, so I'll be gone a while. I'm not exactly sure how long," she fudged. "Marnie talked about hanging out a while and getting to know our new cousin."

"A couple of weeks, just long enough for you to beg for it again."

She couldn't let it pass, she should have, but she couldn't. "You're the one who came to me. I don't want this with you anymore."

He stood and walked out without speaking or looking at her again. But he made sure to use her shower and leave his wet towels on the floor of her bathroom.

Jack, staking a claim, trying to let her know he was still part of her life. Still her husband.

He wasn't.

He wasn't.

He wasn't.

4

Marnie took a moment to appreciate TJ's fine body when he unloaded her car and motioned her into his home ahead of him. She opened the unlocked front door, prepared for full-on bachelor decor. She was wrong. "Your home is beautiful." Rustic but with a contemporary flair.

He set a suitcase and her laptop on his leather sofa. Brown top-grain, not black, softly worn-in, like a favorite jacket.

"It's a mess," he confessed. "Deke's not the easiest man to live with, but I should have picked up before I left this morning." Two extra-large pizza boxes littered his coffee table, but other than the accompanying pair of empty beer bottles, the living area was tidy. Roomy and filled with furniture large enough for sprawling. A good man's home.

He cared about how he lived, wanted comfort and quality in his life. "Looks great to me."

"Thanks, but I admit to using a service every week to keep things straightened up around here." He put his hands on his hips and surveyed the room.

"It's a lot more welcoming than the Friendly Inn." She

shook her head at the name. "I don't know that I've ever seen a business with such a misnomer."

He laughed. "Jon just didn't like people."

"I can't imagine him as a father with young children. My dad's never said much about growing up with him."

"Jon's heart was torn out when he lost his wife. He didn't recover. He said she made him a better man, and with her death, that part of him died, too."

"Now you've made me feel sorry for a crotchety old man who never said a kind word to anyone." She hung her purse strap over the newel post of his impressive staircase and reached to take her bag from him. "The guest room?"

"Upstairs on the left. Make yourself at home." She put her hand on the staircase but TJ covered it with his. She looked at him for a measuring moment.

"Thank you for taking me in," she said. "I'll try not to disturb you."

His gaze heated. "You've disturbed me since you stepped out of your car. I don't see that changing any time soon."

"Likewise, Thomas John."

She trotted upstairs and found her room right away. Functional and tidy, but the bed was stripped of linen. "Tell me where the sheets are and I'll make the bed," she called downstairs.

His expression when she asked was crestfallen. "That door right behind you."

"You didn't think it would be that easy, did you?"

"A man can dream, can't he?"

She chuckled under her breath as she dug out a set of pretty, feminine sheets. Obviously, the man wasn't always here alone. She held the sheets to her chest and looked downstairs. She found him staring back up at her, his black hair falling over his left eye and his chest so wide they'd never walk side by side on the stairs. He took her breath as his gaze traveled up her legs to her sheet-covered chest and down again.

"Leave the sheets; you must be hungry. We can raid the fridge together."

She needed no further encouragement and tossed the sheets on the bare mattress before joining him downstairs.

By the time she reached the main floor, he'd turned his mind back to the Friendly Inn. "When the sign fell over at the end of the drive, I told Jon he shouldn't bother putting it back up. He never did."

"Think it's still in the ditch? We might salvage it." She followed him through the dining area.

He shrugged and she admired his shoulders from the back. Broad and straight, they tapered to a trim waist. "I'll make you a new one," he offered.

"For free?"

"I'll include it with the cabins. A welcome gift." The kitchen was bright and airy with no curtains at the windows. She glanced out to the view. Trees. Nothing but trees starting at about ten feet back of the house. From the wall to the tree line was a well-used, but clean dog run. "No dog?"

"Beau's gone. Been three months and, well, I haven't had the heart to look."

Tears stung her eyes. "I'm sorry. They do mean a lot to us, don't they?" Her apartment was too small and her life too busy for a dog. She had a couple cacti because they didn't need much care. "Thanks for the offer on the sign; I'll take you up on it but it's a shame Grandad's handcarved sign will rot away." She leaned over the kitchen sink to take a closer look at the area outside. "You must see a lot of wildlife here."

"Deer and raccoons mostly. Birds. We see more bald eagles than we used to." The fridge door opened behind her. "The raccoons have been bolder now that Beau's gone."

This had to be a dangerous game for her. To see the way he lived, missing his dog, keeping a nice home, caring about a grumpy old man, all things that pointed to TJ O'Banion having a good heart. She wasn't sure when the last time was she'd met a man like TJ. Certainly not at the club.

"It'll be good to see the inn taking guests," he said as he checked the contents of the fridge. "Since construction costs on the cabins are already covered, you won't have loans to pay off. Between the cabins and the rooms, you should be able to at least break even the first year."

"Someone will," she said as she turned to face him. "I'm going back to Seattle as fast as I can. I've got a club to run and a partner I need to deal with."

He stilled with his hand on the open fridge door. "Partner?"

Her lips split into a grin at the concern on his face. "Business partner. I don't sleep with him." She shuddered so convincingly he gave her a ready smile. "Just like I'm not going to sleep with you." She wasn't sure if she meant it or not.

TJ cupped his ear at her obvious lie. "I couldn't quite catch that. Your eyes speak a different language." As did her smile, her sway and the way she'd unbuttoned an extra button on her blouse.

Her cell phone rang and she dashed to her purse to answer it. "Holly? Where are you?"

The cousin and a partner in the inn. Holly's feelings about the inn could be different from Marnie's. She may want to keep the place. He leaned into the room.

Marnie walked outside to the veranda, looking for privacy. Damn. She paced in front of his living room window while she talked, looking grim. An argument? It wouldn't be the first time heirs disagreed on an inheritance.

She used her hands when she talked. He remembered that trait now that he thought about it. In fact, he recalled a lot more about that summer and her than he'd realized at first. Memories flooded back in a rapid wash of images. He'd liked her, enjoyed her company.

He'd even thought she was smart and had harbored a fear that maybe, just maybe, he'd stumbled on a girl who was smarter than him. At fifteen, that had been a major cut to his ego.

Now, he was impressed. She had a good head on her shoulders, didn't wail and ring her hands at setbacks.

Marnie Dawson also had a body worth waiting for.

He pulled a beer out of the fridge, thought again and dug into the back for a bottle of wine. He walked to the front window and held them up for her to see. She smiled and pointed at the wine. She held up three fingers to indicate the call would soon wind down.

He took the next couple of minutes to set out some cheese, crackers and grapes on a platter. She must be hungry; early evening and dinner was still an hour away.

He wasn't sure how fast she wanted to get back to the inn, but she didn't seem like a woman to put off work.

She walked in on a breeze of fresh air and a vitality all her own. "Thanks, this looks great. I need the wine after that phone call. Turns out Holly was planning on staying for a couple of weeks at least."

"Great, so you will, too?" He pictured her in his bed for fourteen long nights.

"You look like the cat that ate the canary."

"Not yet, but it's definitely on the agenda."

She plucked a grape from the stem and popped it into her mouth. The moment the juice sprayed inside her mouth, her eyelashes fluttered. She moved her tongue around the grape inside her mouth. Sensual in every way. Her eyelids drooped as she licked her lips to extend her enjoyment of the juiciness, and his libido cranked higher.

Lifting her glass in a silent toast, she took a sip of wine.

"Very good." Then she topped a cracker with cheese and munched the snack daintily. "Perfect."

She caught him looking, then she took a seat at his sandwich bar, which only gave him a better view of her cleavage. "Where can I get cleaning supplies?"

The twinkle of humor in her eye sent his temperature to boil. The witch knew damn well she'd stalled him.

"I've got mops and buckets. I'd be happy to call in a cleaning crew. Some of the housekeeping staff at local hotels might want to pick up extra work."

"Tempting as it is not to wear myself out cleaning up that mess, I'll wait for Holly to get here before I spend money for help. We may have inherited the inn, but all of the money and everything else went to the men in the family."

"They could come help." He'd never met her brother. Might be wiser not to. He'd pick up on the scent of lust right away. Not his sweet little sister's, of course, but TJ's.

"Not allowed. Grandad insisted on the three of us working together on the place." She bit her lip as if she'd said more than she wanted.

At least he'd avoid a showdown with her brother. "I thought it was just you and Holly."

She bit her lip and looked resigned. "You'll learn about this soon enough I suppose. Our Aunt Trudy had a daughter out of wedlock so Grandad included her in his will."

"Kylie Keegan," he said. He knew about the stormy meeting between Jon and his newfound granddaughter, but he couldn't bring himself to betray his friend's confidence. Jon had found his own way to make amends. It wasn't TJ's place to judge. Still, he had to say something. "Your Grandad had his own ideas about things and never thought twice about expressing them, no matter how wrong he was."

"None of us have ever known her and suddenly Holly and I have to sort out what to do with the inn with a stranger." She

shrugged. "But neither of us are ogres, so if she's halfway reasonable, it should all work out." She brightened. "And another
pair of hands to work with us will come in handy."

"Not my business to tell you this, but you should know that
the night she stormed away and Jon pulled out the bottle he
told me he said some ugly things to her. She may come into the
family with a chip on her shoulder." He hesitated to say any
more. "But, for whatever it's worth, Jon regretted every word
after she left, but she refused to talk to him again."

"Great, another stubborn Dawson female." Blowing out a
breath, she said, "Thanks, I appreciate the heads up. Tell me
what he said to her."

"No. Jon had his regrets about how he treated her, about a
lot of things. But if anyone's to repeat what was said, it should
be her."

"You're sure this is how you want to play it?"

What she was really saying was that it was early in the game
between them to tick her off. As much as he wanted her, he had
a loyalty to Jon he couldn't ignore. "You'll get over it."

She took a long, very slow scan of his body, from his boots
to the top of his head, that had his cock ready, willing and able.
"Maybe I will. Maybe I won't."

"Hey, you're right. You'll have another pair of helping hands
with the inn and time to get to know your cousin. It's up to you
and Holly to work things out with her." He scrubbed his hair
and decided to add, "Anyone would have lit out of here the way
she did that night. She had every right to be furious and hurt.
Don't let her reaction to the old man get in the way of family."

His own family was almost sorted out after a rough patch.
Deke was off the booze and on the hunt for pussy, while Eli
still hadn't said when he planned to return, but he would.

TJ humped the dusty wing chair to join the other furniture
in the right corner of the inn's large living room. Marnie was

behind him tackling the cobwebs all over the lobby desk. She tsked and huffed and stood high enough on a step stool to allow peekaboo glimpses of her fine butt as she stretched to reach the very top of the shelves behind the counter. When she stretched to reach the top shelves, her butt muscles clenched hard as firm melons.

If he didn't look away soon, he might approach and slip a hand up her shorts. As it was, his hands were clenched.

Women in full cleaning mode rarely wanted to stop for a quickie. At least none of the women he knew did. When they got help with cleaning, they showed their appreciation later. He looked forward to it. He slapped on an easy grin.

"I've got everything stacked here," he said while he admired her trim waist and the flare of her hips. She turned to look over her shoulder. Bright and inquisitive, she smiled when she saw the furniture stacked in one corner. "Will this work for you?"

"Absolutely. Thanks." She stepped down to the floor and walked around the counter. Hands on her hips, she blew at a cobweb that hung off her bangs. It fell back into place and he wanted to sweep it away, but she got to it first. "I'll vacuum the dust off the furniture before we move it back."

"We?"

"You." She had the grace to flush. "That is, if you can spare some time tomorrow?"

He considered saying no, but butthead Deke might be tempted to take his place here and they'd have to come to blows. While it might be fun to kick Deke's ass, it would make working with him all summer a pain. Deke could hold a grudge like nobody else.

"I'll be here."

"Great. I can get the whole room cleaned before you even have to show up." She slipped her hands to her lower back and pushed her pelvis toward him as she stretched out her back. "Oh, it's good to stretch after the drive today and now this."

He picked up the coffee table and carried it to the door into the kitchen. "I'll take this out to Jon's workshop for a sanding. After it's refinished, you'll never see this damage again."

"You're not even winded," she noted, "while I'm bushed. I'm out of shape for this type of work."

He accepted the invitation to skim her figure with his gaze. "You look like you're in shape to me." His cock rose at the temptation he read in her eyes, and when he caught her looking at his biceps, he shifted the table.

She chuckled. "You're something, TJ, you know that?"

"As are you, Marnie, as are you." The push pull between them lightened his day. He put the table on the floor, hopeful.

She ignored the obvious invitation to step closer and headed for the stack of furniture instead. "I run when I can, but I miss my yoga practice. I haven't been to class for a year. If I hadn't given up, I wouldn't feel so stiff."

"There's a soaker tub in my master bath. I'll run it for you when we get home." Another sexy look over her shoulder and he applauded the impulse he'd had to install the tub last year.

She lifted one corner of her mouth. "Toss in some Epsom salts and I'll take you up on the bath." When she picked up her dusting rag, he picked up the table and watched as she dropped out of sight behind the counter to continue cleaning. "Ugh, it's filthy in these drawers and I think I see—whoa—could you come here please?" Her voice went hollow so he set the table down and moved fast. *Thump.* "Tell me this isn't what I think it is."

She'd landed on her butt in the dust, a look of horror on her face. She'd pulled the bottom drawer all the way out for cleaning.

"Oh, hell, we'll have to call an exterminator and the sooner the better, because that's one big ugly rat."

"How long's it been dead d'you think?" She shuddered again. He reached a hand down to help her up. She took it and he pulled her up fast. Her breasts mashed against his chest as he steadied her.

He tilted his head toward the drawer. "It's been dead a long time, but where there's one, there's more. I can't see how it got in, there are no chew marks on the drawer."

She leaned against him. "Did the kids just stick it in there to die of starvation?"

"Not likely." He slipped his arm around her. "No gnaw marks on the inside either."

"I'll have to disinfect this whole area." She stepped away from him and he felt the loss. She dropped to her knees in front of him and slipped on rubber gloves. "Why do I get the feeling this makes you happy?"

She looked up into his face with a suspicious expression. From here it wouldn't take much to peer down her cleavage or slip his hand behind her head and tug her toward—he cut off the thought. No good could come of rushing her.

"Me? No, I'm not glad you've got a rat problem. It's gross." But having rats in the inn would keep her at his place longer than she planned. Which suited him just fine. He opened his hands to take the drawer. "I'll take care of this."

"Thanks, again. Furniture mover, rat remover. You're a multi-talented man." She slipped her palm into his, with a sweetly sexual expression that sent a jolt of lust into his gut. He controlled his movements so that when she stood, he didn't even grab her close. Instead, he played the gentleman and let go of her hand.

Played was the right term. This was a game they'd entered. A sexual game of thrust and parry and come hither looks that could kill him before he got where he wanted to go.

Or maybe not.

She slapped at the dust on her shorts and stepped away with a briskness that showed no interest. Unless dumping a bucket of black filthy water counted. She carried the bucket out to the kitchen and dumped it down the old porcelain sink.

He picked up the drawer and then walked past her out the back door. "I'll make sure that cellar door's secure for the night."

"I'll get a set of security lights with motion detectors first thing in the morning," she called out after him.

Another thing for him to do for her. At this rate, he'd be in sweet clover in no time.

In his pickup truck an hour later, he watched as she buckled her seat belt and released the elastic band she'd used to cinch her hair at the nape of her neck. Her hair fell free and he wanted to run his fingers through it so badly he clenched his teeth to stop himself.

The air and stillness in the cab filled out, moist and heavy when she turned her half-lidded eyes on him. "Thanks a lot for your help. I appreciate it." She slid her palm up his forearm and back to her thigh before he could capture it.

"No problem. I'm here to serve."

"Right. Then take me home, TJ. I'm not going to pretend that soaker tub isn't calling me. I'll be stiff and sore in the morning, but a hot bath will do wonders for me now."

Her phone rang and she fumbled through her bag to get the call. She talked while he drove with half an ear on her conversation. From Marnie's half of the conversation, it was her cousin Holly saying she was on her way in the morning.

"Great, see you then," she said and hung up.

"You didn't tell her how much work the inn will need before you can put it on the market."

She wrinkled her nose and looked endlessly kissable. "I've already done that. She's the one with all the decorating talent. She can make the place look great."

"You said she has more time to spend here than you do?"

"She has her reasons for wanting to hide up here, while all I want is to get back to the city."

"You think living here is hiding?"

"Don't you? With your talent, you could be anywhere, but instead—sorry—I shouldn't have said anything."

"You think I'm hiding here? That I'm not ambitious enough?"

"I didn't say that." But she'd thought it. The guilty gleam in her eyes said so.

"Or do you think I'm afraid of the competition in the city?"

Her silence said more than a phoney denial would. It stung, that silence, but he'd be damned if he corrected her assumption.

He pulled in to his compound and parked the truck beside the bumblebee she called a car and climbed down. By the time he got to her side, she'd landed on her feet. He shut the door. "I would have helped you out."

"If you'd held me while I jumped out, I would have collapsed in your arms. You'd be carrying me inside." A shaky smile accompanied the words. "I shouldn't have said anything about your choice to stay here."

"I chose to come back. It isn't that I never left."

"Where'd you go?"

He smiled but made no comment. Let her stew about it. It would do her good to wonder. So far, he'd been an open book.

She sauntered up onto his porch and through his front door without pressing for an answer.

The mundane details of towels and fresh sheets on the guest room bed and a fresh bar of soap behind them, TJ set the faucets to run into his tub while she got ready for her bath.

When he turned around, he had to pick his jaw up off the floor. She was in a silky, short colorful robe that barely covered the tops of her thighs. Her auburn hair swayed free at the tips of her breasts, and with her sash drawn tight, the lapels showed a sweet line of cleavage.

Steam rose into the room and he stood there like an imbecile, no doubt drooling. She cocked her head and waited, clasping the towels he'd given her.

He cleared his throat. "Oh, yeah, I guess I'll leave you to it, then."

"Yes, I guess you will."

"If it gets too steamy in here, I can crack open the window."

"Thanks, that would be great." She shifted on her pretty bare feet while he took care of the window for her. "An inch should do it."

"I'm sure that's fine."

He sidled out the door, edging his way around her and damned himself for leaving. He should have grabbed her by the waist and pulled her to him, but Marnie Dawson had him by the 'nads and she wasn't letting go long enough to let him think let alone act on his desire.

The next hour flew by as he grabbed ingredients for an omelette and groaned four hundred and ninety-five times at the thought of Marnie covered in bubbles and steam, her breasts bobbing on the surface of his tub.

Her comment still rankled him. He'd never considered that his return to the Peninsula could be construed as a failure, even by someone who didn't know him. He thought back to this afternoon when they'd first seen each other. All he'd said was that the Peninsula was home. Which was true. He hadn't seen the need to explain anything else. He was here now, and here is where he planned to stay.

The sound of water draining from the tub alerted him to her imminent arrival. Distracted, he burned his hand on the kettle when he reached for it to pour her a cup of tea. "Damn it." He flicked his hand and stuck his burnt fingertip into his mouth.

"Poor baby, want me to do that for you?" she asked from behind him. Close behind him. She was light on her feet, or he'd have heard her.

She grabbed his hand away from his mouth.

And damn if she didn't do exactly what she offered.

The feel of her warm wet mouth on his finger blew his mind. What was left of it shattered further with the way she pressed his forearm to her chest, wedging it between her breasts. Her wicked tongue swirled around his burnt fingertip once, twice.

Three times.

She released him with a soft seductive pop and then stepped back out of reach.

The kettle whistled while his pulse pounded in the rush of blood to his cock.

Every male hormone he possessed told him to lean in, grab her and finish the race, but her impish look of triumph stopped him before he made a fool of himself.

She was a witch who knew how to wield every weapon at her disposal.

With a wink, she slipped to the far side of the sandwich bar and took a seat on a stool. Like a prim miss, she gathered the sides of her short robe and propped her chin on her hand. "What's for dinner?"

You.

Two hours after he'd had the life sucked out of his finger, TJ headed for the staircase. His cock had been hard all through dinner and hadn't subsided until Marnie had disappeared into the guest room.

He'd taken care of some business calls and tracked his youngest brother's movements to an island in the Caribbean. Eli answered after three rings.

"There's a woman here, Teeje." He used the name he'd always used as a kid.

"There's always a woman somewhere, Eli. But unless she lives in Port Townsend and knows how to wire a log building, I'm not interested in hearing about her."

"You've got to get a life, Teeje."

He rubbed the back of his neck. Eli had no idea he wanted exactly that. A life. But for now he might have to settle for the woman upstairs. He had no doubt they were in the initial stages of an affair. He wasn't stupid enough to say no to Marnie. But his ultimate goal had nothing to do with a temporary woman.

Caribbean music blared in the background and he plugged his other ear to hear better. "O'Banion Construction's headed into a busy summer. We're finally building those cabins Jon Dawson talked about."

"I heard about old Jon. Sorry about that; I know you thought of him as a good friend."

"I may have been his only one." They'd never seen much of each other, but when they did, they'd packed a lot of talking in.

"You're building these cabins for the new owners?"

"I'm building them for Jon. He's the one I had the agreement with."

"I see. So the new owners are on board?"

"The granddaughters inherited the inn. The first one arrived today, there's another due tomorrow and the third one will get here sometime." He explained that Marnie and Holly hadn't met Kylie Keegan.

"Are they hot?"

"If I tell you they are, will it get you back here any sooner?"

"When you put it that way, I wouldn't believe you if they all look like supermodels. Scratch that, some of them are too damn skinny. Let's say lingerie models. Yes, I'd be on the next flight if they look like lingerie models."

An image of Marnie's soft cleavage flashed behind his eyes. "Never mind what Marnie looks like."

"Oh, ho, sounds like she's a looker. No prob, I'll just call Deke; he'll fill me in."

"If you're not here by early next week when we've got the foundations poured, I'll find another electrician." Eli knew there wasn't enough work for two, so if he arrived late, there'd be no work for him. TJ wasn't a man to hire a skilled trade then let him go without cause. Not for his brother, not for anyone.

"I'll think about it," Eli responded, getting the last word. Like always.

TJ hung up on the dial tone and considered his options for an electrician if Eli chose to stay with the woman he'd found. The pickings were lean because a lot of good men had left the Peninsula for work elsewhere. Still, he'd find someone, even if he had to bring in somebody from north of the border.

He turned off his desk lamp, shut off his laptop and headed up to bed.

As he walked by the guest room, a moan caught his attention. He stopped and cocked his head toward the door. Ah, hell. Never mind privacy, he had to listen.

He shut his eyes to focus on the sound. Panting. And the faint buzz of a small appliance. Hot damn. Another moan.

His cock, never far from hard since Marnie's arrival, responded. Behind his eyes he saw her in his guest bed, covers thrown back, legs open and heading for orgasm. The head of the vibrator circled her delicious pink lips, then touched lightly on her clit.

Was the lube she used strawberry, like her lip gloss had been? He slid his hand to the doorknob, then stilled. If he turned it and walked in, would she welcome him? Ask him to take that vibrator's place? He wanted to.

Scratch that. He'd *love* to walk in, but she'd sent so many mixed signals he hesitated. And he couldn't quite get over the insult to his ambition she'd lobbed at him.

Marnie was driven to succeed. Obviously she expected the same drive in a man she was interested in. But to assume that because he'd chosen to build a business on the Peninsula he was somehow lacking, piqued his pride.

He hated that pride would get in his way, but there it was.

She'd dangled herself like a carrot all day and the move with his fingertip had been the clincher.

After dinner, he'd noticed a slight flush to her cheeks and her nipples on high beam. Then he'd realized that she wanted the byplay, the press and retreat, the game, as it were.

So, was he up for a full-court press? Damn straight.

He turned the door handle and walked in.

5

TJ stepped into his guest bedroom and closed the door behind him. Marnie yelped and scrambled to a sitting position with her back to the headboard. "What are you doing?"

"You want to be in control of where and when with us?" He pressed his back to the door because if he moved so much as one more inch into the room, he'd lose this round. To a woman like Marnie, winning was more important than sex, or need or attraction. If she won now, he'd be nothing but a convenient partner.

He would not be relegated to *convenience*.

The pretty skin of her neck flushed as she gathered the sheet to cover her breasts, just visible in the gloom. He caught a scent exotically, erotically, hers. The burn of need thrashed him, nearly bringing him to his knees.

But the door at his back grounded him as he squeezed the doorknob in both hands.

"Get out. This is private." Her fevered glance slid down his waist to his crotch. "I'm a guest, not a convenience for your pleasure." But her knees were still splayed open and with her right leg still exposed. A rhythmic rocking screamed invitation.

"I would say the same to you. But you're a tease and I'm not." To succumb would be so damn easy, so fun for both of them. "Question is, what should I do about it?"

"Do what you want." She lifted a four-inch silver vibrator into the air and turned it on. Hypnotic buzzing filled the space between them.

He waited to see if she'd lift the sheets and continue, but her eyes took on a hard gleam of daring and he laughed. If he walked out right now, this moment, he'd win.

She'd lose.

And that would make her nuts.

"Think I'll take a shower," he said. "Just so you know where to find me."

He walked out, leaving the door open as he moved down the hall, fighting his raging hard-on all the way. The slam of the door made him grin.

Soon, she'd come to him and plead. Maybe even beg.

If the pressure in his balls didn't kill him first.

With a cock as hard as iron, he could barely slide his jeans off. There was only one thing to do if he wanted any sleep tonight. He didn't need an appliance, not when he had the five sisters.

He turned on the water in the shower stall and stepped in. Warm water sluiced down his body, washing away the grime of the day. He bent his head into the spray as he soaped up. When he got to his cock and balls, he nearly spewed immediately. An image of Marnie slid sexy and hot through his mind and he went back to her on her knees in front of him behind the registration counter. Except this time, the outcome was more in keeping with what he wanted. She smiled and gripped his cock with a firm hand then slid her mouth down, down, down until he felt the back of her soft throat. He groaned and increased his strokes as her mouth worked his shaft. She took his sac and squeezed until he shot deep into her wet, hot throat. He had to slam his hand on the cool tile to stay upright while he shot a full load into the pulsing jet of water. Shudders racked his body while he came.

When he was done, he turned off the water and hoped to hell this was the last time he'd have to take care of himself. He was damned tired of coming alone.

As he dried himself and walked through his dark room to climb into bed, he heard Marnie's steady descent down the stairs.

Naked, he walked to his door and opened it a crack to see what new torture she was bringing to the game. He could just make her out as she walked through his great room and into the kitchen. The fridge door opened and the light made her body glow. Straight square shoulders, fine trim waist, long legs. She wore the short robe again.

She helped herself to a small glass of milk by the fridge light, drank it quickly then rinsed the glass and set it in the sink.

He breathed deep into his lungs and held it while she drifted absently back up the stairs and down the hall to her room, apparently unaware of him watching. Apparently unaware, but probably fully aware, as he was of her.

Then he headed back into the shower for round two.

The next morning, edgy and out of sorts, TJ stood in the checkout line at the hardware store. He'd left Marnie at the inn, deep in a phone conversation with some guy named Dennis. Something about her club. They were apparently in the midst of a staffing crisis and she'd been laying it on pretty thick that it was Dennis's turn to step up and handle things in her absence.

An unreliable partner. He wouldn't wish it on his worst enemy. The stress of covering for him, doubting his word, double-checking his work, putting out fires he'd made, all of it sucked. Working with family wasn't ideal, not by a long shot, but having Deke home, even as broken as he was, was better than being on his own. Eli would settle down soon enough. A good woman would anchor him.

As long as Eli met his woman on the Peninsula, everything TJ wanted for him and his brothers would come to pass. Full-on partnerships in O'Banion Construction. Homes and families would come along in time and their lives would build into something of lasting value.

When his turn to cash out came, he slid two boxes of security lights on the counter at the front of the hardware store.

"G'morning, Thomas John. Lighting up the night?" He was caught midthought by Alice, one of the local single women. She grinned, overbite gleaming in the fluorescent lights overhead.

"The Friendly Inn's had some late-night partying since Jon died. Now that we're working there, I don't want my equipment vandalized the way they've ruined the interior." He shook his head in disgust and Alice clicked her tongue in sympathy.

"You're finally adding those cabins?"

He nodded and handed over his credit card. He waited, knowing she'd wind herself up, wishing she wouldn't.

"I hear the old man cut all his kids out of his will and left it to someone in the city." She leaned in close. "That's not all I heard."

He steeled himself. Right here, in this moment, listening to her giggle in anticipation of sharing her insight, was the reason Alice was off-limits. He held a distinct dislike for stupid women. He let the muscles in his face drop to blank. She didn't even notice, just barreled on, listening to her own voice.

In the typically gleeful voice reserved for the juiciest gossip, she kept to a stage whisper. "I hear he left it to a group of lesbians and that they're going to move in. Think they'll bring a bunch of gays here? Huh? What d'ya think?" Her avid expression turned his stomach. For a moment he wished what she said were true.

"I think that's as true as the last rumor I heard. That the place was haunted by the bodies of *thousands* of hitchhikers old Jon had cut up in the woods behind his house."

Her off-colored eyes went wide with shock. "Really? Is that what that old man was up to?"

"Know what else I think?" *Alice should have hitched a ride with the old man.*

Avid Alice paused, caught by the image of Jon slicing and dicing innocent kids.

"I think you should take payment for these lights and let me get back to work." He forced his jaw to unclench. "Alice."

"Oh, uh, sure."

Barry Fogarty snickered behind him and TJ cut him a glance. The snickering stopped. Barry always was a dickhead.

On his way out the door, he felt the unmistakable relief of seeing Marnie again. Not only was she unbelievably easy on the eyes, she was smart and witty. Being with her made his steps lighter and his day brighter. And God, what a challenge she'd become. He hadn't had this much fun with a woman outside of bed in, well . . . since that summer with Marnie nearly fifteen years ago.

He wondered what she'd think of Alice and the inane chatter that made up most of his days in town. Putting Marnie in a place like this seemed a sacrilege.

Some women were meant to live in the thick of things, in high-powered careers and stilettos. Marnie was one of them. Which meant even if they did share some good times, she'd be gone and he'd be here.

Shit.

He opened his truck door, but Barry called his name. He

might be a dickhead, but they'd made a lot of money together over the years, so he turned and plastered a welcoming smile on his face.

Barry hustled over. "God, that Alice can talk. Sucks a good dick, though." He slipped his hands in his pocket and adjusted himself. "Maybe I should head back in?" He chuckled.

TJ waited, trying to blank out the image of Alice and her overbite sliding over Barry's distended skinny cock. Sometimes high school gym showers gave a guy too much information.

But the whole thing made him think of getting head. *Marnie.* "Not a bad idea, Barry. Alice always liked you and right now, she's peeking out the door. If you hurry you might get lucky."

Barry actually jumped and turned to look while TJ laughed and climbed into his truck. Christ, he just wanted to get out of here. Normally, he was fine with the quirks and idiosyncrasies of the people he'd known all his life.

But not today. Not when Marnie was at the inn and his workday had just begun. He shouldn't have left Deke there with her. His brother wasn't blind. Any red-blooded male would want to take a crack at Marnie. And Deke, with his new plan to *fuck 'em all,* may just go for it.

Barry put a hand on his truck door and stopped him from closing it. "You going to have any work for me this summer?"

Barry ran a painting crew, and since construction starts were down, he was suffering. "Probably. I'll let you know." He'd sit the cousins down this evening and talk about the plans for the cabins and his schedule for completion. He wasn't sure of the details of the will, but if he got two-thirds of the owners to agree, then that should probably be enough.

If he could think straight with Marnie in the room.

He nodded a good-bye to Barry and backed out of his spot. He chuckled when he saw Barry glance left and right before he reentered the hardware store. It looked as if he really was hoping Alice would oblige the way she always had in high school.

She must be pretty good at blow jobs by now; she'd certainly had enough practice.

The racket outside the inn was unbelievable. All morning while she worked in the great room, earth movers shook the foundations of the building, roaring and chugging out back. No birds tweeted, no squirrels scurried, no deer came to graze the way Marnie remembered.

TJ and Deke were in their glory as they tore out the massive stumps left behind by the tragedy they called progress. So okay, it was a churlish thought, but who could blame her?

TJ had rushed in here unbeknownst to the family and started a project of which they'd had no prior knowledge. The whole thing smacked of underhanded greed.

Midswipe, she shifted her shoulders because the weight of the idea didn't settle well. A man who'd challenged her to a duel of wills in a blatant need for dominance over their sexual relationship wasn't underhanded. He'd made an agreement with Grandad and he had honored it. To TJ O'Banion, it was simple. To her, his honoring an agreement with a dead man was a disaster.

Damn it. Holly seemed not to mind about the cabins in the least, which irritated her all over again.

Irritated, frustrated. Horny. She really needed to make up her mind how she felt about the construction, and about TJ. Why he hadn't just slipped into bed with her last night was beyond her understanding. She didn't know of any other man who would be able to resist.

Irritated, frustrated and horny didn't begin to cover her mixed-up feelings for TJ. So mixed up in fact, that after he'd eased out of her room last night, she'd put away her toy. The fun had gone out of the whole evening when he hadn't taken the bait.

She wanted to deny that the land out back should be developed. With only ten rooms to let, the inn was a joke. With development of resorts rampant around the world, a tiny inn had no hope of competing. Ten rooms wouldn't support one person let alone the three cousins.

To buy out Dennis she'd need a sizable chunk of money. That wouldn't come her way with a one-third split on a too small, dilapidated inn with a clear-cut out back.

Traitorous thoughts intruded as she climbed down from her step stool. If those cabins were built with half the skill she'd seen in TJ's magnificent home last night, then guests would flock to visit the Friendly Inn *and Resort*.

No way. She refused to entertain the notion of adding *resort* to the name of the property. To build a proper resort, they'd need to add a spa, a pool, maybe a string of horses for riding, wireless Internet in the rooms and a hot tub on a private deck. Not to mention more than three tiny cabins.

She would not let ambition get the better of her here. She had plenty of ambition for BackLit.

She would not let TJ O'Banion get the better of her, either. He'd watched her from his bedroom door when she'd gone downstairs for a glass of milk. She'd felt the heat of his stare as she'd moved down the stairs and across the great room. She was sorry she'd slipped her robe on. If she'd been naked, he might have stepped out into the hall. He might have followed her to the kitchen, kissed the nape of her neck, cupped her breast and made her shiver when his hand slid to her pussy. She shivered now, just thinking of it.

She rubbed the back of her neck and felt the sheen of perspiration. TJ O'Banion had her on a low sexual boil.

Last night she'd wanted to turn toward his room and capitulate, but pride had come to her rescue. She'd kept her head and had a fitful night with disturbed dreams of TJ wrapping her up in his arms and holding her against her will.

She shivered with nerves at the memory. She wasn't into

bondage, so what could the dream mean? What weird thoughts and emotions was her subconscious attempting to sort through?

She rarely recalled her dreams. Most of them were mundane, colorless things, mere meanderings through her daily chores.

But the dream last night had been vivid, full of strong colors and emotionally charged. She'd been lustful, yearning and wildly turned on, while he'd been himself, but larger, hotter, hornier than a stallion.

He'd held her down on his bed, trapped by his heavy legs wrapped in hers, his cock deep inside her while he made demands she couldn't, wouldn't comply with.

They'd butted heads while he'd taken her so hard and fast she thought she'd split in two. Still, she'd refused to give him what he wanted.

She still had no idea what that was.

TJ was the hottest man on two legs and she wanted him so bad she could taste it. When she'd sucked and licked his burnt fingertip, the taste of him had whetted her appetite for more. Clearly she was infatuated.

So much so that she found herself drawn to the kitchen window over the wide porcelain sink countless times.

Here she was again, ogling him as he guided one of those monster machines into place. He whistled loud enough to be heard from here to Port Townsend and the massive truck stopped moving. Deke shut off the engine and jumped down from the cab. He walked to the back of the truck to talk, the sun peeking through the treetops to glint off his shoulders. His hair was lighter than his older brother's, a deep chestnut while TJ's was crow black.

She considered TJ's younger brother. Why hadn't her body responded to him? Why hadn't his personality and intelligence plucked at her own? He was quieter, had nice friendly eyes and was exceptionally polite considering he'd been raised in the

same family as TJ. She should prefer a man like Deke. All good women should if they knew what was good for them.

But friendly eyes weren't intense, didn't burn her T-shirts off and didn't start a fire in her shorts. Friendly eyes could be had at any pet store or animal shelter.

While TJ was a completely different animal. There was nothing soft, nothing cuddly about him.

This morning, he'd been cool as the pond he'd taken her to that summer so long ago. His conversation was curt and to the point. *Edgy* would cover his whole attitude, from the moment he'd swiped the coffee carafe from her hand, *before she'd poured her own*, to the moment he'd arrived at the front door of the inn, outdoor light set in hand.

He hadn't offered to install them and she'd been too blind-sided by his disinterest to ask.

Stupid to assume he'd offer to help with the lights, in spite of yesterday's help with the furniture.

TJ bent to pick up a three-foot log that was as big around as his thigh. He carried it to a spot out of sight of the window. She leaned close and put her face tight to the glass to see where he'd gone. A heavy thud of wood landing on wood sounded from just out of sight.

Suddenly, he was there, staring back at her on the other side of the glass. "Oh!" Startled, she jumped back so fast she landed on her rump on the kitchen floor. "Ow."

TJ laughed and made his way inside. Massaging her butt, she rose. She had no dishes to wash, but she turned on the water to fill the sink, then just as quickly shut it off again.

She whirled to put the sink at her back and held on to the counter. "Hi. What can I do for you?"

"Just came in for a glass of water." He stepped so close she could swear she felt the fibers of his plaid shirt against her nipples. They rose toward him, like heat-seeking missiles intent on contact.

He leaned around her, grazing her chest with his as he turned on the cold water. Water ran into the sink as he stepped to the cupboard for a glass. His shoulders, his waist, his thighs all made her own seem narrow and delicate. Her pussy moistened and low pressure blossomed in her belly.

Last night, he'd made it plain he wanted to be in charge of when and where they had sex, but this was ridiculous. What kind of man teased a woman *back*?

She released her breath and dragged in another frustrated one. She took one step to the side to give him room while she collected her composure. What was with him? Cold one moment, hot the next. "Holly should be here by noon," she said, ignoring the waves of tension emanating off him.

He stared out the window, took a long sip of crystal clear water then nodded as he swallowed.

Dear God, even the man's Adam's apple turned her on. She white-knuckled the counter at her back, determined not to launch herself at him. Could she really tackle a guy this large? Take him down and have her way with him? The thought made her nipples peak.

Hard.

Harder.

Hard enough to cut glass.

Oh, hell, yeah. He noticed.

6

TJ walked out the kitchen door, leaving Marnie with her panties wet, her nipples hard and her chest heaving. She sagged against the counter and shook her head to clear it.

A tap on the window made her jump again. The light of humor in his eyes undid her.

She strode out of the kitchen without another word. That would teach her to gawk out the window at him. She grabbed the step stool and moved it down a couple feet, kicked over the bucket of water and yowled with frustration.

She cleaned up the spill as fast as she could. The floors hadn't been waxed in ages and she was afraid the water would leave a stain. More work!

TJ should have taken what he wanted last night. He should have thrown off her sheets and just—taken her. A thrill raced up her belly at the idea of TJ dragging her to the floor, wedging his hand between her legs and making her want it so bad she went blind.

She halted dead center of the room. That's exactly what she wanted, to be overwhelmed, taken, in the fullest sense of the word. Forced? She shied away from that word. Not forced but teased to the point of madness, to the point of helplessness in the face of her own lust.

While he wanted control. Was he afraid of wanting her as badly as she wanted him?

She'd brought this crazy game on herself. She'd played a light game of tease and now he'd turned it back on her. And upped the stakes.

That prick.

That glorious, handsome son-of-a-bitch prick. She'd have to play a much harder game before she made him crack. Not only was he physically strong, he was capable of denying himself to get the grand prize. Whatever that was.

She'd always seen herself as strong and dedicated to her goals, but TJ O'Banion was a force unto himself. She'd always had a helluva hard time backing down from challenges.

To let him know the game was on, she dropped her wet rags into the bucket and turned on her heel to find him.

He was outside, chopping logs into firewood. Oh, mama, she nearly lost the game before it began as the steady rise and fall of his arms pounded through the logs. Precise rhythmic thuds sounded next to the workshop as TJ split the wood with an expert's sure stroke.

"Yesterday you offered to install the security lights. Will you have time for that today?"

He kept his head down and attention on the swing of his axe. She leaned on a support beam. "On the way home tonight, would you mind stopping at a store? I, um, need more batteries for a small appliance." She leaned close enough to smell the musky scent of his hard work. Delicious.

He swallowed and missed his next swing. The blade skimmed off a strip of bark, but the log remained whole.

TJ nodded as a deep flush rose from his neck to the top of his head. "Appliance?" He rested his axe on a log and looked steadily at her. A muscle in his jaw flexed as if he were grinding his back teeth.

She nodded. "Mm-hm. You remember. I used it last night. Keeps me humming right along."

He swallowed.

"So, that's it then. If I think of anything else I need, I'll let you know."

"You do that. I'd think batteries would last longer than one short session. If it's eating batteries, I could tweak the performance for you next time you use it."

"Tweak? I think supplement would be the better word." His eyes flared into full blazes. Her mouth went dry and she backed up a step. "The game is on, big man."

"Long as the stakes are what I think they are." He nodded as if they'd just exchanged pleasantries about the weather.

His confusing response rang in her ears for the next couple of hours while she worked out her frustrations on the exterior walls in the living room.

A car arrived out front and Marnie rushed to see Holly emerge from her low-slung rocket. A newfound love of fast cars was only one of the changes she'd noticed in her cousin since her separation and divorce. She had more sway in her hips than Marnie had ever seen.

She looked happy. Or was that relieved? Her expression was hard to read from this distance and she blanked it as she approached the porch. Which meant Holly was hiding something.

"Hey, you," Marnie called as she opened the door and welcomed Holly with open arms.

"Hey right back." She hugged Marnie hard and they brushed their cheeks. "Oh, it's good to see you and to be here." She leaned back. "I mean, *so* good to be here." Her eyes danced with joy and Marnie believed her. Whatever her cousin was hiding couldn't be serious.

She waved Holly inside with a warning. "Brace yourself, it's filthy. I only told you about the trees out back, not this."

Holly dropped her bags in shock. "What the hell happened?" She took a slow twirl and gaped while Marnie filled her in on their theories of teens and parties. "So, later today, TJ, also known as Paul Bunyan the Elder, will install motion-sensitive security lights all around the inn."

"Wow. I've got to see this guy." She raised her brows and waggled them. "He sounds impressive." Her cousin appraised her. "And somewhat intimidating from the sounds of things."

Instead of questioning Holly about her situation with Jack, the tables had been turned back on her. "TJ's a little, um . . . intense." Her belly warmed at the word.

"Sounds interesting and sexy." She purred and looped her arm through Marnie's. "Show me."

"He has a brother," Marnie blurted.

She stopped. "I see." She nodded. "Got it. TJ's off-limits."

"I didn't say that." Now she was sounding defensive.

"No need to say anything. I've known you my whole life, and something's put that wild gleam in your eye. It sounds as if it's this Paul Bunyan look-a-like."

Marnie patted her suddenly hot cheeks. "Is it that obvious?"

"Only to me or any other woman within a hundred yards. A man probably wouldn't notice a thing. Would he?" But her sly look took in a lot more than Marnie's flush.

"He's noticed. But enough about that; let me show you around." She'd wait until Holly settled in before she offered any more information on TJ and the bizarre game they'd begun. Holly's language turned colorful and earthy as they toured the inn.

"Once we've cleaned and painted, we'll decide on which beds will go into which room. We'll have color schemes."

Marnie laughed. "I've always wanted to say, 'we'll put you in the green room, shall we?'"

They leaned on the railing and looked down into the living area. The furniture was still piled where TJ had put it in the corner. "You won't believe this, but it already looks a lot better."

"Can we afford to hire a service for the worst of this?"

"Maybe after we get rid of the dead rats and other bugs. Rodent poop's a health hazard."

Holly scrunched her face into a mask of horror at the news. "Did you get masks and gloves?"

She nodded. "And I've got a call in with an exterminator. Best they can do is two days from now."

"Not bad, I guess. Until then, we'll make lots of noise so they know to scurry out of our way. Because if I see a rat and I'm armed with a broom, look out."

Marnie agreed. "But if you look past the dirt and neglect, there's a lot of potential."

"Tons." Holly stuck her chin in her hand. "I see a woven rug in front of the fireplace. A desk by the window with a great lamp. Are those wingback chairs okay?"

"Just dusty. We could recover them after we vacuum the life out of them."

"Maybe slipcovers would work. Less expensive and they can be swapped out according to the seasons."

Relief that Holly was here and hope about the place washed through her. "I knew you'd have great ideas." She bumped her shoulder in affection. "This will be fun. We'll pull this off, Holly. I'm sure we will."

Her cousin's face lit. "I'm glad to be here, too. Jack's been clingy and he needs time alone to make whatever adjustments he needs to make."

"I thought when you moved into your own apartment you stopped inviting him over." Marnie knew about the booty calls. Big deal, lots of exes had sex. Familiarity often bred orgasm so it made a kind of sense.

Holly winced. "Sort of. He caught me by surprise that time

you called. I didn't call him, and he must have charmed his way in the front door of the building."

"You gave in?"

"A sympathy lay. That's all." But she bit her lip. "You know I've got an overactive sex drive. He takes it personally, thinks it's because of him."

"You sure it's not?" She eyed her cousin. Was this what she felt the need to hide?

"Pretty sure. I come fast all the time, but it's not the same as it used to be." She shrugged. "It's sex by rote, now. I actually counted how many pumps before he came. How boring is that?"

Marnie shuddered in sympathy. "Jack thinks a fast orgasm is good, huh?" She liked slow herself. Slow and womb-deep worked for her. Quickies were fine with BOB.

Holly nodded. "Yes. But they're not much more than a ripple now." She laughed. "I'm going to take your advice and find a BOB."

"With the amount of work we have here, you'll be too tired to indulge anyway."

After a few minutes of planning their team effort on the cleaning, they ended up on the back porch watching men and their big, big machines.

"Oh, mama, save me from my dirty, dirty thoughts," Holly whispered when she stepped outside and took in the view of Deke and TJ rolling a huge boulder to the side of the clearing. "I think I've just found heaven," she said after she hummed low and sexy in her throat. "Which one's which?"

"Blue plaid is TJ O'Banion, the eldest of the brothers. Deke's in red plaid today. There's a third brother, Eli, the youngest. TJ is trying to get him to come home to work with them." She suspected TJ wanted his brother to stay put for a while. TJ didn't seem the type to ever leave the Peninsula. "More's the pity," she murmured. He could make a success of his life in Seattle.

"Why?" Holly asked, confused. "What's wrong with wanting his brother to come home?"

"Nothing. It's just that as hot as TJ is, I'm a city girl and I can't wait to sell this place so I can get back to where I belong."

Holly huffed. "At the club? What's Dennis up to now? And counting on a future with a man, even a business partner, especially one like Dennis, is a lost cause."

Marnie laughed. "I never should have told you what an ass Dennis is." She hadn't thought of Dennis in hours. Thanks to TJ and her constant state of arousal. "My long-lamented partner has a"—she used finger quotes—" 'new direction' for the club, but I'm not sure I even want to hear about it. We've had a brand-new bartender quit and Dennis won't tell me why. He probably groped her or worse." She hadn't meant to get off track, so she put her worry about the club to the back of her mind. She could worry about BackLit anytime.

"Enough about Dennis." She threw an arm around her cousin's slim shoulders. "You sound bitter about men and that's not like you." Holly was a happy person, not given to dark cynicism. That was why she never saw Jack the way the rest of the family did.

Holly slanted her a glance. "Not bitter, smarter. About men and life. I need this time away from home and my routine. My new job's boring and the pay's not as good as I'd hoped. The break here will do me good." She smiled widely as TJ and Deke finally looked up and saw them.

"Come to mama," she said as Deke slapped the dust and dirt off his jeans on the way over to greet them.

Deke O'Banion

7

Deke slapped the dust and wood chips off his jeans and shirt and eyeballed the spectacular blonde that stood on the back stoop of the Friendly Inn. Must be one of Marnie's cousins. "What'd I say the other night, TJ? Fuck 'em all?"

"Yep, that's what you said." TJ's voice held a hint of relief as if he was glad the cousin was a looker. Deke would never step between his brother and a woman, but it was funny to let TJ wonder.

"Well," he said softly, "I just found the first of many."

His brother snorted in derision. "So you say. Way out of your league, little brother. Way out."

Deke punched him in the shoulder, knocking TJ a step to the side. Every step closer brought the new woman into sharper focus. He gave a low whistle just to keep his mouth moist, because it was in serious danger of drying out. A long-legged blonde, the woman at Marnie's side was a lady in red. Red lips, a red halter top and even red toe nails where they peeked out of a little hole in the toe of her shoes. *Fuck me* was written all over her.

Deke'd be happy to oblige. The first of many . . .

He couldn't take his eyes off her light blue gaze, her perfect mouth and her soft glowing skin. The introductions behind them, he knew her name was Holly Dawson and she was Marnie's cousin, the other granddaughter who now owned the inn.

None of which mattered.

What mattered was how he could get her alone. His mind raced while TJ, Marnie and Holly engaged in small talk that had nothing to do with Deke getting this woman into the sack.

"You can share the guest room with me," Marnie offered with a raised eyebrow at TJ.

He nodded, the asshole. "Sure, if you don't mind sharing a double bed with your cousin." But his voice sounded strained. Deke decided to put him out of his misery.

"I've got room at my place," Deke offered. "It's cramped but I can fold out a bed."

TJ stopped and stared at him, shock all over his ugly mug. "It's a camper. You don't expect Holly to—"

"That'd be great, Deke," Holly cut in. He heard a breathless quality in her voice and his cock sang hallelujah. "I'll just go get my things." And damn if she didn't spin on her sexy shoes and come back twenty seconds later with a set of luggage. Red luggage. She dumped them at Deke's feet and went back through the kitchen the way she'd come.

Marnie's eyebrows rose as far as they'd go then settled back down as she frowned at him. She grabbed Deke by the upper arm and squeezed. "You treat her right, Deke."

"Like the lady she is." Then he followed her into the inn. He caught up to Holly in the living room. She bent to pick up her purse from the floor where she'd left it, but he caught her around the waist before she could get it. She straightened in his arms and faced him.

He snugged her close to his hips, looked into her deep blues while his cock spoke for him.

"Mm," she hummed. Then she nibbled her bottom lip. "Nice to meet you, Deke O'Banion." Her eyelashes were soot black and made her eyes bluer than blue.

Mine.

Holding her was like holding a firebrand tied to a rocket ready to launch. Holly squirmed and wedged her leg between his, rubbing her thigh against his crotch. He groaned and dove into her mouth while she gave it up sweet as can be.

Her breasts were firm and high, her hips flared into his palms as he rubbed into her softness. "Let's go."

"Yes, sir."

He picked up her bags and she opened the door and followed him out to his truck. For a hot damn moment, he wondered if he would remember where he'd left his camper. Then it came to him. He'd moved it to his buddy's place. Lyle was away in Vegas.

"I'm assuming my car's safe until I get back?"

"Oh, sure. TJ's installing the lights before nightfall. And, unh—" Crap. Did she expect to come back today? Because once the camper door closed, he expected to rock all night.

"No worries, Deke. I'm a sure thing, because I want it, too," she said with a saucy smile as she climbed up to the passenger seat. "As long as we're agreed." She narrowed her eyes and sized him up.

He must have passed muster because she added, "We fuck like bunnies for as long as we can stand each other, then we part ways."

"Works for me." He shut her door, tossed her bags in the back and ran around the hood, heart pounding, blood in a race to his cock.

TJ watched Deke and Holly hotfoot it through the kitchen. He shook his head, looked at the thunderstruck Marnie and said, "What the hell just happened?"

"I can't say. I've never seen anything like it before, and I've seen some fast hookups at BackLit. But at the club, people are on the hunt and well into their third martini."

She faced him square on, her eyes serious. "I'll only say this once. You tell your brother that Holly's been through a rough time and shouldn't be toyed with. If Deke thinks this is just a good time he could hurt her."

"Hey, she's the one that jumped on his invitation. Your cousin has no illusions."

She gave a woman's version of a snort. Which worked just fine. Discussing his brother's sex life was not on his agenda. Especially when his own was so fucked up. "Where's the box of security lights? It'll be dark soon and I want to get them installed."

"Front porch. Need help?"

"Just walk around the building with me so I know where you want them."

"If there were any trees left, I'd say a couple should go out here, too."

"You can be a snarky wench." But he had to give her credit for getting the shot in.

"I can," she agreed with a spiced-up smile, then led the way through the inn to the front porch. He could barely tear his gaze away from her ass to take in all the changes she'd brought to the room and lobby.

First thing he noticed was the air. He raised his face to the ceiling and sniffed. "Smells a lot better in here. Looks brighter, too." She must have worked herself to a nub. Shame to waste all that energy on cleaning.

"Thanks, the logs on the exterior walls had a deep layer of grey dust on each one. Even the mortar looks brighter."

"You must be beat."

"Exhausted. My arms feel like they've got ten-pound bags

hanging from my wrists. I don't think I'll ever be able to lift them over my shoulders again."

"And this is just one room. Are you sure you don't need me to find you a cleaning crew?"

"Holly's here now. We're still hoping Kylie will help out, but if she doesn't, we'll rethink the crew."

Deke's truck had just left a dust plume in the air. In under an hour his brother would be face deep in pussy. He stepped behind Marnie and turned her to watch the plume dissipate. His hands slid to her shoulders and he massaged deep into the tense muscles. Her head fell forward and she let it hang as he worked his way to those tiny bits of tension that lived next to the fine bones in her neck. "That's good."

"It could be better," he murmured in her ear. She smelled of shampoo and warm skin as he tempted her.

She glanced over her shoulder, her eyes warm and inviting. "I wouldn't want to have you work in the dark installing those lights."

Deke crowded Holly's back as she climbed into his camper. He hadn't been this horny in years. Arousal sparked along every nerve ending while his blood rushed and heat rose. "This is only temporary until I build my own place," he explained.

"A log home?" she asked, and tossed her purse onto the bench seat at the table.

"Is there any other kind?" It had been so long since he'd smiled at a woman with seduction on his mind his face felt rusted.

She looked around the space and nodded. "You've got everything here a girl could need." She ran her hand down his bulging cock to cup him. "Mm. Nice." She gave his package a weighing squeeze that exploded through the top of his head.

He let her slide and tease him for a moment while he got his bearings. *Fuck 'em all.* He undid his belt and allowed her seeking hand to find him under the denim.

He nuzzled her neck, the smell of flowers and sex and woman filling his head. Her ear was delicate and sensitive where he nipped. Her breathing changed, went heavy with need.

"I need a shower." If only to slow things down. "I sure as hell didn't expect this when I got up today."

She leaned in and rubbed her delicate nose against his neck. "You smell delicious. Like a man. Scent is vital to attraction." She squeezed his balls lightly. "No worries." She pulled her hand out of his jeans and licked her entire palm. "Taste good, too. Salty and hot—"

He slammed her with a kiss that stole his own breath and hers. Holly was hot and wild. As wild to have him as he was to have her. If he didn't slow down he'd disappoint them both. He traced her teeth, slid along the soft tissue of her tongue and savored the deep connection. She was more delicate under her flesh than she appeared. Tall, yes, but so much more narrow than he. He tested her shoulders, back, the flare of her waist and hips. When he cupped her ass, she moaned and pressed her soft center to his hips and hung on.

Her bright red halter top let her breasts sway heavily against him. Her nipples were large, hard, and when he suckled one, it popped harder.

She moved the material out of the way, exposing her chest to his mouth, lips and teeth. He sucked and nudged and took while she crooned dark heated words of encouragement.

Cool air hit his knob when she opened his jeans to let him spring free. Her hand was hot against him where she stroked while her eyes were twin flames of need and greed. "I've got to see this."

She'd hiked up her tight white skirt so that his palms were

full of warm upper thighs. Smooth skin covered by a hint of satin. He looked down her body and caught a splash of red at her crotch. Of course.

"Who goes first," she said as her hand gave his cock a smooth easy twist. His breath caught and he was sorely tempted, but greed the first time wasn't his way. Not when he knew he'd want more. He had to give as good as he got. He'd be greedy later. Greedy tomorrow and the next day.

He laughed and walked her backward to his bed at the front of the camper. She tumbled back onto the mattress and offered herself. "I come fast," she breathed and slid her palm to her belly. She pressed down and slowly opened her legs.

Crotchless panties. Red silk rimmed her slit, while her inner lips were deep pink and already swollen and wet.

He had no choice. His knees gave out and he fell to the floor in front of her.

Her palm slid to cover her pussy. "Not yet. We need to set the ground rules." She closed her legs, hiding herself.

Deke nodded, his mouth so dry he wasn't sure he could speak.

"Number one. I need a lot of sex. And since I'll be here for at least a couple of weeks, you'll get a lot, too. You'll get all of it."

Hallelujah. "We're exclusive while you're here?"

She pursed her lips. "Yes. Exclusive. I may have needs, but I'm not stupid enough to spread my legs for just anyone. My cousin vouched for you."

That surprised him, but he nodded. "Good. Agreed. We're exclusive."

She opened her legs again and she seemed even pinker, more wet. More delicious. He remembered her comment about scent and her perfume cranked his cock to steel hard. He breathed deep and let her musk fill him, drive him wild. "Number two," she said and spread her lips with her fingers to show him her dripping trench. "I like everything you can think of, as long as it's just us."

He slipped his hands from her knees to the valley between her thighs. He thumbed the top of her crease to expose her distended clit. It was long, plump and ready to be sucked. "Quite a clit you've got here."

"Number three, if you take pictures I'll sue you for every dime."

"No problem." He bit back a stab of irritation that she'd think he'd be that low. But then, she didn't know him, and maybe she'd trusted the wrong man before. If that was the case, he'd teach her over the next weeks that he was a man of his word.

If Misty had had more faith, maybe they'd still be together. But no, they wouldn't. He'd been the one who'd trusted too much in that relationship.

"I have a rule," he said as he realized it.

"Oh?"

"We start with a clean slate. Zero baggage."

She raised up on her elbows to look him in the eye. "Sounds easy." But she considered for a moment before she nodded. "Okay. We start out even. Whatever baggage we gather is new from here on out. We don't talk about our exes, or old relationships, or old hurt."

He kissed the inside of her knee to seal the deal. Her breath caught, and quick as that, she was back at full-on arousal. Her scent came to him again and he moved closer to the juncture of her legs, nibbling and licking her soft flesh. The down of dark blond hair at her pussy felt soft and silky. He set his nose to her, a millimeter from her entrance and drew in deeply to memorize her musk. Savory and rich. Warm and delicious.

He slid his finger through the fine curls and tugged lightly, lifting her flesh ever so slightly. She sighed with the gentle motion and he had her complete attention.

She quivered and a quick breath of impatience and need made her belly flutter and her fingertip arch down to her clit. She tapped herself once, twice.

He chuckled. "I'll get there. Have patience and you'll be rewarded."

"But—"

He set his tongue to her in a long stroke, wetting the plump bud. Then he blew a light stream of warm air across her moistness.

She moaned and rolled her head on the bed.

"Now, about which of us goes first . . ." he trailed off with a chuckle, feeling indulgent and easy and patient. They'd have all the time they needed.

Jack was always so fast, this would take some getting used to. Exquisite tension rolled in waves from Holly's core, up into her belly as she allowed Deke to take his time. He'd turned gentle and soft and quiet as he'd studied her every reaction.

Her hips rolled and undulated as he licked at her. Whenever he sucked at her clit, she moaned and panted, being drawn nearer and nearer to the edge of reason. She rolled her head from side to side, desperate to beg, but she wouldn't. Jack had always loved hearing her beg for more mouth work. He also loved denying her.

But Deke's gentle seductive swirling and kissing was killing her when they'd started out so fast. She'd expected Jack's speed. Was used to Jack's rougher handling and demands for compliance and fast orgasm.

Sexual teasing had never been part of Jack's repertoire, and as much as she loved sex, she'd never experienced a man like Deke.

A long soft draw on her clit made her breath catch. No baggage. No Jack. No thought of before. Deke had asked her to bring nothing into this, to start fresh. She wanted—OH! She wanted to try.

She deliberately calmed, drew and released three deep breaths. This was Deke, this was new.

She'd start fresh. With Deke she'd be brand new.

"I'm a virgin," she whispered.

"What?"

She felt him pull back. "You are, too," she said with deep conviction. She looked down her body at his surprise and grinned.

His face popped up between her knees. "Excuse me?"

"If we're starting fresh, this is our first time. Ever. No memories of anyone else."

A slow infectious grin crossed his face. Crinkles appeared at the corners of his eyes. "A delicate virgin needs a delicate touch." The tip of his tongue came out and he applied it ever so lightly to her burgeoning clit.

His tongue worked light. Lighter. Lightest. She felt the load of doubt and pain from her time with Jack drift away and her world righted itself as she gave herself up to Deke.

She was Holly again. Not Jack's ex-wife. Not Jack's woman. Just Holly.

"Deke," she said. "Thank you."

At her words, he stepped up the pace, sucking gently at her lips, delving into her with his tongue, eating her wildly, until in a rush so fast, she came with a gush into his avid, seeking mouth. "Oh." *Yes. Yes. Yes.*

As the rolling wave of orgasm receded he came at her again and again, fingers deep, pulling and turning inside her while he crooned encouragement. "Do it again, babe. You're so delicious."

She flattened her palm on her belly to ground herself. She

was afraid she'd float away on sensation, lose herself and never return. Deke slid up to her and kissed her deeply while his hand worked her into a frenzy. She tasted his need and her own, a rich blend that went to her head.

She rolled toward him, her hips seeking his, her emptiness needing his fullness. He covered her, his mouth to hers, shoulder to shoulder, belly to belly. He nudged her to open wider and in one quick slide pressed inside.

She stilled and focused on every sensation. Full and thick, he filled her. She tested the length and breadth of him with a hip flex. "Ribbed?" she whispered.

His eyes glowed with warmth. "For your pleasure."

She sighed deeply and bucked hard to take him deeper, harder, faster. Wild now, he drove into her. She grabbed his ass and squeezed him, nails digging as she pushed him back, pulled him in. Took him all. Was taken.

With a growl, he rocked deep and held her by the hips as he strove for his peak. His deepest thrust brought on another roar of release and she followed him over the cliff into a world of sensation.

One thought came to her as she drifted back to herself. She could like this man.

She really could.

He rolled away carefully and scooped her up to lay across his chest. "You okay?" He smoothed her shoulder. "You being a virgin and all."

She chuckled. "Oh, yes. I'm fine. Didn't hurt a bit."

"Fine? That's a stab, lady."

She stretched up and kissed the stubble of his chin. "You defiled me in a most spectacular way. Now do it again."

This time he was the one who chuckled. But his questing fingers found her breast and plucked at her nipple. Arrows of sensation shot to her womb and she pressed her hips to his. "That's nice. I have sensitive nipples."

"Good to know."

She cupped his balls. "When we freshen up, I'm going to suck you hard. Would you like that?"

"For a virgin, you work pretty fast."

"Hey, I like what I like."

Next morning, Holly straddled Deke and stretched to touch the ceiling. Free, so free. Her breasts bounced, the weight of them pulling at her womb with each fluid movement. She felt her skin, hot, her pussy, wet, her hair as it swept against her shoulders, light and airy. Wild abandon took her as her belly contracted with each exquisite movement.

Deke clutched her hips hard, controlling the pace, his face focused and hard and so handsome it hurt. Every squeeze of his powerful hands made her rock. Made her roll.

He moved his hands from her hips to her nipples and plucked each one with alternate pinches that drove her so high, she flew.

With a scream, her body took over and drove her to full deep orgasm as she clenched his thighs. "Oh, Deke. Yes!"

Deke answered her with his own shout of completion as his cock flexed against her inner walls. Moist skin, salted and tangy, met her mouth when she collapsed on him. She licked his neck, gathering his taste, holding it on her tongue to remember when this time was over.

Her inner contractions faded to gentle pulses while Deke held her close. The pounding of his heart filled her ear. She rolled her hips once more. Repletion.

Deke gave her deep, strong orgasms, when Jack, at his best, had never come close to this. She smoothed her cheek across Deke's pecs and sighed in satisfaction. "Good morning."

"Morning, Sunshine. That was great." His hands smoothed her back then landed on either side of her rump. He squeezed her cheeks. "I love your ass." He squeezed it again to prove it.

"Do that again and we'll never get out of bed." But she sat up and leaned forward to release his cock. "You're so good at this, Deke. We're going to have a wonderful couple of weeks."

He cupped her breasts again, then sat up and suckled her. He pulled her nipple into his mouth and sucked hard. An answering desire skittered down to the deepest part of her belly. She lifted his face to hers for a light kiss before she climbed out of bed and fluffed her hair. "Do you have the makings for breakfast? I usually eat first thing."

Deke propped himself up on his elbows and looked down his body at her. His eyes warmed to affectionate and brought a flutter to her chest. "You shower, I'll make coffee and see if I've got eggs or cereal?"

"Cereal's good as long as it's not too sweet." His long-suffering sigh made her laugh. "You've got a cupboard full of kids' stuff, right?" Typical guy. She made a mental note to pick up some groceries today. To be halfway human before noon, she needed to stoke herself in the morning. Without food, she was a bear, snarly and unpredictable.

She needn't have worried. When she stepped out of the minuscule shower stall, the camper smelled like bacon frying and she heard the crack of an eggshell. "You found real food?" she asked through the flimsy bathroom door.

"No bread for toast, though, sorry."

She stepped out of the bathroom, only half covered by the towel. Her hand held one end between her breasts while the rest fell to just below her pussy. Water dripped from the tips of her hard nipples while she delighted in the chill of the morning.

He stood in front of the two-burner stove top in his jeans and nothing else. The man was built like a truck, solid, square and looming. His jaw was square too and more heavily bristled than she expected. It had felt soft enough on her tenderest flesh. But maybe he'd been careful not to scrape her.

"Sorry," he apologized again. "The bathroom's too small to

store bulky bath sheets so I make do." But his eyes enjoyed the view. "But I have to say, I'm grateful I don't have larger towels."

She ran the rough terry across her nipples, making them spring to buds. Her breasts bobbed with the friction and she loved the flare that reached his eyes when he tracked her movements. His hand stilled with an egg ready to be cracked into the pan. She cocked an eyebrow at him and startled him into continuing.

She slid her hand down to press the cloth between her legs and laughed when he moved the pan off the burner and reached for the towel. He tugged.

She let go.

His cell phone rang. "I'll finish cooking," she offered at his disappointed frown. "You take your call." She pulled his T-shirt on and slid the pan back onto the burner. The cotton smelled of Deke and yesterday's aftershave. She dropped her nose to her shoulder and sniffed deeply. Even his T-shirt could turn her on. The next couple of weeks looked to be shaping up nicely.

In the confined space, she couldn't miss his conversation and he didn't seem to care that she overheard.

"Eli? Where are you?" he said and settled on the bed. He pulled open a drawer and dug out a pair of socks while he listened to a response. "When are you coming home?"

While the eggs cooked, she found a couple of plates and slid them to the tabletop. Two small benches flanked the table in a typical configuration that would fold down into another bed. Good thing she hadn't needed to sleep alone; Deke's bed was much bigger, even with two people in it.

"We're starting the cabins soon," he said. "I suggest you get your ass back here. TJ won't wait forever." He disconnected and tossed his phone on the bed. He patted his flat belly. "I'm starved. You wore me out last night." But he slid into the seat at the table with a sexy smile, his shoulders so wide it was impossible to sit next to him. "But I'm up for more right now if you are."

She liked that he lied. The man was starving for food, not her. "Let's eat first," she suggested, sympathy making her voice warm. She dished up the bacon and eggs. "Was that your younger brother?"

"Eli. He's the wanderer. But he's on his way home to work for the summer." Deke's smile dimmed.

"What's wrong? Won't you be glad to see him?" She took the bench across from him and lifted a fork full of egg.

"I've kept him in the dark about a couple of things. I don't look forward to filling him in when he gets here." He poured her a cup of coffee then one for himself.

"Bad news?"

"Some of the baggage I'm not bringing to *our* table." He folded a strip of bacon and popped it into his mouth.

"Oh, I see." The beer cases stacked outside must be part of the baggage he'd left behind, too. She hoped so. Drunks made for lousy lovers.

"So, you're cleaning the inn today?" His change of conversation made breakfast go down more easily and eased her mind.

She made a face. "I brought my grungiest clothes."

If Deke slipped and talked about his past, she might feel obligated to mention her recent split from Jack, which would lead to talk about Jack and she preferred to move on. Needed to move on.

While Deke showered she checked her messages. Jack. Then Jack. And Jack again. She considered calling to tell him to back off, but decided to send him a breezy email instead. She'd tell him cell phone reception was poor and he shouldn't expect to hear back.

Although she probably shouldn't contact him at all. Her parents had suggested a clean break when she told them about the separation.

She should have listened, but typically, being a Dawson, she'd gone her own way.

She had to make this break stick. It was way past time for Jack to let her go.

The sound of Deke in the shower, the scent of sex from the rumpled sheets, the delicious glow that infused her body combined to make her dewy around the edges of her mind.

She rolled her shoulders and smiled while she poured Deke the last of the coffee. He'd be out of the shower in a moment, and she wanted to move into her day with nothing but cleaning, decorating and sex on her mind.

To hell with Jack.

8

"I spent another night alone in TJ's guest room." Marnie said, as she grasped her side of a wing chair so they could move it back into position in front of the fireplace.

"And that's supposed to be a good thing?" Holly hooted. "Cousin, you need to get your priorities straight. That man's itching to get to you and you're hot as hell for him, too. Where are you heading with this?"

"Death by sexual frustration," she muttered, which brought a gale of laughter into the room. She gave Holly her best evil eye.

"Wonder what the forensic dudes will discover from your dried-up corpse?"

"Very funny." Nice picture. They'd find her with her legs open, pussy all dry and shriveled from lack of use and a sad expression on her face. She could see the forensic dudes shaking their heads as they snapped photo after photo. What would the signature episode line of dialogue be?

Something like, "Pity. She used to be moist enough to eat."

Or something equally pithy. Or funny, depending on perspective.

A cold chill ran down her back, in spite of the heat generated by shoving furniture back into the middle of the room.

The sofa was next and turned out to be heavier than it looked. She grunted in reply to Holly's groan of exertion. She pushed while Holly pulled the sofa until they had it centered in the room. "Last night at Deke's worked out okay?"

"This morning did, too," her cousin responded with a salacious grin. "The man's got stamina."

"Here's hoping it runs in the family," she muttered.

Holly's eyes widened as she leaned in. "So you do plan to discover that for yourself?"

She winced. "I hope so, yes." She swiped her hair out of her face.

"I've never known you to take this kind of time with a guy as hot as TJ. Is there a man you haven't told me about? Would a fling with TJ hurt someone?"

"No, a fling with TJ wouldn't hurt anyone." Unless she counted herself. "He's free, too. Everything looked like a go until I saw the mess outside. I figured a couple of nights in the sack would do us both good, but now I'm as jumbled up as that clear-cut out back." Weeks with TJ might cloud her mind. She couldn't forget how happy she'd been to see him after all these years. "It's not possible for a childhood crush to mean anything years later, is it?"

Holly made a moue and considered before answering. "They say finding a first love can be a strong motivator to end marriages, so yes. Teenage crushes can develop into more when you're both adults."

"Marriages that are already in trouble, maybe, but not a healthy one." She stretched a kink out of her back. "Besides I was a kid when I first met him. Thirteen. First kiss kind of thing. Nothing."

Holly grinned. "Thirteen and a first kiss? I never forgot mine, either, and if he walked in here right now, I'd be dying to do it again."

"Knowing you, you didn't just stop at a kiss," she teased.

"Billy Watkins." Holly sighed with gusto. "Whatever, I don't see why you're not on TJ like moss on trees. The man's got the hots so bad the soles of his very large work boots leave melty puddles when he walks by." She headed for a wing chair and held up the nozzle of the vacuum cleaner. Before she drowned out the conversation by turning on the machine, she raised her brows and waited. "What is it that you're looking for?"

"Fair question." She knew more what she didn't want. No quick and easy sex. No flings. Nothing not real. And if she was going to enter into a long-distance thing with TJ O'Banion that was real, she needed—"I want to be blown out of my socks."

"Seduced?"

"And teased. Wooed. Is that still done? Wooing?" She rolled her eyes at the preposterous word.

"Ah!" Holly nodded as if she understood the lure of the fantasy. "Chased."

"More like taken."

"In the strongest sense?"

Marnie nodded. "In the strongest sense. I want to be so overwhelmed by my body that my brain shuts down."

Holly's eyes lit up. "Ooh. Hot." She nodded her approval. "TJ could do that."

"I'm not sure he should. We're not exactly conveniently located for a relationship."

A choked sound from behind made her turn to see a tall shadow disappear into the kitchen.

Holly dashed to see which of the brothers was scuttling through the kitchen door. Her face scrunched up. "TJ," she mouthed.

Great.

Holly gave her a speculative stare that made her squirm. Family always knew things without being told. Okay as long as Marnie wasn't the one being dissected.

"You always fretted too much before leaping," Holly commented. "Always figuring the odds, planning things. Worrying about unlikely disasters."

"Like the time we borrowed Mom's car to go see those boys in Tacoma?" She grinned. "I'm just glad we got away with it."

"I still can't believe you thought we'd end up dead in a ditch."

Marnie remembered the overwhelming sense of freedom when she'd decided to go for it and drove through the city to the party. When they got there, the boys had already found girls. The disaster hadn't been physical, but Marnie and Holly had felt betrayed. The drive home had been much slower and filled with a lot of cursing out men in general.

A couple of hours later, and with the living room dusted, the furniture vacuumed and the windows cleaned, Marnie freshened up in the bathroom adjacent to Grandad's old room. As she brushed her teeth and took a quick shower she wondered where TJ and Deke had gone. The machines were silent out back and she hadn't seen either man since TJ had inadvertently eavesdropped.

She'd bet her heart he wasn't sneaky. He must have been coming to the room to tell the women something, then when he caught wind of the conversation had done an about-face.

Holly was right. She overthought things too much. Investing in the club with Dennis was a rare misstep. She'd been blinded by her desire to be in charge of her life and had jumped at the chance to get into the club with a partner rather than wait to do it alone. Ambition was a bitch sometimes.

She rinsed and dried herself. If TJ was ever going to chase her, she needed to bolt like a rabbit out of a hole. She could probably find the pond in the woods if she started out from a familiar point. It wasn't more than twenty minutes behind the inn.

By the time she was dressed and ready, the afternoon had moved toward evening and the temperature had dropped off. She found a fleece vest in her pack and slipped into it.

Outside, she tried to recall which side of the clearing would take her to the half-hidden path through the woods to the stream and the pool of chilly water.

The O'Banions had returned, all hot and big and sexy. Desire spiked at the sight of TJ. The air freshened with pine and turned sultry as his gaze raked her. The brothers' conversation stalled out as TJ continued to stare, but she walked toward him without a word.

Each step came slow and measured as she approached the men. TJ's eyes widened to wary as she brushed past him, shoulder a whisper from his sleeve. He moved his arm and she smiled at the response.

If he didn't follow her now, he never would.

Her nipples tightened as the woods beckoned, quiet and dark. She tried to deny the urge to look back as she gained the shadows. The next round in their game of thrust and parry had begun.

TJ watched as Marnie strutted toward him. For a woman dressed in jeans, T-shirt and an ugly fleece vest, she worked her come hither like a pro. His cock rose so fast it nearly broke. She winked as she walked by.

He turned to watch where she went. She veered to the right about three steps into the trees and picked her way along the old path to the pond. She looked over her shoulder to see if he watched. Their eyes locked and no sound penetrated his sex-fogged brain as she lifted one eyebrow and winked.

Another couple of steps and she disappeared, leaving the

snap of branches to remind him she was flesh and blood and not a woodland nymph.

Deke opened his truck door and climbed in. "TJ? You there?" His brother's voice filled with humor. "You got it bad. And she's right there with you."

TJ turned and stared at him.

"Just go get her," Deke suggested. "Then maybe we can get some work done around here."

That snapped like a rubber band. "You're right. Enough's enough."

He turned and followed Marnie into the woods. The irritating sound of his brother's laughter soon faded as branches and undergrowth swallowed him. He couldn't hear her up ahead, but he didn't need to.

When he got to the pond, he leaned against a tree to watch what she'd do next in this ever more interesting game they played. The air had a bite of chill that made it too cold for a swim, so he should be spared a skinny dipping scene. Marnie huddled into her fleece vest and settled on the flat rock that hung over the other side of the pond.

It was more like a wide shallows in a stream. The water was bitter cold even in late summer but now it could kill in minutes. She must know that; the chill rose brisk and damp all around.

She brought her knees up and hugged them, put her chin on her knees in thought.

"You look serious," he said, just loud enough to reach her ears. Her red hair caught a single ray of sunshine and burned bright for a moment before a cloud stole the light.

She didn't even turn her head at the sound of his voice. She knew he'd followed her. With some luck she would invite him to join her on the rock.

"That's the rock where I kissed you," he said.

"I wasn't sure I could even find it, but I came straight to it without a problem." She looked pensive.

"Hard day?"

"I've got a few things on my mind," she replied.

God, he hoped one of those things was sex. "What things?"

"Business, mostly. But other than that, I keep thinking of that mess you call a clearing. How long will it be before the cabins are built?"

"Are you anxious to leave?"

One side of her mouth quirked up. "You could say that. Seattle's home, it's where my business is. I'm needed there." She picked up a pebble and tossed it with a plunk into the water. "I've got staffing problems, a partner who's off the rails." She looked at him across the shallows, her eyes searching his even though he had no answers to give. "And no idea what'll happen when our new cousin arrives." She wished the damn woman would just show up and put them all out of this misery. Waiting was a bitch.

"I can relate to the staffing problems. Lord knows I've got my own." He raised his eyebrows in a silent question. Was he welcome to join her?

She patted the rock and scooted over to give him room.

He picked his way over the stepping stones in the stream and mimicked her position on the rock. Close enough for friendly conversation, but not close enough to crowd her.

She tossed another pebble, watched the ever-widening rings until they disappeared. "I want to sell the inn so I can buy my partner out of the club."

"Let me guess, the banks wouldn't give you a loan. Money's tighter than ever."

She huffed. "Believe me, I've tried. They wouldn't even consider my third share of the inn as collateral." She shrugged. "Besides, my grandfather's will prevented anything but the three of us working together on the place. I wish I understood why he wrapped us all up so tightly."

"We were friends but he never confided anything on that

score." He thought about the wild rumors running through the community and chuckled. "Your grandfather's will has caused a lot of speculation. Not that it's anyone's business, but the locals always thought of him as strange so it stands to reason they'd be more curious about the inn than they would normally be."

"I would imagine most people's lives are an open book around here."

"Pretty much. I see why it's important to you to get the cabins built as fast as possible."

"We can't even open the rooms in the inn because of the construction noise. You will be noisy, right?"

He nodded. "Why the hurry to buy your partner out?"

She rolled her shoulders, made him want to massage her, but he restrained himself. She'd called a truce and needed real conversation, not a move to get laid. "It's not working out with him. I carry most of the day-to-day load of running the club while he's"—she hesitated, then went on—"enjoying the fruits of the situation."

"Picking up women?" There would be a lot to choose from in a dance club. Young, fresh women thrilled with the attention of an older businessman would tempt most men. Easy, fun sex was a strong lure.

For a time.

"I think he's dipping into the till, too." She rolled her eyes. "To pay for the women." Her laugh turned bitter. "He's getting weird."

TJ had nothing to say to that. Small business was fraught with problems, and while a dance club seemed like fun, it would present a host of unique difficulties. "Why a dance club? Seems to me it would be long, late hours, constant challenges in a tight market."

"I put myself through college tending bar and found I had a knack with people."

"Don't tell me they poured out their troubles?" Her scent blew by his nose and he strained for more. Something soapy and delicate. She'd showered. The thought of her fresh and clean made him close his eyes to hold the scent.

She finally turned to look at him, her eyes full of lively humor and intelligence, as if she knew it was difficult for him to keep his hands to himself. "Listening to their troubles comes with the territory but I've never minded small talk. It's easy to give people what they need in terms of atta-boys and support in an easy breezy way." She put her head to rest on her knees as she sighed. Her eyes held him while her voice eased through to his gut. "Talk about pouring out troubles. I can't seem to shut up."

"No problem. I wish I had some suggestions for you."

"Thanks." She leaned close so that her shoulder rubbed his. "And thanks for not going all smoky sex on me."

"I can if you want me to." Hell, he'd love to! "But I think I'll do better to let you talk. There's plenty of time for me to have my way with you."

Her laugh drowned out the burble of the stream. "See? I knew there was a reason you jumped the gun on clearing that acre. You want to keep me here so you can get laid."

"And you don't?" He'd overheard her conversation with Holly and knew she wanted to be taken. But that didn't sit well with him, no matter how hard she made him, how much his cock twitched for her.

In another surprise move, she shoved him sideways just far enough that he lost balance and toppled sideways onto the rock. Next thing he knew, she'd climbed on top of him. He decided he liked it and let her straddle his waist.

Happy and suddenly girlish, she reminded him of what had caught him so thoroughly that long ago summer. He palmed her cheeks, unable to stop himself. "Your skin's so soft. So pretty." He wanted to tell her about how her eyes drew him in, but that would sound poetic, and he didn't do poetic.

She flushed while he marveled at her translucent beauty. The weight of her on his hips distracted and focused him at the same time. She set her hands on either side of his head, which brought her face closer. Her eyes widened as she studied him. "You're as handsome as I thought you'd be. I never forgot you."

Likewise. But she'd think he was lying so he kept the thought to himself. "Does anyone forget a summer like that? You were sweet and pretty and hung on my every word." He'd started out by thinking she was a pest, but as the days had gone on she'd become a friend.

"I loved our hikes in these woods." Her breath fanned over him, sweet and inviting.

He slipped his hands to her waist. "Remember when I kissed you?" She'd kissed him back with fervent attention to detail, as if she'd rehearsed.

She stilled and her eyes filled with memory. "Yes," she breathed. "My first."

Her nipples had gone hard in the chill of this very pool and suddenly an awareness had bloomed between them, an awareness that hadn't existed before. They'd climbed out of the shallows to stretch out on the sun-heated rock. Awkward and full of promise, the moment had stretched as he'd pulled her close to his chest, careful to keep his hard-on away from her. He'd bent his head while she'd tilted her mouth and more by accident than design he'd brushed her strawberry-flavored lips once, twice and on the third swipe, had settled on her mouth.

"Strawberry," he murmured as his hands moved to her back and down to cup her ass. The grown Marnie laughed and leaned so close he lost sharp focus. But that didn't matter, he'd seen desire and affection in her gaze and held on to the image.

"You remember my lip gloss?"

"Your lip gloss, your mouth, how soft your hair was and even how perfect your nipples were under your bathing suit and T-shirt."

She dangled said nipples within an inch of his chest, then lowered them by half. He dragged in a deep breath and expanded his chest to touch them.

She chuckled and finally brought her mouth down to his. The pressure was light, teasing and delicious. He went straight back to being fifteen and so horny he could split firewood. But things were different now. Marnie was no longer one minute from childhood. She was full grown and the way her tongue tipped into his mouth proved it.

She nipped his lower lip and tugged, then licked and nibbled as he tasted her over and over again. Not strawberry this time, but needy woman.

Her skin was smooth and warm as he traced the bones of her spine to her bra. He undid the hooks quickly and felt her sharp intake of breath, but she raised herself to allow his hands to scoop her out of the cups. Full, luscious, her breasts filled his palms to overflowing. He tweaked her nipples, bringing them to hard points. His mouth watered to take them.

She slid down to straddle his hips, increasing the torture. Her soft giving center called to him and he raised his hips to press against her.

"Mm," she moaned and rode him a moment. "You *have* grown," she murmured then slid back up to offer her breasts. He nuzzled beneath her T-shirt and plucked one nipple while he suckled the other. She rocked her hips on his belly, her ass just touching the tip of his cock.

So perfect. So soft. Her breasts filled his hand and mouth while he drank the scent of woman and arousal. Hers. His. It was all the same, a wild keening need that took them both over.

She pulled her mouth from his, then slid her hands to cover his on her breasts and pulled his hands away. She climbed off him and wiped her mouth with a shaky hand.

He tried to take in the sudden shift. "What? Did I move too fast?" His body was taut as strung wire.

She bent at the waist and fit her breasts back into her bra cups and did herself up with a contortion that made him marvel. "No. I just have a lot to do. And this isn't getting it done."

"Believe me, we wouldn't have been much longer." He sank back onto the rock and cradled his head on the back of his arm. She wanted to be overcome, overwhelmed. Taken. He got to his feet, stepped toward her.

Her lips were blue from the cold. That, more than her wary gaze stopped him. It was June on the Peninsula. That meant Arctic flows that brought wind, cold and rain. He could pursue, overwhelm and take her the way she'd claimed to want.

Wouldn't be the first time he'd had sex in the woods, but the wind had a bite now and would only get worse. Also, if things went sour between them, he didn't want all the blame for starting things. No, if she wanted an affair, or something more, then she had to meet him halfway. His heart simmered back down to normal.

"Gotta tell you, though, Marnie. This kiss was way better than our first."

She laughed and gratified him by letting her guard down. When they forded the stream, he reached for her hand and she took it. Simply. Warmly.

The twenty-minute walk back to the inn was filled with easy chat and friendly banter. When they got to where they could see the clearing, they stopped in mutual accord. Deke and Holly were by the pile of firewood TJ had split the day before.

TJ tugged Marnie to face him. "I can't recall the last time I walked in the woods holding hands."

"Me neither." Her smile dazzled. He'd been right to let her

go by the pond. They had time and maybe it would work in his favor. She stretched up and blessed his cheek with a light kiss, then turned and entered the clearing leaving him to wonder if this had been real or just part of the game.

He voted for real.

As he followed her out of the woods, Holly's voice drifted to his ears. "I want the prettiest ones."

"It's firewood. It's not supposed to be pretty. Even's good, but pretty?"

From the question, it was obvious Deke couldn't see the point. "Next thing, you'll want them washed," he groused.

Marnie crossed the leveled clearing and joined the discussion. "We won't burn the pretty ones, Deke. They're for show."

TJ looked hot and bothered and Deke wondered how long this tug-of-war would last between his brother and Marnie. Obviously, TJ had ignored his advice to go after Marnie and get busy. If they had they'd be glowing warm, not still shooting sparks.

Couldn't be good for a body to be so riled up day after day without an outlet. By the time his brother blew there'd be hell to pay.

He hoped Marnie was up to it.

"That's what I've been trying to tell him." Holly shooed Deke away from the stack of firewood. "Now that Marnie's here we'll go through the wood together and I can stop trying to explain staging to you."

The staging thing had something to do with appearances and not looking lived in while still being welcoming. "Fine with me, I'm happy with a flat-screen television and a lounger."

Any chance for more time with Holly disappeared, but TJ took his attention with work and the evening had arrived before any of them realized it.

"I'm starving. D'you think the women would make a run to the store for steaks? We could use Jon's grill."

"The tank's almost full. I checked it earlier." He sauntered inside the inn and a few minutes later came back out with a grin. "They're on their way."

An hour later, the women returned with juicy steaks and the supermarket's version of potato salad. Deke forewent having a beer and settled on the top step of the deck with an iced tea.

He tilted his head toward the newly cleaned kitchen. "They've got a lot done inside now." At this rate, they'd have the place looking great before his two weeks were up with Holly. "They're cleaning machines, the pair of them. They'll have the interior done way before we're anywhere near finished out here."

TJ frowned but changed the subject. "You're not having a beer?"

"Got other things to occupy my time." And he felt so damn good he could cheer. The sun was out all the time, even if the sky was cloud piled on cloud. He tried to wipe the sappy grin off his face but gave up. No use. He'd been like this all day.

TJ frowned and scraped the barbecue grill clean. "Holly's divorced, Deke."

So much for no baggage. But then, it wasn't Holly that tossed this into the mix, now, was it? "No children, though?" His chest tightened in readiness.

"No." TJ shook his head. "You obviously didn't do much talking."

"Not about our lives before yesterday. We've agreed to start fresh. No bullshit from our pasts to muddy the waters." He held up his iced tea. "And I meant it. No more maudlin drinking binges to help me forget Gabriel." It hurt to even say the boy's name. He'd wanted to be the kid's dad, not just his step-father. But Misty had taken him away and changed Deke's and Gabriel's lives forever.

The pain of loss brought him up short. He and Holly were not going down the commitment highway and he had to remember that. It was sex. Free and easy and so fucking hot it scorched.

"I'm glad to hear about the booze, because I won't babysit you anymore."

"You won't have to. She's good for me. Has me thinking about other stuff. Better stuff." Whatever time was left with her would be great. By then he'd be ready to move on from his deepest grief and he'd have Holly to thank.

Holly stepped outside with a plate piled high with meat, putting an end to the conversation. As she walked down the three steps beside Deke, she gave him a heated look. He ran his hand up her thigh in a quick slide of appreciation. All sex, all the time.

No commitment.

That was his new mantra.

And he had to stick to it.

They sat down for dinner at the long cedar kitchen table amid laughter and teasing between the brothers. Deke and TJ told stories designed to get their women giggling and succeeded.

Until, into the midst of another gale of laughter, a woman walked in.

Deke saw her first and tapped Holly's hand to get her to look up from her plate.

"Hello?" the newcomer said, looking from one diner to the next. "Sorry to interrupt, but I'm Kylie Keegan and I belong here."

Shocked silence turned the kitchen into an eerie void of expectation. For his part Deke felt sideswiped by the woman's beauty. She had hair to her hips, tilted almond eyes and a body to kill for. TJ seemed as mesmerized as he was. A woman who looked like her must be used to this reaction.

Marnie was the first to regain her composure. She rose, held out her hand. "Kylie. It's so nice to finally meet you."

The black-haired beauty gave her cousin a tentative smile and shook her hand. Then she tugged Marnie in for a hug and the difference in their heights made it seem like Marnie was swallowed. "You have no idea how glad I am to meet *you*."

Kylie had to be all of six feet and every curvy inch of her was in proportion.

"I'm Holly Dawson and the woman you're hugging is Marnie." Holly rose quickly and got dragged into an effusive hug as well.

Kylie stepped back and released them both. "Sorry, I didn't mean to grab at you. It's just that I've never met any family members other than Jon Dawson." She got a tentative look in her eyes that asked if she was welcome.

TJ stood. "Kylie. I'm TJ O'Banion and this is my brother, Deke. We're pleased to meet you." They shook hands briskly, but Kylie's eyes never left the other women.

"Kylie," breathed Holly. "Oh. We're so glad you're here. Aren't we, Marnie? So glad."

Marnie nodded then waved at the table laden with food. "Hungry? There's plenty. I haven't taken a bite of steak yet so you can have half of mine." She sliced her piece of meat down the middle.

Holly dragged out a chair at the head of the table. From the wear on the seat and back it looked like Jon's favorite. "Sit here. Please join us."

Deke slid the bowl of potato salad down the table.

Kylie looked from Holly to Marnie then nodded once. "I'll just go wash up. And give you all a chance to get over the shock. I should have let you know I was coming, but I kept getting cold feet and then I'd tell myself I was just chicken." She glanced over her shoulder. "Right up until I stepped through the door."

"We're glad you didn't chicken out," Holly said.

"We could use your help around here." Marnie laughed while she got out a plate and cutlery. "This place is an unholy mess."

Holly directed Kylie to the half bath off the lobby and sat back down in her chair with a whump. "Well. She's here."

"And she's beautiful," Marnie said with an air of awe. "And so tall." But her mouth went tight around the edges and Deke figured this family reunion was best played out without witnesses.

"Maybe we should head out." He directed the comment to TJ, but Holly shook her head.

"A buffer might be good. First shock and all."

With a slow nod, TJ finally spoke. "You've got to admire her guts for showing up like this."

Marnie glared at him across the table, while Holly nodded in agreement. "Grandad's initial reaction was unpleasant so she had no idea how we'd receive her."

"She's got guts," Deke repeated under his breath.

Kylie reappeared at the door, ending that line of conversation. She'd dropped the air of hesitancy and took her seat at the head of the table.

She settled in Jon's chair while Deke looked at the three cousins in turn. "All I can say is, there's not a one of you who looks like you could be related to that old codger. Sorry, ladies, but that old man was butt ugly and you three are the most beautiful women to ever set foot on the Peninsula."

TJ held up his glass. "Hear, hear."

"I'm so glad to meet you here. I already love the place and it's great that you've already begun to fix it up so we can open for business."

"Excuse me?" It was Marnie, red faced.

Deke looked at Holly, who gave him a sharp shake of the head: Say nothing, look at no one.

9

"We're not opening for business. We're selling the place," Marnie stated, calm as a windless day.

"Oh, I just assumed you'd—which was stupid of me." Kylie waved her hand to dismiss her suggestion. "I don't want to force a decision on anyone."

Holly nodded. "Of course not, let's take a couple of days before we discuss anything."

Marnie read the familiar look and pinched her lips closed. She nodded and passed the potato salad to Kylie. "Holly's the calm and reasonable one, while I get ahead of myself. I've got a couple more days to think things through." But she'd decided and Holly knew it. Two against one.

Marnie admired guts and Kylie had them. To walk in here and take her place, not ask for it, couldn't have been easy. Confidence like that came from tests. Life tests, and Kylie had obviously passed.

Hospitality demanded she offer her new cousin a room. This was an inn, after all. She drew in a deep breath, gave TJ a cursory glance and spoke as Holly dug into her steak.

"We've got a couple of clean rooms upstairs, so I hope you'll stay here, Kylie. If you don't mind an air mattress, that is." In her peripheral vision, TJ's face went red and disappointment clouded his handsome features. Good. He needed to be put off balance, and this was a perfect opportunity.

"Sure! That'd be fine. I'm not fussy." She rubbed her palms on her thighs.

She prepared to tuck into her dinner. "This looks delicious. I haven't eaten since breakfast. I was too nervous."

"You don't mind staying alone?" Deke asked.

She shrugged. "I'm cool. I spend a lot of time alone."

Marnie didn't much care to leave the inn in Kylie's hands. Who knew what kind of mess she could create. "I'll stay with you. We'll get to know each other."

"I'd like that." The smile she gave Marnie seemed genuine. She took a bite of her potato salad. "This is so wrong, but it tastes so-o good." Which made the men laugh.

"What's the matter, TJ? Disappointed?" Deke ribbed his brother.

Holly and Deke exploded into laughter at TJ's thunderous expression while Kylie shook her head. "I can go to a hotel until—"

"I won't hear of it," Marnie insisted and refused to catch TJ's eye. By her calculations, the sale of the inn would move more quickly under friendly circumstances. She knew of no quicker way for women to bond than at a sleepover. Or shopping.

Kylie's smile widened. "It will give us a chance to catch up."

"You can't do this without me," Holly added.

"Okay."

"Who's disappointed now?" TJ chuckled as he polished off the rest of his steak.

Deke glared. Holly relented. "I'll stay tonight, then I'll go back to Deke's." She winked at him.

TJ grumbled something about bringing over air mattresses and pillows and left, while Deke volunteered to get Kylie's luggage. "I seem to be the resident bellhop," he said with a good natured salute. "But, I'll ask Holly to take care of the tip."

"No problem. I'll see you first thing in the morning."

Kylie flashed Marnie a look that screamed nerves and she understood the battle for the Friendly Inn had just begun.

Two hours later, Kylie sat cross-legged on the floor in front of the massive stone fireplace and passed the nearly empty wine bottle to Marnie, the older of her two cousins. Older by six months, which hardly counted. But it was enough to know that these women were more like sisters. They'd shared most of their lives with each other.

While she'd had no one but her mom.

Her father was no more than a breeze through her life that she didn't even have a photo of. Trudy's memory of him had been fuzzed out by too much alcohol and pot to be of much use. Deep water under a very old bridge.

She snugged her knees under her chin and rested her head there. Marnie slopped a few droplets of wine onto the freshly waxed and polished oak floor. "Damn." She topped off her glass.

Kylie leaned forward and wiped the wine with her sleeve. "Got it."

"Thanks, we spent a lot of time on this floor. But I think it could do with a complete refinish." She surveyed the area around the fireplace and tsked.

"When I was here before, the place looked run down." Depressing and dirty, too. Not that she'd stayed long. "You've both worked so hard and accomplished so much in just a few days."

Marnie looked put out. "If it weren't for that unholy mess outside, we'd be almost ready to put it on the market."

Kylie let the comment pass. She hadn't yet decided what to make of the place or her newfound family. She preferred to let things develop as they would. Trouble and upheaval were often avoided with patience.

Holly sipped her wine. "This was more than run down. It was a pit hole. Our grandfather let it get filthy. I don't know how he lived in here." She was on her third glass of red, while Marnie and Kylie had split a bottle of white.

"He didn't *live*, he existed," Marnie corrected. "But, you met him, Kylie. Did he seem lively to you?"

She remembered only bitterness and ugly words. "As in having a life? No. He didn't have a life. He was nasty and mean. And I think he liked it that way." She blinked as moisture welled in her eyes. From resentment more than sadness, most likely. He'd rejected her on sight.

Holly patted her knee in comfort. "He was a crotchety, lonely old man who had strange ideas. Look at what he did with his will. Let's face it, the man was strange."

"What do you mean?"

"He left us this inn." She waved her wineglass with exaggerated care to avoid spilling. "But left all the money we'd need to fix it up to our dads and brothers. Then, just to be a prick, forced us to do all the work ourselves."

Marnie nodded, a wet gleam in her eye. "He knew we'd eventually all show up here and squabble about this place." She shot Kylie a bleary glance, then looked contrite. "Sorry."

"And," Kylie added, "he stuck you with me, a woman you've never met." A woman he'd hated on sight. "Strange doesn't begin to cover this situation."

"You've never met us, either," Marnie said with a frown. "It took guts to walk in here to take your place. I'm impressed as hell." She tilted toward Kylie and held her wineglass for a clink. Kylie obliged then touched her glass to Holly's as well.

"Why d'you think Jon Dawson split everything up the way he did? And why did he include me when he didn't have to? The old man hated me on sight."

Marnie cleared her throat. "Maybe not." Now it was her turn to pat Kylie's knee. "TJ told me that the night you left here, he stayed with Grandad. Grandad spent the night soaking himself in scotch and talking about regrets. Maybe he regretted talking to you the way he did."

"I doubt it. But we'll never know for sure, will we?" She remembered that a truck was parked outside when she stormed out of the inn. "So that was TJ who came to see him that night?"

Marnie nodded as she took another sip of wine.

Holly piped in. "The weirdest thing was the codicil. He forced us to wait to list the place for sale until after the cabins are built. He paid in advance and TJ promised he'd get started as soon as he could."

Kylie put the threads together. "So, we couldn't sell right now even if we wanted to?"

Two heads wagged.

"Then there's a possibility we could actually open for business?"

They stopped wagging and looked at each other, then at her. Holly brightened. "I don't see why not. I'm game."

Marnie paled. "You are not. You have to get home." She slammed her palm to her chest. "*I* have to get home."

And suddenly the tide turned. Holly looked from Marnie to Kylie and back again. "I've had too much to drink to decide this right now. But, no, I don't have to go home. I can quit my job. I don't like it much anyway."

"You're drunk," Marnie muttered. "We'll talk about this in the morning."

"Why would the old man do this to his own family? Did he have feuds going with anyone but my mom?" Jon Dawson couldn't have loved any of his family. "This is sick, but I don't feel so bad anymore. Maybe his hatred wasn't personal. Maybe he hated everybody."

"Except our dads got along with him fine. He always favored our brothers over us." Until this.

"My mom never talked about him. But I suspect when she told him the truth about my conception, he kind of freaked."

Marnie and Holly went quiet with expectancy. They didn't seem the types to blame a daughter for a mother's transgressions. No harm in explaining.

"I'm the result of a quickie at a frat party." She shrugged. "Mom wasn't very clear on exactly who my father was. I guess the idea of his daughter letting beer and pot get the better of her was a little too much. He kicked her out and she moved as far away as she could."

"Oh." They chorused. "Makes more sense now." The others shared a look that spoke volumes. "Grandad was an unforgiving bastard at the best of times."

Which Kylie took to be an understatement.

"I'm free for the rest of the summer," she said to change directions. She hated maudlin conversations and they were heading into dangerous territory by talking about Jon Dawson. "I can stay until everything's done."

"I don't mind staying longer than a couple of weeks if it comes to that." Holly glanced at Marnie, who looked stricken.

"We'll talk about everything in the morning. No decisions made by wine."

Holly looked thoughtful and grabbed Marnie's knee and gave it a shake. "Maybe that's why Grandad did all this. To get us together. He knew that you're always tied up at the club. He knew I was divorcing and he messed up with Aunt Trudy and again when Kylie visited."

"You think?" Kylie said. The wine had fuzzed out her thinking for sure, but this was improbable even soaked in chardonnay.

"Maybe he figured he'd fucked up all around, so he brought us here so we could reconnect as a family again." Holly drained her glass. Then she leveled a bleary stare at Marnie. "I think I've had enough if I'm making up fairy tales."

For the first time since setting foot on the property, Kylie let a niggle of hope bloom. "Family," she whispered. "Hm."

"That's a horrible thing for him to do. Trap us here. Force us to—"

"What?" Kylie interrupted. "Bond like family?" Ire rose at Marnie's drunken nod. "Whether you like me or not, I'm a full third of this place and my opinion counts." She wanted the inn and everything that came with it. The land, the cabins, the responsibility. Stronger even than that was the need she had for finally having roots. And no one in her so-called family would stop her from getting them.

Her unspoken vehemence shocked her. The wine must have brought out a yearning she'd never acknowledged. "Sorry. We have to work together. We should make the best of it."

Marnie gave her a watery smile. "S'okay. I didn't mean to sound like you're not welcome. Our dads cried about your mom. They loved her and missed her your whole life."

The sting of tears pricked and she blinked. Holly grinned and held out her hand. "Come on," she said. "It's us against the world. All for one, one for all."

Kylie slipped her hand on top of Holly's and looked at Marnie. Eyes half closed, she grinned at both of them. "One for all," Marnie muttered and topped off the hand stack. Then the three of them flung up their hands.

"So, we're here until the work gets done at least," she said. Holly nodded.

Marnie frowned. "I can't be here the whole time. I've got a club to run," Marnie announced for the umpteenth time. "I hate that Grandad forced me to stay here. I hate that he's making us clean this pit hole. I hate that teenagers nearly destroyed the place and I hate that TJ O'Banion is so hot I want to jump him every chance I get." Her eyes went wide. "Oops. TMI, right?"

Kylie grinned and enjoyed her wine glow. "I figured as much when I saw the way he looks at you."

"Don't feel sorry for her, Kylie. She hasn't jumped him yet. She's waiting to be—what was that you said?—oh, yeah, chased and taken. You know, like swept off her feet straight into the sack."

"Shush," Marnie said around a giggle.

"You're a pretty cheap date, there, Marnie," Kylie teased. "Wine goes to my head, too. That's why I rarely drink and only when I feel safe." She'd spent a lot of years not drinking at parties. Not drinking, period. No way was she going to end up in bed with some forgettable man.

"I'm glad you feel safe with us," Marnie said, looking soppy and a little emotional. She crawled onto her air mattress, pulled the sheet up to her shoulders and then waggled her fingers. "Good night, cousins. Sleep well. Dream big."

Kylie's dreams weren't big, but they weighed heavily. She settled onto her mattress, wondering how best to work the wedge that had appeared between her cousins. They'd seemed united at the dinner table, but now Holly seemed more interested in staying long term. There was no doubt Deke had a part to play in Holly's interest.

Kylie wanted the Friendly Inn in a bone-deep way, and she was prepared to fight to get it. Gifts from the universe should be accepted. Eased by the thought, she drifted toward sleep, at peace with how things were going.

At dawn, Deke arched his hips toward a woman's wet, seeking mouth. Half asleep he groaned when she slipped her tongue to the tip of his cock. "Holly?"

Her head popped up as she eyed him. "Who else would it be?" But her voice filled with humor. "Were you dreaming of a porn star?"

"I thought I was dreaming, but I'm glad I'm not." She teased him with light laps of her tongue, making him sweat with need. "Woman, you're killing me."

She chuckled deep in her throat, sending his nerve endings on a wild tear. She released him with a soft popping sound. "Sorry I woke you, but I missed sleeping with you and came over before dawn."

"You're welcome anytime." She slipped out of her clothes and climbed in beside him with a *brrr!* He tucked the blankets around her and held her close.

"Thanks, it's chilly before dawn." She slid down his body to his cock and took him again by degrees. He strained to hold on to his control but the wild slide toward orgasm rolled through his back and into his balls. He was always fast in the morning.

"This is good, but I'm going to lose it." He flipped her and she laughed. Then she wrapped her gorgeously long legs around his waist and held him so tight he could slip in unsheathed. He pulled back to look at her face. "Wait. I need a rubber."

She blinked and a flash of regret flickered in the back of her eyes that made him wonder if she wanted children.

Pained, he let the thought go and focused on protecting them both. By the time he slid back into position, she was herself again: passionate and willing and oh-so-hot she burned the skin of his hips as she rocked him into a raging wave of pleasure.

"Yes, you're deep, so deep." She panted and rolled her hips to reach for ecstasy as he pressed hard to hold himself tight to her. Her nails dug into his ass cheeks while she screamed her release. A wet track slipped down her temple to her ear. Tears?

"Don't cry," he murmured. This was new, a first. Release could bring on tears, but not for Holly. She was in this for the fun, for the sex, for the moment.

Tears were for other times. For other men, and the stab of that shocked him. He smeared her tears away and kissed her with the salt on his tongue and the beat of his heart.

Oh, shit.

He rolled off her and gathered her into his side for a moment. "I made you cry?"

"No. Not you. Never you." Her arms wrapped his waist and she tucked her face out of view. The camper ceiling was beige and he stared into it, reminding himself of their agreement, so he wouldn't ask.

If he pressed, he might invite baggage to fall open and reveal secrets he shouldn't want to know. He didn't want to know. He knew enough. Her tears were not for him. That was enough.

"I want to show you something." The idea came to him from nowhere. But that wasn't true; the idea came so she'd know there were times his baggage floated to the top of his mind, too. In spite of his best efforts to keep it buried.

She raised her face and grinned. "Sure. What is it?"

"Just a place I haven't thought of in a while. Want to see it?"

In the truck on the way over, he asked how things had gone with Kylie. "Think she'll throw any muck in the works about selling the inn?"

"She'd like to wait before making any decisions. She got excited at the idea of opening for business, until Marnie made it clear she wants to sell."

"What about you?"

"I don't know. I see the lure of both ideas. Quick money is always nice. I mean, who wouldn't want one-third of a holiday property with acreage? But once we decided to discuss our situation this morning, she seemed more focused on getting to know us. She asked questions about our families. I have two brothers and Marnie has one."

"She said she's never met any family but Jon. So, it was just Kylie and her mom?"

Holly nodded. "My Aunt Trudy. Kylie didn't know her father. But I don't think she cared much for our grandfather. He made a bad first impression."

"I can imagine." Jon Dawson often made bad last impressions, too. "My brother steered clear of a lot of subjects with Jon. Kept to things they agreed on, like fishing, building, woodwork and tools."

"Guy stuff. Things Jon would consider manly. When he was alive, he seemed to prefer the company of his sons and grandsons to having us girls visit. I can't understand why he'd disown my aunt. What's the big secret? An out-of-wedlock baby isn't the worst thing a daughter can do. And it certainly isn't rare or shocking. Not even twenty-five years ago. She went to college, got knocked up and came home." She shrugged.

"You'd have to know more about Jon to understand. He had some odd ideas is all." The subject made him uncomfortable. "TJ was closer to Jon than anyone I know around here. You should ask him. Or better yet, your father. He'll know. Especially if you send him a picture of Kylie."

She frowned and then her eyes went wide. "It's her looks. It's her—oh, my God—Grandad was a racist?"

He should have let it go. "That's an ugly word, Holly."

Her voice went hard. "He kicked his only daughter out when she was nine months pregnant." Her face twisted. "If it was just the pregnancy, he'd have done it right away when she told him."

"I should have kept my mouth shut." He felt sorry for Kylie. That must have been an ugly meeting with Jon. "And now, we've brought someone else's baggage into what we've got going."

Holly nodded, but her frown said she was still working things out. "All we can do as a family is let Kylie know that we're not like him." When she raised her gaze forward, he saw a sheen of tears that threatened to fall. "I'll take care of that."

Deke's revelation took a while to sink in, but Holly did her best to set aside thoughts of her grandfather's behavior. Such a foolish man to cause decades of hurt and loss. Her father and uncle had tried to reach out to Aunt Trudy many times in the early years of separation, but she'd been every bit as willful and stubborn as Jon. As far as Holly was concerned, it was up to her generation to improve the situation.

From what she'd learned of Kylie last night over wine, cheese and female bonding, it shouldn't be too difficult for the family to heal.

The three of them would reach a consensus on the inn. As Kylie had pointed out, they had time to decide and there was no need to rush into a permanent decision. She seemed very willing to dig in deep to get the work done.

Deke pulled into a rutted lane that swung off TJ's driveway and parked several yards in. "This is it. This is where I want to build my own place."

"It's lovely. Looks like you could build a beautiful home here." Holly jumped down from his truck and stepped to the center of the concrete pad to judge the four corners. Family sized. "I do believe you're a nester, Deke O'Banion." She turned in a circle.

He flushed and finally stepped onto the foundation with her. He paced off the distance from one side to the other. "Not anymore. These days I'm all about good times."

"So? What's the floor plan?" This didn't count as baggage because house plans were part of the future, not his past. It may be a technicality, but she could live with it. His eyes lit up at her question and she was glad she'd asked.

He slipped his hands to his broad waist and frowned. Then he set his arms wide to encompass one large corner. "This will be the kitchen here. With a large window to catch the morning sun, and I figure sliders about here . . ." He rambled his way through the entire main floor while she watched him in awe.

She hadn't seen Deke quite like this. He was *happy*. She'd seen horny, focused, sated, hungry and even ticked off with work and his brother, but not swimming in joy. It mesmerized and held her and very nearly infected her.

Seeing his plans and dreams for a home designed with a family in mind made her heart race with unspoken dreams. Bad idea, this. She looked away toward the trees and saw the dark cool shade and nothing else.

"What about you? What do you see in your future?" he asked, blowing her thoughts of nothingness to brilliant shards.

She pursed her lips and tried not to bring too much of what used to be into the now. "At one time I thought I wanted children, but I haven't considered a family in a long while." Jack had been dead set against having a baby. He didn't want to ruin a good thing and told her he wanted her to himself. She ran her hands up her chilled arms. She had always hoped Jack would change his mind one day.

When he'd opted for a vasectomy without discussing it with her first, she demanded a separation. He'd betrayed her trust that they'd always share in decisions. Once she'd left him, she'd felt more optimistic about life. She got her groove back, so to speak, and the separation had moved into divorce.

Except for sex, of course, but even that was over now.

"Are you okay?" He pulled her into his chest and wrapped her in his arms. "Cold?"

"Just a chill."

"Someone walk over your grave?" But he turned and kept her close to his side as he led her toward his truck.

"More like a memory," she tested.

"Sorry, I shouldn't have brought you here. I didn't mean to bring up anything painful." He reached for the passenger door and opened it. He waited while she stewed about mentioning Jack and the reason for their divorce.

"No worries. There's no baggage about a family. I just haven't thought about one for a while. Things didn't work out that way for me."

"Doesn't mean they can't though, right?"

"Right." She grinned and, for the first time in over a year, felt happy about her options. "You're absolutely right, Deke. There's nothing to stop me from getting everything I want for myself. My future's bright and rosy again."

She saw affection in his eyes and it didn't scare her.

Not a bit.

A looming shadow of Jack's comments about wanting her all to himself brought her back to reality with a thump. If she wanted to move ahead, she had to clear her path. "I need to make a phone call, Deke. I doubt it'll be a pleasant one. But it will feel good to have it behind me."

"Anything I can do to help?" Concern shadowed his eyes.

"Just be here when I'm done, okay?"

"Always."

She stepped away from Deke and the truck and walked a couple yards into the heavy brush around his foundation. The air in the cool shade turned to a fresh pine scent while birds twittered overhead. She walked in far enough that the trees and bushes would absorb the sound of her voice while she spoke to Jack. She may raise her voice and didn't want to be overheard. She listened to her voice mail messages to gauge his mood.

They were angrier than the last time she'd checked. If she had to shock him into listening then she'd yell loud enough to rattle the trees.

She took three deep breaths to calm her nerves but her stomach still clenched in dread. He answered on the second ring. The roar of traffic told her he was in the car. "Took you long enough to get back to me," he said without so much as hello. Jack's way of saying he was disappointed. She refused the bait.

"Hi," she said in a breezy tone. "You called?"

"Yes. I called. Every day since you left. When are you coming home?"

"When I'm ready. This is not the way to make me want to

talk to you, Jack. Your messages were nasty and uncalled for. I told you before I left that you've got to move on. Things are different now."

"Different? *I'll* never be different, Holly. *I'll* never move on. Never. Now when the *fuck* are you coming home?"

She straightened and went still inside. Wary and aware. "I'm not coming home. Not to you. We're divorced." She'd assumed her voice would get louder if she got this angry. She was wrong. Her words came soft but hard as forged steel. "You signed the divorce papers. I'm free of you. Stay out of my life, Jack. I mean it." She was shaking when she hung up and shut off her phone. By the time she stumbled out of the brush, she was fighting back tears of anger. She must have looked like hell, because worry washed over Deke's face.

He rushed to her but she put up her hands to ward him off. She got control through sheer force of will. Jack's fury had reached out like a psychic slap. She told herself it was over, but a small voice reminded her Jack hated to lose. Had he been faking when he'd signed the divorce papers? Maybe he'd played her for a fool.

Maybe he'd never intended to let her go. The dark thought came out of nowhere and everywhere at the same time. She shook it off.

"What's wrong? You look like someone died." Deke wrapped her into his chest and she hung on, waiting for the fear to ease and the shaking to stop. She buried her nose in his plaid shirt and took comfort from his heat.

She shook her head, determined not to bring Jack into this time with Deke. "Baggage has a way of weighing you down, even when you try to leave it behind."

"Tell me, Holly."

She wiped her hand down her face, pulled herself together. "No. It's over now. And like I said, my future's bright and rosy again. This should have been dealt with ages ago. My family told me to make a clean break, but I wouldn't listen. I wanted to be nice. I hate confronting ugly feelings and I screwed up."

He nodded. "You're divorced?"

"Yes, and I let him hang on instead of dealing with leftover feelings."

"Leftover feelings. Huh." A frown filled his face as he struggled with what to say next. He'd been hurt. The hurt was in his eyes, the way his shoulders stiffened and the way his arms dropped from around her. "I drowned my leftover feelings in beer."

She nodded. "I saw the cases. But you haven't had much to drink since I've been here." One at a time seemed to be his limit. And he drank iced tea just as often. "But then, maybe you've moved on?" *The way Jack should.*

"I have." He glanced over his shoulder at the foundation of his future home. "And it feels good."

"It's healthy. And that's why I'm concerned about—"

"What spooked you, babe. The ex?"

She shook her head. Some small part of her still held a loyalty to Jack. She didn't want to discuss his inability to cope with their divorce. It seemed petty to talk about him when Deke had never met him. But Marnie knew him and it may be time to share more about Jack with her. "It's nothing, really. Nothing to worry about."

She lost the conviction in the words when Deke turned back onto the road to the Friendly Inn and she caught a glimpse of a car similar to Jack's. "It's so gloomy this morning," she said, "is that car grey or silver?"

"Looks blue to me," he said. "Why?"

"It seems familiar, but the color's wrong." Still, it unsettled her to know that Jack had been driving when they'd spoken. She hadn't thought to ask where he was, and normally he'd be at his desk at this time of day.

10

Marnie hugged her first mug of coffee to her chest and leaned against the kitchen table, prepared to be reasonable. She started with a simple question for Kylie. "You seriously think we can make a go of a business together?"

"It's worth a shot. I've never done anything like it and I'd like to try."

"But the inn is in bad shape. I'm afraid we'd find ourselves in a hole so deep we'll never get out. I've already got a business partner that's a pain in the neck. I don't need another one." She hated being difficult but she had to be straight about this. "In business, there's no room for guessing games and innuendo. We need to be straight with each other."

"You think because I haven't run an inn before that I'll make a lousy partner?" Kylie slammed the carafe back onto the warming plate.

"Now you're insulted and that's not my intent. I don't know how you'll be to work with. But running a business is harder than you think. People always think there's no boss to answer to."

"Right."

"Wrong. Every guest who walks through that door and signs in is the boss. You need to think of nothing but their comfort, their needs, their pleasure. And you have to think ahead of them." The inn was shaping up inside and she could see how Kylie's inexperienced eye could want to make it homey and welcoming. "Going into a business shouldn't be an emotional decision. There's a lot to consider." And the people you had to work with and around was a big part of the decision. "I just don't know you well enough to trust that we could make a go of this."

"If your partner in the club is so hard to deal with, why not dissolve the partnership and give this a try?"

"Giving it a try won't pay my bills. The club's about to take off." She heard Dennis's whine about how long she'd been saying those words. "I just need a little more time with it." If Mike the DJ didn't leave because they couldn't afford to give him a raise. And if they could find a loan, and if Dennis would actually handle his side of things and—

"What if you left the inn to Holly and me? Would that work?"

"No, it wouldn't." She needed the money, plain and simple. "Unless you pay me my third. Do you have that kind of money? Because Holly doesn't."

"Of course not. My mom lived well and put me through school, but when she died I cleared off her car loan and paid for the funeral. I can afford to put in a year here, but after that, the inn will have to support me or be sold."

"If the inn was a success, would you want to live here?"

But Kylie didn't need to answer, because the glow in her eyes said it all. She wanted the place, wanted it bad. "I don't know."

Holly walked in. "Morning, ladies. I got up early and went

to give Deke that tip I mentioned last night." She poured herself a coffee. She took a sip while her gaze bounced from one to the other. "I see you've started the discussion without me. Let me guess, Marnie still wants to cut and run and Kylie wants to give running the inn a whirl."

"If Marnie wasn't so stubborn—"

"If Kylie would listen to reason—"

"Does anyone want my opinion?"

Finally she'd get Holly's support and it would be two against one. "Of course," Marnie said. "Kylie, this doesn't mean we'll go our separate ways. We'll still get to the family bonding—"

"I want to stay," Holly said.

"—Just because we won't be working together doesn't mean we won't play together." She froze. "Like hell you do!"

"I want to stay," Holly repeated in a firm voice Marnie hadn't heard before.

"Why?" she asked, when she already knew. "It's Deke, isn't it? I thought this was all about sex and fun and good times."

Holly hid her mouth behind her mug. "This isn't about Deke at all."

"If it's not Deke, then why?" She thought back to the moment Holly arrived. "I knew you were hiding something. You looked so relieved to be here when you climbed out of the car, but then you smoothed your expression when I answered the door. What's really going on with you?" She focused on Holly and tried to see the truth behind her eyes.

Holly shrugged. "I think we can give this a summer. You can be here on your days off."

"Which is never." She couldn't leave the club to Dennis. A band of pressure formed across her forehead as she turned and walked out, too stunned to talk about it anymore.

But she wasn't stunned; she was hurt. Betrayed by her own flesh and blood. Her cousin. The one family member she'd always counted as a best friend.

* * *

Holly turned to Kylie. "She's stressed. Worried about a lot of things that have nothing to do with the inn."

"I think it's me. She hates the idea of sharing her inheritance with a stranger and I can't say as I blame her."

"That may be a part of it, but she'll come around. Marnie's got a good heart and loves family. It's that club. Her partner's such an ass and she's desperate to be rid of him."

"Why are you willing to stay? Don't you have a job and a life in Seattle?"

"I have a new job I don't like much. A new apartment I think is fine, but my ex is a pain. The time I spend here will give him time to believe we're over."

"But you're divorced."

"To the world we are, but to Jack, I'm not so sure. I may have messed up badly by continuing to sleep with him."

Kylie's understanding nod eased her mind. "My mom did that with a long-term guy once. Big mistake. We had to move in the middle of the night because he started coming around drunk and demanding to move back in."

"So she couldn't convince him to move on?"

"Not after she caved in and slept with him a couple of times. Some men think it's the way back into your life." She shrugged. "I guess some women think so, too. Sex messes up a lot of people." She dug out the cleaning supplies and looked at her.

"You take the back bedrooms and I'll tackle Grandad's suite today."

"Good luck with that." Kylie turned to leave. "No, wait. I'd like to do his suite. If that's okay."

"Sure. No problem."

Holly found Marnie on the veranda, painting the chairs they'd discovered in the basement. "The red looks great. Kylie was right about the color. It warms the veranda and makes it cheery."

Marnie sighed and wiped the back of her hand across her nose. "I hate to admit it, but she's been right about a lot of things around here. She has an eye," she admitted.

"I like her."

Marnie made a face that soon dissolved into a begrudging grin. "So do I. She's got a lot of guts to take her place here with us and demand to be heard. I guess she's a Dawson even if her mother did try to hide behind a different name."

"It's not that I want to disappoint you, but being here has opened my eyes to a couple of things."

"Like Deke?"

"Yes, but actually, it's more than him. I was so wrong to continue seeing Jack. I should have moved on right away, but I held on out of fear."

"Of being alone?"

"No, if I were afraid to be alone, I'd have stayed married. I was afraid of the possibilities. It's a big world outside of a difficult marriage to a controlling man. I took small steps away from him, but now I'm ready to run into the future and part of that run is this place. I'm full of what ifs and wants and excitement for a different future from anything I ever imagined."

Marnie's face went from sympathetic to surprised to delighted. "You're ready to fly?"

"Headlong into the future. I want to quit my job, give up my new apartment and give this place a shot. I want to learn if this thing with Deke has the power to hold me, if I can handle the pressure of running a business."

"And when it fails?"

"You can't be sure it will. But if we fail here, it won't be because we didn't try."

Her cousin nodded and set her red-tinted brush down onto the paint tray. "Better to have tried and failed than never to have tried at all?"

"Something like that." She couldn't tell Marnie about the

conversation with Jack and about seeing that car that looked so much like his. Marnie would tell TJ and word would get back to Deke right away. This was her problem and no one else's.

In the spirit of moving headlong into her future, she kept her thoughts about Jack's whereabouts to herself. If she got any inkling that he was going to cause a scene or otherwise interfere with her life, she'd deal with it then.

For now, Marnie had enough to think about. "Are you going to the city soon? You might want to take a couple days away from here for perspective."

"You call dealing with Dennis getting perspective?" She snorted.

"Sure."

She nodded. "I'll finish these chairs, then give the jackass a call."

"What about TJ?"

She laughed. "He'll wait. The problem is, can I?"

Three days later TJ felt the ache of defeat. He'd tried like hell to get Marnie alone, but she was quick as a mink and either dashed away or had someone with her. The logs he'd traded for would soon be delivered, and once they got here, he'd be swamped with work.

Every night, he thought of her at the inn, *bonding* with her cousin, when what he wanted was her bonding with *him*. He'd never been so frustrated.

Celibacy was easier when there weren't any interesting women. But now that every sense he had went on high alert whenever Marnie was within view, his lack of sex was killing him. Slowly, painfully killing him. He wanted to tear the woods apart, tree by tree.

The kiss on the rock had been explosive. A tease of the worst kind. And now, nothing. Made him grind his teeth.

He'd been pushed to his limits before the kiss, but now, he

was way past reasonable. Not only was she avoiding being alone with him, she was looking at him whenever they were in the same room.

She looked at him with desire.

With invitation.

With lust, not caring who was with them. Deke laughed so hard he could barely work and Holly and Kylie gave him sympathetic glances but quickly ducked their heads when he glared back.

He hated this game. It had been good fun and hot, silent foreplay when he'd thought it would last twenty-four hours, but this was ridiculous. *She* was making him ridiculous.

Didn't mean he could stop playing though, because as ridiculous as they were being, it would be worse to lose.

He stared at her bags on the floor by the front door and then raised his eyes to watch her descend the staircase.

She was dressed to kill. "You're leaving?"

"Yes."

He tried not to track the way she moved, like a cat on the hunt, but he couldn't tear his eyes away. He crossed his arms over his chest and waited, hoping she'd pounce like the feline she was.

No go. She stopped at the foot of the stairs, one hand on the newel post. Her knuckles went white as she held on. Good, he wasn't the only one on alert. He eased away from the front counter and stood straight. She stiffened, ready to run back up if he moved closer. "Right now?"

"I've got to get back to head off a disaster." She looked hot enough to sear. A short tight skirt, long legs that ended in stilettoes. She wore her hair down and the tips brushed just below her shoulders. A wide-belted green blazer topped off her outfit and put the city stamp all over her. She was high fashion, high maintenance and he could almost taste her.

"I had plans for this weekend." He spoke softly so she wouldn't spook.

"Did you now?" Her knuckles tightened and he smiled his response. She loosened her grip.

"You know damn well I did. You've been staying here all week *bonding* with Kylie, when I wanted you at my place."

"I've been happy here. Kylie and I have come to some agreement over the last couple of nights."

"I don't give a rat's ass about—" He ground his back teeth to stop from giving her any ammunition.

The smile she gave him was pure come get it.

So he did.

In one step he had her in his arms, his mouth on hers, his hands cupping her ass and dragging her hips into his. He pressed his erection against her as he held her tight, felt the press of her pubic bone, the softness of her thighs. She sighed into his mouth and slipped her tongue along the length of his in a drag race they could both win if she'd only allow it.

He'd planned to get her into his bed come hell or high water and not let her out until they were both drained. From sundown Friday to sunrise Monday, he'd wanted to be buried in her, awash in Marnie.

Instead, he was kissing her good-bye. *Fuck!* Life went to shit sometimes.

He broke into a sweat as she coaxed him for more. He tore his mouth from hers. "Don't leave." He held himself rigidly away from her.

"If I don't go, I'll lose everything. This time, my partner has messed up so bad I'm not sure I can fix it."

"I had plans for this weekend."

"You won't believe me, but so did I."

He growled. Sounded like an asshole, but he couldn't help it. She was tearing him apart.

"It's not as bad as all that, is it? I'll be back as soon as I can. The bedrooms will be well on their way to done. We'll be ahead of schedule."

"Which means you'll be gone permanently all that much sooner."

She jerked. "Now, now, that sounds as if you—"

"Want you to stay?" No woman had ever frustrated him on so many levels all at once. He hadn't even slept with her yet and here he was ... wanting. More than she offered, more than they'd shared, more than he'd ever wanted before.

She stepped back. "Maybe. Do you?"

"How could I want you to stay? We haven't done anything more than kiss." What the hell did he want?

"That's right. Nobody makes decisions based on a kiss."

Kylie and Holly walked in, with Deke trailing. He wanted to wipe the smirk off his brother's face. Instead, he set her away and nodded. "I'll see you when I see you, then. Good luck."

Kylie gave her a tight hug and a warm smile to see her off. "I'll have all the bed frames put together and the headboards stained by the time you get back. And I'll start sewing the curtains for the bedrooms, too. You'll see. They'll be lovely."

Marnie hugged her cousin back, then smiled for the group before Deke grabbed her bags and escorted her to her tiny car.

Each of the women had brought special skills to the inn. Marnie knew business, Holly had a decorating and cooking flair, while Kylie knew her way around handiwork, including sewing, painting and some renovation work.

The three of them made a great team. He wondered if Marnie saw it or if she was too focused on the club to realize she had a shot at making the inn viable.

Holly was next with a breezy wave and easygoing wish for a safe drive back to the city. She closed the door and spun to glare at him. "You need to do something, TJ. She's stubborn to a fault. And she won't give up on that loser partner of hers until it's too late."

"That's my choice? Convince her to walk away from the business she's built? The life she loves?" No one with half a brain made decisions on the strength of one kiss.

No one.

He growled again and stormed out the door after her. He watched as the bumblebee she called a car disappeared in a cloud of dust. He stopped with his hand on his truck door. Chasing her when he had work to do. Pathetic bastard.

"Deke!" He strode around the building, furious with himself. If he got the cabins built, Marnie would see the potential in the redeveloped inn and change her mind about leaving.

Now that would be a big enough thing on which to base a life-changing decision: potential, and the inn oozed it, especially with these three women running the place.

But unless she saw it herself, it was a stupid plan. If she left the city because of him, she may grow to resent the way he'd forced her hand.

His body thrummed with disappointment when he thought of another whole weekend without easing himself into her. But the cabins wouldn't build themselves, and with Eli still not home, it wasn't fair to dump the load on Deke.

He caught sight of his brother and hollered again. "Where the *hell* is Eli? And why isn't he home yet?"

"What's been shoved up your ass and got your guts in a snarl?" Then he laughed. "Oh. Never mind."

"Fuck off." He strode past his smirking brother and headed out for the pond. As soon as he hit the water's edge, he knelt and stuck his head in deep, letting the icy water shock him nearly senseless. For a second there, all he wanted to do was float downstream to the ocean.

Maybe he'd be swept over the strait and into Canadian waters.

But he'd still have this hard-on and he'd still want that exasperating woman. He rose straight up out of the water with a huge gasp and shook off droplets like a dog. He wanted to howl.

Another whole weekend.

Nope. Couldn't do it.

Marnie pulled into her reserved spot behind the club, edgy and out of sorts. "Please," she muttered, as she climbed the back stairs to her office, "don't let me find another threesome." If she saw anyone getting laid and it wasn't her, she'd scream.

Nothing this week had been harder than walking away from TJ O'Banion. That kiss at the pond had fed her dreams every night since it happened. Damn this club and damn Dennis even more. She should be at TJ's place right now. This was an idiotic game of frustration she'd started. What kind of moron pushed a man to his limits when they wanted the same thing? But once she'd teased him and he'd teased back, her competitive side had come to the fore.

Damn her Dawson bullheadedness. Why couldn't she have just slept with the man when he made it clear he wanted her? What was the big deal?

But the wiser side of her head said that sleeping with TJ O'Banion would change her life and not for the better. Once she had a taste of him, she might not be able to let go.

She had to remember her priorities. She'd be a fool to get involved with TJ. Sex with the man would bind them in ways too deep. He wasn't the kind of man to keep things light.

Leaving him was the right thing to do for herself. And likely for him, too. He didn't need a fling with a woman determined to leave him behind.

At the top of the stairs she held her breath and opened the office door. No Dennis. No threesome. The lights were on, but the security monitors were blank. "Great. What now?"

She couldn't find an obvious reason for the monitors not to

work, so she called her security company and sicced them on the problem. Was a simple phone call too much for Dennis to handle? He knew how important security was in a club.

She headed downstairs and threaded her way through the Friday after-work crowd. She found him at his favorite table on the back wall nursing a bottle and a shot. "You're back," he said and downed his glass. "Good thing."

She slid in beside him on the banquette and watched the customers, rowdy after work and ready to party. They'd be busy tonight, and they were short staffed.

Thanks to Dennis. "You assaulted our new bartender?"

"Grabbed her tit, that's all." He shrugged.

"You admit it?" She sagged into the banquette and waved away the bottle when he offered it. *Overload.*

"Well, she shouldn't wave them in a guy's face."

She wanted to slap him, but no matter how much power she put into it, she didn't have the strength to kill him with one blow.

Pity. But maybe a quick death was too merciful.

Besides, if she started slugging him, she might not stop. The idea gained merit as she watched his put-upon expression. He really believed this was the bartender's fault.

"Damn, I wish I could remember her name, but I'm too angry with you to remember my own." She unclenched her hands and let them rest flat on the table.

"Why blame me? She's the one who came into the office in a low-cut top and smiled like she wanted it."

She held on to her composure, afraid not to. "She's new. It was her first week." She enunciated every word to try to get the lummox to hear her. "She wanted you to like her. You know, Dennis, like a *person*. She wore the top to encourage tipping and she smiled like a regular human being." She couldn't resist a moment longer. She smacked his shoulder. He didn't even grunt, the slimy bastard.

An image of TJ by the water wafted through her mind. He wanted her and even with her teasing him, he would never try to force his advantage. TJ would never treat women the way Dennis did. He'd never intimidate a woman, or flat out grab what he wanted. She was proof positive. She'd flirted and challenged and tantalized him, then left him high and dry. He hadn't been nasty or snide.

He must be furious that she left him. Maybe she should have invited him here. But if he were here, she wouldn't be able to focus on anything but TJ. He was a distraction she couldn't afford.

Right now, rather than dream about what she'd like to do with TJ all weekend, she needed to fix this mess Dennis had created with his grabby hands and cheesy expression. She smacked him again for good measure. His tequila slopped out of his shot glass. "Clean that up," she snarled as she left him. "And you're tending bar." She took the bottle and handed it off to Jeff, promising him a bonus for the extra load he had tonight. "Make sure Dennis helps you." She couldn't believe she'd been forced to include Jeff in this spat.

She waited until Jeff nodded at her and Dennis slouched his way over. She wanted to tell him to grow the fuck up, but that was not the way to handle a man-child. Dennis would pout and dig in his heels. Jeff controlled his expression, but laughter lurked under his control. Damn.

It had been wrong to let Jeff know she was furious with the other owner. But clearly, the entire staff knew about this mess and were waiting to see how it played out.

After all, if she screwed up with this, they could be out of their jobs.

"I'll be back as soon as I can," she promised Jeff. She shouldn't have argued with Dennis in front of the staff, but damn, it felt good to let off some steam.

She stalked through the gathering groups of people. Tables

were filling fast. She had a couple of part-timers she could call in a pinch.

After that, she'd call Tisha for an appointment to see her. *Tisha.* Yes, that was the bartender's name. How stressed was she that she'd forgotten?

Maybe she could make this go away before Tisha found a lawyer and sued them right out of the club. But at this point, it would almost be a relief.

She found Tisha's personnel file, called and left a message. Then and only then, Marnie sank into her chair. Tired of putting out Dennis's fires, she missed the mindlessness of cleaning and sorting. The work at the inn had been physically demanding but mentally freeing. While she'd scrubbed and wiped and vacuumed and polished, she'd had time to ponder and to dream. Her grandfather had forced her, Holly and Kylie to work together. After the initial disagreement and disappointment with Holly, Marnie had come to understand that something was going on in her cousin's life that no one knew about. Whatever it was, Holly seemed determined to handle it herself.

If she needed to stay on the Peninsula for a few months to get things sorted out, then so be it. Not everyone's life was as straightforward as Marnie's.

The mindless work had given her mind time to roam. It had been far too long since she'd been able to do any free thinking and she missed it. She got her best, most innovative ideas when she let her mind wander, open and free. That's when possibilities walked in and grew into solid ideas.

The other day at the inn, she'd been waxing the wood doorframes and the lemony scent of the polishing cloth and rhythmic movement of her arm had opened her mind to the resort idea again.

There were acres and acres of trees behind the inn. The clearing for the three cabins had barely made a dent in the available land. What if the three cabins were just the beginning of a meandering trail that led deeper into the woods to cul-de-sacs of cabins interspersed with play areas and tennis courts and bike trails?

The dream was all well and good, but her future was here in Backlit, not at the inn.

She walked to Dennis's desk and rifled through the stack of mail he'd left sitting unopened. Resisting the temptation to leave the mail for him, she settled back at her desk and pulled out her letter opener.

The shaft shone and flashed as she opened each bill in the quiet of the office. In under an hour, a stifling cloak of pressure enveloped her. Her desk was now piled with paperwork. She had myriad details left undone, the blank, staring monitors she couldn't fix herself, the stack of unpaid invoices Dennis hadn't bothered to pay.

She mindlessly flicked a corner of a supplier's invoice. This one was for foodstuffs for the bar. Pretzels, peanuts.

Crap.

Crap, crap and more crap. She lowered her head to rest on her folded arms and thought of the waxy scent of lemon on wood, the smooth rhythmic strokes. The same rhythm she'd like to use on TJ.

Desire rose as she thought of him. She should have indulged her needs every time she'd had the chance. Foolishly, she'd played games that left them both hot and yearning.

She sighed. A full-bodied I-don't-give-a-shit-anymore sigh.

She was horny. She was lonely. She wanted TJ and she'd *left* him.

A sound at the door startled her into straightening.

And there he was. TJ O'Banion in the flesh. She blinked as he bristled with seductive energy. Edgy and hot. His shoulders filled the doorway, his expression went hard, his jaw firmed as he glanced around the office, then let his gaze rake over her face.

"You're here. Really?" She couldn't believe he'd made the trip. He must have left right after she did.

His hands clenched at his sides as if he itched to grab her out of her seat. His eyes burned as he raked her body.

She half stood, every nerve ending alive, arced to his in mutual need. Her heart slammed in her chest and everything but TJ left her universe. He was all there was.

Him and his need. One step inside, then he kicked the door shut.

"Lock it," she said. "And turn out the lights."

"Fuck the lights."

11

TJ got to her before Marnie could do more than nod her head. Grabbed her by the forearms and pulled her the rest of the way out of her seat.

Slammed his mouth to hers and took. Goddamn, she tasted good.

Apparently so did he, because she rolled her tongue across his and got into his pants faster than the next breath. He nearly buckled when the heat of her hands touched the head of his cock.

Color exploded behind his eyes, starbursts of need narrowed his vision as he pushed her against the wall, hoisted her to his hips and pressed her hard. If he didn't get inside her soon, he'd lose his mind. And even if he did, he'd lose his mind.

Either way, he was going to have her so fast, so hard, so deep, she'd never forget it.

Her hands flew around his clothes. His belt fell away, his fly widened as she nipped his lower lip with urgency that filled him. He felt cool air on his cock as he sprang out of his jeans. She cupped him with both hands and stroked once. He felt the pressure build in his balls. "Stop. Fuck."

"Oh, yes," she breathed, as he yanked down her skirt, then dragged her panties off. She stepped out of everything that was in his way and then wrapped her legs around his hips. So close. Her wet heat grazed his cock, making his flesh slip and slide along her juicy cleft.

Blind with need, he clasped his cock to guide it in when she froze. "Wait. Condom. Top drawer on the left."

The fog lifted long enough to let the word *condom* sink in. He reached for her desk drawer but she grabbed his hand. "Not my desk. That one. His."

She left him, stunned and shaking, while she tore into the drawer and came up with a packet. "Here. At least he's good for something."

TJ pulled her into his arms while she opened the packet and hurriedly slipped the rubber over his distended cock. He ground his back teeth to hold on when her sly fingers cupped and squeezed his sac.

"You're so hard. Ready."

"My balls've been blue for a week." He laid her out on the desk and stepped into her cradle with a thrust that buried him to the hilt. She scrabbled backward at the pressure, but he held her until she rocked against him, open and wet. He thumbed her clit and watched as she gathered herself then flew apart and off into ecstasy. She shattered and rocked, crooned and groaned. Her hips stilled as she held on to every pulse.

"Oh, TJ. That is good. So very very . . . good."

He shuddered at the sound of her guttural cry, the inner clench of her walls. Orgasm rolled through the small of his back and through him as he spun out of control and fell. Fell. Fell as he followed her into the little death.

"Marnie." Her name came from somewhere else. Some other place near his heart. He sagged onto her, only vaguely aware that she clung to him and crooned near his ear; softly and in gentle words he didn't deserve.

"I'm sorry. I rushed you, took you like a—"

"Sh, TJ." She dug her fingers into his hair. "Never. You could never . . . be like that."

He raised his face, her sweet grace a balm. "I hurt you," he pulled back, suddenly aware that he'd slammed into her on her desk, not caring that she was spread eagle on the hard flat surface. That he'd spread her so wide, he must have touched her womb. "Marnie," he whispered again and wanted to kiss her, hold her.

Rock her gently until she let him do it all over again.

"I'm a bastard." But his cock was already hardening, never really went down. "But I want you again."

She laughed as if his guilty admission pleased her. "Yes. Again and again." She hitched her hips higher, reached around and tapped his sac with a naughty finger.

He felt the condom, full and slippery and pulled out. He kissed her belly. "Washroom?"

"In there." She pointed over her head and he saw a door. "While you're gone, I'll get another condom."

Satisfaction rolled through him as he heard her light step across the office. When he returned, it was to find her fiddling with a set of three monitors. "Security system down?"

"Seems to be okay now." Her sexy ass peeked out at him from under her blazer. He hadn't even given her time to get comfortable. The front hung open as she clicked a remote control aimed at the screens. Her cheeks were full and round and he slipped his hand to cup her there. She glanced over her shoulder with a grin. "Hi, there."

The images cleared and he saw various views. If the monitors had been working, she'd have seen him come in through the alley door. "That door was unlocked when I got here. I just walked in, but I was too focused to think about how unsafe it is for you."

"It should have locked behind me," she said. A frown formed on her brows. "That's odd."

"Your partner not on top of things here?" Stupid question. She'd had to leave the Peninsula to come back and mop up a mess he'd caused.

"Never. Dennis is"—she hesitated—"a challenge." But she looked satisfied with what she saw on-screen. "At least he's lending a hand at the bar. And I called in some reinforcements for waitstaff and they've all arrived."

Anyone with eyes could see the club was packed. "You need to get down there." It wasn't a question.

"Twenty minutes?" She bit her lip, but her eyes tracked down to his jutting rod. "Then we can go to my place. Have the whole night together." The promise in her gaze zipped along his spine. He nodded.

"Sure." He reached for his clothes, pulled them on while she did the same.

Her twenty minutes turned into an hour, but he enjoyed seeing her in action. She was a superb people person. The staff all liked her. She didn't hesitate to pitch in, but didn't hover over the casual staff, either.

She kept a sharp eye on the guy she'd pointed out as Dennis but said little to him. Whatever beefs she had with him were private and not for public display. At least not now. While they'd dressed, she'd admitted blasting him in front of the bartender earlier.

He sat at the end of the bar, watching her work. His gaze never left her, not when a busty blonde sat down and tried to start a conversation, not when her friend flanked his other side, not even when they sandwiched him in tits.

"Sorry, ladies. I'm happily attached and loyal as a retriever." By now he figured his eyes were pleading for rescue, but Marnie was biting her lip to keep from laughing at him while she sorted the cash in the till.

"But you're so big, there's plenty enough to go around." Her whisper in his ear went sultry and he finally turned his gaze to the blonde. Avid eyes met his, calculating her chances of success. She swept her hardened nipples across his biceps and moved in to kiss him.

He dodged.

She missed.

The other woman hissed because his dodge mashed her breasts. "Let's go, Cissy; he's pussy-whipped."

The blonde pouted as they moved away and suddenly he was free. He sipped his half-warm beer and watched Marnie approach with a full-on grin splitting her face. Goddamn, she was beautiful. Her hair shone, even in the muted lighting, her eyes glowed with suppressed laughter. She leaned across the bar and kissed him, licking the beer from his lips and creating a hard-on the size of a Douglas fir.

"Apparently I'm pussy-whipped."

"You are?"

He shrugged. "Seems so."

"Good." She kissed him again, opening his lips with her tongue and swooping in. He let her and wanted more, but she pulled back before he could drag her across the bar to him. "I won't be long now and we can go to my place."

Thank Christ.

"Will you stay with me for the whole weekend? Tonight's not enough."

He tugged her closer and leaned in for her ears only. "Is there such a thing"—his voice sounded strangled, but the noise level of the bar hid the wobble—"as cock-whipped?"

She laughed. "There is now."

At least he wasn't in this alone.

"Walk with me to the office. I have to take some cash upstairs."

Her partner kept his wary gaze on Marnie as she collected the cash from the till. TJ dogged her every step as she made her way through the crowd toward Dennis. He was directing human traffic near the door. "This place is hopping." A roar from the dance floor crowd drowned him out.

A quick glance over his shoulder told him the DJ had taken his place. The guy bowed to the groups of people cheering, then took his place behind his equipment. The whole place went darker as he started his patter. Then a thrumming beat began that would soon drive his eardrums into hiding if he was forced to stay.

Nights on the Peninsula were full of quiet and he liked it that way. He knew what the other customers saw when they looked at him. A hick. A small-town man in a plaid shirt and work jeans. Hell, he was still in his construction boots. The club was upscale, full of professionals in suits while he sat like a mountain of trouble at the end of the bar.

Marnie was in her element. Laughing with customers, pouring drinks, moving smoothly behind the bar while keeping one eye on the entire place.

She juggled everything beautifully. Capably. While Dennis kept a malevolent eye on her every move.

TJ wanted to have a word with the jerk, explain the niceties of working in a partnership with a woman like Marnie, but he refused to take a chance of ticking her off. She wouldn't want him dealing with Dennis. He wasn't sure he could keep a cool head with the guy anyway.

Marnie talked into Dennis's ear for a moment, while he listened, eyes darting around the people coming into the club. He nodded a few times, leaned in to her ear and spoke.

TJ couldn't catch a word, but she looked satisfied with whatever he said. She turned, put her hand on TJ's arm and smiled in relief. "We can go."

In the office, he was tempted to put her over the desk and take her just as fast and hard as he had the last time, but he reconsidered when she closed them inside. "I think I hate him. I really do. Tisha called *him* back instead of me."

She crossed the office at a brisk, no-nonsense pace. "We're having a meeting Sunday morning after I see Tisha. He's going to have to prove he's worth all this effort."

"Good luck with that." He feigned interest in the monitors as she knelt behind her desk to open the safe. No business owner wanted anyone looming over them while they were using their combination.

The moment he heard the safe door click close, he turned and drew her to her feet. She leaned into him, let him kiss her.

Marnie.

He fell into her mouth over and over again until she moaned with want. Desire prettied her up all over, made her flush and pink, her pussy wet and breasts swollen. He hadn't even seen her fully naked yet.

"Take me home," he said, his voice a gravel bed of need. "Now. Before I'm all over you again. This time I want to take things slower."

She nodded. "You're right. There are lots of things I want to do to you, too."

A week of denial hung between them, a curtain of frustrated nights and daytime longing. "We were stupid to wait this long."

"You think so? By waiting, I know I want to take you home. I know I'll want to see your face in the morning. I know everything we do will be good and right for us both."

He dropped his head. She was right. He couldn't wait to see where she lived, and how. He already knew she was snarky before coffee and easy to laugh after. He knew how she sounded when she came and knew the taste of her mouth.

And none of what he knew was enough.

"Let's go."

12

Holly and Deke stood in the cashier's line at the hardware store and watched as the woman chatted and flirted with every man she waited on. She looked about Deke's age, but hard ridden, which Holly thought was a harsh way of putting it, but it seemed accurate. Cheap mascara had flaked off onto her cheeks, and her eyeshadow, in a shade that had been popular a decade ago, had settled into creases in her eyelids. Her mouth turned down at the corners and her hair needed a good salon job. She'd way overestimated her ability with store-bought color.

Still, she seemed friendly enough when she spied Holly with Deke. "Hey, Deke. How's TJ?"

Which was why the woman didn't mind that Holly was with Deke.

"He's fine, Alice. Yourself?"

"Can't complain. You boys must be busy at the inn?" The question included Holly, so she smiled and nodded.

Curiosity flared in Alice's gaze. "Maybe you're the one he was looking for?"

A chill skittered down her back. "Who was looking?" she asked.

"A man. Kind of skinny. Black hair."

"Pointed chin?" her voice came out hollow, as fear crept along her arms, raising the hair. Jack. It must be.

"Yeah, kinda." Alice mimicked a narrow chin and Holly felt sick. "But good lookin', too."

Deke watched Holly closely. "You all right, babe?" At her nod, he looked at the cashier. "What'd you say to him?"

Alice shrugged and took his credit card. While she slid it through her machine she dug through her memory. To Holly it seemed like a slow process, but eventually the woman perked up. "Since I hadn't seen her yet, that's what I told him. That I'd never seen her. Unh, you." She nodded at Holly and looked pleased with her report. "He asked where the inn was though, so I figured he must be either looking for work or maybe he's family?"

"He used to be family. He's not anymore." Her sharp retort startled the woman and her expression closed.

"Well, I didn't know."

What the hell did Jack think he was doing? The car *had* been his, and she'd been stupid not to trust her instincts at the time. When Deke had said he thought it was blue, she'd been only too willing to agree.

"It's okay, Alice." Deke leaned in closer to the woman, his voice soft. "Don't tell him you've seen us though, all right?"

"Uh, okay. Seriously, Deke, I didn't think there was any-thing wrong with giving a friendly stranger directions to a con-struction site. The inn's going to open for business later this summer, right?"

Holly broke in. "You didn't tell him that, did you?"

Alice blinked and her mouth turned down even farther. "I may have. I'm not sure." She looked confused and tried to recall more details. But gossip didn't come with details, just vague embellishments and innuendo. "We chatted. He was nice and kind of hot."

Jack had an appealing side to him. Prickly around the edges, but his nearly black eyes oozed sex in a way that some women found hard to resist.

Holly should know; she'd been one of them.

Alice piled their purchases into a reusable cotton bag Holly had insisted they take to the store, then slid it into Deke's waiting hand.

He grabbed Holly's hand none too gently and led her out to his truck. She followed quickly, keeping her eyes down. Stupid, really. She should look around to see if Jack watched from somewhere nearby. "I wonder when he got here?" she said, which seemed like the natural thing to say. She didn't want Deke to know that she thought she'd seen Jack's car the day before. This business with Jack was all hers.

She'd never shared her problems with him, with anyone; she wasn't about to start now.

Deke slammed to a halt in the parking lot, not caring that other customers walked by openly staring. "This is your ex-husband. He's here for a reason, Holly. Are you really through with him or does he have reason to believe it's not over?" His face looked thunderous. Angry and defiant.

"Don't look at me as if this is my fault." Deke was a big guy, but now he loomed large and hard and furious. She refused to be cowed and stared just as heatedly back at him.

The breeze kicked his dark hair into waves, making him look even angrier. "You heard me: How over is this?"

"Very." But her answer made her uncomfortable. She'd slept with Jack just before she got here. She shifted with her guilt and Deke noticed.

He stepped back as if he couldn't bear to be near her. His

face closed, his body went rigid. Shit, she'd never been much of a liar. And Deke had definitely been lied to before. "Why am I doubting you, Holly?"

"We haven't even seen this man yet. It may not be Jack," she hedged. Then she got riled. "So what if I have an ex? We're divorced. It's over. End of story."

The heat of anger rose as she stared at him. "You can't tell me you don't have some woman in your past you cared about."

He narrowed his eyes but she didn't heed the warning. "You didn't put in that foundation for nobody. You had plans, Deke. And they were broken, just like mine. Are you saying you've made it to thirty-two without ever having cared about someone?" She couldn't believe it, Deke was too good a man, too kindhearted not to have fallen for some woman somewhere.

He blinked and set his jaw at a stubborn angle. "It wasn't a woman I fell for." His eyes went bleak. "I know that now."

"But—" This was not something she could have seen coming. "But, you're—"

He held up his hands, the bag dangling in the breeze. "I'm not gay, but I'm not bringing my baggage into this. This is about yours."

Baggage. Jack.

"What the hell is Jack doing here? You told me there was nothing to worry about." He stepped away, yanked on his truck door and climbed inside, his face a mask of stubborn denial.

"There is nothing to worry about," she snapped, still stunned by the force of his anger. "Jack's harmless. He's probably just here to—" He started the truck, so she leaped into the passenger seat to avoid being left in the hardware store parking lot, an honest-to-God spectacle. She couldn't believe she'd been about to say Jack was here to get laid. *Yeah, that's exactly what Deke wanted to hear.*

Deke was so large and intimidating she wasn't sure what to

expect once they were alone, but she'd give her last breath knowing he'd never hurt her. He wasn't that kind of man. So she buckled up and turned her face to the side window to avoid the steaming heat of anger that rose all around him.

"I didn't ask for you to handle this for me, Deke. If this is Jack, I'll talk with him and send him back to the city."

He grunted and pulled out of the parking lot. He turned left toward the inn. "Turn around," she said. "Take me to your place so I can get my things. I'll move into the inn with Kylie. You won't have to deal with me or my ex-husband ever again."

"Goddamn it." He slammed his palm on the steering wheel, then white-knuckled the thing as he pulled a U-turn. "I got into the middle of a legal battle between a woman I cared for and her ex. I'll never do it again. She used me. Convinced me of all kinds of things that weren't true." He glanced across the cab at her, his eyes dark pools of pain. "In the beginning, she told me the same thing you are. That there was nothing to worry about, that she'd handle everything. But then, occasionally, she'd mention some of the things he'd done, some of the shit he was pulling to hurt her and her son. I fell for it, hook, line and sinker."

And then she saw the source of his pain. He'd wanted a family. He'd cared for this woman and her son and she used Deke's feelings for the boy to her own advantage. "Oh, Deke, I'm sorry. You wanted that little boy to have a dad. A real dad."

He stiffened and she knew the pain was still fresh. That was why he'd been drinking so hard. He was grieving the loss of a son. She wanted to ask what happened, where the boy and his mother were now, but Deke was still raw and it wasn't her place.

He needed to understand more about her and the divorce so he'd see she wasn't a repeat of this other woman. "I went through my divorce without even getting my family involved, so I'm not about to ask you to get between Jack and me now."

"You divorced without telling your family?"

"I told them after I left but kept the process to myself. They never warmed to Jack and I didn't think it was fair to blame him for the whole thing, which is exactly what they'd have done." The death of her marriage had been painful enough without going over it in intimate detail during every conversation. And her father and brothers would have been in Jack's face. "I was always their little girl and baby sister." Having anyone else deal with Jack would be admitting she couldn't stand on her own two feet. As stubborn as Aunt Trudy? Maybe. "I needed to deal with my divorce in my own way." She still did. "And I'll deal with Jack without your help now."

She wasn't sure if this argument signaled the end with Deke. Not everyone wanted to share their vulnerability so soon in a relationship. If he'd said too much too soon, and was already sorry for talking about his recent painful break up, the end could be on them without warning. Intimacy needed to be earned and she had no way to know how far along that path they'd gone.

None of this pain would have surfaced if Jack had just stayed home. "This is exactly the kind of shit Jack loves to pull. He's ruined what you and I have and I'm so sorry about that, Deke. I didn't want this to happen. When we promised to leave our baggage out of this, I took my promise to heart. I never meant for this to happen." Her voice wobbled in the middle of her speech, but she pulled it together admirably by the end. If Jack knew the way he'd ruined a good thing for her, he'd be happy enough to crow.

"I don't want us to part on angry terms, Deke. We have to see each other at the inn. It'll be uncomfortable for TJ and Marnie, too." The distance to his camper was eaten by the tires on the damp road. Another misty rain morning.

When he didn't respond, she turned to the window again and stared out at the passing trees. Trees and more trees. She wanted to look out the other side, but Deke would think she was staring at him, so she subsided into her seat and let her mind wander.

She refused to let her thoughts settle anywhere, because if she did, she'd get angry again: at Jack, at herself and at Deke, when none of this was his fault.

Deke drove on autopilot. Good thing it was midmorning with little traffic. Holly sat beside him stonefaced and staring out the side window to avoid looking in his direction.

He couldn't blame her. He'd really lost it back there. But he had the right to be sick and tired of women and their baggage. He tried to get back his *fuck 'em all* attitude but he wasn't built that way.

And there, right *there*, was his problem.

He wanted a woman, a family, a home. A life.

Why couldn't he find a woman who wanted the same things? Who came without baggage? Losing Misty's son Gabriel had kicked the shit out of him, plain and simple. He'd loved the boy like his own and he wanted to hate Misty for tearing them apart.

A sniffle from Holly brought him back from the simmering sense of loss that had never gone away.

The moments spent with Holly at his building site had been filled with a future again. He glanced at her and caught the sag in her shoulders as she did her best to ignore him.

It must be like ignoring an angry bear inches from your face. "What do you think Jack's up to? Why would he be here?"

She turned, her face a furious mask, her blue eyes snapping. "I don't need your help. Did I say one word about being helpless? This is my problem, Deke."

"So some guy comes around asking questions and looking for you and I'm supposed to ignore it?"

"Yes. I said I wouldn't bring anything to our table and I

won't. I don't go back on my word, and if you're bringing a woman who did go back on her word to *our* table, that's your shit. Don't lay it on me."

He jerked in his seat and the truck veered for a second. When he righted it, he still couldn't think of what to say. So he said nothing.

When the turnoff for Lyle's place came up, he turned in. She was right, he was taking on her concerns about her ex when she hadn't asked him to. His downfall was wanting to rescue women. This one clearly didn't want or need his help.

He should be relieved. This was exactly what he'd wanted when he struck the no-baggage bargain. It was stupid to push at her, demanding to be let in to her problems. He'd said he didn't want to know and he should stick to that. He pulled to a stop in front of his camper.

"Thanks, I'll get my stuff," Holly said. "It shouldn't take long."

She was leaving. He put his hand on her arm when she opened the door to jump out. She looked at him, wary. "I was wrong to assume you wanted help. Jack is your problem, not mine." It was hard but he knew not to ask any more about her break up. Whatever was going on with her ex, it was none of his business. She'd made that clear even when he'd been an ass. "I'm sorry about bringing Misty's lies into this. It was wrong."

She blinked and her eyes looked misted.

No way would he ask another question. But still, something was off about Jack. If Holly hadn't told him where she would be, she had good reason. "I'll keep out of your business. But I'd like you to stay with me." It would be safer if she were with him, but he couldn't say it. She did not need to be rescued and she'd spit nails before asking for help.

"I'll think about it," she grumbled. Her expression was just as dark as it had been before so he expected to be on pins and needles for the rest of the day.

"Let me know when you've decided." He tried to keep his tone light and easy but it was tough. "I'm sure an air mattress is plenty comfortable."

She lifted one side of her mouth in a half grin. "Plenty soft, too."

He slipped his hand to hers. "The idea of you sleeping anywhere but with me feels a lot like heartburn." He rubbed his chest. She let her gaze slide down his chest to his lap and back again. She turned her hand over to clasp his.

"That's rough."

He nodded.

She smiled and shut the truck door. "We'd better get to work. Marnie'll give us hell if she comes back and we're behind schedule."

Marnie. He'd ask Marnie his questions. Holly may not have told her parents and brothers what had happened in her marriage, but Marnie would know.

When they were heading back toward the inn, Holly's mood shifted to horny. She hated confrontation and make-up sex was the best. "Tonight, we'll shut the door of the camper and lock out the whole world." She ran her fingers up the inside of her thigh in suggestion.

Deke's firm mouth kicked up and he slanted a sexy glance her way. "Oh, yeah? And how will we do that?"

She leaned on the passenger door and opened her thighs. Her khaki shorts gave plenty of room for his fingers to roam. He couldn't mistake the invitation.

He patted the seat next to him. "Slide on over here."

With a grin she felt in her heart, she slipped into the middle seat, belted herself in and set his hand on her knee. He grinned and drew circles up the inside of her thigh, sending whorls of intense sensation to her sex.

Her breasts rose and her nipples peaked. She pulled the material over her crotch out of the way of his fingers. Soon his touch would scorch through anything that stood between them. The truck veered in the lane again as he watched her. He swore and corrected immediately.

"Touch me, Deke. Right there where I'm wet." She slid her finger into her mouth and sucked. He squeezed the fleshy part of her thigh in his large palm and the flare of desire in his eyes made her wetter. He stretched his little finger north toward her center. "Pull over," she breathed. "Please." Pressure built in her lowest reaches and need overrode her good sense.

Midday on a rain-slicked road was a dangerous place to play this game. The danger heightened her edgy need.

But Deke was still able to think clearly and turned the truck onto an overgrown driveway entrance. "This is a summer home. No one is here yet." But he didn't drive the length of the lane. Instead, he parked the truck in the deep shade, out of sight of the passing traffic.

She undid her seat belt and gave him a delighted whoop.

"You're not fooling me, Holly. You want me to forget about your ex. You want to distract me."

"I want sex, Deke. I told you I have a strong libido. That's all there is to this."

He narrowed his eyes and she felt the burn through her chest and held her breath. "I don't want to talk about Jack. I don't want you to be concerned."

He turned in the seat and she took that as a good sign. If he was facing her fully, she could drag him down onto the seat and get his mind on her and off their disagreeable discussion. "What I want," she said, "is you. Now."

Suddenly his hands were on her thighs, opening them. He slid his fingers up to her center and moved the crotch of her shorts out of the way. Finally. She melted as moisture pooled and heat rose between them.

He tugged her down to the seat, shucked her out of her

shorts, then set her left foot on his headrest. Thrilling at his touch, she arched her hips toward him in total surrender. He made her feel this way, made her want to give him everything, made her want to abandon herself to him.

He set her legs wide as he gazed at her. Cool air touched her heated slit as a warm pool of moisture grew with each second. Blood rushed to her labia and her flesh opened to receive him. How much more could she surrender?

How much more could he want?

She shied away from the answer. Not her heart. Surely, not that.

And then he was there, his lips kissing and licking her fleshy mound. She clasped his head, burrowing her fingers in his hair and held him to her. Intense pleasure rolled up through her belly and out the top of her head and he hadn't actually touched her core. But anticipation brought orgasm closer as she rolled her hips up to meet his audacious mouth.

He teased her by blowing air across her sensitive flesh until she dug her hands into his scalp and moved his head to bring him to her.

She felt his lips move against her and his muffled voice came from between her thighs. "Why me?"

He stopped. Just as she'd begun to crash against a wave of release. She groaned in desperate need. She cried out. "What?"

"Anyone could get you off, Holly." He lifted his face, his eyes glittering hard as diamonds, his lips and chin wet with her juices. "You said it yourself. You're a slave to your needs. Anyone would do, anyone *could* do this for you. So why me?"

Why not him? But that was too cavalier. In the few short days and nights they'd been together, Deke had come to mean more to her than she'd planned. Desire ebbed as she pulled her sex-filled mind back from the brink of letting go.

She thought of the laughs they'd shared, the intense attraction that had steamrolled her into his bed that first day. His expression of pride in his future home where he'd shared the floor plans and for just a smoke-moment of time, she'd wanted the home to be hers, too.

"I don't understand," she whispered, but it was more to herself than to him because she wasn't sure what she wanted with Deke.

Being Deke, he nuzzled his chin against her soft belly. "If you're not happy with me worrying about your ex, then that's too bad. I know about him now and I can't unknow it. We can't just fuck each other anymore. We lost that free-and-easy time. It's gone. So, we chuck the whole agreement about no baggage and accept that we both have some."

She nodded and blinked away a tear. He was such a gentleman.

Dare she think of him as a keeper? Her heart hammered a tattoo that rattled her chest. "Oh, God, Deke. You're right. We've moved past the beginning now, haven't we?"

He licked her clit and suckled it gently, pulling her straight back into orgasmic waves of sensation. "Oh, Deke. Yes," she panted between strokes of his tongue, arching and needing more. Dying a little as more waves rolled through her. "I'm coming."

He entered her with three fingers at once, then turned his hand to make her scream with a deep, forever orgasm that roared up through her belly, into her chest and down her arms. Her head swam as she let the sensations take her to the sky and back again.

She was limp as a rag doll, but Deke was able to lift her to straddle him as he slid to the center seat. The feel of him, full and hard, brought her back to awareness as he rocked up into her. The strain of control made his lips firm, his eyes dark and his face flushed.

So she took him over the edge with her again, clinging and rolling her hips in time with him.

She shattered on him again and when she opened her eyes, he buried his face in her neck. A wet sensation where they were joined warned her they'd been rash.

"Bareback?"

He mumbled against her skin. "I'm sorry." His head whipped back, his eyes stark. "I'm healthy. I got checked a while back and haven't been with—"

"Then we're okay. I've been very careful since my divorce."

A roar of tires spewing gravel startled them. Deke looked out the cab window. "That blue car. It's him! He saw us. He must have."

"Maybe this is a good thing. He'll know I've moved on," she said, doubting every word. "Maybe he'll leave now and never come back." Jack had always been possessive, but she truly thought he was past the worst of that behavior. He'd been easing back, letting go, she would swear it. Unless that was wishful thinking. She'd spent a lot of her early years with Jack in that very pursuit. She'd wished her family liked him, wished they could settle in one place, wished he was happy with his work, wished he was more social, wished for a child to help open his heart.

Eventually she'd given up the wishes. Hard reality had finally moved her to leave him. Her love had been slowly, inexorably squeezed out of her by his demands and pettiness.

When he'd shown up at her door one night, horny and lonely and needy, she'd taken pity on him and let him in. The sex had been some of the hottest they'd shared.

After that, she'd allowed him the odd visit and even made a call or two herself. Sex with Jack was easy and reliable and the biggest mistake of her life.

Instead of being brave and looking toward her future she'd clung to that one piece of her past. She'd fooled herself into thinking Jack felt nothing more than sexual convenience where she was concerned. How stupid.

She should have refused him the night before she left to come here. If she'd cut him off in the hall he might have come to terms with the end.

But no. She'd let him play her the way he always had. She rubbed her arms to ward off the chilling dread and hoped Marnie got back soon. She needed to talk about this.

Calling her family would be a mistake. Her brothers Seth and Damien would be here in a flash and heaven help Jack if they found him. If they got an inkling that Jack was stalking her, there'd be hell to pay.

She couldn't quite believe Jack would go that far. She pulled out her phone and checked her messages.

Nothing.

If Jack had gone quiet, maybe it was because he'd finally accepted the end. She hoped so.

"Did he leave a message?"

She closed her eyes and squeezed them tight. "No."

"You have to stay with me. You can't be at the inn, vulnerable. Kylie should move out, too. TJ's got that spare room and since he left to see Marnie, there's room at his place."

"Maybe you're right. It couldn't hurt to make sure Kylie's safe at TJ's. And I never really wanted to get my things out of the camper. I thought it was what you wanted."

"Since we've moved from the beginning of this thing into the middle, then we're in it together."

She wasn't stupid enough to be alone where Jack could find her. He'd want sex just to prove he could get it. What he thought of as seduction most people would see as emotional blackmail at best, coercion at worst. She shuddered to think how forceful he could become if he was angry and jealous.

Eli O'Banion

13

Eli O'Banion stood in front of the Friendly Inn with his knapsack at his feet, his hands on his hips and his head cocked. The place looked different in ways he couldn't believe. He hadn't asked for details on the transformation and now he was blown away by the changes. It was as if Jon Dawson had never lived here. Except for the solidness of the building itself, all reminders of the old curmudgeon were gone, replaced by feminine touches.

Flower baskets hung from the veranda overhang. Leaf litter was a thing of the past and the Adirondack chairs on the veranda had been painted a bright red. A matching swing hung from the rafters on the other side. It had bright white and blue striped seat cushions. The windows shone clean, too.

Change had come to the Friendly Inn and Eli would be part of it. Cool. He loved change. Always.

That's why he traveled. He loved new challenges and couldn't wait to see what was around every bend in the road.

His next stop was the Himalayas. And he could barely wait

to get there. Just as soon as he got the money he needed, he'd be gone.

A woman in a bedroom window on the second story stretched to reach the top of the glass, a paper towel in her hand. She was the source of the shiny windows on the main floor.

His cock twitched as she mashed her breasts against the window in her need to stretch as high as she could go. Black hair to her hips, luscious breasts and a tiny waist. Her skin was dark gold and exotic.

He'd seen a lot of lovely women in his travels, but she was a blend of beauty that defied a label.

Maybe she belonged on a cleaning crew from one of the local hotels. TJ had talked about picking up some extra help.

He waved up at the window but the woman was engrossed in finding spots she'd missed. She was digging at something on the glass with her thumbnail. Fly specks most likely.

He knew all about fly specks, had counted them on a window in a Jamaican police station. Two hundred and forty-seven tiny brown specks.

He bet Jon Dawson had accumulated just as many on each and every window in the inn.

Nothing like cleaning fly shit to piss a woman off. He gave up waving and decided to knock on the door instead. As he walked up the steps to the veranda he cleared his mind of her luscious breasts moving across the glass.

He knocked several times, then opened the door and poked his head in. The first thing he noticed was the fresh scent, then when he stepped all the way inside, the clean and welcoming living room gave him pause.

A feminine squeak sounded from above and he turned to look up. The window washer pulled ear buds out of her ears. "Hi, can I help you?" A stream of black hair threatened to fall across her face so she scooped it back and out of her way.

A real-life Rapunzel.

"I'm looking for TJ," he said. Oh, shit. Now that the hair was behind her he could see that the window had been damp. Her dark nipples were clearly showing under the twin wet spots on her T-shirt. He swung his knapsack to cover his sudden woody and watched as she bounced downstairs. Braless.

It was good to be home.

Her breasts were teardrops. Heavy on the underside with a gentle slope down from her shoulders. They swung with every step she took. She stopped halfway down the staircase and froze. She watched him warily. "Who are you?"

"I'm his brother, Eli."

"You three look so much alike, it's weird."

"My hair's lighter than either of them. And I'm smarter, better looking and—"

She held up her hand. "I didn't ask for a glimpse into your sibling rivalry."

Eli had seen some exotic beauties in his travels, but none could match her. She was tall, for one thing, and moved with a dancer's grace. Her hair swung heavily to her hips. Most women would have tied it back for cleaning chores.

He expected her to have dark brown or black eyes, but hers were a strange blend of green and gray, which added to her mystery.

"TJ's not here," she said. Damn if her nipples didn't pucker and make his mouth go dry.

"Deke around then?" He had to stop staring, but it was impossible. He'd traveled the world only to land back here and find her? Crazy.

He ducked his head, aware he'd been gawking like a fourteen-year-old boy. He offered her his hand, half afraid he'd pull her into his chest. When he got tongue-tied and awkward, anything could happen. He'd always followed his instincts and, so far, they'd worked.

But the cynical measuring look in her gaze made him think twice. No, whatever his instincts said wouldn't work on this one.

She didn't move, effectively refusing to shake his hand. He stepped back and let his hand drop to his side. "You part of the hotel cleaning crew?"

She set her expression to bland. "I've been mistaken more than once for a cleaning lady, but no."

"Sorry. No offense, but I saw you working on the window upstairs," he explained, feeling like he'd stepped in something smelly. "The place looks great." He spun and made a gesture that included the living room and registration nook. He turned back to face her and caught her staring. "Look your fill?"

"Actually, yes. You're smaller than your brothers, right?"

"Not where it counts."

A flush raced up her neck from her chest, but she ignored his parry. She stepped down into the room and brushed past him. He caught a whiff of ammonia, clean and sharp. Under that, the scent of a shampoo with flowers in it. He'd always liked shampoo scents. They were always more mysterious on women than in the bottle.

She walked to the draperies. "I made these. The others were nearly rotted through."

He nodded. "The whole inn's impressive cleaned up this way. Very homey and welcoming. Jon made most of the furniture, you know."

"So I've heard."

He waited and when she didn't speak again, he said, "Well, I guess I'll catch up to my brothers when they get here. Nice to meet you?" The question hung for a long moment while he waited with clear expectation.

"Kylie Keegan. I'm the prodigal cousin."

"Jon's granddaughter?" Suddenly the thing he'd stepped in had an odor all its own.

She shrugged. "Not that he cared."

"Oh, he probably cared, but not in a good way."

"So you knew my grandfather. Yes, he took one look at me"—she pointed to her exotic face—"and went white as a ghost. No pun intended."

"Jon had some strange ideas. No argument there." The old man was all kinds of wrong, but it was a shame such a beauty had been exposed to him. "I'm sorry. Your meeting must have been strange."

"Stranger is the fact that I'm here now. He included me in his will."

"I heard something about that, but no one told me the circumstances." He put his hands up. "None of my business, of course."

She narrowed her gaze and sized him up. It took all of ten seconds to see that somehow, he was lacking. In character? In looks? In whatever way a woman sized up a man, he guessed. Fine. She didn't feel the spark he did. Fair enough.

But something flashed between them, some essence of dislike or surprise. And then he understood. "You've got his eyes," he said, surprised he'd notice. "He had that same piercing quality and color, although it looks better on you."

She stepped back. "No, I have nothing of his. Nothing."

"Jon could look at a person and see right through whatever bullshit you thought you were giving him." He shook his head in memory. "He caught me with a girl once and—never mind." He'd thought Jon would call her parents, set her father onto him. But Eli waited for days before he realized Jon was all bluster.

"Am I doing that now?" she asked quietly.

Pulled back from the memory, he asked. "Doing what?"

"Piercing you with my gaze and seeing behind the face you present to the world? The charming, sexy traveler who's breezing in and out of here?"

"Yeah. You are." Her assessing glance made him feel small. He shifted his gaze from hers and found himself focused on her chest again. Great, now he really did look like an ass. He shifted his bag onto his shoulder. "I may travel a lot but this is my home. And I'm always happy to come back to the Peninsula." He shrugged. "Always glad to see my family."

"Huh."

She apparently didn't believe him. Not a word. "My brothers probably whined about me. You shouldn't believe everything they say. They're jealous as hell I come and go as I please. They both got rooted way too early. TJ's stuck with this business, and Deke fell for Misty until she tore his heart out." He didn't know the details but the effect on Deke was clear.

She looked shocked. "So, wanting roots is a bad thing?"

"I didn't mean that—"

"Yeah, well. When you've been rootless most of your life, you get a different perspective." She turned the tables on him and took her own measure down his chest, waist, then snagged her gaze on his knapsack. Then she moved down to his legs to end off at his well-worn sneakers. "The happy-go-lucky globetrotter."

"You say that like it's dirty." His brows knit together.

"I don't care for men who go in for the sex tourism trade. It's disgusting."

There it was, the reason for her instant dislike. Not that he gave a shit. "I'll just head out back, maybe Deke's out there by now." He left on an Arctic-cold blast of anger and headed to the kitchen. Once outside he took a deep, clean breath of cedar-washed air.

The ground rules had been set. She didn't like him, nor would she ever. In a way, that made this visit easier. She was interesting enough to pique his interest. This way, he could keep a lid on it.

And when it was time to leave, nothing would hold him back.

Kylie returned to the front bedroom and tackled the rest of the window. She scrubbed and sprayed window cleaner, then scrubbed some more. Finally, with a sense of accomplishment and tired arms, she could stop scrubbing and focus on giving the glass a shine. She'd left her ear buds dangling onto her chest in case Eli showed up again. She didn't want to give him the chance to sneak up on her.

TJ and Deke had spoken of their brother several times in the last couple of days. Eli was a footloose loser who wandered the globe in search of pussy. Any guy who spent as much time as he did in places like Bangkok and Amsterdam was a hound, plain and simple. When she'd blurted out her opinion of such men, she'd felt his shock, but she wasn't sorry.

She'd let him know her opinion and that was that. He wouldn't try to charm her again. She saw through him and he knew it. The problem of the charming Eli O'Banion had been solved, and quickly.

She'd seen the way his eyes had lit with interest when she'd been at the top of the stairs, the way he'd followed every movement of her breasts as she'd walked down to meet him.

Her nipples had gone hard because the window she'd been cleaning had been cold and damp. This early, the front windows were shadowed, the glass still dewy.

She hadn't expected an audience, let alone a sex-starved behemoth of a man. It took a lot of man for Kylie to think in terms of behemoth, but every O'Banion she'd met qualified. She'd never seen such big men before.

He'd certainly looked his fill, but that meant nothing. Men were fickle, randy and always looking. What was peculiar was her reaction to *him*. She hadn't felt her sex drive rev up for either of his brothers.

Must be something in his bearing or his eyes. Or maybe it was just the way he looked at her, as if she were the only woman to ever get his full attention.

For the first time since arriving, she felt a shiver of alarm at the quiet seclusion of the inn. They were alone here. No one else was on the property. He could come upstairs behind her and wrap his bear-sized paws over her mouth so she couldn't scream.

Then he could drag her off the chair, to the floor . . .

Ridiculous.

Wouldn't happen. Charmers relied on charm, not brute force.

But there had been that one guy in college who'd charmed her into a first date. All night long he'd whispered sexually loaded comments into her ear, thinking to arouse her, when all he'd done was turn her off. When he'd driven her home, she'd had a hell of a time getting out of the car intact. She'd managed to escape his grasping, grabby hands, but she'd made sure to avoid him and his friends after that.

She'd never felt like a victim, but just more wary than before. While she'd seen interest in Eli's gaze, it hadn't been lust-filled like college-dude. Eli had been interested not scary.

When he'd turned around to check out the living room, she'd checked out his impressive backside. Nice butt! Strong thighs, trim but solid waist and shoulders broad enough to swing from.

Yes, much like the other O'Banions. He'd ducked his head and she'd seen the intriguing tail end of a tattoo curled up behind his ear. A snake? Maybe. But definitely reptilian.

Now *that* made Eli different from his brothers. She couldn't see TJ with a tat, no way. He was too staid, too serious. While Deke might very well have a tattoo, it wouldn't be a reptile. He'd have something warm-blooded or of special significance to him. A tattoo for Deke would have to have an emotional connection.

Eli had a grin that could charm a Siren and she'd been wrong to compare him to TJ and Deke. The man had way more charm.

Charming, not forceful. That was Eli.

Now that she'd thought about it, she may have been wrong to tip her hand so soon. A guy like him might see her as a challenge and set out even harder to win her over.

She sprayed ammonia cleaner on the glass and wiped with vigor. Being compared to Jon Dawson had been odd. Hard to believe she could share any of that man's DNA, let alone carry it forward. Had the old man seen his own eye color looking back at him that day she'd visited? If he had, he might actually have been offended.

All she'd seen in his eyes was shock, then anger and hatred. She'd left before things got worse. She couldn't believe TJ's story that Jon had been regretful after she'd left. If he'd regretted any of his actions, he'd have done something about his regrets before he died. Before her mom's accident. Before Kylie had been born, grown up and become an adult.

Her mom had always told her Jon Dawson was an unforgiving bastard, but Kylie couldn't believe her own grandfather could look at her that way. No. She'd had to see it for herself.

The sting would fade eventually, and in the meantime, she had a life to build.

And if she had anything to say about it, that life would be here.

She wanted the Friendly Inn. She wanted to grow old here, be part of the walls, the floors, even these fly-specked windows. Her blood, her sweat would make this place hers in spite of Jon Dawson's hatred. She would succeed here. And success was the best revenge.

The Friendly Inn would be hers. Now and always.

She didn't care why her grandfather would include her in this inheritance. So what if he wanted to atone for what he did to his daughter. The regrets in his past had been his problem.

Kylie's future was hers.

She surveyed the window and decided it sparkled enough to move on to the next room. Unfortunately, the next room was at the back of the inn. Where Eli was.

She dipped into her closet for a sweatshirt to cover her dampened T-shirt. She pulled it on and headed downstairs for fresh water for her bucket and a new scraper for the fly specks. At the bottom of the stairs, she looked outside and saw Deke's pickup pull in and park.

Holly jumped out, looking flushed and satisfied. Those two could hardly keep their hands off each other. She considered Deke and wondered why the youngest O'Banion irritated her, while Deke didn't at all.

TJ was masterful and decisive, but not arrogant nor a blatant charmer, although he had Marnie tied in knots. Maybe even literally in knots, considering how he'd torn out of here looking like hell on wheels the other day. She wondered how her cousin had reacted when he'd arrived in Seattle. She'd often compared him to Paul Bunyan and Kylie had to agree.

She snorted at the image of a plaid-shirt-wearing, axe-wielding giant of a man in a downtown dance club. TJ O'Banion with sex on his mind . . . *my, oh my.*

Marnie was just the kind of woman to handle a man like TJ. She'd held him off for the better part of a week while driving him mad with lust. Something about the scenario titillated Kylie.

But Eli was arrogant enough to believe that women would fall at his feet. His big feet.

Outside, Deke swooped in behind Holly and wrapped his arms around her belly. He nuzzled her neck while she lifted her arms to hold his head. She gave a half turn to kiss him and in a wink they were face-to-face in a deep kiss that curled Kylie's toes.

To have what they had together. To let something that hot take root and grow would be a dream come true. She hoped Holly understood the rarity of her connection with Deke.

She left them to their moment in the rare morning sun and continued into the kitchen to fill her mop bucket with fresh soap and water. When she returned to the living room, Holly stood there, shiny and sated and flustered.

Lucky woman. The mop bucket slopped water onto the floor so Kylie set it down and wiped the spill, acutely aware of Holly's bounty.

"How did you get the windows so clean?" her cousin asked.

"Hot water and a scraper. It's gross but effective." She warmed at the appreciative glow in Holly's happy, satisfied face.

"You've been so busy." Holly bounded upstairs and headed into the bedroom where Kylie had just been working. Kylie followed. "The curtains are gorgeous." Holly fondled the material.

"I have to expend my energy on something."

Holly appraised her. "Yes, you should. Are you a workaholic? Or a perfectionist? Or both?"

"None of the above. But I'm motivated more than I've ever been before."

"Marnie will come around. She's already come to terms with having the cabins out back."

In a couple weeks standing walls, completed roofs and windows installed meant the buildings could be locked. Talking Marnie into working on the interiors with them was next on Holly and Kylie's agenda.

"I wonder what's happening with her and TJ?"

Holly grinned. "I'm betting plenty. TJ peeled out of here with the look of a man who'd refuse to take no for an answer." She looked horrified. "In a good way, of course."

"In the way that Marnie guided him toward."

Holly hooted with laughter. "Pretty much, yes. She teased and squeezed that man."

Holly took the cleaning supplies. "Why don't you take a break. You must have started at dawn." But when she hefted the heavy bucket she set it down fast. "Ooh, a twinge."

"Are you okay?"

"Deke's got me bent out of shape." She laughed harder. "The man's a pretzel maker." Her cheeks flushed.

"Really? How so?"

"Pickup trucks look roomy, but if you're making out in the front seat with a man the size of Deke you'd better be limber. These O'Banion boys are big." She flushed even redder.

"Hm." Kylie didn't want to hear any more. "That reminds me, the youngest one has finally deigned to make an appearance. He went out back."

"Eli? What'd he look like?"

"His brothers. He's within a smidge of both of the others, in height and width. His hair's lighter and his eyes are a piercing blue. Too big and brawny for my taste."

Holly gave her an odd glance. "What do you mean, deigned?"

Kylie examined her toes in her flip-flops. She needed fresh polish.

"Kylie? What's he like?"

She shrugged and didn't know how to get around the topic. "He just, you know, thinks he's special."

Holly leaned in, raised her eyebrows. "If he's anything like Deke, then, um, he probably is special." She waggled her brows for emphasis.

"Maybe, but I'm leery of men who assume a woman's going to swoon at their feet." She hadn't liked him ogling her breasts like a starving man at a buffet. Although that analogy didn't quite work. A starving man would dive in and take what he wanted. Eli had only admired what he couldn't have.

Wouldn't have.

Definitely wouldn't have.

Her nipples peaked into pearls, damn them.

"I see," Holly teased. "You didn't like him, but your body did?" she guessed. "I've got to see this guy."

"He's out back. You can see him from the back bedroom window." Holly hotfooted it to the back bedroom and Kylie followed more slowly.

Below them, the brothers clasped hands and did a man-hug by patting each other on the shoulder. "I told him he was shorter and smaller than his brothers, and being the youngest, he hated it. Do you see a difference?"

"Nope. Eli's as brawny as the other two."

"Yeah." Her breath caught at the sight of the two men, clearly happy to see each other, grinning and clapping each other on the back. The claps turned into playful punches and before she could blink, they were wrestling and grappling, testing each other.

"Are they bears or men?" Holly laughed and tapped on the glass. They didn't hear her.

"Next thing, they'll be butting heads."

Holly snorted. "Locking horns."

"Like stags." But the power in the men was certainly something to see, even in play. Eventually, they stood apart, chests heaving, faces split in grins.

"My God, they're impressive," Holly murmured.

"Too bad Eli's such a dog. From what I can figure he's one of those men into sex tourism. He travels to all the sex hot spots, right?"

Holly gave her a surprised look. "Not likely. He teaches English to underprivileged children. Lots of people go the private school route, but Eli goes into orphanages." Holly waved and got Deke's attention. She motioned that she was heading down and turned to leave. "Kylie? Are you coming?"

"I don't think Eli really wants to talk me right now."

"What happened before we got here?"

"I insulted him."

"Do tell," she said and wrapped her arm around Kylie's and coaxed her into a lock step.

"I have to change first," Kylie said as a means to escape. Then she dashed into her room and changed into a bra and clean, dry T-shirt. Then, as an added precaution, she topped it with a light sweater.

Even if her nipples did betray her, no one would see through three layers. Not even a man who looked. She hated that she owed Eli an apology, but she wasn't about to let it go unsaid. She was not *that* much like her grandfather.

Deke and Holly were holding hands by the time she caught up to them outside. Deke introduced Eli to Holly, while Kylie hung back and watched. Eli didn't ogle Holly's breasts or trail his gaze hungrily down her body. In fact, he was a perfect gentleman.

Until he turned his gaze on her. Damn, there it was again. That look that said she was the only woman he'd ever focused on. But this time it was tinged with disappointment. She'd been wrong about him and the sex tourism.

If he'd defended himself at the time, she wouldn't have believed him.

"I, ah, would like to speak to you," she said. "Privately." She ignored the surprised glances between Holly and Deke. Holly pulled Deke to the side and murmured something for his ears only. Deke gave Kylie a sharp look.

Eli nodded and motioned her to join him on the far side of a large crane they would use to set the logs into place. He settled his shoulder against the crane and waited. An interested but wary expression lit his bluer-than-blue eyes.

"I apologize for my comment about the sex tourism. I shouldn't have said it."

He crossed his arms, his biceps bulging. "How do you know I don't indulge while I'm away? Just because I help out at orphanages by day doesn't mean I'm not at sex clubs and whorehouses at night."

"Maybe you do hang out in those places, maybe you don't, but making me feel like a fool is rude. I'm done." She spun to leave, but she felt his hand on her elbow to stop her.

He slid his fingers through her hair for a few inches. "Wait. You can't really blame me for getting a bit of my own back." He combed a wider swath. "This is like silk. It's almost dangerous."

"What do you mean?"

He dropped his hand to her arm again. "It invites the touch. You wear it like this to get noticed." He ran the back of his hand from her shoulder to her elbow in a soft caress.

"I like it long. And it's very forward of you to comment on my appearance when we've just met."

"Worse than your assumption about me?" He moved his hand back up to her shoulder. "Too bad you put on this sweater, I'd like to feel your skin."

Heat rose in her cheeks, but she didn't shrug him off. It would only entice him further. "I've already apologized. I won't do it again."

He stepped so close behind her she felt the heat of his body along her back and flashed on the memory of Deke nuzzling Holly's blond hair aside to kiss her neck. She tilted her head a millimeter.

She waited, breath held to see if he'd notice the infinitesimal invitation, but all he did was whisper next to her ear. "I shouldn't have teased you, Kylie. I don't want to start off on the wrong foot, either."

"So we start again?"

"Any way you want." Damn the man. He was rough, he was hard, he was sex personified. And the worst part was, she was *charmed*.

She walked away before he figured it out.

14

Back in the front bedroom, where Eli wouldn't see her, Kylie picked up the curtains she'd made and began inserting the rod through the rings. Holly came in when she heard the rustling.

"Kylie? Everything okay?"

"Yes, of course."

"You said before that you insulted Eli, but from what I saw he's definitely interested in you. He looks at you the way Deke looks at me. There's something primal about these O'Banions, don't you think?"

Primal. "That's it, yes." She slid the last of the rings onto the rod and lifted it to the brackets over the window. "I apologized for something I said and he accepted. End of story."

Until and unless Kylie learned her cousins could be trusted, she'd be safer saying, and giving, nothing of herself. Much as she wanted to talk easily about her feelings and her life, she had to tread carefully. Trusting too much too soon could be painful.

"Okay. Well, if you ever want to talk about Eli and you, I'm here." Holly's breezy acceptance that there was something to talk about regarding Eli made Kylie grin.

"Thanks. If I need advice, you'll be the first one I ask." She placed the end of the rod in the bracket and stretched to fit the other side. "I doubt there will ever be anything between us. I want roots and he moves around too much. I did that all my life with my mother. Time for that to stop."

Holly nodded. "Must be nice to be so tall. I'd need a step-ladder for this."

"We never needed a kitchen stool after I turned twelve," she quipped, relieved her cousin had changed topics. Kylie would prefer to mull over her attraction to Eli. She was rarely impulsive when it came to men, which was why it had been out of character for her to insult him at first sight.

"Speaking of advice, I'd like to get your take on something," Holly said. Her cousin's usually sunny expression dimmed.

"Sure, what's up?" As long as this wasn't about sex, she'd be fine. Her expertise would fit on the head of a pin.

"My ex is stalking me."

"How? I mean is he here? On the Peninsula? Or is this more like cyber-stalking?"

"He's been belligerent on the phone, leaving me nasty messages and being an ass when I call back. But I saw his car. And he may have seen Deke and me together."

"Oh, that's not good. My mom had a weird ex-boyfriend once. We moved out in the middle of the night and left the state."

"You're suggesting I run away?"

"No. Not in this case. If he's seen you with Deke, it's probably too late to avoid a confrontation. I'd call the police and ask advice."

Holly agreed. "But I won't tell Deke I've spoken to the police. This is my problem, not his."

"But—"

"No. He got involved with a woman in the middle of a nasty

divorce and custody battle. It nearly broke him. I'm the first woman he's been with since then. I feel terrible that Jack's pulling this shit. But more for Deke's sake than mine. Jack's harmless, really."

"More hot air than action?"

Holly nodded and a spring of tension inside Kylie eased. "Well, that's different. Deke will come to terms with this in his own time. In the meantime it can't hurt to have a private talk with the local police and ask about the process for getting a restraining order."

"Jack's not a man who responds to intimidation well. That's one of the reasons I didn't tell my family about the divorce until I'd already made my decision and moved out. If my father and brothers had seen me unraveling and fighting with Jack, they may have stood up for me. Believe me, that would have been worse for me. As long as it was kept private, Jack didn't feel as humiliated by the divorce. It was easier all around."

Kylie nodded. "I can see that. Sometimes family drama feeds off itself and can get ugly." Maybe that was part of her mother's reason for cutting herself out of her family.

Holly suddenly drooped around the eyes and her shoulders sagged. "You're tired of this," Kylie guessed.

Holly nodded. "I am. I want Deke, Kylie. I do. More than I ever thought possible, but if Jack doesn't go away soon I don't know that he'll stick with me."

The afternoon after he chased Marnie to Seattle, TJ slipped his hands to Marnie's wrists and held them over her head. She grabbed the headboard and held on. "I like you this way," he said, drinking in the sight and scent of her. "Ready and wet and open."

"I like you hard," she responded. "And big. And oh—yes! Just like that." Her belly and cradle softened against his hips as he slid into her. She had the most intriguing habit of widening her eyes in that first thrust, as if she were surprised to find him inside.

Wet heat enveloped him, body and soul as he pressed and retreated. Her slick inner walls gave with every push and clasped with every pull.

He tightened his hold on her wrists and tugged so she arched her breasts. He took one and sucked her nipple deep, then scraped it with the back of his teeth as he released slowly. She gasped at the friction and bucked her hips up to meet his thrust. He felt her ankles high on his waist. "Higher, take me deeper."

"Greedy bastard." Marnie bucked, then did as she was told. He slid deeper and she swore but never released the headboard. She liked the powerful strokes, the deep thrusts as he reared back, grabbed her ankles and set them on his shoulders.

The slide in was sin itself. Every millimeter pulled back on his sensitive skin, each pull made him groan.

"Fuck me," she screamed. "Hard."

But slow was so damn good.

When she screamed it again, he chuckled and held himself still. He felt the throb of his cock, the wetness of her channel as she pulsed lightly around him. "Orders? You think I'll take orders?" But he gave her what she wanted and bucked harder. Sweat pooled between his shoulder blades as she flew apart in his arms. Her orgasm rumbled through her shuddering body and into his chest. He thumbed her clit to keep the pressure on as she strained against him.

He pulled out quickly while she spasmed and put his mouth to her, lapping fresh cream as she came. He tore off the condom and turned head to tail so she could finish him with her mouth. She took his cock deep in her throat while he buried his tongue in her fresh wet pussy. "Delicious."

Her tongue caressed him lightly until his balls contracted with the first spurt. He filled her throat in a powerful rush.

Heart pounding, he slid his hands to her ass cheeks and squeezed the soft flesh with a gentle shake. She took all he had and reached to press his sac for more.

Moisture seeped at her slit as he lapped at her. Her clit engorged as he worked her toward another orgasm. "You're one juicy woman." He rubbed his face across her thighs and reveled in the softness.

She finger-combed her curls and gave her labia a shimmy. "Mm, yes."

"Do that again. I want to see you come that way."

She obliged as he darted his tongue between the apex of her fingers to her clit. She moaned and arched as he encouraged her into one last shivering cataclysm.

He slid to her side and gathered her close.

"You taste good," she said as she licked her lips with a mysterious smile.

"You put honey to shame."

"Flatterer."

"Are you sore?"

"No, are you?"

"I think my tongue's blistered," he said, sticking it out.

"Well, I'll be. A callus," she teased. "As good as you taste, I think I need a shower and food." She rolled off the bed and headed to her bathroom.

He followed. "We'll do both together." His stomach growled. "I need food."

"We should go out to eat or we'll end up back in bed with empty stomachs. I pretty much cleaned out my fridge before I left for the inn."

"Know a good steakhouse?"

"Several."

"My kind of woman," he said. "Even if you do love the city."

She frowned. "At this point, with Dennis being such an ass and a lawsuit brewing, I'm not so in love as I once was."

He let the comment pass. No sense pushing her; she'd buck. Between coming to some consensus with her cousins about the inn, and now Dennis pushing her stress buttons, he decided to let her come to her own conclusions. It was safer that way.

Thirty minutes later, clean and shiny, they headed to the door, intent on food. Marnie's phone rang.

She pulled a disappointed face but answered without looking at her screen. "This better be important, Dennis." She frowned. "Oh, sorry, Holly, what's up?"

He hoped it wasn't a problem with the site, but Deke would've called. He pressed the call button for the elevator while she talked.

"He is? I'll tell him. Yes, he's here with me." She rolled her eyes. "Shut up." She put her hand over the receiver. "You'd think I'd never had sex before. But she's calling to say your youngest brother arrived today."

"Good. I'll call him." He stepped a few feet away and dialed Eli's cell. "Yo, the prodigal son and all that," he said when Eli answered.

"Yeah, yeah. Good to be home, Teeje. I like what you've done to the inn." He laughed. "What was that the women were saying? Oh, yeah, it's decluttered out back."

He snorted. "You've met Holly and Kylie?"

"If I'd known there was a babe fest going on, I'd've been back sooner. But it seems all the friendly ones are taken."

He laughed. "Kylie's seen through you that fast, huh?" He hooted. "She's a smart one."

"Marnie must be desperate to take up with an old guy when she could have waited for me."

He accepted the dig about his age. "But she likes her men fully grown, not runty."

"Jeez. Missed you, Teeje."

"Missed you, too, *boy*. Now get to work. I'll be on site first thing Monday morning." He was smiling as he disconnected. Eli was home, Deke was happy and off the booze and Marnie was giving it up big time. Life couldn't be any better.

He turned as he heard Marnie locking her apartment door. Life might be fine with him, but she looked worried. "What's up?"

"Holly's naive sometimes."

"How?" He kept his voice soft. If this was about his brother, he wanted to hear it, but he'd have to tread carefully.

"Her ex, Jack, is on the Peninsula. He didn't tell her he was coming, but a woman in the hardware store said a man fitting his description was looking for Holly." Her eyes went wide as she looked up at him. "Jack's got a couple screws loose, in my opinion. The family was relieved when she left him."

"She divorced the guy. She must've had a good reason. How long has it been?" Relieved Holly hadn't complained about Deke, he slung his arm across Marnie's shoulder and pulled her into his side.

"The divorce is final, if that's what you're asking."

"So he let all that happen without freaking out, why assume he's out to do her harm now?"

Her face fell and she chewed her lip. "She felt sorry for him, I guess. And . . ." she trailed away, looking guilty. "I shouldn't betray a confidence."

His belly sank. "She kept sleeping with him," he guessed. A couple he knew kept that up until they got back together. "She gave him hope that she'd let him back into her life." Now she was sleeping with his brother. And he was hip deep into someone else's divorce.

Again.

"I've got to call Deke."

"He was with her in the hardware store, so he knows. And I would prefer that you leave it to Holly to explain about the rest of it. She's independent to a fault when it comes to her private life. In fact, I'm surprised she told me this much."

"She didn't have a choice if Deke was with her at the hardware store. Once Alice gets her gums flapping on a juicy bit of gossip, the whole Peninsula will know there's another man looking for Deke's new woman." Although he admired Holly for trying to keep a lid on Deke's involvement.

The elevator doors opened, revealing a mother and two young children, putting an end to their personal conversation.

At the lobby, he held the doors open while the mother held her youngest on her hip and the toddler managed on unsteady legs to exit. He refused to hold his mother's hand, insisting he could walk alone. The kids were sandy-haired mop tops and the little girl's smile brought one to Marnie's lips. She waggled her fingers and the girl giggled.

With the doors closing, TJ called his brother. "Deke, were you with Holly in the hardware store?"

"This about the guy looking for her?"

"Marnie says he's got a screw loose. Keep a sharp eye out for him."

"Holly told me she can handle this guy herself."

"Maybe, but Marnie says he's a lit fuse. Everyone in the family saw it except Holly."

"I'm pretty sure he's already seen us together."

"Then be careful."

"I will."

"Good. Do you want me there?"

"No. Eli's here if I need help. Holly's prickly about this and I don't want her thinking I'm sticking my nose in when I said I wouldn't."

"You told her about Misty?"

"Yes."

"And about how you don't get involved with divorced women?"

"Too late for that now."

"I figured."

"Speaking of involved, how are things on your end?"

"Great. We're heading out for a steak."

Deke laughed. "Don't let her finish her meal. Women get sleepy on a full stomach."

TJ disconnected as they walked to her car. "You know this guy, Jack; do *you* think he's dangerous?"

"I'm not sure, but how many times are neighbors surprised when some guy goes wacko? If you're friendly with the police up there . . ."

"You're right, I'll call Chuck. It couldn't hurt to ask him to swing by the inn on patrol." The call was short and succinct and made TJ feel that he'd done what he could without interfering too much. He stopped beside her car. "There's no way I'm going to fit in there."

She looked at his shoulders, then let her gaze slide south. "You're right. We'll use your truck. After dinner would you mind dropping me at the club?"

"As long as I can park myself at the end of the bar and watch you work."

She slid her hand into his. "I'd like that. There's nothing like a mountain man in a plaid shirt, blue jeans and work boots to bring in the pretty young women."

"I kind of liked that blonde last night. The one with the boobs down to her lap."

She pinched his ass so hard he jumped out of reach. "Hey, that hurt."

"Did it?" She said, all wide-eyed innocence.

15

Tisha Campbell was one piece of work. Why she hadn't seen it during the interview, Marnie couldn't say. Tisha had played the part of college student to perfection. But one glance around her expensive condo apartment and it was clear Tisha was nothing like she appeared to be during her job interview.

She was no broke college kid trying to make ends meet.

Tisha may be the right age for college, but either she had wealthy parents who provided for her, or she had a law firm on speed dial.

Marnie would bet her last dime the woman's law firm of choice was *Blow-Em, Screw-Em and Sue-Em.*

Tisha sat slouched on her brilliant white leather sofa in a tight white mini skirt and boobalicious tank top. She'd paid well for her boob job and her tan.

Marnie suppressed a grin at TJ's reference to the blonde with boobs down to her lap. Tisha wasn't far behind. Give her a couple of years and gravity would win. It always did. "I have to give you credit, Tisha, you hid those puppies pretty well during your interview." Marnie settled on the only other chair in the room, a low-slung rocker with no arms. She steadied herself and looked around the young, hip condo. "Is white the new cream?"

Tisha arched her eyebrow and lifted her breasts. "Like them? Everyone does. And my boyfriend likes white and I always give him what he likes best." She smiled with her mouth, while her eyes remained wary. Cold. She flicked her nipples. "I thought I'd lose some sensation, but I didn't. Not if the suction's right, anyway."

"I'm not here to discuss your tits." Marnie leaned forward, more aware than ever that she was in the room with a shark. What she couldn't figure was why Tisha hadn't already called her lawyer.

"Are you going to fire me? Or are you here to see how I'm feeling?"

Hm. They didn't seem to be on the same wavelength. She waited to see if Tisha would reveal more. Marnie tilted her head and waited with an expectant half-smile.

Tisha drew circles on her bare knee. "I thought Dennis would come to check on me."

"Check on you?"

"Yeah, after the other night in his office . . ." Her eyes went wide. "Oh. Sorry, I didn't realize you two—"

"Dennis and I?" Marnie shook her head. "We're partners in the club. That's all."

Her eyes lit with interest. "Oh. Then why are you here? I called in sick the last couple of days, but I planned on coming in for my shift tonight."

"Sick?"

"Yeah, didn't Bernadette tell you?"

Bernadette, another new hire. "She didn't relay the message. You need to call Jeff with plenty of notice for us to find someone else. This last-minute stuff doesn't fly. The club's too busy." She should fire her, but that grope still hung over the room like a hammer. Sooner or later, Tisha would expose her real purpose.

Tisha pouted. "I was hoping Dennis would come over to check on me, but it's good of you to come." Her knees parted slightly as she slouched lower.

"You're feeling better?"

"Much." She opened her knees and revealed her hairless pussy. She paid a lot for her Brazilians, too. When her fingers skimmed her inner thigh and headed north, Marnie stood.

She had a clear memory of Dennis saying Tisha had waved her tits in front of him. Now she could well believe it.

"Like what you see?" Tisha splayed her legs wide. "Because I do. You're hot, Marnie." Her eyes were avid, her slit moist.

Marnie rolled her eyes and bent to pick up her purse. "Why did you expect Dennis to come check on you?"

"I was hoping. I've heard he's got it going on. Word gets around about a guy like Dennis."

Marnie barely managed to contain a grossed-out shiver. "I'm sure it does." Maybe Dennis's penchant for group sex was drawing attention. The blonde told two friends, the brunette told two friends and so on. And that was only the pair from last week.

Tisha gave her a considering gaze. "You mean you've never tried him on? I hear he's real open-minded."

"Like your boyfriend?" She couldn't resist the reminder. Tisha was a sexual predator, or an extortionist who preyed on legitimate businesses. Or she was an attention-crazed slut.

Whatever. The club needed to be protected. To do that, Marnie wanted to see Tisha in action. She'd left for the Peninsula without actually seeing her interact at the club. That had been a mistake. Marnie would be sure not to make any more. "I'll see you at work tonight. Dress appropriately and don't go into the office for any reason. With anyone."

Tisha gave her a porn queen pout and stood up. "I'll see you to the door."

"No need. I know my way out." She had to get cameras installed to cover the office, the stock room and anywhere else two people could be alone.

No way would she let Tisha get away with seducing Dennis in order to claim sexual harassment. Marnie would fight tooth and nail to save BackLit from the likes of Tisha.

Dennis was in the office for once, dressed and alone, with his ankles crossed on his desk. He had his hands behind his head and face to the ceiling.

"You're here, good. I spoke to Tisha. You wouldn't believe how she lives." She described the exclusive address, the expensive furnishings, the quality of the electronics. "Top of the line everything."

He dropped his feet to the floor and sat straight. "So?"

"She's either got a sugar daddy, or she extorts businesses for hush money. Settlements on sexual harassment would be my guess." She walked to sit at her desk.

"Shit. And I fell for it."

"She even tried seducing me."

Dennis barked a laugh. "I'd've liked to have seen that."

"I'm sure you would." She leaned forward and folded her hands on her desk. "I'm installing cameras everywhere in case she tries to seduce anyone else on staff. That way, we'll have it on tape and she'll either go away or we go to the cops and expose her extortion attempt."

"Works for me," he agreed. "I've been thinking . . ." he trailed off and waited, looking hopeful. Her belly sank; Dennis hopeful was a bad sign.

She tapped a pen on the desk to expend some of her nervous energy. "What about?" She'd hoped to have the inn listed for sale so she could forestall him. As it was, she'd have to listen to the new idea.

He leered. "I want to turn BackLit into a fantasy club."

"What kind of fantasies?" But his avid expression said it all.

"Groups, swaps, BDSM. Cameras, too, if people want to do live feeds. Private rooms for that, of course." His voice took on a dreamy quality. Dennis was on a roll. "We could provide doms and subs but I doubt that'll be necessary. There's enough of those around to keep people coming back."

"Yes, I'm sure." The images that filtered through her mind were darkly sexual. She understood the need, but she was not the person to get behind this idea. She cleared her throat. "That's a lot of renovation. An expensive proposition."

"We'll need partition walls, new lighting. I want to exchange the banquettes for platforms. We'll install swings and brackets for other gear."

She closed her eyes. Tried to see his vision and came up with TJ trussed up with a ball gag. *So* not him. He liked to use his mouth too much.

"I've worked out the numbers." Dennis broke into her thoughts.

"Of course you have." She should have seen it coming. Hell, he'd been priming the pump, so to speak, for months. He already had clientele lined up. She looked at him and said as much. "Now I know what Tisha meant when she said word was getting around about you and how open-minded you are."

He had the grace to flush, at least. Months, he'd been planning this for months without telling her.

He shrugged. "I'm into the scene. So what? Why not make it a business, too?"

"Why not?" She kept her tone noncommittal. "I agree that it's best to work with what you know." She'd known how to tend bar, how to sling drinks and get people in a party mood. This? This was Dennis's forte, not hers. She stood. "Give me the numbers, I'll go over them."

He smirked and slid a file across his desk toward her. "Get back to me in a week?"

"I'll see what I can do." A week wouldn't be nearly enough time to get him the hell out of her club. Money from the sale of the inn was months away. Maybe longer.

Aside from the inn, she had TJ to consider. She shouldn't have slept with him. She should have sent him home when he'd arrived. But TJ seeing her in her element was probably for the best. He would understand selling the inn was strictly business. He would see why she didn't want to walk away from her club. She'd put too much of herself into this place. Her blood, her sweat, her heart.

Odd how she wanted nothing more than to find TJ O'Banion and fall into his arms. He'd offer more of his level-headed advice and let her vent her frustrations without trying to fix everything.

She took the file from Dennis and walked out, feeling as if her legs had been shot out from under her.

TJ waited for Marnie at the bar, watching Tisha turn her sharp hazel eyes on Jeff, the bartender.

"Jeff, a word, please." It was Marnie, looking worried and upset. Jeff followed her to a spot by the door, out of earshot of the rest of the employees.

When they returned, Jeff looked grim. Marnie settled onto the stool beside TJ and leaned against his arm. "Take me home, TJ. I've had enough for one day."

"You want to leave your car here?"

"I forgot we took separate vehicles. Did you get some clothes?"

"Sure, doesn't my shirt smell new?"

She rested the tip of her nose on the flannel. "Now that you mention it, yes. When you said you needed to pick up some clothes, I assumed—"

"What? That I'd buy a suit?" he teased.

She closed her eyes and took a deep sniff. "Never. You'd never buy a suit."

"Too city," he said.

"Damn straight." The warm look she gave him melted his heart.

"You okay?"

"I've been better," she said ruefully. "Take me to bed, TJ, make me forget."

If Marnie decided to stay in Seattle to keep an eye on that partner of hers, it might be the end of them. She'd get so wrapped up in keeping her club afloat there'd be no room for him.

But then, half of him thought if the club was what she really wanted, then maybe it would be smart to let things peter out before either of them got hurt.

The other half of him thought: *No fucking way it was over.*

He kept her tiny car in his rear view, but still, he called her. "You okay back there? You had me worried."

The sexy warmth in her laugh hit him low in the gut. "Of course, I am. I've got some things to think over, that's all. I'll tell you about it when we can talk."

He took his exit. "Right." When he tossed his phone on the seat beside him, he grinned. Goddamn, he liked that woman. He liked that she trusted him enough to share her stress. He knew how to help her relieve it, too. His cock stiffened just thinking about her.

He called her again. "If you need any help with Dennis, let me know, I'll head back to the club. Have a chat with him."

"No need for that. Is there anything I can help *you* with? You keep calling."

"I seem to have developed a huge growth in my jeans. I could use your help with *that*."

Her laugh was a throaty promise as she disconnected.

* * *

The Saturday after Eli returned home, Holly lifted the empty propane tank onto the deck of Deke's truck. Everyone else was out back discussing the landscaping Kylie wanted to put around the cabins. The concrete slab foundations had cured and the logs would be delivered tomorrow. The sky had brightened throughout the afternoon and consensus for dinner was grilled burgers.

She only felt slightly guilty for skipping out alone to get the tank filled. They hadn't heard from or seen anything of Jack in days and she needed some solitude. The impulse to disconnect the tank from the grill and run this small errand had hit suddenly and she'd grabbed her shot at a few minutes of freedom.

The local gas station included a propane fill station and it was only a mile or so down the road. She'd be gone and back before anyone missed her.

She needed the time alone to think without the distractions of everyone else's ideas on what was best for her. For themselves. For the inn. So many voices, so many needs, she doubted any one of them would be completely happy.

The O'Banions were close as brothers could be. The grousing about Eli's travels was a bluff to hide how much the older brothers missed their younger.

As for her own cousins, Marnie still wanted to sell the inn as soon as they could, while Kylie seemed determined to hang on and make a business out of it.

Holly wasn't sure what she wanted if life here didn't include Deke.

She liked the Olympic Peninsula. The people, including Alice the hardware store clerk, were quirky but kindhearted. She felt at home already. A feeling that would only increase as she settled into life at the inn with Kylie.

She hoped that life included Deke, she really did, but it was still too soon to tell. Unless she could put an end to the nonsense with Jack.

A young man directed her to back into a spot near the large propane supply tank and then accepted her payment in cash. "I'll put this into the truck. Keep the change."

"Thanks, lady. You're one of the new owners over at the Friendly Inn, right?"

She smiled and looked at his earnest expression. "Yes, I am, why?"

"You doing a lot of construction?"

"We're adding cabins out back and tossing around some other ideas."

"I'm not getting enough hours here and I'm trying to save for college. I'm Sam Whitaker."

"Check with Deke or TJ O'Banion. Tell them you talked to Holly. They may not have work for an untrained laborer, but it can't hurt to ask."

"Okay! Thanks!" He turned and left with the spring of hopeful youth in his step.

She secured the tank with a couple of stretch cords and closed the tailgate. Burgers tonight, with a sideshow of Eli and Kylie ignoring the fireworks between them. She smiled. She and Deke were smart to have their arrangement.

"Who you playing house with Holly?" Jack's soft voice startled her.

"Jesus, Jack, you scared me." She jerked and spun to face him. Jack never used a soft tone. He used his arms to trap her against the tailgate.

"Don't bother lying, wife-of-mine. I already know his name."

"Back off." She shoved him off her and stood her ground. She glared at him, fighting hard not to scream that she wasn't his wife. Instead, she used the same calm no-nonsense tone he used. "You have no right to be here, no right to question me and no right to put your hands on me. Do it again and I'll call the cops."

She turned to raise the tailgate, but a painful yank on her arm stopped her. "I mean it, Jack."

Instead of letting go, he pulled her back against his body. His hard cock pressed into her ass. "Feel that, Holly? You want it, I know you do. You always fuckin' want it." His hand slid to her crotch and pressed her there while he kissed her on the neck. His teeth nipped hard enough to hurt.

He was quick with his hands and had the tab of her jeans undone before she realized his intent. His fingers delved into her pants and found her clitoris. He rubbed her with a lover's knowledge of the perfect stroke, the perfect pressure. "See? You're wet already."

"Not for you, Jack." This was a physiological reaction to stimulus, nothing more. She hated that she moistened, hated that she had so little control over her own body. Hated that she'd given herself to him after her affections had fallen away.

She pulled back from his hand, but that brought her into contact with his cock. She had no choice but to talk her way out of this.

"Jack, you're hurting me. We're not into pain, Jack, and this hurts. I don't want you this way, not anymore."

He eased back and stilled his fingers but instead of removing his hand he cupped her mound. "Holly, you don't mean that. I'd never hurt you. I love you."

"This is love? Taking what I don't want to give?" She knew his next move. "And don't do that jiggling thing you do." But it was too late, she felt the shimmy in her mons, along her slit and labia. "Stop it, Jack." She tried pushing his hips back but he didn't budge.

She dragged in a couple of deep breaths while her belly began to sing with response. Not so long ago, she'd have opened herself to him, taken what she needed and given him what he wanted. But this ugliness shamed her.

"Jack," she coaxed. "I'm sorry. I was wrong to keep sleeping with you. The sex was a mistake. We should have ended our marriage clean, but we—*I*—didn't. I'm to blame for letting you think . . ." her voice went husky, as she opened to the tap, tap of his forefinger. "Stop that."

He kept up the pressure, and her hips moved involuntarily. If she didn't stop him soon, she'd come and she'd never be free of him.

"Don't, Jack. I *don't* want this." She relaxed against him and kept her voice reasonable. "You're not a man who hurts women. Please. Step back."

Her heart stampeded blood and the first frisson of fear made her break into a sweat, but she forced her muscles to loosen. She wasn't sure she could hold on long enough to escape her own body. But she had to. She turned her mouth into his biceps and bit.

Hard. Before orgasm rose and swamped her.

"Jesus!" He stepped back and she stepped forward, pulling his hand out of her pants. She buttoned and zipped quickly, dragging in three deep breaths to steady herself. She slammed the tailgate closed and held on to it for dear life.

"What'd you do that for?"

"You weren't listening." She searched for any sign of another customer or the gas jockey looking their way. No luck.

Jack was busy rolling up his sleeve and didn't answer. "Are you okay? I didn't break the skin. I couldn't have." He had on a long-sleeve sweater and light jacket.

None of the gas customers looked her way and she'd parked next to a stand of trees. If she wasn't careful, Jack could drag her out of the parking lot and no one would see a thing. She stepped around the side of Deke's pickup in full view of the other people going about their routine.

But this was Jack and he'd never actually been violent. Even now he looked more confused than angry. She'd hurt him.

"I'm sorry, Jack. This isn't working anymore." She waved her hand from his chest to hers. "You have to move on. Please. For your own good." She hesitated, then touched his cheek. He dropped his gaze to the ground and for a flash she saw the man she used to want a life with. But not now.

"There's so much good in you and another woman can bring that out. It's time to find her."

He shuttered his eyes against her, let them go cool and assessing. "So you can fuck this guy"—he rattled the tailgate—"with a clear conscience?"

"This has nothing to do with Deke. He's not important right now. You are. Your dependence on what we used to have is misplaced. Set yourself free, Jack. You deserve to be happy, not trapped in our past. If you think about it enough you'll see that you weren't happy, either."

He nodded and backed away. Relieved, she turned and scooted around the front of the truck and climbed into the driver's seat. Thank God Deke hadn't come with her. She wouldn't have had a chance to be reasonable and all kinds of shit could have gone down.

With a little thought and time, Jack would see reason and finally move into his future.

She could tell everyone to stand down now. Jack wouldn't bother her again.

The best part was, she'd managed the whole thing without Deke or her family getting involved. She locked the door and started the truck, finally at peace. Jack still stood where he'd been and she watched him grow small in the rearview mirror.

"Good-bye Jack. Take care," she whispered, and meant it.

16

Kylie and Holly parked themselves at the foot of the staircase to take a break from painting the back bedrooms. Kylie held her hot mug of tea with blistered fingers. She showed them to her cousin with pride. "Blood, sweat, tears and blisters. Does this prove I'm committed?"

"Nobody's ever doubted you," Holly responded with a sympathetic moue. "And thanks for the tea. I like it." She held her cup in a salute.

It had been a week since Holly's successful confrontation with Jack and the worry had eased for all of them. They'd had a full week of peace, hard work and bonding. Trust had built and Kylie's comfort level over sharing confidences had evened out. Marnie had told them about her partner's idea for BackLit. She hadn't asked for opinions, so neither Kylie nor Holly had offered theirs. "TJ's happy to have Marnie back," she said, "and Deke finally seems back to normal."

Holly smiled a private smile at the mention of Deke's name. "That man can hold a grudge. It took him two days to get over the fact that I sneaked away with the propane tank." She bumped Kylie's shoulder. "But the sex was smoking hot." Holly shivered theatrically then took a sip of tea. "I'll have to remember to tick him off every once in a while. It was like he needed to put his stamp on me."

"Sounds hot."

"Believe me, it was. A focused demanding lover creates all kinds of fantastic opportunities. He dragged me around the bed, put me into positions without asking, he even caught me in the laundry room off the kitchen while you were serving lunch for the work crew. Hot, dirty, sweaty sex with people in the next room—" She broke off with a quick loud sigh.

"And I thought the dryer was overloaded."

"It was." She sighed.

"TMI, dear cousin." Kylie held up her free hand, mind ablaze with possibilities. "Too much information."

Holly chuckled. "How's it going with Eli?"

"There's nothing to *go*. He insisted on staying here because we weren't sure what Jack's next move would be. But now that Jack's gone home and he's stopped calling you, Eli doesn't need to stay here. I'm fine alone." She always had been.

"Do you want him to leave?"

Kylie shrugged. "It's no bother having him around. He stays at his end of the hall and I stay at mine."

"No accidental collisions in your nightie? No trips to the kitchen at the same time? No bathroom doors open a crack while you shower?"

"No!" She wasn't a fool. Eli would see any one of those things as invitations. And the man was difficult enough to deal with in the daytime. "Well," she confessed, "last night we ended up in the kitchen at the same time. He always gets a glass of milk and I had to wash my favorite teapot."

"Had to? Right when he happened to be in the kitchen?" Her gleeful expression said she read a lie.

"Yes, and I got there first. I hate the brown tea stain at the bottom of my best teapot. Makes me think my tea won't taste fresh." Eli had walked in on her while she'd been at the sink, hands deep in soapy water. "Come to think of it, he did brush up against me when he got a glass for his milk."

Holly eyed her with suspect humor.

When Eli's hips had caught her backside, her nipples had responded and she'd shifted to avoid another brush, but he'd also moved and they ended up colliding again. She hoped he hadn't been able to see the flush that had moved up her neck.

Marnie called downstairs. "The logs are here!"

Sure enough, they heard the sound of trucks arriving in a rumble of squeaking brakes and powerful diesels. Marnie flew downstairs to join the race to watch the delivery. All three women careened to a halt on the back porch.

The first of three trucks arrived and the women were awed into silence as the driver backed into position behind the inn. Some logs were notched in half moons close to each end, while others had angled ends and square notches. Some were short, some long, but each was of similar girth. The sun split the clouds and turned the logs to a buttery color. "Beautiful," Marnie sighed. "Aren't they beautiful?"

Kylie nodded. "It feels like a dream come true. The only problem is, it's Grandad's dream. He ordered these cabins."

Holly wrapped her arm around Kylie's waist. "Maybe, but he knew we'd be the ones to see the dream fulfilled."

Marnie's arm settled across Kylie's back from the other side, and for the first time since her mother's death, she didn't feel bereft. She felt connected. "This is a good thing, then, right?"

"Right."

Marnie blew out a breath. "Right," she agreed. "A good thing." She looked at Kylie's profile, then tucked a lock of hair behind Kylie's ear. "I'm glad you're here. I'm glad we're together to watch this."

The truck settled, the brakes sighing, and Eli and TJ took up positions on the first foundation. Deke climbed into the crane.

Holly spoke in a heavy breath. "How do they know which log goes where?"

"Eli told me they're marked. The cabins were preassembled and each log will go back into the right place. They're like kits at this point," Kylie explained. She'd asked Eli the same question last night when they'd bumped into each other in the kitchen before bed. When they talked about anything that wasn't personal, they managed not to snark at each other too badly.

The more impersonal the conversation, the better they got along.

"Wow." Marnie put her head on Kylie's shoulder in a show of solidarity and affection. "Did you ever imagine we'd be here, like this, watching this?"

"You mean the logs or the men?" Holly asked, her mind seemingly never far from sex.

"Both." TJ was in red plaid, Deke in green, and Eli in blue. "Good thing they're color-coded, I can hardly tell them apart. Look at those tool belts."

"And hard hats," Kylie agreed with a sigh, as TJ stopped long enough to roll his sleeves to his elbows. He lifted his hard hat and smoothed his hair off his forehead.

"Oh, mama," Holly breathed. "With any luck it'll get hot enough to take those shirts off."

Three fervent prayers drifted upward.

An hour later, the four walls were outlined and the notches made sense as each log settled on top of the one below, guided into place by Eli and TJ. Deke handled the crane like a master and didn't release a log until TJ gave the sign.

The brothers weren't the only men on the crew, but to the cousins, they were. Kylie couldn't tear her gaze from Eli. He performed impeccably, taking the end of each log and guiding it, notch down to its proper resting place.

Soon, shorter logs were manhandled into place and the openings for the windows became clear.

The women settled into chairs and watched from the safety of the porch, their feet up on the sturdy log railing. The split in the clouds had grown and now the sun blazed down in one of those rare Northwest moments of dazzling sunshine that heated the air.

"Hallelujah," Marnie breathed.

Kylie agreed and opened her knees and closed them again when she realized her unconscious action. She bit her lip to keep from moaning as first TJ and then Eli stopped to remove their shirts.

Their muscles bulged and bunched as another log lowered toward their heads. Their strong legs stood braced on top of the previous log as they reached to position the newcomer. Perspiration brought their lightly tanned skin to a high sheen. Gentle as a bird landing, the log settled into place and TJ released the straps so Deke could pick up the next log.

The other crew members attached the straps and the process began again.

"Dear heaven," Kylie murmured. Eli was a god. A titan, perfectly sculpted and shiny with the heat of exertion. She loved the shadow of hair on his chest that fanned wide at the top and narrowed to his waist. It took little imagination to *see* what lay beneath his heavy leather tool belt. She sighed. "If we're lucky, they'll ask for water and douse it over themselves. Like Hugh Jackman in the movie *Australia*. I think I've hit rewind on that scene six hundred times."

Holly laughed. "Is that all? It must be a thousand times for me."

"Ditto," Marnie murmured.

Kylie wanted to hoot, to catcall, but she feared the men would put their shirts back on or be distracted enough to get hurt.

The work continued for another hour, with Kylie moistening more with every log that Eli manhandled into place. She dipped her fingers into her iced tea and took out an ice cube to run over her overheated neck. The sudden shock was more exciting than calming. Her only ease came from the butterfly motion of her knees. The press and release of her upper thighs eased the pressure momentarily, but then Eli's back muscles would bunch and he'd bend over and she'd be lost in a haze of desire again.

She moved her glass to sit on her mons and pressed lightly, convinced she'd pass out without some small measure of relief. An icy trickle of condensation slid under the thin crotch of her cutoffs. Dear heaven she was so *hot!*

"If they don't stop soon, I'm going to walk out there, grab Deke and fuck his brains out in the crane. I'll crawl onto his lap and have at him."

Marnie hooted and high-fived her. "You do that and I'll take TJ out to our favorite pond. There's a nice flat rock out there that catches the afternoon sun. Mmm-mm."

They both looked at Kylie simultaneously with twin expressions that screamed for a comment. She shrugged. "Well, if the chance were to come up, so to speak, I—ah, hell—I'd have at Eli, too. But I'm not sure he feels the same way."

Her cousins looked at each other and burst into laughter, which drew TJ's attention. "Hey, ladies, you going to hog that iced tea all afternoon?" he called. "Everyone take twenty."

The crew scattered into the shade of the surrounding trees while Deke jumped down from the crane, shirtless, and joined his brothers. The three of them walked in step toward the porch, shoulder to shoulder, talking about the morning's progress. They looked animated and happy, oblivious to the effect they were having on the women.

Incapable of speech, Marnie, Kylie and Holly watched their advance.

Eli glanced Kylie's way and caught on her position on the porch immediately. She kept her feet up on the railing, short cutoffs exposing the backs of her thighs. This time, when she opened her knees she knew exactly what she was doing. And why. When Eli's step faltered, she did it again, more slowly: a direct and blatant invitation.

Out of the corner of her eye, she noted her cousins weren't far off from her own behavior. Marnie slid her fingers along her thighs while Holly pressed her breasts together.

Clearly, men in tool belts operating big machines, manipulating logs large enough to crush them in near ballet precision was a major turn-on. Not to mention the bare chests and hard hats.

"Gentlemen, start your engines . . ." It was Holly, naturally. She finished off with a low-pitched purr.

Kylie chuckled and did another butterfly that stopped Eli in his tracks. A hot spear of desire bolted to her sex as he narrowed his gaze from ten feet away. For a measured moment there was no one in the yard for her but Eli.

Her pussy melted for him as she let him look his fill as her knees opened and closed as delicately as fluttery wings. She had good legs and she'd caught him watching them before, so now that she had his attention, she meant to keep it.

She'd let go of her attitude toward him as the days and nights alone in the inn with him had worn on. He'd been polite and completely nonsexual all week.

But tonight would be different. Tonight would be hers.

He advanced to the porch slowly. At five feet away, he lifted his hard hat and ran his forearm across his forehead to swipe at the sweat on his brow. He replaced the hard hat, leaving her wondering how his sweat would taste.

Tonight. Yes.

She'd find a reason to call Eli down to her end of the hall. If she worked things just right, he wouldn't leave again until they were both wrung out and useless.

A sexual shiver let loose inside as she realized his eyes were boring into hers. She accepted his look and gave it back tenfold. *Tonight.*

Eli watched Kylie's curtain of ebony hair swing forward as she dropped her feet from the porch railing and stood. Whenever they were within yards of each other, she couldn't move without him noticing. She laughed, he heard her. She walked, he saw it. She showered down the hall and he smelled the fruity soap she used, felt the steam when she walked out.

Problem was when she spoke, he more often than not disagreed. Maybe his back got up because he didn't like hearing, seeing, smelling her twenty-four seven. Especially when he knew touching was out of the question.

The Himalayas were looking better every day. Maybe there he'd put her out of his mind.

As she stood, she wrapped a knot in her hair with a deft flick of her wrists and threw it over her shoulder. Even that motion irritated him. Did she never use a clip? The knot always eventually slipped south, until it disappeared and she'd have to do it all over again. The inefficiency and wasted effort piqued his anger.

With a sway in her hips and a determined gleam in her eye he'd never seen before, she walked toward him while his brothers skirted past her to get to Marnie and Holly. The gleam intrigued but couldn't be good. She was up to something and Kylie on a mission was a dangerous woman.

His cock had twitched to life as she'd opened and closed her legs at his approach. Now, seeing her stride with her breasts fluid and unrestrained, his cock engorged to full. Her cutoffs were the shortest she'd worn since arriving and the bottoms of her pockets peeked out at the top of her thighs. Her nipples jutted like erasers, small and tight.

Even so, it was her gaze that caught his. He couldn't look away as she approached.

"You should wear a hard hat," he managed around his dry mouth. "This is a construction zone," he said as she drew near enough to touch.

"I wanted to see the cabins up close."

As much as she irritated him on every level, he wouldn't expose her to falling logs. "TJ, toss me your hard hat for Kylie."

The yellow hat sailed across the yard into his hands and he passed it to her. When she took it, she brushed the back of his hand. "Is this on right?" she asked.

He adjusted it to sit more evenly on her head, aware of her fruity soap and underlying woman's scent. Before he could pull his hand back, she turned her mouth to the inside of his wrist and pressed her lips against his flesh. An electric jolt snapped and crackled down to his groin.

"Thanks," she said lightly. "Show me the cabin wall?"

He did but kept well away from her. This was not the time to touch her again, because once he did that, he'd be lost, unable to do anything but continue. Tonight. He'd touch her all he wanted tonight.

The invitation was clear in her eyes, her body, the way she moved, even in the way she smelled. He didn't much care why or how this had happened. His raging hard-on was in full control.

"Do you have the floor plans?" she asked.

"Not here."

"Because Holly says she hasn't even seen them." She crossed her arms under her breasts and his mouth went dry. "Can you show me the plans tonight?"

"Sure."

"Good, I want to start work on a different theme for each cabin."

"Themes, sure." This must be like decluttering. "We can take a break and look at the plans right now. Holly and Marnie may already have themes in mind."

"They're leaving that to me. So far, they've been happy with everything I've done in the bedrooms." Her eyes widened and said he'd be happy, too. His belly dropped as her message ricocheted through his chest. "We'll look at them later. Alone."

He cocked an eyebrow and grinned. Her nipples rose. "Chilly out here?" He said with an obvious glance.

"Not at all. It's warm." She lifted her silky tank top away from her chest and flapped it, giving him a glimpse of cleavage. "Some might say it's hot."

· "Hot. Yes." His brain shut down by degrees as control shifted south of his waist. "It'll cool down tonight though," he said. Her breasts jiggled with another shake on the material. His cock went into overdrive. A trickle of sweat slid down his temple to his cheek.

Out of the blue, she thumbed the bead. In brazen invitation she looked at her damp thumb, then licked his sweat clean off. "Mm. Tasty. I bet you're tasty all over." She moistened her lips and stared heated come-get-me into his eyes.

He pulled her thumb away from her lips to inspect it. "A blister. You need to take care of that." She blinked when he kissed the spot with a feather-light touch of his mouth.

Her eyes drifted closed then open again. Her breath hitched. "It's nothing. Proof of how much I want this place. I'm willing to work hard to get what I want." Her green eyes darkened in promise.

He checked the rest of her fingertips on each hand, every blister earning another kiss. "No one should have to work this hard." By the time he was done, she was shifting her legs and squeezing her upper thighs.

He loved the idea of her panties getting wetter with each tiny blessing of his mouth.

"Everyone should work hard for their dreams," she murmured.

Amused at agreeing with every word, he said, "For once, you'll get no argument from me."

He had two choices. Drag her behind the log wall where the crew might see or walk to the inn. He chose the inn and took off at a quick clip, her hand firmly in his.

"Where are you taking me?" she asked as he strode across the lot. He should steer clear of her, but he couldn't. She didn't even like him. He wasn't sure he liked her!

He dropped her hand, letting her choose to follow or not. "I need a drink of cold water. In the kitchen."

Her throat worked and her eyes pulled at him. That talk about working for her dream had set off a chain of thoughts he hadn't had in years. He always thought he'd find his dream out in the wider world. But now, he wasn't so sure.

"I'm thirsty, too," she said with nod.

He couldn't touch her again, not until they were alone, so he set off at an even faster clip. His balls tightened with each step.

His brothers settled their butts on the porch railing as they talked with Holly and Marnie. The women each had their feet on his brothers' knees. The closer he got, the more he read the sexual tension between the couples. Deke, never a man to hide his sexuality, ran his hands up Holly's calves.

Eli averted his gaze. "Must be something in the air," he muttered as he bolted across the porch and into the cool quiet of the kitchen.

He pulled a glass out of a cupboard while Kylie walked in after him. He turned on the cold water faucet and slipped the glass under the stream. The water ran clean and cold. "In the third world a glass of clean water can be hard to come by."

He shut off the water and leaned against the counter, facing her. He raised his glass and drank about half while she watched. God, she was fine. *Fine.* And tonight . . .

He let his eyes wander to her chest. "You sure you want to wait for tonight to go over the plans?" He dipped his fingers into the cold water and flicked droplets across her chest. She jerked at the cold shock. Before she could sputter and ruin the moment, he said, "You looked so hot, I thought you needed to cool down."

She wet her bottom lip with her tongue, then she dipped his fingers in the water again. In a deft move, Kylie slid his water soaked fingers across her left nipple, then her right. Each one budded harder.

"In for a penny," he said and snagged her upper arms. He dragged her close, slipped his hand into her hair and tugged her head back. When her neck tilted enough, he took her mouth in midgasp.

Kylie tasted like nectar and need as he slipped his tongue against hers. Blood rushed, leaving his brain on autopilot. She welcomed his tongue, lips firm and coaxing. She used her hips in a full-on body press and the metal edge of the counter bit his naked back. Her hands fluttered down his naked chest to land on the heavy leather of his tool belt. She moaned and pressed her soft belly against him.

Her softness pressed against his rising cock while she opened her thighs in invitation.

He kissed her deeply and allowed all the sensation he could muster. Grabbing her hair, he bent her head back to trail his lips down her neck to her collarbone. He cupped her breast and stroked her nipple with his thumb until she moaned assent and nipped at the skin behind his ear.

Kylie was tall and fit against him without adjustment. A first for him and the idea of stretching her out naked, her long limbs ready to entwine with his, made him harder still. He slipped his hands inside her tank top and lifted it to expose her nipples. Like black rosebuds, her nipples stood erect. "Teardrops, like I thought," he murmured.

Heavy on the underside, her nipples slanted upward, inviting his mouth to suckle. He accepted the invitation and rolled first one then the other with his tongue and lips. Salty and warm, her tits filled his mouth and brought another slide of rocket-fuel heat to his back.

She responded with a gasp and slid one hand to the back of his head to hold him to her. Her other hand slid along his turgid rod. When she reached beneath and cupped him with a definite squeeze, he nearly lost control. She fondled him as he tucked a finger up the leg of her cutoffs to her crotch.

"You're wet," he whispered with a groan pulled from his deepest fantasies of her. Too many days of denial called and teased as he circled the prize of wet folds. She sucked his lower lip, mashed her full breasts against his chest and slipped her arms around his waist.

His cock rose higher, her scent came to him, jasmine-sweet and aroused.

"Unh," she groaned with a nearly imperceptible movement downward on his hand. "Yes, do that." She shivered in his arms.

"You're ready to come so soon?"

"Close," she muttered between kisses. "I've thought of this a time or two." The confession rang true and must have cost her. She was so hot, so wet. Something had turned her on. Not that he cared what it was, he was just glad to be on the receiving end.

He set one finger to her center and pressed inside her slick heat. She shivered around his hand and gasped with urgent need as he worked his finger inside her. She shuddered again as another slide of moisture coated his hand.

She tugged at his fly, brushing against his erection with clumsy speed. "Yes, touch me there. I want—"

A hard rap on the glass startled them both. "Christ! It's TJ." Eli stilled his hand, while she groaned against his lips.

"Can he see anything?" Her voice was breathy and high.

He turned his head enough to catch sight of his brother's ugly profile in the window. "No, he's not looking inside, he's looking at Marnie."

Kylie sagged in relief as TJ's voice barreled through the window. "Break's over. Back to work." TJ sauntered off the porch toward the cabin.

"Tonight," Eli promised and released her.

She gasped again at the sudden loss of his hand between her legs. "Eli, you can't leave me hanging."

"If I don't go now, TJ will come looking for me. One glance at you and he'll know what we've been doing."

"And what have we been doing?"

He chuckled as he washed his hands. "Finally agreeing on something?"

She tilted her head in surprise. "We are." Her hands grabbed his butt and she squeezed hard, then tugged his tool belt. "Wear this tonight," she whispered in his ear. "I find it . . . inspiring." Her breath warmed through to his belly and he grinned before sidestepping her to reach for the hand towel. He should have washed up before touching her but the moment had called for inspiration not logic.

"I'll wear it. Anything to help inspire you." He winked at her. "I love the scent of the fruity soap you shower with."

She nodded and patted his ass as he walked out on leaden legs. Leaving her was the hardest thing he'd ever done.

17

TJ tossed his hard hat to Eli so Kylie could put it on. The sparks between those two would cause a lightning strike if clouds rolled in. He wiped his brow with his forearm and focused on his true objective.

Marnie. She sat with her feet on the railing, her chair tilted back and a look in her eyes that screamed come and get it.

The rhythmic trail of her hand along her thighs was a sure-fire sign that she wasn't thinking of the cabins or the work being done.

He wasn't sure what had triggered her train of thought, but he didn't care. Fact was, she wanted him and that always brought on a firestorm.

Deke walked beside him and sucked in a deep breath. "I'm not sure we're going to get much work done after this break."

"You just keep your eyes on your own woman." He cut Holly a glance. Whatever had affected Marnie had Holly in its grip as well. "What the hell got these women so—"

"Horny? Who the hell cares?"

He followed Eli onto the porch. Marnie dropped her feet to

the floor to allow his brother to pass. The second TJ settled his butt on the railing she bracketed his hips with her feet. From this angle, he had a clear view up her creamy thighs to her crotch. Deke was in the exact same position.

"Those logs are big," Marnie said. Her eyes looked fevered, her voice husky. "Slipping them into place like that takes a lot of strength." Her knees drifted together, then apart. She let her gaze roam across his chest and down to his lap.

He braced his hands on either side of her feet.

Holly spoke next. "And I had no idea you were so talented with that crane. Such precision work. You really know how to handle those logs, Deke."

Suddenly Eli stormed across the porch and into the kitchen as if the hounds of hell were after him. But it was only Kylie, intent on catching up.

A look passed between Marnie and Holly, followed by suggestive smiles tossed at the men. Holly stood and held out her hand to Deke.

He dogged her steps around the corner of the inn, leaving TJ alone with Marnie. "What's going on?" But the glow in her eyes was all the answer he needed.

For the first time since that summer all those years ago, he saw the light of admiration in her eyes. He'd bask in her appreciation all day if she'd let him.

He never wanted that light to dim. He wanted it in his life from now on.

She stood and flowed into his arms with a kiss that rocked through to his soul. "Thomas John. You don't need instructions, do you?" Then she took his hand and tugged him along the porch and into Jon Dawson's woodworking shop.

"Jesus, Marnie. The place is full of people . . ." The protest died as she shoved him against the closed door and dropped to the floor. She worked at the buckle of his tool belt, then looked up at him with a grin.

"I think I'll leave that on." She opened his tab and fly and yanked his jeans down to his knees.

Already erect, he leaned back against the shop door and closed his eyes with anticipation. Her mouth slid over his full tip and down his shaft in a smooth slide. Sensation rolled in waves up his back as he clasped her head to hold her there. Heaven! She suckled and tongued him and eventually opened her throat to take every inch.

"I love your taste," she said between slides. "So salty. So you."

He braced her shoulders between his knees and rocked into her mouth again and again in an easy rhythm. When her hand cupped his sac, he nearly lost it, but there was no time for finesse and he wasn't going to come alone.

Not like this, not with her. Not today when he'd finally seen that look in her eyes.

He coaxed her off her knees. "Take off your shorts." She obliged in silence while he draped a heavy leather apron across the top of the workbench. He lifted her naked butt to the bench and fitted himself to her entrance.

"Do me, Thomas John. Fuck me hard and deep." She draped her knees over his elbows and scooted closer. He fit his thick head into her pussy and let the sensation overtake them as she opened to receive him. "I need you. Now."

She was wetter than she'd ever been before. Wetter. Hotter. More swollen. She shuddered when he didn't move. He felt the inner clenching of her channel as he slid in another millimeter. "I'm not going to last, so you'd better be ready to come when I'm in deep."

Her eyes flared into twin flames of need as she reached for his hips to draw him in. "No worries, partner, I'm ready."

He thumbed her clit and watched as she rolled her head back and braced herself on the bench. He cupped a breast and squeezed and plucked the nipple as he slid his shaft in to halfway.

He pulled out and saw the gleam of her juices coating his cock. The sight took him over the edge of reason and in one deep stroke he plunged in.

She crooned at the pressure and bounced her ass to take more. He rubbed her bud harder in wider circles and moisture flowed over his scalding flesh.

The rush took him over then and he pumped without thought, without reason until her breath hitched and her vaginal walls clamped and released in orgasm. She bit her lip and groaned as sensation rose and he spewed into her with a wild burr of release. "Marnie, God! I love you. I love this."

When he opened his eyes, she kept hers closed for a moment to savor the glow. He pulled out and stepped back. "Are you okay? We forgot protection."

She closed her legs quickly. "I'm healthy, if that's what you mean. And I use birth control." She slid off the bench with a little hop.

"I'm healthy, too. Regular blood donor." He tucked and zipped and grinned. "Great way to spend the break. What gave you the idea?"

She slipped a finger into his tool belt and tugged. "Are you kidding? Men really have no idea, do they?" She kissed him before he could answer.

When she was done blowing his mind again, she opened the door and sauntered along the porch to the table and chairs. She raised an empty tumbler, filled it with ice cubes from the ice chest and then splashed tea into the glass. She cocked her hip and raised the tumbler like an offering, her eyes full of sexy promise.

It was then he recalled she hadn't said it back. The big *L* word.

Hm. Too late to take it back, and he didn't want to. She had huge decisions on her plate and she needed all the facts in order to make the right one for her.

And the fact he loved her was salient. At least to him.

Hm.

He'd be patient. She was still getting used to him. Still more in her element in her dance club than here in the quiet trees and the sighing woods.

She passed him the drink. "I'm going to set up a Web site for the inn. If Holly and Kylie have their hearts set on running the place, even for one season, then it's the least I can do." She lifted the corner of her mouth in a sheepish gesture. "I know how hard it is to get a business off the ground. If I dig in my heels, I'm only being a bitch."

"And if you help with the Web site, you'll feel better?"

"You got it. I love Holly like a sister and I don't want any hard feelings over my decision on the inn."

"So, you think you want to let Dennis change the focus of BackLit?"

"I didn't say that. I'm still going over his figures, asking questions. It isn't the kind of business you can find in a phone directory. But there are definite possibilities for profit there." She put her hands on her hips and blew out a frustrated breath. "There, I said it. I'm intrigued by the profit margins."

"Profit makes the world go round."

She chuckled. "Spoken like a tried-and-true capitalist. And I happen to agree."

"You've got a lot to consider."

She set her palm to his cheek and stretched to bless his cheek with a kiss. "Yes, I do." Her eyes shone and he knew she'd heard his too-soon declaration and had added it to her considerations.

"I know you'll work this out. You're smart enough to know exactly what you want."

"Thanks, Thomas John."

The use of his full name made him think of sex again. She only used it when she was feeling warm and friendly, like those first moments of recognition when she'd arrived. Once she'd seen the clearing out back, she'd reverted to TJ.

"Let me see the Web site when you're done." Creation would give her a sense of ownership of the inn, in spite of her desire to sell. That emotional connection to the place would act in his favor. "You'll want to link to the locals. Chamber of commerce, the tourist association."

He drank the icy tea then peered into the kitchen. Eli had his arms full of Kylie, and from the looks of things, they were about to finally set off that lightning storm. He could leave them be for a few minutes. Or not and drive Eli batty.

He rapped once on the kitchen window, keeping his face averted so as not to embarrass Kylie for her lack of taste in men. Hah! Take that, little brother.

"Break's over," he called. "Back to work." He gave Marnie a wink and a soft squeeze on her ass before he sauntered back to the cabin. "Hey, boys," he called to the crew. "I hope you're ready to get back to it. Nothing like a short break to revive a man."

Deke watched Kylie stride out to meet Eli, who'd suddenly fallen out of step and lagged behind. A second later, TJ tossed his hard hat across the yard. Deke shook his head. About time Kylie and Eli sorted out their shit. They'd been in heat for days, but too stubborn to admit it.

He liked the arrangement he had with Holly. They'd started with hot sex and continued that way. The things she could do with her tongue drove him wild.

His next glance at Holly nearly felled him in his tracks. She had her feet on the porch railing about hip width apart, like Marnie did. He'd been with her long enough to read her signals and one of them was the habit she had of pressing the sides of her breasts together with her arms. The effect was a line of cleavage that drew a man to thoughts of soft flesh surrounding a hard cock. "I'm not sure we're going to get much work done after this break."

After that he went on automatic as he drew close enough to read the full-out arousal in Holly's gaze. He stood between those elegant legs of hers and watched as she pressed and released her tits. Asking for it. Just begging.

Eli rushed into the kitchen in a burr of male need with Kylie quick as a mink on his heels.

With TJ and Marnie shooting sparks of their own, he took the lead and tilted his head toward the corner of the inn. Holly stood, took his hand and they left the porch without a word.

Her hand was hot in his, and she leaned close to brush her nipple against his bare arm. "It was hot in the crane," he said. "I'm a little sweaty."

"You smell like a man. My man. And that's all I care about. Now, take me somewhere we can be alone."

He couldn't help being surprised. He'd been a pig all week, demanding sex whenever, wherever the mood struck him. He wasn't sure why, but he'd needed to fuck her time and again. *Fuck* being the operative word. He hadn't been gentle. He hadn't been kind.

He'd been driven by some primal need to possess, a need he'd been powerless to overcome alone. The fact that she hadn't kicked him to the curb made his head spin. "Are you sure? I haven't been the easiest man to live with—"

"Shut up, Deke, and follow me."

He didn't need to hear it twice. She led him through the front door of the inn and up the stairs with a speed that made him wonder what he was in for. Once inside the front bedroom, she closed the door, pushed him onto the bed and straddled him.

"Holly?" She'd been aroused quickly many times. She'd teased and coaxed and flirted his cock into full erection time and again, but she'd never been aggressive. Not like this.

He couldn't believe the speed in her hands as she undid his jeans and stripped them down to his knees. He tried to kick his jeans off and undo his tool belt at the same time but he was trapped. She pushed his hands away from his buckle. It was the oddest feeling to be trapped in his own jeans, unable to free himself.

But this was Holly and the lust in her gaze made him settle in for a great ride. "Won't the buckle on my belt hurt you?"

"No. I like the belt on. Leave it." She ran her hands over the leather. "Yes, I like the belt." She stripped off her shorts in a deft move and licked the sweat off his belly. "You taste good, Deke, like a man." Her fingers swirled through his chest hair and pulled a few strands taut.

He felt the pull and his hips jerked in response. "Like that, Deke? Do you like that I'm taking you instead of the other way around?"

He nodded without speaking, half afraid he'd say the wrong thing. Her scent wafted up from between her legs, so heavy with desire he wanted to ask for a taste, but this new version of Holly might say no, so he asked for nothing.

"You lay there and take it, Deke. Like I've had to all week. You've fucked me raw ever since I saw Jack and it's my turn now."

Jack! That bastard had bullied and frightened her and Deke had been a hair's breadth from that same behavior all week. Ashamed, he settled back to let her have her moment.

Not that it would hurt him any to be under her thumb for a change. He deserved this slice of comeuppance. "Okay, you've got my attention." And her taking charge was kind of hot. Correction, a whole lot of hot.

"Good." She spit on both hands and spread the saliva all

across her delicate palms, then braced each hand on either side of his cock. She rolled his shaft between her wet palms. Quick strokes while his skin slid and pulled.

He arched, shocked by the wild twist, but she didn't stop, just worked him harder, faster until the tip of his cock wept with pre-come. His balls contracted and flexed.

"No, you can't come until I say so." She gave him a powerful twist that racked his balls into hard nuts. "You will eat me now and like it."

No problem there! He wanted to howl, "Yes!" but her avid expression stopped him. She walked on her knees to straddle his face and settled her open slit on his mouth. She held on to the headboard and rocked against him. He flicked his tongue in a mad assault on her inner lips, her plump clit rubbing against his nose. When he pulled the engorged nub between his lips and sucked it, Holly arched and cried out. "Yes, that's right! Suck it, lick it. Rock it."

Her turgid bud engorged further, long and thick. She had the largest clit he'd ever seen and he made the most of it. He spread her labia with two fingers and gently wedged her clit behind his front teeth. He massaged it with his tongue, sending her into a shattering orgasm that sent fluid gushing over his chin.

His cock burned for her touch so he slipped his other hand to his shaft for some relief. "No, don't touch yourself. That cock's mine." She grunted and more juice slid onto his face as she pressed her open slit to his mouth.

She wanted rough and fast so he shoved three fingers into her at once. When he turned them and pulled out she jerked and came in another rain of wet cream.

She spasmed on his fingers as he ground his teeth to keep from shooting his load. Holly sighed above him as her shudders eased. "Deke, one more thing," she said firmly. She leaned back and tweaked his left nipple.

He jerked, afraid to ask what she had in mind.

With a scramble, she turned and moved back down to straddle his cock backward. She raised herself so she was on her feet in a full squat.

Her ass cheeks parted, soft as a peach, to expose her wet swollen lips. Her scent was heady and fresh. Her juices had smeared across her backside and upper thighs.

His balls contracted in preparation for whatever came next.

"Now. You come," she ordered. She rose above him and grasped his cock to hold it at her entrance. "Look, Deke. Watch your cock spear into me. I take you, Deke. I take your cock. It's mine because I take it."

He bit the inside of his cheek to keep from blowing his load in a shower of spurts. Her lips were swollen and red while her slit opened so wide the head of his cock slipped inside in a tease so intense he nearly choked on his tongue.

He couldn't take any more torture. He cupped her ass, the tips of his fingers just grazing her outer lips. The juice scent made him wild as he helped her keep her balance as her lips slid in millimeters down his shaft.

He saw spots before his eyes as she rose to the tip and back down again. "Unh," he groaned, trying to bite it back.

"You're so wet. I can see you taking me into your pussy. I see you take it, Holly. Is that what you want? To show me how you take it?"

"Yes, yes," she hissed. "Watch me take it deep and deeper." She dropped suddenly, sending a spark through his balls that ignited his need to pump. His hips moved up into her. "Yes," she hissed again.

Her slick folds took him in deep and straight to the hilt. Wet suction and the pull of her inner walls was too much. On her next slide to take him all, he arched straight up into her and let orgasm thunder through his balls as they flexed and shot true. "Holly!" He lost it, lost himself, lost his mind as she pressed and took him deeper still.

A hip roll and shudder signaled another orgasm as she cried out with him. "Yessss!"

After the storm passed through them both, he sat up and cradled her limp body in his arms. "Babe?"

"Yes?" She hung her head, refusing to look at him while he held her.

"You can take me any time."

"Oh, Deke." She sniffled and rubbed a damp cheek on his forearm. "You've been so raw all week." She turned in his arms, her eyes brimming. She slid her palm to his cheek and gave him a tentative smile.

"If I've been too rough with you, I apologize. I don't know why I've been behaving like some caveman."

"It's okay, because I think I do know. You wondered if I had feelings for Jack."

He frowned. "Maybe." He thought about it. "Yes. I hated that you saw him alone, that you gave him a chance to try to talk you into going back to him."

"Wrong. I needed to help him see the futility in pursuing me. No one can tell him what to feel, but he can be shown the path toward acceptance. Now that he has, he'll move on. It was a gradual process, but I've finally succeeded in getting through to him."

Wrong! Jack was a controlling bastard with an agenda and Holly refused to see the truth. But as long as Jack stayed away there was nothing Deke could do about the guy. He took comfort where he could. "At least he's not calling anymore."

"That's a big step for Jack, believe me." She kissed the tip of his nose. "You overwhelm me, Deke, with your broad chest and brawny shoulders. The way you focus on me takes my breath sometimes. I wanted to show you today that my feelings for you are just as powerful and primal as yours are for me."

"Primal?" That about covered it. "Not animal?"

She grinned. "Well, maybe a little. And as long as I can show you my animal side once in a while, we're good."

18

Tonight. She'd have to wait until tonight for Eli to finish what they'd started. He'd shaken her to the core. She'd been kissed plenty. Hundreds, thousands of times, but never like that. She leaned on the counter over the sink and watched Eli follow his brother back to work.

Eli was potent, strong and so sexual he burned. Burned *her.* She massaged her arms where he'd gripped her before he'd lifted her tank top. She smoothed her shorts, letting her fingers drift across her mons. Tonight.

The promise of tonight with Eli would sustain her for the rest of the afternoon.

Marnie gathered the empty iced tea jug and glasses and stepped into the kitchen. She flushed as they each took their own inventory. Marnie arched an eyebrow at the twin damp spots Eli had left on her tank top.

Confidences were not for strangers, and Kylie had moved so often as a kid that she'd never bonded deeply with any girl-friends. But still, this was Marnie. Family.

"*Now* do you have something going with Eli?" she asked with a smirk.

"I don't know. It depends. Does planning on having sex later count?"

Marnie dealt with the empty glasses and jug. "I'd say so. But what about afterward? You'll still be under the same roof, seeing each other every day until the cabins are done."

She shifted, uneasy. "I'm not sure we even like each other."

"Don't you think you should decide that before you sleep with him?"

"What is this, the third degree?" She wasn't used to sharing this much with anyone.

Marnie stepped close, put her hands on Kylie's forearms in a light mimic of Eli's grip. "Did I push a button?"

A worm of guilt cruised her chest looking for a place to settle. "Maybe," she hedged.

"Good. That's family, Kylie. I've known Holly's buttons all my life, just the way TJ knows his brothers'. But you're new to the fold and I've had a such short time to study you. So, I'm glad I can read this much about you."

"You wanted to make me feel guilty?"

"No, although guilt operates freely in the family zone. But I wanted to know what kind of stuff makes you feel guilt. I can't tell if it's the sex or sex with Eli that's got you in a knot."

"It's Eli. He makes my head spin. One minute I want to hate his guts and the next I want to fuck him senseless."

"Holly and Deke took off for the sack within minutes of meeting each other."

"No!"

"They moved so fast they blurred. Instantaneous heat."

"She told me Deke's been wild all week."

"He has!" It was Holly, tousled and flushed, as she stepped into the kitchen from the living area. "We were upstairs," she admitted with a shrug. "But it was my turn for wild." She sighed, a fulfilled glow oozing from her pores.

"As I was about to say," Marnie continued with an appreciative smile, "I think with Deke and Holly the sex has turned into much more. Right, cousin?"

"Yes. It has. I'm quite taken with Deke. He's even shown me his home's foundation. He's planning a future and I'm pretty sure I want to be part of it."

Kylie wanted to cheer at the news. If Deke and Holly decided to live together or even marry, then she was that much closer to keeping the inn in the family. "So you'd stay permanently?"

Holly held up her hands. "Patience, cousin. We're a long way from permanent commitment. I've been married and it's nothing to rush into." She looked from one to the other. "So what's this about?"

Marnie gave Holly a measured look. "Just be sure of Deke. And let the rest of the family meet him first. You married Jack way too fast."

"I learn from my mistakes. No worries. Stop avoiding the issue. You two look like you were sharing a heart to heart and I want in. Now, what's going on here?"

"Eli and Kylie are planning on sex tonight."

Kylie rolled her eyes and Holly patted her shoulder in commiseration. "Welcome to the family, girly. You can't hide a damn thing."

Kylie surprised herself by realizing she wanted to share her thoughts on Eli. "I'm not hiding, I'm wondering aloud." She shifted over to let Holly get at the faucet.

"Thanks, I'm parched."

"This is difficult for me. I've spent most of my life only confiding in my mom. We were a team. Us against the world." She felt rueful with her next admission. "Mostly it was us against men. She held some bitterness toward my father and her own."

"Our fathers tried to reach out."

Kylie shook her head. "Maybe if they'd waited for the bitterness to ease a little, but forcing my mom too early just made her more stubborn."

They nodded in tandem. "Push and you get pushed back," Holly said softly.

"I learned to keep my thoughts to myself and work out my problems on my own. Going to my mother just brought on bitter rants and I didn't want to live that way. I've tried to be open, but just look at what I said to Eli at first glance!" She'd been unforgivably rude to condemn him the way she had.

"He's not nearly as bullheaded as Deke," Holly offered. "Eli's watched you all week. He sees every move you make, and every word you utter, he hears. He's as tuned to you as TJ is to Marnie."

"And Deke is to you," Kylie agreed, amazed that they'd seen the building tension between her and Eli when they were so involved in their own lives and decisions. No one knew which way Marnie's mind was going and no one dared ask.

She understood sexual attraction, she understood the idea of opposites attracting, but this thing with Eli was stronger than anything she'd ever felt. Why sleeping with him had become inevitable was beyond her ability to understand.

"Eli's so wrong for me." He was a wanderer and would never settle. He would never pick family over wanderlust. "I want a man who wants a family and roots."

"You think Eli doesn't want those things?" Holly leaned against the counter and watched her closely.

"He walked away from his roots." And kept walking away. "If it weren't for the need to earn money, he wouldn't ever come back."

"Nonsense," Marnie blurted. "He could work anywhere in the world, but as soon as TJ calls him, he comes home."

"All I want is to stay put with a man who's happy to stay put with me," Kylie insisted.

"Here, at the inn," Marnie clarified with a clouded expression.

"Yes, here. For the rest of my life." Her eyes danced to Holly's for agreement, but Holly's gaze was locked on Marnie.

Marnie nodded. "I understand how important this is to you. To prove it, I'll create a Web site for the inn. Just a page or two, nothing fancy, but it's the least I can do."

A small concession Kylie was thrilled to take. "Thank you! I've been hoping to get one done, but I'm lousy at knowing what to say and how to say it. I had no idea you had the skills."

Marnie shrugged. "Don't get excited. This will be very basic. And it doesn't mean I'm staying."

After Eli caught up to TJ at the cabin he asked, "Any word from Chuck on Holly's ex?"

"Chuck hasn't seen or heard about him hanging around. Yesterday, Marnie called his work and he picked up, so we figure it's over and done. And Holly doesn't know we even checked on him, so don't say anything."

"Sure thing. I'm glad he's given up."

TJ made a point of looking back to the building where the women stood together in the kitchen window. From here the conversation looked animated and happy. Kylie especially, and Eli warmed just seeing her smile. Tonight, that smile would be all for him. "Don't tell me you want to move into my guest room and leave the inn? Because that's not the way it looked to me when I saw you through the window with Kylie."

"I don't know what's going on with her. Sometimes she really bites my ass and other times—"

"She's hot as blazes?"

"Yeah. Like that. You wouldn't think a woman who could tick me off as fast as Kylie can would also turn me on." He looked to the sky. "Clouds are moving in." He found his shirt and slipped it on.

"Just be careful," his brother warned. "Kylie's putting her all into this place. It's like she wants it more than her next breath."

Eli looked at her through the window, her smiling mouth, her happy expression as she chatted with her cousins. "Yeah, I know what you mean." He'd give her this place on a platter if he could. "Let's get these cabins built." For her.

Sam Whitaker stepped up and waited for his chance to ask TJ a question. "We don't have enough screw jacks for all the corners."

Eli nodded to the boy and finished tucking in his shirt while TJ answered him. "We don't use them on the corners. It's only for vertical logs. They shrink with time."

Sam's confusion brought out TJ's patient side. He loved to teach a willing student. "Logs don't shrink much in diameter so the walls themselves will stay level. It's the uprights that need to be jacked, and that's only once a year or so."

"So, it's just the supports for the roof over the front stoop?"

"Right," TJ agreed. "You got it."

The boy nodded his understanding and went back to work. "I'm glad Holly found that kid at the gas station, he's got a good head on his shoulders."

"Seems so," Eli agreed. "He keeps his nose clean and his eyes open."

"And he'd rather ask a question than make a mistake by thinking he knows it all."

Eli rubbed the back of his neck. "Well, Teeje, you make it easy to ask. Some bosses aren't so willing to teach."

TJ cut him a surprised glance. "Thanks. Sam's okay. He's still working the gas pumps in the evenings, trying to save for college. I'll give him as much work as I can through the summer."

Deke suddenly rounded the corner of the inn, looking well

ridden and worn out. He grinned as he walked up. "Back to work?" Eli handed him his shirt. "Thanks."

"I was just telling Eli that Jack seems to have given up," TJ said.

Deke nodded and looked over his shoulder at the women in the window. "There's nothing for him here. The pecker head lost and he knows it." When he faced them again, his expression went cocky.

"If he does show up anywhere near here," Eli said, "Chuck will hear about it. One look at him and Jack will run back to the city with his tail between his legs." The cop was a bodybuilder and, since his nose had been broken in high school, had a face that could stop a truck. He'd perfected his scowl back when he and Eli played football together.

Deke grinned. "Good, I'm glad Chuck's on it. But for the first time in a week, I'm hopeful Holly really did get through to that loser. Maybe he won't be back."

TJ nodded. "Now can we get to work? We're burning daylight. And I think Eli's got a big night planned."

Eli landed a halfhearted punch to his asshole brother's shoulder.

Holly spent the late afternoon running errands, free of Deke's watchful eye. Free of worry that Jack might pounce. Relieved that she'd cleared the air with Deke, she found herself humming as she wandered the grocery store and picked up brochures at the tourist kiosk on the edge of town. Marnie would want to check out all the other recreational Web sites in the area.

She'd either want to have the same look and feel or go with something different.

She scrunched her nose and hoped her cousin didn't want to use photos from the hunter green room. There was a deer head on the wall of that room and Kylie had done nothing more than dust it and brush the fur. Poor thing. But since the inn was surrounded by forest and built of logs, it only seemed right to have one room with a hunting theme. Still, she didn't have to like it.

She'd been wild with Deke and she still glowed from the sex but already looked forward to more. Emotionally, she was way beyond just having a good time with him and now he knew it.

She grinned as she turned into the driveway that led to the inn. She stopped the truck and got out near the road to check on something she'd never noticed before.

In the ditch beside the road was a carved, badly weathered sign. "The Friendly Inn." She trailed her finger over the lettering carved by her grandfather's hand. He'd made a mess of his relationship with his only daughter. But repairs had begun with Kylie and she couldn't help but think his crazy will had created the chance. He'd always been a wily old codger.

She tried lifting the sign but it was too heavy. She'd ask Deke to pick it up out of the ditch next time they drove by. Maybe it could be sanded and refinished. They could hang it up on a new post. The idea brought a fresh smile and she hopped back into Deke's truck and rumbled down the drive to park in front of the inn.

Inside she found a blueprint spread out on the kitchen table, with Kylie and the O'Banions standing over it. Kylie looked thoughtful, the men apprehensive.

"And the fireplaces need to be here," Kylie said and pointed to a spot on the paper.

Eli bristled. "No way. These plans are perfect as they are. Your grandad agreed to them and that's all there is to it."

Her cousin gave Eli a baleful glance. "Huh. I'm supposed to give a shit what that old bastard wanted?"

"Kylie wants to change the cabins," Eli told Holly while glaring at Kylie across the table. "The operative word there being, *cabins*. Not luxury palaces."

Kylie glared right back at him. "I'm asking for minor changes to individualize them." She slammed her hands to her hips and turned to Holly for support. "The fireplaces are wedged into the corners. I thought that if we put them in the center of the cabins they could be open to more than one room."

Eli cleared his throat. "Cabins this size only have two rooms. The living area and one small bedroom with bath."

Intrigued, Holly moved to the table to stare down at the plans. "These cabins are tiny. Don't we have anything large enough for families?" She did a quick mental inventory of the rooms upstairs. None of them had connecting doors, so people with children would either have to share or get a separate room.

Kylie frowned. "Was this place supposed to be couples only?"

They all looked from the plans to TJ. He shrugged. "Who knows what Jon was thinking? I doubt he ever planned to operate. He spent years just woodworking."

"He didn't like people enough to want anyone to stay here."

"I hate that I'm related to him. What if I carry a gene for reclusive asshole-itis or something?" Kylie complained.

Eli laughed and nodded. "I don't know that you're just a carrier, you—"

Kylie glared so hard Eli bit off his words.

Deke glanced Holly's way and nodded toward the door. She sidled out to the hall with him while TJ slipped out the back door. No one else wanted to be caught in the crosshairs.

"Marnie's at TJ's working on the Web site already," Deke explained when they were out of the line of fire.

"That was fast."

"She's got to get back to the city. Her partner Dennis has been calling. I guess he wants an answer."

"Kylie and I want to know what she's decided as well." Holly had come around completely to the idea of running the inn for guests.

"I want to know what you've decided," Deke said, pulling her around to face him. His pupils dilated. Arousal? She didn't think so. Fear?

"What's wrong?"

"I'm ready, Holly."

"You're always ready." She slid her hand to his fly, but no erection greeted her. He lifted her hand away and kissed her palm. He bent his head, his lips brushing against her. Once, twice. When he looked at her again, she saw a glitter in his eyes.

"I want to finish building my house. Make it a home with me, Holly. You wanted a family before. Make one now with me."

She shook her head. "So soon?" She'd married Jack in haste. "I made a rotten mistake the last time I married."

"I won't push. We'll take our time. I just want to know you feel the same way I do. That we have possibilities."

A smile lit her soul. "Major possibilities." She gave him a nod that went on and on, until he palmed each side of her head and planted a deep kiss. "Love me, Deke."

"I will. Love me?"

"I do." This time, she'd do it right. Her family would love Deke, Marnie and Kylie would vouch for him. Jack was behind her, the mistake she'd learned from. She and Deke could move into their future, free and unfettered.

Without baggage. "Let's keep the camper, Deke, so we'll always have to pack light."

"No baggage for us, babe."

Raised voices came from the kitchen and they took the cue to leave. They could share their news after the dust settled between Kylie and Eli.

At the road, Holly asked him to pull over. She climbed out of his truck and walked to the ditch. "What are looking for?"

"The old sign. I saw it earlier. It was too heavy for me, so I thought you could get it into the truck." The only evidence that it had been there was a dead patch where it had lain for years. "Deke, it was here less than an hour ago. Who could have taken it?"

She spun and searched both directions along the road. Dark still trees filled each side. "Why would someone steal it?"

Eli leaned out his window. "Firewood? We'll make a new one."

"But Grandad made it."

"He built an entire inn and all the furniture in it. Are you really going to miss one sign?"

She shook her head. "Of course not. It's just odd that it would be gone right after I found it."

19

"Why'd you have to say that?" Kylie lashed out at Eli the moment they were alone in the kitchen. "You practically called me an ass!" And in front of his brothers, too. And Holly. They'd been so hot for each other earlier, she'd had high hopes their snarky ways were behind them.

"Sorry, it slipped out." But he didn't look sorry at all. He looked edgy as he crept to the kitchen doorway and glanced out into the hall. He motioned for her to stand behind him and peek with him. She held her ground.

He grabbed her hand and tugged. When she looked where he indicated, she saw Holly and Deke in midkiss in the hall. Arms wrapped around each other, bodies aligned, their posture was seriously intimate. Their murmured words and gentle kisses were more than sexy, they looked soul deep and yearning. "I didn't think they'd ever leave."

Clearly, he didn't see the kisses for what they were. Declarations. Touched and oddly embarrassed by the show of soul deep intimate feelings, she pulled Eli away from the doorway.

By his expression, he was oblivious to Deke's blatant display of his deepest feelings.

"I don't think they're ever coming up for air," he said.

She pinched his arm. "Never mind them. You won't distract me from the cabin plans or what you said."

"We can argue again," he let his gaze drift slowly down her body, "or not. Your choice." After the expression of love she'd just seen, Eli's sexual innuendo felt raw and shallow.

She wanted more. She wanted the intimacy and the trust Holly had with Deke.

"Don't try to distract me with sex. It won't work."

"Fine." Eli stepped around her. With exaggerated care, he made certain not to brush so much as her arm as he left the kitchen. He sauntered in a fluidly powerful stride out to the log truck. Heat blossomed between her legs as she watched him move.

The man was a spectacular pain in the ass.

She went back to studying the floor plan. There was no reason to deny the change she wanted. It seemed simple.

There must be a logical reason for Eli to argue against the change, but she'd been so fast to take offense she hadn't given him a chance to explain.

From the kitchen door she watched Eli climb onto the logs still left on the truck deck. He scampered across the pile of logs, obviously checking for something. Fear clutched her heart. By moving about so quickly, he was asking for a fall.

Afraid to call out in case she spooked him and the logs tumbled, she sidled out the door.

She blinked, aware of choking fear as she imagined the worst. She wanted him on solid ground, safe. Wanted him where she could touch him, talk with him, fight with him if necessary but safe on the ground.

She approached the truck slowly, hoping that he'd see her.

If he startled and jerked, the logs could shift, trapping his leg or worse.

"Kylie," he said on a wry note when he spied her slow steady pace. "What are you doing out here?" He sat on the log at the top of the pile. The sharp scent of cedar heightened her awareness. Her heart thudded so hard she felt the pulse in her ears.

"I'm wondering what the hell you're doing taking your life in your hands by climbing around on a pile of logs." Looking hot and adorable and so manly she could barely stand it.

She stared at his feet braced over three feet apart on uneven logs. His jeans pulled taut across his crotch, and from her worm's eye view, the man was, well, built. His chest widened from his hips to his shoulders, clad in plaid, blue today, like his eyes. Eyes that narrowed and gave her as good as he got in the inventory-taking.

Moisture pooled as her hands itched, her mouth went dry as her lips tingled at the memory of kissing him. At the way he'd had her at the brink of orgasm with nothing more than a brush of his fingers. She was crazy, wanting a man this much.

He could make her angry in a heartbeat with nothing more than an insolent look. But there was another side to the man, too. A capable, solid side she responded to on many levels. *No.* Everything about the man was wrong.

She needed roots, permanency, the feeling that her life was finally on an even keel. She didn't need a man with itchy feet who wouldn't look back if his home was on fire.

But what she *wanted* was sex. For the first time, she *wanted*, with a desire that reached into her marrow, hot, her ligaments, icy, until everything melted and oozed and ran with need to pool in her panties. She squeezed her thighs together.

Eli slid his hard hat higher on his forehead but kept his gaze trained on her. The moment stretched. Electric. Needful. Taut. "You wait right there," his voice came hard, throaty and firm.

She couldn't have walked away if he'd been breathing fire with talons for hands. She wanted to be scorched, scratched, taken. And since he wasn't some mythical creature, but a flesh and blood man with need in his gaze and sex on his mind, she would stand and wait. And want.

He scrambled down off the truck to stand two feet away, facing her. "What can I do for you?"

"Take me. And shut up about it."

Kylie Keegan was crazy as a loon. He'd offered not five minutes ago. "You changed your mind about tonight and you were right. Sex with you will likely kill me. Or both of us." He ran his hand through his hair then stared at his fingers. The tremble he saw would only get worse if he stayed. "I'm moving my stuff over to TJ's."

"Are you? Right now?" She crossed her arms and took hold of the hem of her tank top.

"You wouldn't." He looked around the clearing, but it looked as if everyone had left. Blood pounded down to his cock. Soon he wouldn't have enough left in his brain to think with. "We already don't like each other. After sex, we'll hate each others' guts. Believe me, it happens."

She lifted her top over her head and dropped it to the ground. "Then we have nothing to lose, do we?" Her breasts were free to the cooling air, nipples dark purple and hardening as he watched. Infinitely kissable.

She had a tiny waist for such a tall woman and hips he could ride for hours. "Come here, Eli. I'm cold."

She wedged her hands into the pockets of her cutoffs. The bulge of her hidden fists emphasized her flat belly. Her breasts jiggled and he didn't need to hear any more.

He drew her close to share his heat. "To be clear because we have a habit of misunderstanding each other: You want sex. With me?"

"I want sex with you." She wrapped her arms around his waist, her breasts soft against him. "Don't get me wrong. What I really want is permanence. I want marriage and children and I want the Friendly Inn. But for now, sex with you will be enough."

Her words rattled around in his brain, his empty, bloodless brain. "Why?"

"It's going to end anyway, because you'll be leaving soon. Which means I can relax and enjoy myself and not worry about trying to, um, like you."

He knew there had to be something wrong, but he was beyond trying to sort things out. She was offering and he was willing. "Maybe we'll be friends."

"Don't hold your breath."

Her smile, the first one she'd ever directed at him, blew what was left of his brain to smithereens. He cupped her exquisite jaw between his palms and kissed her.

Her lips went soft, giving, while her mouth was moist and invited him in. He took the invitation and pressed his tongue inside to find hers. She played and coaxed and tantalized.

Different from before, this kiss held no rancor, no anger, just heated invitation and welcome.

He lifted his head, watched while her eyelids drifted open. Her green eyes clouded with desire. "There, I knew we could get it right," she breathed.

Half his mind said to leave her be, that he had no right to take a woman who wanted the things she did. No matter what she thought, sex between them would change things. She'd start to see him as the man who would give her the home, children and roots she craved.

While the Himalayas waited, he would never be that man. Without thought, he caressed her breast and plucked at her engorged nipple. She felt so fucking good pressed against him.

With her offer fresh in his mind, his other half said Kylie was an adult, fully cognizant. She was the one who'd asked. "Are you sure you want this?"

Another lift of her lips that bounced around his belly and lodged in his cock. "I'm sure. Take me, Eli, take me all night long."

Marnie listened to Dennis's whine, letting the sound grate along her last nerve. "I want you back here this weekend; I've got things to do."

She saved her work with a click of the mouse and thought of hanging up on him. "What happened with Tisha? Last I heard she was back at work with no problems."

"She's fine. She's great. We worked things out."

"How?" Dread and suspicion made her grip the phone harder. "Dennis? How did you work things out with her?" But she knew, in the marrow of her bones, that he'd slept with her.

"Did you look at the figures I gave you? Did you talk to those people?" he asked. The people were other club owners in various parts of the country. They all claimed to make terrific profits and even more so since the economy tanked. People need relief in hard times and they were willing to pay and play hard to get it.

"It's tempting," she hedged. "You were right about getting the renovations done quickly." Mike, their DJ, couldn't hold them for ransom with his claims of bringing in the crowds. She was sick of hearing how the place would be dead without him.

"We'd be open in under a month," he promised. "Word of mouth would have us full in no time. Believe me."

"Like I said, it's tempting."

"So, *now* will you be here this weekend? We can go over the finer points."

She looked at her laptop, made some rapid calculations on

how fast the cabins could be built. Holly and Kylie were better at decorating than she was. She trusted their judgement with the cabin decor.

"I'll be there late tonight. We'll spend the morning going over everything. Be ready."

"I'm always ready, baby."

According to the people she'd spoken to, Dennis had done his homework. His concept for the club was solid. He'd always been good at ideas and start-up. It was the day-to-day grind of a business where he fell down. If the new version of BackLit took off in a way the dance club hadn't, she'd be able to buy him out sooner.

The sound of TJ's pickup truck drew her attention to the living room window. As she watched him climb out of the cab, she was struck again by his size and breadth. Absentmindedly, she reminded Dennis of the early morning meeting and ended the conversation.

TJ had opened his plaid shirt and removed his hard hat. His tool belt was gone, too. His shoulders sagged with weariness, but he opened his tailgate and tugged out a thick square of weathered wood. He had to stretch to get both hands on either side as he pulled at it.

When she took a closer look, she gasped. He'd remembered. She warmed at the sight of the weary man making good on a promise made weeks ago.

She dropped the phone to the sofa and yanked open the front door. "TJ! The sign! You remembered."

"Of course." He looked at her curiously. "I said I'd fix it up for you." A man of his word. He tightened his grip and carried the heavy wooden sign into his garage as if it weighed nothing.

Some small piece of her heart broke off and sailed out across the yard toward the eldest O'Banion.

"Oh, TJ," she whispered. "You sneaky thief."

Freer than she'd felt in a long while, Marnie wandered out to the garage.

She watched TJ for a long time as he sanded the sign Grandad had made. It had been in the ditch for years, a victim of wind and weather. The whine and burr of the sander hid her presence as TJ focused on the work. At the first break in the noise, she moved in. "Hi."

"Hi, yourself." He lifted his protective glasses and watched her approach. "Get a head start on the Web site?"

"I did. And then I called Dennis."

"Oh." He froze and stared at her, curiosity warring with cool objectivity in his eyes. He wanted her to explain but didn't want to ask. How soon she'd come to read his fleeting expressions and body language.

"Just for a couple of days." She walked her fingers from his belt up to his shoulder and back down. Slipping her hand to the bulge in his crotch, she licked her lips. "But first, I thought I could thank you for the sign."

"My pleasure," he said, running his hand across the carved lettering. Tension rested across his shoulders.

"You look tense. Let me take care of that for you."

"Here?"

"Why not here?" This is where he'd stolen so much of her heart. "There's no better place."

"I can think of a few. My bed, for one." She opened his belt buckle and jeans. "I'd love to reciprocate in the house. After a shower."

She chuckled, amused that he still didn't get it. His cock was already hardening as she dropped to her knees.

It wasn't hard to make him surrender. His protests died the moment her wet mouth enveloped him. He leaned against the bench at his back and braced himself as he accepted her offering.

Salty hot flesh filled her mouth. Earthy scents surrounded her while guttural groans rained down from the solid man she could bring to his knees. A flick of the tongue, a light suction, a stroke of her fingers across his scrotum, and TJ O'Banion was hers to do with as she wished.

She kissed the length of heavy vein that ran from root to tip, tasted the slick bead of essence that wept at his eye. Deep wet strokes of her tongue, fluttering kisses from her lips and sly coaxes from her fingers took him over as she stole control.

"You're so good," he groaned, as his cock flexed in her mouth. She loved the moment right before she took his seed, the anticipation, the heady sense of power, knowing this man had lost all reason. Had given his mind and body completely over to her.

When he'd said he loved her, she'd put it down to the heat of the moment, but now she wasn't so sure, because she was perilously close to saying the same thing as he cupped her head. Orgasm overtook him as she groaned and encouraged him with light flutters of her tongue.

When she looked up into his gaze, he looked troubled. "TJ? What's wrong?"

"City girl," he called her and stroked a fingertip from her earlobe along her jaw to her chin. He tilted her to look him squarely in the eye. "You spoke to Dennis. This feels a lot like good-bye."

"It might have been," she said, afraid he was right.

"Take the time you need to decide what you want, and call me."

TJ sat in the dark of his den, his feet up on his desk, the house silent around him. A bottle of scotch kept him company as he drained a crystal tumbler. He reached for another shot and the moonlight caught the label. Jon Dawson's favorite. This was the same scotch they'd shared that night Kylie had stormed out of Jon's life.

Regrets. Jon's life had been full of them. Whenever anyone had asked what those regrets were, TJ denied Jon had ever listed them. They were too dark to share with Jon's family and the one he needed to talk with most was already dead. Jon had accepted his unmarried daughter's pregnancy until she'd told him the truth.

She couldn't even guess at the baby's father. The night she'd partied in the fraternity house she'd been drunk and high. Vague memories of several men slipping into the room with her would be the legacy she passed to her child.

Sickened by his only daughter's confession, he'd roared and thundered and threatened until Trudy Dawson had walked out of his life. For years, Jon had denied he'd even had a daughter and wouldn't allow his sons to speak of her. If her brothers had caught wind of news of Trudy, Jon had refused to hear it.

As dark and as hard a man as Jon could be, TJ was shocked at the reception he gave Kylie. After she drove off in a high lather, Jon had spit on the ground in a vile display of hatred for her exotic looks. To Jon, her almond eyes and straight black hair were the ultimate insult.

TJ had been hard-pressed to even stay with his friend that night. Disgust at the old man's ranting had nearly sickened him, until he'd seen tears and loss fill Jon's eyes. "My baby girl," he'd said, "my baby girl is gone. And I just destroyed any hope of making things right. I wanted her to look like Trudy. I wanted to see my little girl in the child. I saw the face of a man who walked into a room and took advantage—"

"My little girl was incapable of consent. It was rape. I see that now and I . . . Trudy was right to leave me to my hate. I'd have infected that child."

TJ had stayed in the end and watched the old man cry his pain away amidst a wash of scotch and tears.

A week later, the cagey old man had called and had TJ meet him at his lawyer's office. The deal for the cabins was struck and once everything had been agreed, TJ had read farewell in Jon's eyes. Within a month, Jon was gone and the wait for the granddaughters' arrival began.

If TJ had had any idea that seeing Marnie again would have this effect on him, he never would have agreed to build the cabins. He'd have talked Jon out of his crazy codicil. The entire Dawson clan would have sold the property, split the money and gone on with their lives.

Kylie would never have known of her grandfather's legacy.

Deke would still be drowning in beer after Misty's betrayal.

Marnie wouldn't have climbed out of that ridiculous car and swept his heart out of his chest.

Life would have continued on the way it was going. Saturday nights would be spent driving Deke home drunk, weekdays would be spent working and wondering when the hell Eli would show up.

He considered chasing after Marnie the way he had before, but it was time she decided. She knew how he felt about her. If she didn't choose him over her life in the city, it would be for the best. He had no right to talk her into coming back. This had to be her decision. He held out hope that the deep affection he'd seen in her eyes in the garage would count for something, but he couldn't tell.

She'd had plenty of time to tell him how she felt and she'd chosen not to. Instead, he'd gone back to work on the sign and she'd headed into the house to pack her bag for Seattle.

He shifted the phone to the middle of his desk next to his feet and stared at it, willing it to ring. Marnie was going over the sex club idea with her partner in the morning.

So why was he staring at the phone right now?

20

The scent of Kylie's fruity bath soap drew Eli along the hall to her room. After working hard all day, he'd insisted on a quick shower. She might still change her mind; the woman had mercurial down pat and she had more to lose than he did with this arrangement. He knew he'd be leaving. He knew he could walk away.

He knew he would move on. He'd spent years perfecting the art of the short-term relationship.

Her bedroom door invited, so he slipped inside to stand with his back against the wall. Steam billowed out of her adjoining bath, water thundered into the tub. Splashing sounds and Kylie's light singsong voice came to him as he pictured soapy water sliding down her long tanned neck, between her sloping breasts. Some would cascade off her delicious nipples and bounce off the tub floor by her delectable feet.

She'd been royally pissed with him earlier. Furious because he'd refused to entertain the idea of new floor plans. Building with logs had it's limitations. Holes for electrical and cable wiring had to be predrilled in the logs. Each log had to line up exactly to provide space for running the wire.

You couldn't blithely rearrange the interior once the walls were up. He should have explained when he had the chance, but she'd been too riled to talk with.

She might actually listen after they were too spent to argue.

The water stopped running and he crossed his arms over his chest to wait for her. With one towel wrapped around her body and another in a turban on her head, she stepped out of the steamy bathroom to face him. He held up the bottle of wine he'd brought. "Peace?" he offered. "No arguments or snarky comments. At least for tonight."

"Tonight's about our pleasure," she said breezily. "We can fight tomorrow." She crossed to the bed to pick up her robe. Turning her back to him, she let the towel drop, exposing her straight shoulders and trim waist. Her legs went on forever to the floor. It was the first time he'd seen her without her hair swinging free. She was beautifully formed; feminine but strong.

He could have bitten his tongue at the incredible play of muscle and silky skin that shone in the light from the bathroom door.

Unfortunately, she slipped on her cotton robe to cover herself. Damn, things had been looking up for a moment there.

She tied the belt and reached up to unwind the turban that held her mass of hair. With the towel undone, a black tangled curtain of hair swept to her hips. "I have to comb it," she said and walked to the dresser where she picked up a wide-toothed comb.

"Let me, Kylie." He wanted nothing more than to get his hands on her. To stroke and separate the heavy strands would feel like heaven.

She cast him a glance over her shoulder. "Yes. You may comb my hair." She handed him a spray bottle that smelled like her soap. The label announced it as leave-in conditioner. He took the comb from her other hand and stood her squarely in front of the dresser mirror.

"Start from the bottom and work your way up."

God, he wanted to and when he reached the top of her thighs, he'd . . .

"Oh, you mean your hair," he muttered and lifted the tips of the left side. He sprayed the conditioner liberally along the hair shafts then held a hank of hair. He combed out the bottom third with long sure strokes. The well-lubricated hair separated more easily with every pass of the comb. Live silken threads. Beautiful thick sheets of hair draped his hands as he worked. Eli loved the erotically repetitive action.

Sensual and elegant, her hair wrapped around his palms until he tugged her head back with easy but steady pressure. He exposed the shell of her ear for a nibble and he heard the most delicate sigh as he tasted her. "Like that?"

"Mm." She tilted her head even more, offering her neck.

He slid his lips down from her earlobe nearly to her shoulder. With a light nip, he saw her nipples bud into hard points and she moaned. He brushed his palm across first one then the other. "My hair," she reminded him.

In the mirror, he saw them entwined, her robe half open, the belt loose and all that glorious hair in a cascade of black heat.

He continued with leisurely strokes of the rest of her silken fall until it shone in the golden glow from the bathroom light. She reached up behind her head to lift her hair in a sensuous sigh of movement that took his breath.

His cock rose hard and insistent. She shifted to face him with the satin of her hair twisted into a loose twine. "Show me your cock, Eli."

He'd never been so eager as he released himself to her scrutiny. With a flick, she wrapped the twine of silk around his shaft. She began a slow steady slide of hair on his hot flesh, wrapping him up tight and releasing the pressure just when he thought he'd scream for release. "Kylie, that's—"

"Hot?"

His brain had mushed out and he could only agree. "Yes." He watched the mirror for their profiles then looked down his body to see her focused attention. She clasped her hair with both hands and created a thick wall.

She held the curtain half an inch from the dew-slick tip of his penis. "Now, push through," she whispered.

The sensation was like nothing he'd felt before. Not wet, but so soft, so tight and giving at the same time. Her robe fell wide open and she leaned in close so that his cock head kissed her pubis through the curtain of hair.

He wanted to shoot this way. Spray his load all over her flat belly so his seed would drip down to coat her landing strip. "I could come this way."

"You will." She looked at him, her eyes a promise. "Sometime."

He kissed her with open-mouthed greedy kisses, catching her naked waist under her robe. She shrugged it off, the hair play forgotten in a blast of need that swept him to the bed. He laid her out and took his time studying her length. Long, strong limbs, exotic beautiful eyes, soft kissable lips and golden skin, Kylie took his breath away.

He trailed a fingertip from her bottom lip, down her neck and between her ample breasts. The softness of her belly gave under the gentle pressure of his touch until he ended at the apex of her thighs. A thin line of hair guided him to her clitoris. She closed her eyes and arched toward his finger in a silent plea.

She wanted him. She wanted this.

Kylie waited while Eli undressed. He'd showered and had only half dressed for his stroll down the hall. He dropped his shirt and jeans in a pile, never taking his eyes from her. No socks and no underwear. She knew he was large and had admired him many times, but now, as he stood before her buck naked and ready, she saw him completely nude for the first time.

Eli O'Banion was a lover to be reckoned with. He was solid from his shoulders down and that included his package. Long, thick and fully aroused, he was a wonder.

"I like what I see," she said. "You'll do."

He grinned and his brown hair fell over his brow while his laser blue eyes burned with the hottest flame. When his finger had brushed her clit, she'd wanted to open for him, but it seemed too much too soon. She was glad she'd waited.

Once she felt his hands on her again, there would be nothing but Eli, and the anticipation felt exquisite.

Her knees moved restlessly as he gazed at her from the bedside.

She wanted more than a quick rough tumble. "I want long and slow and thorough."

"Whatever you want," he promised. "I'm your man."

She patted the mattress and he joined her with a heavy sigh. For the first time since this idea had formed between them, she had an attack of nerves that must have shown on her face.

"You don't have to be afraid." He scooped her close and she let Eli's heat steam along her nerve endings.

"I'm not. I just don't know how to tell you to shut up. I want to do *this*"—she waved her hand between their naked bodies—"I want to *like* this, but I don't want to like *you*."

"I should be offended but I'm too horny to think."

The quip was exactly the right thing to say. She grinned and relaxed as he bent to kiss her. His mouth was toothpaste, and Eli coaxed her tongue to tangle.

"You're so beautiful when you're happy. Your face lights up and your eyes shine."

"Most men don't focus on that."

"That's where real beauty begins." His eyes took inventory and his hands roved. "You have luscious breasts. I love your dark nipples and your black curls here." He skimmed her mons, making her breath catch again. "So golden," he said, "your skin's smooth as velvet over sleek muscle. I want to touch you all over. Inside and out."

To test her, he slid his fingers to her curls. "You're so wet."

"Have been since we were in the kitchen together," she confessed against his lips. "Touch me."

Her outer lips bloomed as he swirled her moisture over her rubbery flesh. As hard as he was, she felt soft and open. He slipped a finger inside and she gave him a throaty moan of approval. She rolled her hips toward his questing hand, then bore down to take more.

So hot. So needy. "Eli, now!"

Still he swirled his tongue around her turgid nipple. He plucked the other until she threw her leg over his hip in blatant invitation.

"Kylie, look how wet you are." He slid two fingers into her in one smooth stroke. "You could take another finger, but I'd rather have my cock inside."

He rolled to cover her. "You fit so well." He slid his palms to her ass and tilted her up to receive him.

He brushed her slit with his sheathed cock. "Clever man," she said as she grabbed his ass and widened to take him in.

"Fully charged." He nodded. "You're so fucking soft, like slippery hot satin."

Enough talk. She hooked her legs around his hips. "Now."

"Now," he said. He kissed her with deep need. He pressed his full head in an inch and her inner walls softened in welcome.

She hitched her legs higher. "I'm full. I feel so—"

"Right. You feel so right," he said against her lips.

"Yes." She sighed.

He rocked and slid in deeper. His cock throbbed inside her as his heart hammered against hers. He lifted her hips higher and stilled.

So deep, so thick. So hard.

Oh, yes, the man was thorough to a fault. She kissed heat and hard man. To slow herself, she set her face into the crook of his neck to breathe him in. His palms settled on her hips as he measured the span of her from waist to hipbone. The sexy feel of him testing her went to her head and she moaned.

Eli kissed Kylie again and again while keeping his pace slow. Buried inside her sweet wet heat, his balls contracted hard as walnuts. "Can you move?"

She rolled up, then down, pulling on the head of his cock with each tight millimeter. "Oh. That's good, so good."

He pulled out to his tip, then slid in again, watching her eyes widen with the new sensation. Her hips rolled with his and soon picked up his new rhythm. Her breathing changed, quickened, as her eyes rolled back and closed.

He licked his thumb and used it on her clit. He rolled the nub with each buck of his hips.

"Yes. Do that again." Her breath went ragged as moisture flooded her pussy. He felt the slick slide, scented the fresh arousal.

She was fully with him now, open and yearning and rocking her pussy along the length of his cock. She cried out and he felt contractions surround him. Deep, strong, her walls grasped and clasped and eased and took, milking him.

"Hold me. I'm coming!" The words burst free as his first surge began. She wrapped her legs tighter, held him in her arms and rocked him into the abyss.

Heart hammering, he lost all control and slammed into her. He shook with the power of orgasm and held her tight. Her face shone with joy and surprise and something close to affection filled her gaze.

If it were any other woman, he might believe it.

In the first blush of the aftermath, he dropped his lips to hers once more. She grinned against his mouth. "That was wonderful. Thank you." She wriggled her hips as if to suck even more sensation out of him. "You're very good at this."

He rolled off and tucked her into his side. "You're a natural. And it's I who should thank you."

Her hand trailed down his belly, bringing a clutch to his gut. He could take her again, right now. "You like that?" she asked.

He nodded. "Don't you?" And he ran his hand down her warm silky belly to her curls. He grinned when he felt her muscles jerk in response. His forefinger found her round nub and swirled. She sighed and let her legs fall open. "Greedy already?"

He didn't bother to wait for confirmation and slid his finger into her. He rested his head on her belly and plunged in as deep as he could go. "You feel okay? This isn't too intense?"

"It's wonderful."

"I'll be right back. Stay just like this."

Once in the bathroom he disposed of the condom, then returned to her. He set his hand palm down on her belly to hold her in place. "We're not finished yet."

"We're not?"

He shook his head, and when her eyes glowed with heat, he said, "You need more."

"I do?"

He couldn't tell her how much more he wanted. This may be their only time, especially if they went back to sniping at each other.

"I'll give you whatever you need." He knelt at her feet, opened her legs and hooked them over his shoulders. "You're rosy pink and luscious." He parted her outer lips to expose the deeper darker pink of her slash. "I'm going to kiss you. Right here." He touched the tip of his finger to her clit, then rimmed her labia. "And here."

She jerked.

"And then, I'm going to slide my tongue in here." He slipped a finger into her sexy little hole and turned so she felt the pull of his knuckle.

"Oh, God," she muttered. "Yes. Do that."

"You'll come again. Do you want to?"

She nodded.

He parted her labia with both thumbs and held her open for his tongue. He swirled and licked her clit until she moaned. Fresh moisture slid to his mouth, delicious, spicy and all her own. "You're so tasty, I could eat you all night."

Her answer was another moan accompanied by a raise of her hips in offering. So giving.

Eli gave her more than she thought he could. Sensation was a riot that overtook her, a temptation to which she'd never fallen.

Here, with Eli of all people, she felt safe. He didn't care for her, didn't so much as like her, so if she gave herself the freedom to let go, it didn't matter. He wouldn't care. He wouldn't be around long.

A pulse rose from her depths as he suckled and licked. Awash with need, she pressed up for more of his mouth. The sound he made as he lapped at her, the deep and wild sensations helped her float away, adrift. Above herself, and free, Kylie wasn't Kylie anymore.

She was woman, fecund, rich with earthy needs, willing to give and take and feel the ripeness of completion.

Another pulse, stronger now, swept up, up, up into her chest, her heart as she crowned. "Oh. Eli." A cry tore from her lips as he pushed her higher and higher toward the sky.

When she fell again, it was into the safety of his arms. His lips worked her as she cupped the back of his head to keep him there so she could wring every last sensation from his mouth and tongue.

Her bloodless legs sagged as tension flowed away and Eli let her settle back to the soft mattress. She closed her eyes to enjoy the last of the orgasmic pulses. "That was spectacular."

She stretched her arms over her head and touched the iron bedstead. Clasping the metal bars, she arched her back to enjoy a languorous stretch of muscle and ligaments.

Eli's breath caught and she peeped an eye open. He was caught by the sight of her stretched out, his eyes glowing with primal need. Hard planes and tight control, his face went rigid as he watched her stretch and arch. She'd seen men gaze at the length of her legs, her long waist and heavy breasts, but this was different. He'd tasted her secrets, been inside her, had cleansed and licked her.

Eli had kissed her with gentleness and swift desire in turn.

She liked the way he looked at her, as if he could do it all again.

Then she noticed his cock, strained full and ready. A dew drop seeped from his tiny slit. She licked her lips and his eyes caught on her mouth.

"Let me do that to you. What you did for me," she offered. This would be a first for her. "Bring yourself to my mouth."

The mattress moved as he settled his knees on either side of her shoulders. She plumped the pillow behind her head and took the tip of his cock against her lips. The silky dew tasted salty on her tongue. "You're so hot here."

The soft ridge around the cap fascinated her and she spent long moments enjoying his moans of encouragement. "Yes, do that," he implored. "More, yes, scrape your teeth—*Jesus.* This is—"

She stroked his shaft while she tongued him. A glance to his face proved his enjoyment. Experimenting with technique brought more groans until he rocked slowly in and out of her mouth.

His balls felt like rocks when she reached for them. A slow, pumping squeeze made the bed quake with his shudders.

His cock flexed while his body stilled just before she felt his balls go rock hard. Spew, salty and hot, filled her mouth. His releasing spurts at the back of her throat startled her, but his cry of intense pleasure pleased her.

She swallowed everything he gave her and jerked when his stealthy hand found her pussy. The man was insatiable.

He rolled to the bed beside her, his fingers lightly stroking through her curls. "Fuck," he said, "you're unbelievable."

She opened her legs and let him rub her into another orgasm.

He wasn't the only one who felt greedy.

She was voracious and spent the rest of the evening proving it.

Three hours later, they rinsed soap off each other in the shower and stepped out to dry off. She wrapped her ropes of hair with a towel while they shuffled and twisted around each other in the tight bathroom. "How long will you be here?" she asked.

He had one foot on the rim of the tub while he dried his toes. "I could stay the night or go back to my room. Whatever." He turned his head to catch her response.

"No, I didn't mean tonight." She felt the heat of a blush. "How long will you be on the Peninsula?"

He rose to full height and faced her. She clutched her towel a little tighter over her breasts. His eyes turned assessing. "I don't know how long I'll be here."

"Well, then, when will the cabins be done?"

"You in a hurry to see me leave?" His brows knit and his voice went harder than it had been all evening. "Or do you want to pretend that I'll stay?"

"No, yes—NO!" She swallowed and tried to form her question in a different way. "I'm just curious." This is why she didn't like him. He confused her.

What's worse, he liked it.

"Or do you ask because you want this over and done already?" He slipped his hands to her waist. "Or because you've already had enough of me?"

If she admitted she might never get enough of him, he'd run off even faster. Men never stuck with clingy women. "Just tell me when the cabins will be finished. And then you can move out to your brother's place. Deal?"

He raised both brows. "Deal. Although moving out at that point seems premature, considering I'll be here through the entire tourist season. I need the work."

That said, he walked, stark naked, back down the hall and into his room. He couldn't even bother to spend the night in her bed.

21

The next morning, Kylie looked for Eli in his room, but he was already gone. At least he was tidy. He'd made his bed and his towels were neatly hung in the bathroom. She guessed he'd learned in his travels to be a considerate houseguest.

The smell of bacon and coffee told her where she could find him and she skipped lightly downstairs, ignoring the twinges between her thighs. She should have expected this, since he was so broad in the shoulders. It seemed all three O'Banions were proportionate. Deliciously proportionate.

But he wasn't in the kitchen and the bacon was only a lingering scent. He'd eaten breakfast and cleared his mess. At least there was still coffee in the carafe.

The crew was arriving out back, so she checked the front of the inn. Eli turned from the deck of TJ's truck loaded down with extension cords and power tools. When she opened the door, he looked up and frowned when he saw her.

Oh, mama! Men on the Peninsula were born to wear plaid. Her heartbeat went thready as she took in the morning sun on his hair. Sun-bleached tips caught the light and brightened his brown hair and made his blue eyes bluer.

"I'd like to talk to you, if I may," she said. "Please." She'd been rude before and wanted to start the day on a more pleasant note.

"Why?" His tone was suspicious. She couldn't blame him.

"I don't want to holler out the door. Please come inside." She turned, not giving him the chance to refuse. He set the tools down on the veranda but kept the extension cord looped over his shoulder.

She held her hands over her belly to keep from touching him. "I've been rude and deliberately aggravating to you. I don't understand why, exactly. I'm not usually so prickly."

His lower lip was swollen. "Did I do that to your lip?"

He patted it. "You're the only woman I kissed last night. And you're the only woman who clamped her teeth on my lip when she came." His gaze turned sexy in memory.

But she was mortified. "I'm so sorry. I didn't break the skin, did I?"

"No."

She palmed her shorts. "I have a plan."

"That is?" He pursed his lips, winced and immediately loosened them.

"I did hurt you. I'm so sorry. Let me get you some ice to help the swelling."

"No, I'm okay. It's already come down a lot." It was unexpectedly kind of him to reassure her. But when she opened her mouth to say so, he spoke quickly. "Before we mess up any more than we have, we should just avoid each other."

"That's not what I had in mind," she blurted. "I want—"

He held up his hand to forestall her saying more. "Sex with you was unbelievable. Smoking hot, Kylie." She warmed at his praise and opened her mouth. Again, he cut her off, this time with a finger to her lips. She badly wanted to draw the tip into her mouth and suck, but he spoke again. "We talk at cross purposes, mix up our signals, have some kind of weird chemical reaction that creates tension. We should just agree not to be friends, or even try. That way, no one gets hurt." He shouldered past her and went into the kitchen.

She heard the freezer door open. He did need ice for his lip and it was her fault. She walked to the doorway and leaned on it with her arms crossed. "You're right. You bring out the worst in me. I don't know why, but there it is." She watched as he tested an ice cube on his lip.

"I could kiss it better," she offered. She wasn't about to give up on her plan, not yet.

He narrowed his eyes. "See? Here we go again. You're talking about kissing me with your eyes all huge and innocent. What I want to do, Kylie, is bend you over the kitchen counter and fuck you raw."

The graphic image burned into her retinas and she stared at the counter, then caught the movement of the crew at the cabins. "They'd see," she said.

"Right there, that comment. You make me think with my dick and that doesn't work with our situation."

"How?"

"Instead of being shocked or put off by the idea of me fucking you in the kitchen, you're only worried about the men outside seeing us. It makes me think you want me to do everything I want."

"I do." There, it was out. He'd finally said what she'd come downstairs to tell him. "I have a plan that might work for us."

He dabbed the ice cube to his lip. "I'm all ears, but keep in mind, I already know your low opinion of me so I don't need to hear it again."

Her blood heated but not with desire. "I've apologized for the sex tourist remark." She forced herself to calm. "My plan is that we don't spend time in each other's company until after dinner when everyone else has left for the day." She shifted her hips, aware of his sudden and complete stillness.

"So, we have wild sex every night, but ignore each other all day?"

"Pretty much, yes. Why ruin good sex with miscommunication?"

He pursed his lips as he considered. Then he shrugged and tossed the ice cube into the sink. "Works for me." He walked back out to the veranda. As he picked up his power tools, he grinned. "Tonight, be naked by nine."

Moisture slid to her crotch. "Don't talk to me at dinner," she warned. She didn't want to ruin her chances of having another night like last night. Eli was wondrous in bed, even if he did leave for his own room when it was over. "I'll be tired by dinner. Maybe even cranky."

"No kiddin'." He rolled his eyes, then whistled tunelessly as he strolled along the veranda and around the corner of the building.

In Seattle, Marnie rose on Saturday morning later than she planned and raced through her routine. After the busiest Friday night in recent memory, she'd tossed in her sheets, stressed over her lack of decision about TJ.

She'd been shaken with TJ's assumption that she'd been saying good-bye. Was he right? Were things over between her and TJ? If they were done, it wasn't TJ's doing, because he made it clear in every gesture and glance her way that he cared deeply.

When they made love, there was no doubt that it was lovemaking. If she were honest, they'd never actually just had sex. From the first moment she'd climbed out of her car at the Friendly Inn, she'd been drawn to TJ in ways too complex to grasp.

In midshampoo she set her hands on the wall tile, overcome by the memory of seeing him for the first time again. The moment his name popped into her head and she'd said, "Thomas John," a quiet *tick-tick-tick* had begun. A countdown to when she'd kiss him, hold him, sleep with him. Fall in love with him.

The shampoo suds ran down her face and back as she let herself enjoy the memory of those early moments of greeting. She'd been impressed by the man her old friend had grown into.

She still was. Steady, secure, strong. TJ O'Banion proved every bit of the promise he'd shown at fifteen. She touched her fingertips to her lips as she recalled the thrill of that kiss at the pond all those years ago.

That thrill was still between them today.

Oh, God. Was she going to walk away from him to pursue her dream? Was it possible that she could be so focused on her idea of success that she could leave him?

Last night, the club had been hopping from the moment she'd arrived. Drinks flowed, Mike had the crowd jumping with his new dance mix. She'd had to stay later than usual because people flat-out refused to let him stop.

Even Dennis had pitched in throughout the night, never once leaving for a break. Surely he'd see that BackLit had taken off. They'd reached a new high last night. Things would only get busier from here.

In a few weeks, she could approach the banks again. Her mind raced with possibilities in a way it hadn't in months. Positive possibilities and opportunities abounded.

She finished rinsing her hair and the rest of her routine went by in a flash as she realized Dennis would be waiting for her. No matter what he said about the sex club idea, she'd throw some of her new thoughts at him.

He'd see the same opportunities she did. By the time she'd dressed and stepped out of her apartment, her thoughts were clearly focused on BackLit and her future.

She called Dennis as she exited her parking garage. "Are you on the way?"

"ETA ten minutes. I'll meet you there." His voice vibrated with energy. He was ready for their future, too.

She dropped her cell phone on the passenger seat before she gave in to the temptation to call TJ. She couldn't think of him now; she needed to keep her head clear for the meeting with Dennis.

Excitement traced through her veins. Decision time. If Dennis agreed to wait for the inn to sell, she could buy him out of their partnership. BackLit would be hers.

The inn was her ace. He still didn't know she held one-third of the place. Once the cabins were finished they could put the property on the market.

Holly would be fine. She could find a job she enjoyed, maybe go back to school. Kylie would stay in their lives, a fully accepted member of the Dawson clan.

That was what her newfound cousin really wanted. The family connection would soon outstrip her desire for the roots she craved. Roots weren't about place, Marnie told herself, they were about relationships.

Everyone would win in this plan of hers. Everyone but TJ.

The light at the intersection straight ahead suddenly turned red. She slammed on her brakes in a squeal of tires.

Horns blared, traffic whooshed by. Cars swerved. When she slid to a stop with only inches to spare, her knuckles showed bone white on the steering wheel. Even in a fishtail her car was too short to swing into the other lane.

Her cell phone slid off the seat and hit the floor. In the eery first seconds after the near-accident, all she could think was that she hadn't told TJ how much he meant to her. How much she loved him.

The car behind her honked once to get her attention and she saw that the light had changed to green again. The rest of her short commute she stayed hypersensitive to every light, pedestrian and especially all the other cars on the road.

Dennis's car was already in his reserved spot, a sign that at least he realized the seriousness of the meeting. Their office door was unlocked and she stepped in to see Dennis at his desk, head thrown back as he studied the ceiling.

"Hi, you're here already." She breezed in and set her purse on her desk and made for the coffee. "Thanks for making coffee," she said. "But I nearly got creamed coming in here today and I need something to calm my nerves, not wake me up!" She dug out a bag of herbal tea from her desk drawer.

"I've thought long and hard about this sex club idea of yours," she said, as she pulled out the single burner hot plate they kept for just this kind of morning. She walked to the bathroom to fill the small kettle with water for her tea. "The profits are there, Dennis, as is the interest in that kind of club. We've got a great location, too." He'd been right about word-of-mouth, especially within the lifestyle.

When she returned with the full kettle, she caught a look of ecstacy on her partner's face. She'd missed the cues again. When did Dennis ever study the ceiling to think? He jerked and grunted, then ended off with a chuckle.

"Who's under your desk?" Maybe the blonde from before. Or the brunette from his threesome, or maybe both again.

The blonde, she realized as a woman's head appeared from under the desk. "Thanks, babe. Took the edge off," he said as he zipped up, then helped the woman crawl out into the room.

Marnie nearly dropped the kettle where she stood as Tisha rose to her full height and patted him on the shoulder. "No problem." She turned and tidied the corners of her mouth, her eyes assessing Marnie with chilly dislike.

"And here I thought you were an afternoon kind of guy," Marnie said dryly. *What next?* To Tisha, she said, "Nice to see you again. Now, excuse us, we have business to attend to."

"Be nice to me," Tisha said with a pout. "I told you I wanted Dennis. I'm willing to share."

"Get out."

"You'd better go, babe," Dennis agreed and stood. He walked her to the door, handing her his car keys.

As soon as the door shut, Marnie said, "Jesus, Dennis, you're more stupid than I thought."

"You think so?" His smile moved into predatory. "Didn't you just say I had a great idea on the fantasy club? That you could see the profits even from that tree museum up in no-man's land?"

She set her kettle on the hot plate while she gathered her thoughts. Motioning him to his desk, she took her seat and then folded her hands in front of her. "As far as the fantasy club goes, I think it's viable. But last night, the club was screaming. Mike had the crowd eating out of his hand."

"That crowd was mine," he said, studying his manicure.

She thought back over the crowd. Most of them were regulars, but some she'd never seen before. "Maybe they showed up because you're putting the word out." The kettle whistled and she rose to pour the water. "But they stayed for the dancing and the music." And the atmosphere.

She brought her steeping tea back to her desk and sat again. As she'd so often seen, he steepled his fingers and looked at her with interest. Not male interest, but flat curiosity as if he'd never quite figured her out and no longer cared to. "Tisha doesn't have a sugar daddy like you assumed. The money's hers."

"Surprise, surprise." She remembered now that Tisha had hoped it would be Dennis who visited her. "Maybe I was wrong about Tisha after all."

"She wants to buy in."

He couldn't have surprised her more if he'd said he was going into a seminary. "To BackLit?" If she wanted two partners instead of one, she'd choose her cousins before she'd partner up with Dennis and his girly.

She closed her eyes and a picture of the inn popped up. Not rundown and filthy, but clean and fresh, the red door and furniture on the veranda welcoming and warm. She dipped her tea bag as she considered the image. Swirls of color ran through the hot water and the scent of chamomile filled her nose. "Tisha wants to buy into the club with us? She's got that kind of money?"

"Yeah, that's what she says. Except—"

"She doesn't want it to stay a dance club."

"Right."

"She's into the lifestyle, as you call it."

"Riiiight." He looked pleased that she'd caught on so easily.

"Then good luck." Her first sip of tea was always the best and she savored this one.

Dennis dropped his feet with a heavy thud. "You're shittin' me."

"Good luck with Tisha and your new fantasy club. If she's got enough to buy me out of our partnership, then more power to you."

"What?"

"You look surprised." More, he looked thunderstruck, then he blustered and a whine built in his throat.

"But I can't do it without you. I'm no good at the day-to-day shit and you know it." He stood and paced, much the way she had countless times when money was tight and they could barely pay wages.

Keeping Dennis under control had become a full-time job. He had as much personal restraint as a boy with a girly magazine when it came to spending money. He could blow through a weekend's profit in no time. To see him on edge and actually worried felt oddly satisfying.

"Careful, Dennis, those frown lines might stay on your

face." He was already coloring his hair. He thought she didn't know, but three months ago he'd lost the silver at his temples. Overnight. "I'm sure Tisha can pick up the slack, just the way I always did."

"You have to stay," he blurted. "Everything you have, everything you ever wanted is here!"

"Everything I've ever wanted is"—the realization came softly and fell with the light tinkling sound of a fairy's laugh—"is in a tree museum." Starting with TJ O'Banion.

Late Saturday afternoon Kylie and Holly dragged and pushed their grandfather's furniture into the middle of his bedroom. They could have asked the men for help, but they were busy setting the remaining logs on the first cabin. The walls were expected to be done by dinnertime.

"It'll be brighter in here once we've cleaned." The exterior wall was the only one with exposed logs. Like the log walls in the living room, dust had settled, turning the light-colored cedar gray with dust.

The interior walls were smooth drywall and easier to wash. Still, when Kylie had run her hand down the wall, she'd seen streaks of dirt on her fingers and palm.

Holly grunted over the nightstand and shoved it toward the pile of other furniture. The foot of the stand caught on a raised nail in a floorboard and nearly toppled. A drawer flew open and she swore. "Catch that stuff, Kylie. It could be important."

She picked up a book of crosswords, never started. A sheaf of sketches of furniture pieces. "The old man had a talent for this." She held up a sheet of graph paper with a sketch of the coffee table.

Holly took it and gave it a long look. "I didn't know. This is exactly how the table turned out."

"The rest just looks like letters and notes." She set them aside on the floor by the door. "We'll recycle everything later."

But a name caught her eye and she crouched to read more. "This is a letter . . ."

"Yes, so?"

"To my mother," she said, only half-hearing her own voice. She shuffled the top sheet to the side and looked at the next page. "And another. 'Dear Trudy,'" she read aloud. "On the next one he starts with 'My darling daughter,'" she looked up from her crouch at her cousin's stricken face.

"He wrote to her?"

Kylie nodded. "For years. Look at the dates." She fanned the letters out. "But he never mailed them. A lot of the letters are unfinished."

"Oh, Kylie, he never found the words, but at least he tried."

Kylie hardened her heart. "No, he could have phoned. He could have got her a message through her brothers. He didn't care to, that's all." But she knew the truth now because she'd seen the hatred in his eyes. He'd never been in touch because of Kylie. Because of who her father may have been. She could hardly stand to be in there with his sorrow and loss.

Not for her. Never for her.

"Stupid old man, he was stubborn to a fault," Holly declared.

"I guess he kept his thoughts to himself. He probably figured there was time to set things right with my mother." But her car accident had ended any hope of reconciliation.

Holly made a doubtful face. "Maybe he hoped she'd show up at this bedside for a deathbed father-daughter lovefest. Reunions like that are rumored to happen."

"Well, it sure wasn't going to happen with *me*!"

"I'm sorry he behaved so badly when you came to meet him."

"Me, too."

"I'm more sorry for him because he missed out on knowing what a great person you are. You're talented, smart, funny and so gorgeous it would be easy to hate you if you weren't so warm."

Kylie squeezed her eyes shut so tears wouldn't leak down her cheeks. "That's so sweet, Holly. I appreciate it."

Holly moved in close for a hug. "You'll always be family, Kylie. No matter what happens with the inn, we'll never lose touch."

"Have you heard anything from Marnie?"

"Not a word. I've called but her phone's shut off. It's not like her, but she's deep into negotiations with her partner, so she may want time to think."

"About TJ?"

She nodded. "I just hope she's thinking clearly. Sometimes we Dawsons are too stubborn for our own good." She sighed and collected the rest of the papers that had fallen out of the drawer. "Like me. I should have been more open with my family about Jack, starting with my marriage going sour. I kept my problems to myself and didn't ask for advice or help. Look what happened. I allowed him to manipulate me into sleeping with him again. If I'd only shared my troubles I might not have made that mistake."

"Don't blame yourself. Sometimes it's easier not to share the bad stuff in our lives. Besides, Jack's behind you now. And Deke's a great guy," she assured. "Much easier to get along with than Eli."

Holly hooted with laughter. "I have no problem getting along with Eli. I think he scares you."

Kylie grinned. "Maybe a little. He arouses me in ways I can't describe." She put up her hand to stop Holly's next comment. "He brings out the worst in me." Her reaction to Eli wasn't all about sex. "Arouses my inner bitch, so to speak."

"No kidding." Holly's dry comment hit home.

"Do you think I'm afraid of him?"

"Maybe he's the kind of man you imagine your father to be. A rolling stone, a ramblin' man, for want of a better term. But Eli has deep roots here and he's strongly connected to his brothers. Sooner or later, he'll settle into a more normal life. Do you want to offer that to him now or let him find it with another woman?"

"I do like the sparks we strike." She hated the idea of Eli finding another woman on his travels. "We've reached an impasse. No conversation but great sex. The less we speak to each other, the less likely we are to argue. Even if I do miss those conversational sparks . . ." She leaned in. "Make-up sex is the hottest."

"It sounds to me as if neither of you wants to say anything to ruin a good thing."

She shook her head. "Everything I want is here on the Olympic Peninsula. My new family, my new home, a business—okay, I can dream, can't I?—if Marnie does the sensible thing and gives the inn a chance, then yes, everything I want is here."

"Including Eli?"

"He's leaving at the end of the summer. He let it slip out about the Himalayas." She shrugged. "It's not as if we've really connected." It pained her to say it, because she felt Eli down to her soul, while he, typically male, felt next to nothing. But maybe Holly was right. Maybe Eli felt happy to travel because he had deep roots. No matter where he went, he always had his home and family to come back to.

Holly watched her closely. "But you feel more than casual," she guessed.

"I do." It felt great to release the truth. At least to her cousin.

"It can happen faster than we'd ever think possible. With Deke, I went into overdrive at first sight. My mouth watered, my knees went weak and when he walked across the back lot toward me, I didn't even register that TJ walked with him. Imagine not noticing TJ!"

"I had a lot of that, too, when Eli showed up. I reacted badly and insulted him. I felt like such a fool when you told me about how he teaches in orphanages."

Holly shrugged. "The whole thing's physiological and, in a lot of ways, beyond our control."

"Being out of control with men is one of my worst fears. My mother spent a lot of time warning me off them."

"Are you afraid of men?"

"Not men specifically, just the damage they cause." Eli was hurricane force. "Some women bend, but others can be broken like twigs."

"Was Aunt Trudy broken? She had men disappoint her at her most vulnerable point."

"It's not right to talk about my mom. She had a lot of guilt over how I was conceived. She says she knew what would happen at the frat house, but she went anyway, got loaded and high and went into the bedroom willingly."

"She told you that?"

"My mother was brutally honest about that night. Her behavior appalled her later, but by then, all she could do was hope for the best and get tested for STDs. She was clean, but also pregnant. When I was born, she figured it was likely the Hawaiian guy, but there were others that night. She made no bones about behaving stupidly, but she did go speak to him and he blew her off." She sniffed and blew out a deep breath. "My mother loved me and I loved her. If you'd been raised with only one parent and no other family, you'd understand."

"You mean she was raped while she was passed out?"

"Actually, no. She made it plain she'd partied hard several times when she got to college. She was an easy drunk and an

easy lay when she drank. She was acting out after a strict up-
bringing. Grandad watched her like a hawk in her teens."

"She was very brave to confess all that to him. I can see how
she would feel that it was just the two of you against the
world."

Kylie nodded. Her mom had done her best under rotten circumstances. "Sometimes I wonder if instead of protecting me
from bad choices, she gave me no choices at all. I grew up afraid
of losing control, and with Eli I have no control whatsoever."
Oh, God. She'd said it. A look, a sexy move, an unintentional
innuendo and she wanted him.

"Oh, Kylie. Don't be afraid." Holly dragged her into a
fierce hug that Kylie gratefully accepted. "Your mom didn't
want you to make mistakes or be foolish, but I doubt she
wanted you to live like a nun. My dad always said Aunt Trudy
had a backbone of steel and as much pride as Granddad."

Kylie sniffed again. "He was horrible to me when I came
here. He hated me on sight and I understand why she stayed
away. I'm sorry about her brothers, though. She never gave them
a chance." Maybe Trudy thought they'd reject her as well, so
she did it first.

"She never talked about them?"

"No. I knew she had family because I found an old photo
album, but that's all. When I asked, she said the people in the
photos were from a previous life and weren't connected to our
lives now."

They pulled apart. "She was right. We weren't connected.
You know now that the estrangement was her choice. We've already put that behind us."

"A fresh start," Holly agreed with a nod. "It helps to know
her father missed her. Maybe he did design his will to take one
last stab at fixing his mistakes." And Trudy's.

"He brought us together. And we'll stay together."

Kylie gathered her nerve. "I want more than the summer. I

guess that's obvious." She grinned. "Do you think Marnie will see the potential in the inn by then? The three of us make a good team." Kylie didn't know Marnie as well as she'd hoped to by now, but she admired her tremendously. "Or is she so committed to her dance club that she can't see what she's got here?"

The distant sound of a vehicle in the parking area of the inn broke through Kylie's musing. "Maybe she's back," she said and headed for the sound. Holly followed and dashed to the living room window. "Is Eli in the doghouse?"

"Not at the moment. But wait a minute, that'll change," she quipped. She *did* miss the sparks. Maybe he did, too.

"We've got a flower delivery coming in," Holly said. "Maybe it's for Marnie from TJ. I'm sure it's not from Deke." Her voice thrummed with excitement.

Kylie opened the front door as Holly slid to a stop beside her, excitement making her bounce on the balls of her feet. Holly accepted the heavy vase while Kylie signed the delivery slip. "Wow, these are all incredible." Tall and full, the bouquet would span the entire coffee table. Lilies, roses, orchids and more exotic flowers than Kylie could identify filled out the bouquet.

"These are perfect," she said as Holly slid the vase to the center of the coffee table that TJ had returned to the inn just this morning. "We'll have to get more for the registration desk when we open for business."

"I love fresh flowers!" Holly confessed. "I know some people have allergies but I'm always drawn to the fresh scents. And the colors brighten my day."

Holly fussed over the blooms as she unwrapped the cellophane wrap and spread the stems to show off the flowers to their best advantage. "In the winter, we'll lay pine boughs across the mantel on the fireplace. The woodsy pine scent will make the whole inn smell fresh and cozy at the same time." Her eyes glowed. "I found a card!"

"Open it," Kylie urged.

Holly hesitated. Her fingernail flicked the corner of a small square. "There's no name on the envelope. Maybe it's for all of us." Still, she hesitated while Kylie balled up the cellophane and stuffed it into the cardboard carrier the florist had used for the base of the vase.

"Open it, I'm dying to know which of the O'Banions is sensitive enough to send such a lovely gift." TJ? Maybe, but he was the practical man who saw to things like removing the cigarette burns on the coffee table. It could have been Deke, he was more open about his feelings for Holly and the most likely candidate for a grand gesture like this. "It can't be Eli. His apologies are private." And since they rarely spoke other than before and during sex and about sex, he had nothing to apologize for.

"These are my favorite flowers. Every one," Holly said. Her mind raced with possibilities as she stared at Kylie. Her finger still flicked the envelope as her nerves clanged.

The full display weighed at least ten pounds and took up a three-foot circumference. This thing had better not be from Deke; she'd wonder what he'd done that he had to make up for.

Unless this was how he brought his affairs to an end. Her belly dropped. He wouldn't. Not so publicly and not out of the blue. "If it's from Deke, maybe—" She passed the card to Kylie. "You open it."

"If it's from Deke, it's because he loves you, not because there's anything wrong." Kylie patted her shoulder and tsked. "Men don't spend this kind of money to say good-bye."

"Thanks." She gave Kylie a weak smile. "Now, open it."

She watched as Kylie pulled the card out. She frowned and gasped. Then handed the card over without a word.

The world tumbled away as her eyes fell to the precise handwriting. Jack. A parting gift.

A match made in heaven gone to hell . . . burn, baby, burn.

Her belly may have dropped when she thought Deke was

sending her a kiss off, but this felt *off*. "It's Jack and it's not like him to be extravagant." He'd always picked up single flowers or small bunches at the grocery store.

"It's big enough for a funeral arrangement. They're lovely though." She sniffed a rose. "I guess this is Jack conceding defeat?"

"Yes, of course, that's it. His final good-bye." She folded the card to hide the words and slipped it into her front pocket. "His idea of a joke. He always had a flair for drama. No worries." She grinned at her cousin, wishing she didn't feel cold all over. "He picked all my favorite flowers."

She centered the vase on the table and stepped back to admire the burst of color, ignoring the dread that grew in her chest. Must be heartburn. Jack had always given her heartburn.

"Hey, what's this?" Deke came in and wrapped his arms around her from behind.

"Flowers for the great room. I thought they'd add color and scent. Maybe in the winter we could bring in pine boughs for over the mantel."

Kylie frowned. "Flowers are just what we need in here," she said with a curious glance at Holly. Thankfully her cousin didn't correct the impression Holly had given Deke.

"The winter, huh? Does that mean you'll be here that long?" He nuzzled at her ear and tightened his grip around her waist.

"If you'll have me," she said and wrapped her arms around his as he rocked her side to side. If the rigid cock at her back was any indication, Deke was a happy man.

She wouldn't call Jack. That was exactly what he wanted. She refused to play his game.

This time she'd call in reinforcements.

22

Marnie still hadn't called, and at nearly four thirty in the afternoon, TJ's patience was shot. Her meeting with Dennis had been hours ago. The temptation to phone her rode him hard, but he forced himself to resist. But the waiting was torture.

He gripped the end of the last log and settled the notch into place on the log below. "We'll get the roof done Monday."

"But the women are in a hurry," Eli said.

"We can take one day off," TJ snapped and climbed down the logs. "The crew's exhausted. Besides, Kylie's not happy with the floor plan."

Eli made a disgusted face. "She's only happy sometimes."

"Then it's time you two settled things. You've got everyone walking on glass around you." Did he have to take care of everything himself? Frustration made him snap again. "You're the electrician, if you think we can rearrange the walls, then we will. Just man up and talk to Kylie."

Eli followed and landed with a thump beside him. "We haven't discussed it. We've agreed to avoid conversation. Makes sleeping with her a lot more fun."

"Brother, you are fucked up." He shook his head in disbelief. "Most women like to talk to the men they're sleeping with."

"Most women aren't Kylie. She's so prickly I never know what'll set her off."

"It can take a while to figure that out, but in the meantime, don't make promises you won't keep."

"Now you sound like her. She's convinced I'm never going to settle down."

TJ sat on a bundle of roof shingles. "Shit." He stared off into the distance. "Here's me, wanting Marnie, ready, willing and able to offer her anything she wants. While Kylie's the one who *wants* to be here and she's stuck on you!" A sick and twisted irony.

"Well, if there's any woman who could make me hang around, it's Kylie." Eli studied his boots. "She's a challenge every day. Keeps everything inside me hopping. I could spend my life trying to stay one step ahead of her."

"You told her this?"

"Like I said, we don't talk."

"Marnie and I talk a lot. We agree on most things and she's smart and ambitious and—aw—fuck it. She's going to stay in the city and I want to be here. I don't fit in Seattle any more than you and Deke do."

"You got that right. I've only traveled because I've been free to come and go. If Kylie wanted me to stay, I would. But she's convinced I'm like all the other men in her life. A rat bastard. Did I ever tell you what she said about me the first time we met?"

"No."

"She called me a sex tourist, like I'm some pervert who travels the world abusing women. She said that and she didn't even know me."

And yet he still found her doable. "Women, they do what

they do. We'll never know why." He'd said much the same to Deke about Misty and her betrayal.

Eli studied him then ducked his head. "Marnie's too smart to walk away, Teeje. She'll make the right decision. You should go after her."

"I did that once. I won't do it again." He'd sat at the bar in his plaid shirt and new jeans like some grizzled, strange mountain man. Marnie had noticed that he didn't fit in. "She has to decide for herself in her own time."

"Go home," Eli suggested. "We're done for the day. Deke's already gone off to get Holly. He can't keep his hands off her."

"At least one of us is on track."

"Yeah." Eli nodded.

A shout and loud crack from the other side of the cabin brought their surroundings home. The crew was still here and unsupervised. Blue curses split the air overhead. TJ was the first to tear around the far side of the cabin.

A near miss with an axe. Sam Whitaker lay sprawled on his back, red faced and cursing. "Sam, take it easy, I don't see any blood and your foot's still at the end of your leg." The kid's eyes were stark with fear.

"Really?" His face flooded red as he caught his breath.

"Really." Eli gave him a hand up.

"Thanks," he said when he stood. He shook his leg. "I don't know what happened. My hands slipped, I guess."

"We're all tired. It's been a long week," TJ said. "Get some rest tonight."

Sam shook his head. "I'm working at the station tonight and tomorrow," he said as he bent to pick up the hard hat that had slipped off in the fall. He slapped the dust from his jeans and headed toward his mom's sedan.

"Adjust that hat so it fits properly," TJ instructed. "I'd hate to lose a good laborer."

Sam nodded as his face split into a grin. "Thanks!"

* * *

TJ took off right after Sam did and left Eli to his thoughts.

Until Kylie, the only people who had ever succeeded in making Eli feel like an awkward kid were his brothers. He'd spent his younger years running to catch up with them, hoping to be included. Eventually, he'd grown enough to simply run away.

Kylie tied him in knots. He didn't know from one minute to the next what new hell she might concoct for him. She piqued his interest and his anger.

He used a tarp to cover the roofing materials, because even though the weather report called for sunshine, on the Peninsula that could change in a heartbeat.

"Eli." He knew before he looked it was Kylie come to torment him.

He secured the end of the tarp with a chunk of wood to hold it down and then faced her. "Kylie." Her face held a secret, but he'd be damned if he'd ask. He kept his expression impassive and waited. She'd get to the point eventually.

"I'm happy with the cabins as they are. I'm sorry I insisted on changing the floor plans."

He nodded, wary at her new attitude. "I should have explained about building with logs. The holes—"

She held up her hand to cut him off. "Deke explained it all. You must think I'm such a bag, always being so mean and difficult."

"And rude," he said, wondering what new aggravation she had planned.

"And rude." She stepped close and palmed his pecs. "I don't want to fight with you."

"What do you want?"

"You." She bit her lip. "I want you. Not just sex with you. I want to talk and argue and be myself with you." She shrugged and looked pensive. "I mean, you know, if you want to be yourself with me, too, feel free."

"Okay, you have to explain, because I'm missing something here. I thought we weren't going to ruin the great time we're having by *talking* about the great time we're having."

She ran her curious fingers up to his collarbone. She kissed him there and murmured something hot and dark and sexy. "Your chest hair is perfect." She nuzzled the *V* at his throat and opened his top button. She scented him like a cat with a morsel of food.

"I like your chest, too," he said and cupped her breasts. He tilted his head. "This is where we usually shut up, Kylie." He was already hard enough to take her, but he couldn't be sure that's why she'd come out to see him. "Why don't we take this inside?"

"Let's go. And afterward, we'll make dinner together. I hear you make a mean pasta sauce."

"I do." He pursed his lips, then gave her a quick nod. "Dinner afterward. TJ's gone home to wait to hear from Marnie."

"Deke and Holly left right after TJ." She towed him like a dinghy toward the kitchen door. He followed her through the inn and upstairs.

At her urging, he stepped into her bedroom. "Are you sure?" Something was off with her, he was sure of it.

"Yes, now take off your clothes and join me in the shower."

His mind blanked at the idea of washing Kylie's hair with that fruity shampoo, watching the suds slip and slide down her exquisite body. "I'm game if you are."

Once in the water, words weren't needed and he finally relaxed and followed the line of soapy water down to the apex of her thighs. He dropped to his knees and burrowed between her legs to find her plump clit. He suckled lightly and let her moans join the sound of the water, thrumming, thrumming.

If any woman could make him hang around, it was Kylie.

Her moisture filled his mouth as he suckled and licked her to orgasm. She clenched her thighs around his face and groaned as she held him to her. "Eli! Yes! Love me, Eli, just like that."

The words filled his ears, his heart and he knew he'd give her whatever she asked for. She claimed to want more than sex. She claimed to want him. For the rest of the evening, that's what she'd get.

A couple of hours after Eli's fabulous spaghetti and meatballs, Kylie left the shower for the second time and tiptoed to the bed. A soft snore rose. Eli was sound asleep in her bed for the first time. They'd never even cuddled after sex and now they'd done that and more.

He'd cooked for her, talked with her and even planned some outings with her. He wanted to show her around the entire Peninsula as if he accepted that she would always live here.

But what she wanted more was Eli.

She slipped in beside him and realized she hadn't shared a bed with anyone since her last sleepover as a teen.

He took up so much space. But the warmth under the sheet felt awesome. The man was a furnace. She lay flat on her back, arms and legs stretched out straight, so as not to wake him. They'd worn each other out and his deep breathing proved it. Weary to the bone and sore between her legs, she waited, stiff and silent for sleep to claim her.

He was a side sleeper and kept one knee bent, the other straight, the way she did.

She rolled to her side, facing him. No room. If she bent her knee, they'd bang kneecaps all night. She rolled to her other side but her knee hung over the edge of the bed and she felt as if she'd fall out.

She eased toward the middle, hoping she didn't nudge his

knee and wake him. There. Better. She tucked her hand under her pillow and settled in.

A snuffle from behind gave her minimal warning that she'd disturbed him. He moved with a light grunt and flung his leg over hers while tugging her back against his chest.

Caught between the rock of Eli and the soft give of the mattress she finally understood the idea of spooning. She wiggled her butt closer into his heat while his hand stole to cup her breast. His breathing barely changed as he held her in slumber.

Finally at ease, his warmth surrounding her as his body draped hers, she joined him in sleep.

The morning found her still wrapped up in Eli, except now his hand had moved south of her waist and into her pussy. "Good morning," she muttered on a sharp sigh. She raised her leg to give him more room. He took quick advantage and slid his rigid cock between her legs.

"Sore?" he asked at her ear.

"Not anymore." She was wet and slippery and very aroused already. Her sleep had been filled with hot dreams of Eli taking her in a variety of ways she had yet to experience with him.

"Good." He flipped her to her stomach and brought her to her knees. He wedged her legs apart and parted her butt cheeks. "You're wet. So fucking wet."

"What are you doing?"

But his finger in her pussy told her where his interest lay. He slid in a second finger and pumped her until she moaned and pressed for more.

"More. Please."

A third finger took her higher, closer, as tension rose. She buried her face in her pillow and moaned louder.

She heard the tear of a condom packet and grinned in anticipation until he rubbed her clit with his wet fingers. She pressed back when the tip of his cock slid into her opening. She bloomed in urgent need.

Eli took her fast and hard. Deep, so deep. She came quickly, then reached between her legs and stretched to cup the tight knots of his balls. He fit so perfectly with her. She was tall, but he was taller. She was strong, but he was stronger and they matched each other stroke for stroke, buck for buck.

Eli plunged again and again, gaining speed and depth. She squeezed him until he growled with orgasm and pressed her flat to the mattress.

When it was over and they'd caught their breath, he nipped her skin at the shoulder before he collapsed on the bed.

"Wow," she said, "I've missed out on a lot of great mornings."

He chuckled and tilted her chin up to meet her lips in a light kiss. "Better than coffee any day."

Sunday morning and TJ rolled out of his empty bed, determined to get through the day without calling Marnie. It had been almost twenty-four hours since her meeting with her partner.

It had to be bad news. People shared good news right away, and hesitated when it came to hurting someone. He was half convinced she wouldn't call at all.

He had to keep busy. The only way to avoid calling her was to be productive. The crew had the day off and it was too dangerous to work alone so he was stuck at home. He knew exactly what his brothers were doing.

Of the three of them, he was the one who wanted a wife and family. He was the one who'd built a business to support that dream. Hell, he'd built the house he was standing in with children in mind.

And which woman had knocked his socks off at first glance? The only Dawson granddaughter who didn't want to be here. He wanted to tear his bedroom apart, but instead, he thumped downstairs to grab his first cup of coffee. Thank God for automatic timers.

He had the sign to work on. That would keep his mind off Marnie. He headed out to his shop, slipped his ear protection on and started the sander. But the muffled sound only gave his mind time to work him over but good. After an hour of torturing himself with doubt and hating his brothers for finding what he so badly wanted, he pulled the plug.

There weren't enough woodworking projects in the world to keep him from thinking about Marnie. He finally understood what had driven Jon Dawson to build an entire inn and all the furniture by hand. He must have had a mountain of regret. Too many for one man to bear and, in the end, when he'd had one chance to square things with Kylie, he'd fucked up all over again.

TJ hung his head in acceptance. Whatever it took, he had to try one more time with Marnie.

"TJ?"

He raised his head, convinced his name had come from inside his head. The buzz from the sander had affected his hearing, in spite of the ear protection. He turned and blinked.

"Marnie!" He wanted to grab her to his chest, but her face stopped him.

She glowed. Just glowed.

"God, you look good." So fucking good.

"Dennis offered to buy me out of the club."

"I see." Everything stopped. The distant birdsong, the wind in the trees, the beat of his heart. "Did you accept?"

She slowed her approach, put some sway in her hips and a light of sexy anticipation entered her eyes. "He'll come up with some numbers. We'll discuss it."

"I see," he repeated, unsure of her signals. She could just be here for a few days, like usual. This didn't mean she wanted to move here. She could have other plans for a new business in the city.

"You don't seem happy." She drew closer. "I told Dennis I had a lot to consider. My dreams, my goals, my feelings for you."

"For me?"

She stood kiss-close and looked up into his face.

He was afraid to believe what he read in her eyes. That light of love might be something else.

"I also need to consider your feelings for me."

"You know how I feel. Do you need to hear it again? Because I'll yell it from the treetops if that will convince you."

"I'd love to hear it again, but let me say it first. I love you, Thomas John O'Banion, and I want you for the rest of my life."

He grabbed her to his chest so tight she gasped. "I was blind to the possibility of selling out to Dennis. I never even considered walking away because I only thought of myself. My ambitions, my dreams. I'm sorry I didn't call you, but my phone was destroyed and I wanted to tell you in person."

He kissed her, but she tore her mouth off his. "I love you, TJ, and I always will."

"Took you long enough," he breathed against her lips.

"Give me a break; I was only thirteen when this started."

23

_____

Holly held the end of a tape measure for Deke as he paced off the length of his envisioned kitchen. They'd spent most of Sunday morning here, going over his plans for the house. Her phone rang and, seeing her brother's number, she answered immediately. "Hi, Damien! How'd it go?"

"Are you sure Jack was at work all week?"

"As sure as I can be." Marnie had confessed to calling Jack at work. *Family.* "When he picked up, dear cousin Marnie disconnected. Why?"

"Because he's not home and it looks like his mailbox is stuffed full. I'm not sure he's been there lately."

"Jack was never efficient with routine stuff, like mail. Besides all his bills are paid online." Hearing Jack's name, Deke looked over, a frown clouding his features. He approached with a wary expression. She covered the mouthpiece. "My brother, Damien, checked Jack's place for me." To Damien, she said, "Thanks, yes, I'll let you know if I see him."

"And when do we meet this new guy?" Damien asked.

"Just as soon as we can take a day to come visit." She smiled at Deke and touched his hand. "You'll like him, Damien, I promise."

Her brother gave her a "we'll see" hum and one more word of caution. "If Jack shows up there, Holly, you call the cops."

"I will. I promise. I love you, too," she said. Not that Damien ever said the words, but she always felt them. They disconnected at the same time.

"My brother, Damien, wants to meet you soon. The silly codicil says none of the men in the family can come to the inn for a year, so we'll have to go to Bellevue to visit him. The rest of my family will probably be there, too, so be prepared."

He grinned. "Fine, I do okay with family. I may even pull out a white shirt, cords and a sports jacket."

"No plaid?" She feigned horror.

He chuckled. "That's all fine, but what's happening with Jack?"

"Don't get upset, but he sent this card along with that huge bouquet on the coffee table at the inn." She hated having to tell him, but they were past the point of arguing about how much she should share. He needed to know about Jack's newest attempt to get her attention.

"He sent those flowers? I figured one of you women picked them up." Then he read the card that had been tucked so innocently into the bouquet. He glared at the words, then at her. "You're saying you've had this card since yesterday? And you didn't tell me?"

"I called my brothers. Which is probably what I should have done months ago when Jack kept"—she was *so* not going to tell him how often she'd slept with Jack since the divorce. Or that sometimes, she was the one making the call for a hook up.

"Jack kept what?" He looked at her with suspicion.

"We slept together for a short time after the divorce. I thought it would ease the transition. There. Now you know. Feel better?"

"I feel like shit! You should have told me about this!" He shoved the card at her. She grabbed it and slid it back into her pocket.

"Yelling at me won't help. The thing is, Jack doesn't seem to have been home and now, I'm wondering if he's here again."

"But Marnie called him at work."

"That was midweek, this is Sunday. He's off today. He could be here right now."

"Call the flower shop," he ordered. "Ask when the order was placed and whether or not it was in person."

He clasped her hand and hurried her into his truck. "We'll go to the inn, check things out. Eli planned to take Holly on a tour of the Peninsula. They've probably already left."

"Huh. They've likely shoved each other off a cliff somewhere." Her dry humor brought a smile to Deke's mouth. She climbed in and dug the card out of her pocket again. "The number for the shop must be on the envelope. We threw that out."

"We'll dig through the trash until we find it."

She called information, but none of the store names sounded familiar. She pulled up her memory of the truck. "It came from a grocery store! Some of them have florists and also deliver."

"I've used them myself." He looked sheepish. "I sent some to Misty, on the off chance—"

"You could get back together with her?" She finished his cutoff thought. "You keep that in mind when you feel like judging me," she said.

With a half-grin, he pulled the truck onto the road and headed toward the inn. She made more calls. One to Kylie, the next to Marnie.

"Kylie and Eli are about an hour away and heading back now. Marnie's phone is still messed up or something."

"Try TJ's place," he said and gave her the number.

Marnie answered.

"Hey, Marnie. You're there."

"I am. What's up? You sound agitated."

"We've kind of lost track of Jack." She explained about the bouquet and the warning on the card. "But it's pretty vague. I mean it's sort of nothing, you know? A match made in heaven and all that. I mean, it's a common enough saying about married couples and it was one of his favorite things to say after we fought."

"Typical of you to ignore the *burn, baby, burn* part. Meet us at the inn right away."

After Marnie hung up she looked at TJ. Concern filled his eyes. "Holly. She called about Jack." She sat on the side of the rumpled bed, a cold trickle of alarm skating along her nerves. "She always gives that man the benefit of the doubt. None of the rest of the family does. Her brother went to his place and says it looks like he hasn't been there in days." But he'd been at work when she'd called the other day.

TJ leaped to his feet and grabbed his jeans, shirt and socks to dress. "I'll call Chuck and put him on alert again. Can't hurt."

"Thanks," she said through the sweatshirt she pulled over her head. She felt safer just by TJ being there. "We shouldn't overreact," she cautioned. "But the note on the card was ominous, even though Holly doesn't agree."

She pulled on the rest of her clothes and followed him out to his truck while he called his friend, Chuck. Just hearing him advising the police officer of the situation warmed her heart.

TJ was the man. The man for her.

Thomas John O'Banion finished what he started, did what he promised and took care of his own. With him, she could have a full and fulfilling life.

She'd be part of a real team, a true partnership. He'd known from the beginning what they could have together. Halfway to the Friendly Inn, she slid across the seat to sit close. "I love you, Thomas John, with everything I have."

He looked at her with seriously sexy focus. The man was killer gorgeous. "I love you, Marnie Dawson, with everything I am."

Eli pressed the accelerator to ten miles over the posted speed limit. An urgent tattoo in his brain thrummed, making it hard to sit still as he drove. "I've got a bad feeling, Kylie," he said.

"Me, too." She looked worried. "I should have said something yesterday, after the flowers came. Holly's face went white when she read that card. But she was so private about Jack before that I let it pass." She bit her lip and looked guilty.

He slid his hand over hers. "Don't beat yourself up. You didn't know all their history. You're new to the family, remember?"

Her face glowed with happiness. "Thanks." She leaned in and kissed his cheek as he drove.

They'd hiked a short trail in the Olympic National Forest and discovered another thing they had in common. "Hey, we've gone over three hours without a cross word between us," he commented.

"A record. And we only stopped for sex once," she said, followed by a sexy purr. "Holly was right, though."

"About?"

"Sex in a truck with an O'Banion is not easy. You guys are huge!"

A warm flush rose. "I hope you mean that in the best way, but let me know next time if I hurt you. I'll slow down." They'd gone at it fast and furious.

She stretched her legs and pressed her feet against the floorboards in response. "I'd tell you if it hurt. I feel great." When she kissed his cheek, he eased up on the gas pedal. "But two tall people in a truck cab makes for cramped quarters. That last maneuver, though?"

"Too much? Too deep?" *Too fast, too rough.*

She grinned. "Really hit the spot." Her eyes shot sexy sparks and he relaxed. Sooner or later, he'd learn her signals and their communication outside of bed would be just as good as in. She slid her hand from his knee to his crotch in the best style of communication they had.

His cock responded the way it always did to Kylie. "Easy there, we'll be home soon."

"Good, I'm tired of talking," she teased. She turned her face to the passenger-side window. "When you go to see the Himalayas, will you go alone? Or do you have a travel buddy?"

"I travel alone, unless you'd like to come?" The invitation slipped out easily. "We could go for a couple of weeks. Maybe after the inn's doing well enough that we can afford a trip like that. I've got to get back into a work routine."

She removed her hand from his leg. "Don't talk like that, Eli. It's not fair." She went rigid. "Show me the courtesy of being honest."

Stunned, he turned to stare at her. "Now, see, this is where we end up in an argument. I say something nice and you take it wrong. What's the matter with suggesting a vacation at some point in the future?"

"You want me to believe you'd like me to join you, when we both know that in a few weeks, you'll be itching to leave."

"Why do you think I travel?" His curiosity was simple, but he doubted her answer would be.

"To escape responsibility. Like all men!" she blurted, then immediately looked contrite, but he didn't care.

A burn started in his gut and worked its way to his face. Her eyes widened and she clamped her jaw tight. He faced the road, hit the accelerator and white-knuckled it back to the inn.

Just as he passed the "Welcome to Port Townsend" sign, his phone rang. "What?" Beside him, Kylie jerked at his gruff tone.

"Eli? It's Sam Whitaker."

"Sam, yeah, what's up?"

"I'm working at the gas station today." He sounded out of breath. Excited.

"So? You want tomorrow off? Can't come in?" Eli wanted Sam off the phone in case one of his brothers needed him.

"No. It's kind of weird . . ." He trailed off.

"Sam, I'm tied up right now. Busy. What can I do for you?"

"I saw this guy again today. He was buying gas. He filled five jerry cans." Eli sat up straighter, looked over at Kylie and tapped her leg to get her attention. The burn of anger was doused with icy dread.

"What guy bought jerry cans full of gas?" he said to bring Kylie up to speed. She blanched.

"Remember that Holly told me to call about the job with you guys?"

"Yeah, sure, Holly turned you on to us." He nodded while Kylie hung on every word.

"A guy was kind of in her face that day. He grabbed hold of her behind Deke's truck when she put her propane tank in the back. I never said anything, because it looked sorta personal, you know, and once I saw her with Deke, I figured I should keep my mouth shut. I don't want to get in anyone's business."

"What do you mean you saw Holly with a guy and it looked personal?" he repeated for Kylie's benefit. "Exactly what did you see?"

"He had her from behind and, you know, slid his hand down, you know, under her—"

"Jeans? He molested her?"

"I figured he *knew* her, that she *liked* him! Then when I saw her with Deke, I thought I should keep my mouth shut. The guy didn't hurt her or she would'a called out for help, right?"

"Right, Sam. If he hurt her she'd have called for help. But are you saying you saw this guy today and he filled up jerry cans with gas? Did he say what it was all for? That's a lot of gas."

"That's what I said, you know, that it was a lot of gas, and he told me to shut the fuck up and looked a little, you know, wild-ass crazy. Kinda mad."

"When did he leave?"

"About fifteen minutes ago. Church just got out and we've been busy like always at this time on Sunday and I just now got the chance to call you. I didn't feel right not saying anything."

"Thanks, Sam. If this guy comes back, let us know right away, but don't tell him you called me. I'll see you tomorrow. I appreciate you calling me, Sam. You did the right thing." When he slid the phone to the seat beside him, Kylie grabbed it.

"We've got to call the others. Jack has jerry cans full of gas?"

"And Sam said he had a wild look in his eyes. He's dangerous and doesn't care who gets hurt." But she was already on the phone with Holly. What the hell was the bastard up to?

If he was crazy enough to immolate himself for Holly's sake, one can would be enough. But if he wanted to burn down the inn . . .

"Call 9-1-1. Tell them there's a possible arson at the Friendly Inn. Make sure you say possible. Never mind, just give me the phone when they answer." When she didn't quibble at being given an order, he lifted her hand to his mouth and kissed her knuckles. "Thanks."

TJ heard sirens in the distance before he even reached the turn that would lead him into the inn. A glow of light through the trees that lined the driveway said the firefighters would be fully engaged. "Oh, shit. Look over there; does that look like firelight?"

"Oh God. Yes! Go faster!" Marnie cried.

"We can't block access for the fire trucks," he said as he pulled to a stop at the side of the road. He opened his door and jumped out into the ditch. He left his four-way flashers on and helped Marnie down.

Deke's pickup roared up and TJ waved him over. As Deke rolled his window down, TJ said, "We'll have to go in on foot." Sirens wailed closer and Deke inched his truck as far off the road as he could. The light from the fire grew brighter and a distant crackle urged them to move faster.

Marnie and Holly looked stricken as they all ran up the drive toward the flickering light ahead. The first fire truck overtook them and roared past. A water tanker followed.

The veranda was already engulfed by the time they got to the clearing where they normally parked. Staying well out of the way of the working and focused fire crew, they stood in shocked silence as the red swing reduced to glowing cinders and collapsed under the chains they'd used for support.

Eli and Kylie joined them by the time the water hoses attacked the flame. "Think they'll save the building?" Eli asked.

"Maybe. But this doesn't seem big enough for five cans of gasoline." TJ's comment fell into a moment of horror as they all saw flames lick along the veranda roof.

"We should check the cabin," Deke said and started to run. The others followed immediately.

When a fifth man caught up to them as they edged the drive that led around to the back, Eli grinned. "Chuck! Glad you could make it."

The officer tried to tell them to stand down, then gave up. "Never could tell you boys diddly squat. Smart asses, all of you!" His partner trailed behind.

TJ had never been so glad to see his old football buddy. "We think we've got an arsonist."

Flames leaped inside the unfinished cabin and Chuck pulled out his radio. He called the fire department dispatch to send men with hoses behind the building. "Faster than running back to get the truck through here," he explained to his young and dazzled-looking partner.

"Think the hoses will run this far?" TJ asked as they crashed to a halt in the eerily beautiful light from the cabin fire.

Deke ran to the garden hose and unwound it while Holly turned on the water. "I'm so sorry," she shouted to everyone. "This must be Jack but I can't see him, anywhere. Deke, what if he's inside the cabin or the inn?"

Chuck grabbed the hose from Deke and aimed it at the outside walls. "I'll soak these good and maybe it won't spread to the trees."

At Holly's words, TJ took off at a dead run toward the cabin. Deke followed, which caught Eli's attention and all three O'Banions disappeared around the corner of the burning cabin.

Kylie screamed. "Eli!" She started to run, but Marnie caught her by the elbow.

"No, if they're after Jack, they don't need us in the way."

"Marnie's right, Kylie. I'm so sorry I brought this on. I'm—" She broke off as the firefighters appeared, dragging a hose. "Thank God," she said. The women backed away to give the fire crew room to work. They huddled together, comforting each other, focused completely on the smoky haze on the far side of the burning cabin.

"I can't see anything, can you?"

"I thought I heard TJ yell Jack's name, though, did you?"

"Yes! Then I heard Eli, too."

"Should we go look?"

"There's nothing we can do about the cabin—"

"I vote we go."

"Maybe they need us."

"Maybe one of them's hurt—" Kylie broke off and tore away from her cousins. "I'll kill Eli if anything's happened to him!"

Marnie and Holly exchanged a look and followed.

* * *

TJ tackled the man first, the smell of gasoline overwhelming. With loud grunts the two men went down in a pile of cedar chips and pine needles.

The spout of the jerry can sprayed gasoline in an arc across the ground. "Gas!" TJ shouted as he grabbed a fistful of gas-soaked shirt. "Stay back!"

But Eli and Deke paid no attention to the warning. TJ wanted to retch from the gasoline smell as he rolled closer to the burning cabin with the arsonist in a strong grip. "You're not getting away!" He grunted in the guy's face, but the eyes looking back at him were wild and he knew he wouldn't get through to him.

"Get back!" he screamed at his brothers as the madman's overwhelming strength threatened him. Terror licked at his insides. If his brothers were burned, he'd never forgive himself.

He could feel the heat edging higher. How hot could it get before his gasoline-soaked shirt went up in flames?

"Holly's gonna pay! She's gonna fuckin' pay!" Jack screamed in TJ's face. But the last word ended in a howl of pain that rattled through TJ's head. Had he caught fire? TJ struggled to get clear of him and scramble backward.

Suddenly hands grabbed his shoulders while another pair had him by the ankles. Both pulled and twisted him away from Jack, but through the haze of rising smoke, he saw Jack being pulled back from the burning wall.

Chuck flipped Jack flat to the ground and snapped cuffs on him while Jack howled in frustration.

"Get your clothes off! Now!" Chuck ordered. "You, too, asshole!" He stripped Jack's pants down his legs.

Gasping for breath, nearly overcome by the stench, TJ unbuckled his belt and slid his jeans off as fast as he could. He did the same with his shirt, while his brothers undressed as well. Adrenaline pumped through him and he leaped into the air with a wild shout, fist raised.

His brothers joined him in a victory stomp as Marnie, Kylie and Holly ran over. Each woman grabbed a brother and dragged them out of the firelight.

"You're okay?" Marnie asked, checking TJ over for welts and burns. Her hands felt cool and sexy as they ran over his chest and arms, down his back to his ass.

"My knuckles are bleeding, but they're fine." He'd landed a couple of good blows to Jack's face, but the guy had been so wild, he wasn't sure he'd even felt them.

As Chuck dragged Jack to his feet, TJ saw a split lip and cheek. But Jack just screamed his rage at Holly. Chuck shoved him toward his partner and they escorted him away.

Holly collapsed against Deke. "I brought this here. This was all my fault."

"Your fault for refusing to see the worst in a guy? He never hurt you before, did he?"

She shook her head. "No, not once."

"He snapped, Holly," Deke comforted her. "He snapped and lost control." The flames crackled behind them as firefighters worked to dampen the walls. The trees that surrounded the clearing were sprayed with water. The cabin was lost, but the surrounding woods were safe.

"Eli!" Kylie kissed him hard and clung to his neck, her soft breasts spots of warmth against his chilled chest. "I'd have died if you'd been hurt. I'd have killed you first, though!" She sniffled against his neck. "Don't leave me, Eli. Please. I love you."

He cupped her cheek and held her still for a kiss. "I've wandered the whole world looking for you, Kylie. If I'd found you anywhere else, I'd have brought you here to live with me. Believe that."

"I do. Oh, God, I do."

Epilogue

Six weeks later, Marnie, Holly and Kylie stood behind the registration desk of the Friendly Inn and Resort, balancing on the balls of their feet. Excitement and edgy anticipation filled the room. TJ, Deke and Eli feigned interest in the tourist brochures set out on Jon Dawson's hand-carved coffee table.

Each man took up a station when the first car rolled up the drive. TJ leaned nonchalantly on the log mantel set into the stone fireplace, while Deke and Eli positioned themselves on the recovered love seats. They'd completed the veranda only an hour before. New furniture was on the schedule for next week.

"Are we ready?" Marnie breathed, nervous and excited and completely committed to the partnership.

"Ready as we'll ever be," Holly said, happy with her future with Deke.

"I'm breathless," Kylie said with a glance at Eli. "Thank you all for this."

This was her dream. The Friendly Inn *and Resort*, staffed by her own family, her partners, the people who loved her. The people she loved in the place she belonged.

The front door opened and a couple strolled in. Their faces lit when they looked around the inviting space the women had created. "Welcome to the Friendly Inn and Resort," the women said in unison. "We're your hosts . . ."

Don't miss any of these steamy stories by Bonnie Edwards!

"Slow Hand" (from *Pure Sex*)

Is that a furious runaway bride marching down the beach? Caribbean charter captain Jared McKay to the rescue. She's ready to pitch her wedding shoes overboard and sail away. Aye, aye. Whatever the lady wants. Hey, was that a garter flying by? And wait a minute—a white lace thong just hit the deck. His wildest dreams are about to come true . . .

"Bodywork" (from *The Hard Stuff*)

Lisa Delaney's classic Cadillac coupe needs work and she knows exactly who to call: Tyce Branton. The man has a reputation for making temperamental engines purr like kittens. And when it comes to women, he has some *very* satisfied customers . . .

"Rock Solid" (from *Built*)

Florida carpenter Jake McKay can't resist the honey voice insisting he travel cross-country to renovate a historic Seattle estate. When he meets Lexa Creighton, it's lust at first touch and skin-scorching pleasure all the way. But it's going to take a little help from some amorous ghosts to keep this rock-solid man where he belongs—in Lexa's bed.

JUST TELL ME WHAT YOU WANT

Faye Grantham doesn't quite know what came over her except that her body was on fire. She knew what she wanted, craved, needed—hot sex. Right now. Tonight. But nice girls don't get to do whatever they want, with whomever they want . . .

Faye feels like someone's trying to tell her, *Go for it!* The long-gone ladies of the old bordello she inherited are with her in spirit—sexual spirit, that is. If the walls of Perdition House could only talk . . . oh my. But in fact, they do, and their ghostly tales of amorous encounters are awakening Faye's desire for flesh-and-blood men. Who is she gonna call? Mouth-wateringly sexy Mark or hard and handsome Liam? Her wildest fantasies are about to get very, very real . . .

Midnight Confessions II

ONCE IS NEVER ENOUGH

Living in a former bordello definitely has it pluses—especially when the house comes with the bawdy, opinionated ghosts of the women who once worked there. Faye Grantham's sex life has never been hotter, even if her *love* life is twice as complicated.

Because Faye has two in-the-flesh men to choose from. There's smolderingly sexy Liam, the lawyer who wants to help her get to the bottom of Perdition House's mysterious past. And there's Mark, the businessman with the gorgeously sculpted body, who's decided to settle in town for good. Two irresistible men, two times as many wildly delicious fantasies to play out . . .

Thigh High

TRIPLE YOUR PLEASURE...

An enticing collection of irresistibly erotic stories by Bonnie Edwards that reveals its delicious secret inch by inch—and goes deep into the very heart of desire...

"Parlor Games"

Total strangers Matt Crewe and Carrie MacLean have one thing in common, and it's brought them both to the mysterious Perdition House. When Carrie wins Matt's services as a sex slave, the amorous adventures that follow will lay bare the secrets of the house—and the exquisite ecstasy of all who pass through its gates...

"Thigh High"

Kat has been harboring a crush on her hot-but-shy neighbor, Taye, for ages, so when a pal dares her to seduce him, Kat can't say no. It's the perfect chance for Kat to try out the sex toys she sells—and, as luck would have it, Taye's a man who *loves* to play...

"Twinkle, Twinkle, Little Thong"

Late-night DJ Daniel Martin knows he has some eager female fans, but it isn't every day one of them shows up on the gangplank of his boat, looking for a diamond-encrusted thong. Yet Frankie Volpe is here, breathless, and, yes, missing her very valuable underwear. The search begins...and they're both getting hotter...

Breathless

"Let go. Let go for me . . ." *It was a house of sizzling seduction with satisfaction guaranteed. Now the notorious bordello Perdition House bares all its secrets—and ignites your wildest fantasies . . .*

Blue McCann longs to feel desired . . . needed . . . wanted. Now, thanks to a mysterious corset, she's a lush-bodied beauty back in 1913. And she's going to reward the caring, oh-so-capable hands of Dr. Colt Stephens with all the pleasure he can take . . . Tawny James has legs—and secrets—that won't quit. And since she likes her men big and bad, private investigator Stack Hamilton is uncovering *all* her luscious desires . . . And when Mariel Gibson needs artistic inspiration, she calls hard-bodied carpenter Danny Glenn to work his masterpiece—over and over again. Because you can never, ever reveal too much . . .